THE VERMILION TRIANGLE

THE VERMILION SAGA
BOOK 3

HAYLEY PRICE

HAYLEY PRICE
BOOKS

A catalogue record for this book is available from the National Library of Australia.

National Library of Australia Cataloguing-in-Publication entry

Author: Hayley Price

Title: **The Vermilion Triangle**

ISBN: 978-0-9756238-6-2 (Print)

ISBN: 978-0-9756238-8-6(ePub)

ISBN: 978-0-9756238-7-9 (PDF eBook)

❀ Created with Vellum

This book is dedicated to my baby brother, Andy.
I wasn't always there for him, but I love him.

At times this book will change point-of-view. Please note that each new scene does not necessarily follow the same timeline as the last.

A note for my American readers. This book is written in UK/Australian English. Many of the words will be spelled differently from what you're used to - colour, centre, grey, etc. We pronounce the 'h' in 'herb,' so it's 'a herb,' not 'an herb.'

In addition, we do not share your fondness for the letter "Z". I realise you may find this difficult and offer my humble apologies. We make up for this by using a plethora of "L's where you would make do with one. Marvellous

---

All the writing and artwork in this book was created by a real person. No AI was used at any time.

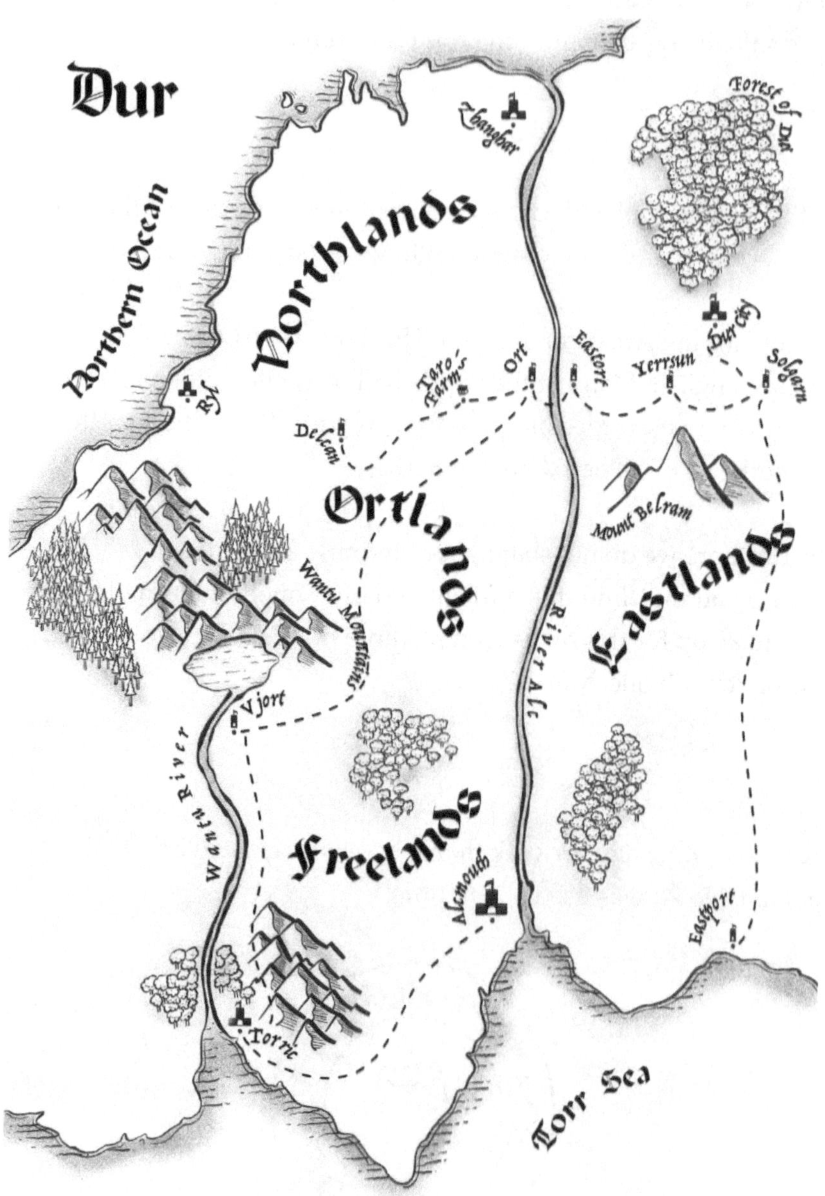
Dur
Northern Ocean
Northlands
Tbangbar
Forest of Dal
Dur Ey
Ryl
Taro Farms
Ort
Eastorf
Yerrsun
Solgarn
Delcan
Ortlands
Mount Belram
Wantu Mountains
Eastlands
Vjort
River Alc
Wantu River
Freelands
Alcmouth
Eastport
Torric
Torr Sea

ONE
STYRRACH MEETS THE BAILIFF

MOONLIGHT SHONE ON THE STREETS AND HOUSES AS ANOTHER NIGHT IN Dur's capital city crept by. The moon believed the streets to be empty, but it had been deceived, and the lone figure who slid with great stealth through the shadows, unseen by moon or eye, moved with such skill, nobody marked their passing. From time to time, the figure turned back the way it had come, only to disappear into a darkened alleyway or stand, motionless, in the blackness of a door-way. Nobody noticed the figure, clad in nondescript clothes, as it travelled on silent feet through the poor quarter toward the more affluent part of the city where the Riverside Tavern plied its busi-ness. The good people of Alcmouth failed to notice Styrrach, and how fortunate for them they did not encounter him, a man cold, ruthless, and cruel. Instead of a warm greeting, the warmth of their blood spilled into the street might be the only welcome from him.

He pressed on until the light from the tavern's windows threw bright square patterns onto the compacted dirt of the street.

With one last furtive glance around, Styrrach strode into the tavern. The Bailiff would await him, doubtless irritated by the length of that wait, as Styrrach had intended. He did not order a drink and did not deign to speak to the innkeep. At the door of the room where meetings with the Bailiff had always taken place, three men in the distinctive tunics of the Bailiff's men stood guard, no weapons visible. They would carry daggers at their belts, concealed from view but available in a heartbeat. Long ago, Styrrach had insisted the Bailiff's men carry daggers and had swept away the man's vain wish for his men to be armed with swords, as the Duke's men were. Swords might frighten a drunken imbecile who fancied himself able to tackle an adversary, but they were almost useless at close quarters.

The men at the door stiffened as he strode toward them. Two reached behind themselves, where Styrrach imagined their daggers lay concealed, but the third held up a hand. The man's face seemed familiar, which suggested he had been in the Bailiff's employ for some time. Styrrach did not speak to them as he pushed open the door and entered the room.

The Bailiff, Glailam, had an emissary with him who lounged in a chair to one side of the room while Glailam paced at the far end. Styrrach imagined the Bailiff paced from frustration and impatience, but he did not care. "You do not deign to take meetings with us any longer?" Styrrach wasted no time on preamble. Preamble allowed time for others to form thoughts and opinions. In any conversation, the thoughts and opinions of only one person mattered, and that person had already spoken.

Glailam stared at Styrrach, and expressions of surprise, fear and contempt followed one another across his face as he composed a suitable response. "I will not meet with the simpleton you left behind."

Styrrach could not deny his admiration for the response. Glailam might be Styrrach's puppet, but he had not risen to become the Duke's Bailiff on the back of his pliability alone. His shrewdness and quick-wittedness set him apart from most other men. Styrrach respected those qualities, more so when he could employ them on his own behalf.

He chuckled. "None will meet with him again, unless they do so wherever he has travelled to afterward." The Bailiff raised his eyebrows, and Styrrach raised a hand to his mouth in mock horror. "Woe. I have confessed to the murder of the buffoon who failed to represent me. Will your men drag me to the gallows for my crimes?"

A grim smile split Glailam's face. "It is good you have returned. Balgow had become a stone in my boot, and I welcome his relocation to whatever lies beyond, if there is anything. The death of the Portreeve's man in the alleyway meant I missed more than one dalliance. The Duke felt compelled to interfere and wasted my time in the control of an incident your emissary had not the wit to prevent."

Styrrach bristled at the hint of criticism. "I have no emissaries. He served as Guildmeister." Glailam held up a placatory hand, and Styrrach adopted a friendlier tone. "Nonetheless, he failed us."

"When did you arrive? Will you stay to manage affairs here?"

Styrrach tutted. He loathed to be asked more than one question at a time. It created the potential for confusion in the answers and wasted his time while he sorted through the questions for priority. "I stay, and things will be as they used to be. I arrived today, after an incident you must resolve without further delay." Glailam raised his eyebrows again. "Raolos. Do you move to impeach him from office?"

Glailam sighed. "These things take time. Is there a need for greater expediency?"

"That there is." Styrrach pulled out the nearest chair and sat. He hooked out another with his boot, rested both feet on it. "I encountered unpleasantness in Ort. I took a meeting with the man, and it turned awry. Four men were lost, Porl among them."

Glailam knitted his brows and lowered himself into a chair. "That is a sorry turn. Did the Portreeve's men kill them, or is Raolos himself a brawler of unequalled ability?"

Styrrach paused. It went against his instincts to admit to any hint of weakness. Corelle's involvement cast him in an unfavourable light—a mere woman, and a deviant at that. To acknowledge she had bested him would bruise his pride, but how else could he explain what had turned? He disguised his answer in a half-truth. "Traitors from Zhanghar aided him."

"The same names that came to me in excuses from Balgow? The woman?"

Styrrach sucked air through his clenched teeth. "She is a jade. I will have her under my knife." His temper worsened as he told the tale, but he did not want Glailam to perceive any weakness he could exploit, for the Bailiff would exploit it if he could. The Guildmeister fought down his anger. "The Portreeve must be removed without delay. We need Ort. Some from the south wish to sail no further than Ort—Malkartas for one. It grieves their poor hearts to sail on to Zhanghar with goods destined for the north."

"Why does it concern them to sail a trifle further?"

"Time is coin, they tell me. It is better for them if the ships return sooner, and if they avoid Zhanghar it saves them four days at the least. More, if they avoid the need to re-provision in Ort or Alcmouth. I cannot fault their logic. They also reason they can increase the weight of goods they carry if they avoid the extra provisions needed to sail direct to Zhanghar. We need Ort."

"Why do they not unload in Alcmouth and leave us to ship the goods north?"

Styrrach tapped a finger on the table. He alone ran the enterprise, and it irritated him when others seemed to feel they could venture suggestions as though he had not already considered and discounted their ideas. Did they think him as simple as they themselves? "Our costs will increase if the goods are unloaded in Ort and we ship them north, but I wish to minimise these increases. If we ship them north from Alcmouth instead, it adds four or five days to the voyage, and those additional costs are borne by us, not our southern friends." He waved a hand to dismiss the subject. "These matters are best left for me to attend to. We need Ort because there is coin to be made there and because it sweetens the tempers of our trade partners. Impeach Raolos." Glailam need know nothing of the complicated negotiations with southern merchants who already badgered Styrrach for higher prices. If he added Ort to his business, he could offer them the compromise of shorter voyages and minimise any additional expense to himself.

"Incompetence takes time to prove. Evidence must be gathered, and it must stand the test of scrutiny. It cannot happen overnight."

"He attacked me. His men slew four of mine, and he consorts with wanted murderers. He should hang for this. Impeachment should be the least of his concerns."

The Bailiff sat with his head bowed, deep in thought. He looked up at last. "A bold claim from a man whom nobody in Dur would recognise if they stumbled over you in the street, and against a well-liked Portreeve. This will not do."

Styrrach stared at Glailam, numb with disbelief. Had he heard aright? Did the man have the audacity to challenge him? "Three times I have told you we need Ort. As a rule, I do not repeat myself, yet it appears you fail to hear me. Do we need a new Bailiff along with the Portreeve in Ort?"

To Styrrach's chagrin, the Bailiff laughed. "My dear Styrrach, I hear you. I do not agree with you. The two are unrelated. We risk much if we bring these accusations against Raolos. You may be called to testify against him. Everybody will ask, 'Who is this man who challenges such a popular leader and accuses him of murder?'

Will you tell them you are a businessman? They will ask, 'Where is your business?' Will you tell them you lead a clandestine band of callous murderers? That will turn ill for you, and you will have little time to regret your claim as the noose is lowered around your neck. We must be more certain of our accusation than this."

It would be simple enough for Styrrach to kill Glailam and his emissary. The Guildmeister's blood ran as hot as a smith's forge at the Bailiff's contradiction, and he pulled out his dagger. The emissary blanched, but the Bailiff held up his hands again. "Bloodshed has not served us well in recent times. Let us avoid it if we may."

The emissary coughed and Styrrach glowered at him. He had not spoken since the meeting began but now ventured a suggestion. "Raolos is rumoured to have entertained dalliances outside his marital bed. This is not the decorum expected of one in so high a position."

Glailam nodded. "That it is not." He laughed, and Styrrach smiled at the irony. The Bailiff had a formidable reputation as a womaniser. It would be delicious if he removed the Portreeve for infidelity, then went to the bed of one of the many consorts he kept at his beck and call around Alcmouth.

The emissary stared at Styrrach as he continued. "We would need several women who would attest to these dalliances."

Styrrach acknowledged the covert suggestion with a small nod. "You shall have them. How soon can the papers be served?"

Glailam replied with a shrug of his shoulders. "They will be aboard a ship in the morning. Raolos will be ordered here to answer his accusers, and within days, he will sail home with impeachment papers in his pocket. Ort will be ours."

Styrrach pondered all aspects. He would kill Raolos as soon as Glailam removed him as Portreeve, payment for the four lives lost in Raolos's office. Another idea occurred to him, one that gave him great satisfaction. Styrrach would kill the man's wife and son even as he journeyed to Alcmouth. "I will send a trusted messenger to carry the letters, who will wear your tunic. He will be at your offices at the sunrise."

Glailam scoffed at the proposal. "He may well be. I shall not, though he is welcome to await my arrival. I do not arrive at such a preposterous hour."

Styrrach did not raise his voice. He did not need to. "Tomorrow, you will." The Guildmeister did not care how the Bailiff planned to spend his night. It mattered not if Glailam left the meeting and headed for a night of debauchery with a thousand women—the papers would be in Styrrach's man's hands at the sunrise, whatever the cost to the Bailiff.

Glailam's face reddened, and Styrrach imagined he wondered whether he could resist the edict. Styrrach spun the dagger on the table, a casual gesture with an unmistakeable meaning. The Bailiff did not meet Styrrach's eye as he replied. "Very well. Are there other matters?"

Styrrach had suggested a new Bailiff might be required, and he may not have been far wide of the mark. This one would suffice for now, but further impudence would not be well received. He picked up his dagger, stood, and slid the blade into his belt. He turned and left without a word. The man had his answer and needed no other. With his usual caution, Styrrach strolled back toward the Guild building, convinced Ort would be in his control soon enough, and he turned his mind to Wilash and Corelle, or whatever she called herself these days.

Corelle had evaded him and disrupted his plans for too long, and he longed to have her in his hands where he could make her pay a terrible price for her interference. She and Wilash would not remain in Ort now the Guildmeister knew they were there, but he doubted they would risk another trip to Alcmouth. The docks must be watched, nonetheless, to alert him if they did arrive and to ensure he received word of Raolos's arrival. He would send his best man to Ort in case Corelle might still be there, but he felt certain she would have left already. She must know he would search for her, and she would not risk a confrontation with his members.

He glanced around before he entered the Guild building. He had returned via a different route and taken numerous random turns. He had the utmost confidence nobody followed him, but he still sought to assure himself no one lurked in the shadows to watch for him. Satisfied, he entered the building.

Gill perched on a chair in the parlour where he had been when Styrrach had left. He stood as Styrrach entered and appeared anxious to speak, but Styrrach addressed him first. "Something is awry?"

"Word has come in the last hour. Corelle and three others took ship to Ort under the token. The name of the ship is known to us, The Friendship. Wilash used his token and passed off the three women who travelled with him as his family, it seems."

Styrrach digested the information. He had ordered them apprehended if they used the token, and his order had not been carried out. "Why did the master not take them into custody? Women who travelled under the token were to be brought to me."

"One of the women—Corelle, my guess—threatened the master. She claimed to be your friend, bent on the capture of the woman you sought. Also, some unpleasantness took place on the trip. They called her Jorinda, but we can guess it must have been Corelle. She became embroiled in an altercation with several of the crew and went ashore in Ort with tempers frayed on both sides. Another woman with her may have been injured when she fainted or fell on the journey, and Corelle and this other became involved in a great argument over something."

Styrrach sifted through the noise for the gems of information he could use to his own benefit. He did not recognise the name Jorinda but would remember it against future reports. She could have killed several members of the crew in a fight, but they appeared to have made no effort to apprehend her. He imagined she cowed them with threats of violence. He understood the tactic, for few had mastered it better than him. The crew had failed him, nonetheless. "The master and two others are to be killed. The reward is five regals for each. See to it." Gill nodded. "My word is not a delicacy on a table to be picked over or ignored. It is to be obeyed, and we must make a clear example of those who do not grasp this."

Styrrach entered his office as Gill moved toward the outer door. "One other matter." Styrrach's shout stopped his Senior Aide before he could leave the building. "Rouse your best man and send him to me, no matter the hour." Gill hesitated for a moment before he nodded and left. Gill had been Senior Aide for less than a day and might have delayed as he pondered who might be the best man. Styrrach would allow him the benefit of the doubt this time, but should he hesitate to carry out orders in future, the man would not be granted such leniency. A memory of a conversation with Porl came into his mind, and he smiled. *I am too kind.*

He stood with his back to the door of his office for some time while he replayed the conversation with the Bailiff in his mind and stored up any slight he recalled. He never forgot a name, nor a grievance. Within an hour, he heard the outer door open and a knock at his office door.

He said nothing, and in time the door opened behind him. He did not turn to face whoever had entered. He did not smell fear, and it surprised him. Fear had a smell, and he could recognise it. "Your name?"

"Synna." The man said nothing more.

"Gill has sent you?" The name sounded familiar, but he could not place it.

"That he has. Is there an urgent gest?"

Styrrach turned to face Synna, a short, wiry man, like a great many of the members, with a familiar face. Doubtless the man had worked for him here in Alcmouth before, but Styrrach dismissed the thought. He had no sentimental attachment to the members, and he required nothing from them but complete obedience. Synna wore his hair too long for Styrrach's taste and sported bushy sideburns that appeared comical to his new Guildmeister's eye. "How long have you been a member of this Guild?"

"Several years. Is there a gest?"

Styrrach clenched his teeth, irritated by the brief responses even as he admired the man's focus on the reason he had been summoned. Such focus would be useful under the pressures of the gest Styrrach had for Synna, so he moved on to that matter. "Present yourself to the Bailiff's office at the sunrise, where you will be handed letters and a Bailiff's tunic. You will sail to Ort and pass yourself off as a Bailiff's man to deliver the letters to the Portreeve there. Raolos is his name, and you will hand them to no other. Then you will watch him until he takes ship to Alcmouth. Afterward, go to his house and ensure that when he returns to Ort, a Portreeve no longer, he will find his wife and child dead in their beds. Then return to Alcmouth. For this gest you will be paid twenty regals."

Faint creases appeared on Synna's brow as he appeared to consider the gest. "A child?"

"Did you mishear? The man's wife and child are to be killed. They are no innocent bystanders. They are casualties of unpleasant business. Are you too squeamish for this gest?"

Synna hesitated, drew in a breath, then nodded, turned, and closed the office door as he left. Styrrach tutted. He had hoped to use his favourite line, but Gill appeared to have chosen the right man, despite Synna's question about the death of the child. As the outer door closed, Styrrach pressed open the secret passageway and entered the house next door. He pushed the passage closed behind him, lay on the cot that stood, forlorn, alone in the room, and fell into an untroubled sleep.

TWO
THE GARDENER FROM RYL

After they left Taro's farm to return to Ort, Jorinda and Deineike decided to spend another night at The Ortlander. Deineike had not questioned Jorinda on the ride from the farm, but Jorinda guessed her lover must wonder what prompted the change of heart that now led them back to Ort a mere three days after they had left. They had revisited Taro's farm, where Jorinda had first met Deineike a year ago or more, and where they had become lovers, bound up in fates that became ever more violent and fraught. The visit to the farm re-opened old wounds in Jorinda, and she now regretted she had ridden down the lane at all. Deineike had urged her not to do so, but some compulsion for which no rational explanation could be found had prompted her to point her horse toward that wretched farmhouse where terrible memories preyed on her guilt and forced her to return to Ort.

The next morning, they rode on toward Ort. Jorinda owed Deineike an explanation, and she attempted to put her jumbled thoughts into words. "You must wonder why we ride for Ort when we left there a few days ago."

Concern filled the blue eyes that gazed into Jorinda's. "I believe I understand, but if it will help you to explain it, you should. It may be good for you to tell me, to arrange your thoughts in your own mind."

Jorinda took a deep breath and gathered her feelings together. "It shocked me to find Taro still on the bed where he died a year ago. I feel unbearable guilt for his death, and that we ran from the farm. He did not deserve to die. When I first arrived there, I did not intend to stay long, but inertia took hold, and I remained. When you appeared, I killed him by accident, but now his death torments me and persuades me I cannot abandon Raolos and his family to Styrrach and Guild justice. You are endangered by this decision, and I will understand if you are frustrated with me, but I must return. I cannot abandon them. I cannot run from Styrrach for the rest of my days."

Deineike's smile lit a small fire in the cold depths of Jorinda's misery. "If you are with me, what harm can befall me? I did not want to leave Raolos, Pettra, and Raopul at Styrrach's mercy, in truth. Whatever his motivations are, Styrrach seems bent on their ruin. He may see it as part of his vendetta against you. I do not understand his obsession with you, in truth, nor why he longs to see you dead."

Jorinda shook her head. "I cannot grasp it either. I slipped through his fingers in Zhanghar and killed Arella as I did so, to my shame. At first, I thought I had incurred his anger because I killed another Guild member, but he pursues me with such ferocity, and I am baffled. His ire seems to grow each time I slip through his fingers."

Deineike took Jorinda's hand and kissed her fingers. "I am glad I did not slip through your fingers."

"As am I."

They rode on, and by the time they entered Ort through the same gate they had ridden out of three days ago, the sun had already sunk low in the sky. The day had been cloudy, but a breeze sprang up late in the day to blow the clouds away, and the sun put in a welcome appearance for the first time since they left Ort.

The pair rode through the town with no urgency. They had already discussed their priorities. They would let Raolos know they were back in Ort to help him, return the horses to the stable, arrange for Raolos to have his coin returned to him, and find somewhere to spend the night. They would take the horses to Raolos's house first and seek his opinion about their return, since he had paid for them and could do with them as he wished.

Once past the stable, they rode along two further streets, then turned the horses into the street where Raolos lived. They had almost reached the iron fence that surrounded the grounds of his home when Jorinda noticed a flicker of movement ahead and reined her horse to an immediate stop. Deineike had lagged a little way behind her and rode level with Jorinda before she stopped her horse. Jorinda gestured for Deineike to be silent and turned her horse around. Deineike followed her into a different street, then whispered in concern. "What is wrong?"

Jorinda did not want to frighten Deineike. "Somebody takes a late stroll around their garden across the street from Raolos's house. Wait for me here while I go ahead and check."

"Are you sure you have not become so paranoid about the Guild you see danger where none exists?"

Jorinda considered the suggestion. "Better safe than sorry, I believe. I will be but a moment." She handed her reins to Deineike and slid from the horse. She peered around the corner, cautious. A high wall built around a home some way down the street would hide her from the sight of anybody in the garden opposite Raolos's house, so she hugged the shadows and ran as the sun sank below the roofline. She reached the wall, calmed her breaths after the brief exertion, then lay on the ground and crept forward a span at a time until she had a view down the street. Any who looked around for movement might miss her at ground level.

The large house opposite Raolos's carriage path had an ornate garden, and close to the road the owner had planted a stand of tall, colourful flowers. She thought she had seen the movement among those flowers, but she now wondered if it had been nothing more than the movement of the bright, coloured heads of the flowers. She saw the movement again at that moment; she had not been mistaken. A figure in dark clothing crouched low amid the flowers, hidden among the stalks. The figure stared at Raolos's house, then turned to glance behind them, a small movement, but it had been enough to catch Jorinda's eye as they rode toward the house.

At first, she could not decide why the figure glanced behind, then she noticed the shadows of the flower heads, which almost reached across the street to the iron fence. The figure checked the sun as it slid down the sky and waited for darkness. Slow and careful, Jorinda moved back, and once the wall hid her again, she dashed back through the shadows to where Deineike stood with the reins of both horses in her hand.

Jorinda panted from the exertion and forced words out between heavy breaths. "Somebody watches the house from the garden opposite."

Deineike looked anxious. "What will we do?"

Jorinda checked the position of the sun, which had now all but reached the horizon. "I do not know whether Raolos's house is guarded, but we cannot take any chances. There may be others hidden where I could not see them. I imagine it is the Guild, an attempt to kill Raolos in reprisal for the deaths of Styrrach's men.

Time is short. You must ride to the Portreeve's Offices and bring as many of his men as you can."

"Why must I go? You can better describe what you have seen."

"You are a better rider than me and will get there sooner. Leave now and impress on them the urgency of the situation."

"What will you do?"

Jorinda pointed toward the square. "Deineike, go now, for pity's sake. My actions will depend on what turns. Go."

To Jorinda's relief, Deineike did not debate the matter any further. She climbed onto her horse and kicked it forward down the road toward the square. As horse and rider turned a corner and vanished from sight, Jorinda tied the reins of her own horse to the low wooden fence of the house nearest to her and ran back to the shelter of the wall, dropped to the floor again, and peered down the street. The light deteriorated as the sun set, but she could still make out the figure crouched among the flowers.

Should she wait for the Portreeve's men to arrive? They would not be silent, and the figure might slip away when it heard them approach, and they would not learn why he or she—he, in all likelihood—lurked there. She could walk along the street past the figure and wait in a carriage path further along the road. The mystery person might also abandon their vigil when they saw her, and she might be in no position to prevent it. Since she could not approach from the street unseen, she needed an alternative to move closer to the hidden figure. She pulled back and looked up at the wall she hid behind.

When she jumped upward, she could not reach the top of the wall, even with her arms extended above her head. As she considered her options, a door opened, and a man stood in the doorway of his house. He drew in a breath to speak when he saw her, but she rushed forward to cover his mouth with her hand.

She whispered a hurried, urgent explanation she hoped the man would believe. "Your Portreeve is in danger. Do not speak." His eyes widened but he nodded. "Is this wall a part of your property?" He shook his head. She scanned the area but saw no other option. "Help me climb this wall."

Jorinda took her hand from his mouth, and he wore a quizzical look, but she dragged him over to the wall and held him close to it. "Help me." She pointed to the top of the wall.

"What sort of danger? Why should I trust you?"

The man wasted time on details while Raolos's life lay in peril. "I am Jorinda, if that name means anything to you."

"I have heard your name in connection with the disturbance at the Portreeve's Offices." He seemed to come to a decision and knelt on the ground while she watched him, perplexed. Although he whispered, his voice sounded too loud, and she scowled. "Get onto my shoulders." Baffled, she lifted a foot to one of his shoulders, but he raised a hand. "Not like that, put my head between your legs."

"Do you mock me? Raolos is threatened, and I am his only—"

He interrupted her snarls. "That I do not. I will stand, and you can reach the top of the wall."

Jorinda cursed, but the dark of the night deepened, and she had little time to act. With no workable alternative, she turned her back toward him, and he thrust his head between her legs. He gripped her shins with his hands and stood. If she stretched her arms above her, she could reach the top of the wall, so she clung to the top edge and pulled one leg up until her foot rested on his shoulder. He released her other leg and she stood, convinced she would fall to the ground at any moment. He held her feet and moved about in small steps, unsteady as he supported her weight, but she pushed off with her feet from each of his shoulders and hoisted herself up until she lay on the top of the wall.

Jorinda crawled forward along the wall until she could once again look down the street. She could not see the shadowy figure in the garden and feared she might be too late. An abrupt commotion broke out below her as the man who had helped her climb the wall stepped out into the road with another man. They yelled and pushed at each other. She cursed them, for now the figure would be sure to notice them.

Jorinda glanced toward the flowers and saw the figure rise to stare at the fuss as she had anticipated. At once, she smiled to herself at the man's imagination. He tried to beguile the would-be assailant, who would be distracted by the brawl. The momentary disruption might cover her movement. She stayed low and crawled as fast as she dared along the wall close to the street, then turned at the corner, the street now at her back.

The noise from the men stopped, and the figure disappeared back into the flowers, but Jorinda could now approach from behind. Beneath her, a low hedge ran close to the wall, so she swung her legs over the edge and lowered herself as far as she could. The sun had set, and she hoped the figure would not glance backward again. Her feet did not reach the ground, so she must release the top of the wall and drop behind the hedge, as quiet as possible.

With luck, the figure would not mark her movement as she dropped to the ground, but as she glanced once more toward the figure, a light sprang up in a window glass on the third floor of Raolos's house. If the light distracted the shadow visitor, they might not hear her drop, so she released her grip. She made an awkward landing and almost fell, but she heard no movement from the figure as she crouched low behind the hedge.

Near total darkness had spread across the town. Either the night had turned cloudy, or the fates had stolen the moon to aid her. The darkness would not be an ally to her alone, of course. The figure could also move unseen in such darkness—the perfect night for a gest. She hurried along the length of the hedge until she came to a gap and passed through it toward the road before she crouched as low as she could, pulled her dagger from her boot, and stared toward the flowers.

Down the street, beyond the wall she had crawled along, she heard shouts. Somebody yelled, "Portreeve's men," and the figure raised its head to look toward the sound. In Raolos's house, somebody came to the lighted window and obscured the lantern's glow behind them.

Jorinda's mark pushed the flowers aside and moved away from the direction of the noise. They must have decided to flee from the potential arrival of the Portreeve's men as Jorinda had guessed. She, of course, had now moved closer, and she ran after the figure. She closed the gap with ease as the other moved away with care, but the white flash of a face told her they had glanced her way. The person must have spotted her, and no doubt pulled a dagger.

Jorinda launched herself forward, stayed low, and caught the legs of the figure as it turned toward her. A man's voice grunted, then they rolled on the ground, entwined. She slashed with her dagger but made no contact until her hand struck the ground, and the dagger flew from her grip. She heard a whoosh as an arm sailed past her face in the darkness, and she scrabbled for something she could cling to. The man pushed at her and extricated himself from the tangle. As she swung her legs around to scramble to her feet, she kicked him.

He let out a howl of pain, so she reached for him again and managed to grasp an arm. She rose to her knees and heaved herself toward him. He aimed another blow that connected with her shoulder and knocked her askew. He knocked one of her hands loose from his arm, but she grabbed for it again. He had punched rather than slashed with his dagger, so she guessed he either had not pulled it or held it in the hand she clung to.

The voices drew close, and lanterns waved in the air. Jorinda yelled, "Here," and figures turned toward her in the lantern light. The shout betrayed her, and a powerful punch connected with her head. Lights flashed before her eyes, her thoughts vanished into clouds in her mind, and she cried out in pain. Jorinda struggled to retain her balance, swayed backward, and fought not to lose her grip on her opponent's arm as dizziness overwhelmed her. Before he could land another punch, other figures leapt on them. The scene grew more chaotic as hands reached for them in the lantern light. Somebody jerked her backward, and she yelled in protest, but two figures now held the man she had fought. She lost her hold on his arm as whoever held her pulled her further from him.

Arms wound around her body, and she heard a surprised gasp as a hand touched one of her breasts. Breathless and shaken from the fight, she managed to cry out. "My name is Jorinda, if you recognise it."

"That I do." The voice came from behind her, and the man released his grip.

Anxious, Jorinda yelled, "Do you have him?" More lights waved in the darkness, and Jorinda thought six or more men in the red tunics of the Portreeve had arrived, but she could not see Deineike.

A voice ahead of her cried out, "That we do." She exhaled in relief.

Somebody yelled for the man to be brought to the road, and the men who held him pulled him without ceremony into the road as he continued to struggle against them. His hands were manacled behind his back, but it still took four of them to manoeuvre him out of the garden. Jorinda glanced down the road, saw a knot of people and two horses near the wall she had climbed along, and guessed Deineike must be among them.

More urgent matters concerned her, and she stepped over to the captive. Torches now illuminated the scene along with the lanterns, and the splutter of the torches mingled with excited chatter. The man Jorinda had fought stood little taller than her, with long hair that extended in scruffy bushes down each of his cheeks. His clothes were muddy, and her own had fared no better in the tussle.

He glared at her, his face twisted in a mixture of anger and surprise. "Corelle. Why are you still here in Ort?"

One of the Portreeve's men punched him in the stomach, and he let out a gasp and fell forward. They pulled him back upright.

Jorinda snarled. "You are with the Guild. How else could you know me?"

He appeared to struggle for breath after the punch. "We all know you. You are marked for death. It is an honour gest, and fifty regals to any who brings your head to Styrrach."

One of the Portreeve's men barked at him to be silent, but Jorinda held up a hand. "Have you come here in search of me?"

He spat blood out of his mouth. It seemed the Portreeve's men had been none too gentle in their apprehension of him. "That I have not, although I would have claimed the reward if I had killed you."

If the man had not planned to kill her, he must have a different target. "Have you come for Raolos?"

He laughed. "Raolos is aboard ship, headed for Alcmouth, as you well know."

The reply puzzled Jorinda, and she turned to the nearest Portreeve's man, who confirmed the story. "It is as he says. Ibie and five others are with him. We have fewer than twenty men left in the town. Every man available rushed here when your message came to us."

"Jorinda, are you hurt?" Jorinda snapped her head around toward the sound of Deineike's voice. The tall woman still held the reins of both horses and had walked forward to stand on the edge of the crowd of Portreeve's men who surrounded Jorinda and the captive.

"I am unhurt. We have captured this—"

"Jorinda?" Pettra ran across the road, accompanied by a woman in servant's garb. "You return, but what has turned here?" She embraced Jorinda for five heartbeats, then stepped back and placed a hand on her cheek. "You are a mess." She gave Jorinda an affectionate smile, and her hand remained at Jorinda's cheek for long moments before Jorinda reached up to pull it away from her.

One of the Portreeve's men turned to Pettra. "This man lurked here for reasons we do not yet know."

Pettra seemed to notice the captive for the first time. "What business have you here?"

He laughed. "You were to be my business, and now I see you, I declare I would have taken great pleasure from that business." Pettra covered her mouth with both hands. The man's words appeared to have terrified her.

Jorinda needed to understand more. "You have been sent on a gest for Pettra?"

The man spat out more blood. "That I have if that is her name. And the child."

There were angry growls from the men around him, and one of them cuffed the back of the man's head. Jorinda again held up a hand, anxious for them to allow her to continue her questions.

She stared the Guild man in the eyes. "The child? You would take a child? You have sunk low if you would accept such a gest."

His blood dripped from his chin onto the street as he lowered his head. "I have sunk low." His head snapped up, and he stared at her as fury blazed in his eyes. "You know who sent me. Would you defy him if he sent you?"

Jorinda drew in a sharp breath, the nuance of his question not lost on her. He meant Styrrach, and she knew the terror he could instil in anybody. "I cannot say. My heart says I would take a dagger first. My head says I might have feared the reprisals if I refused that order."

One of the Portreeve's men spoke. "You rave." Jorinda shook her head in sadness. They could not comprehend Styrrach's menace. To stand before him and defy him, just he and you; in truth, few could say they possessed that level of courage. He gave off peril and threat, even when he said nothing. His intimidation of everyone who met him would not be easy to explain to those who had not.

Jorinda turned her attention to the Guild member again. "He sends you here to do his work, yet tomorrow he would as soon sell you to the Portreeve if it served him better. He is despicable."

"I know this." The Guild man's quiet voice sounded almost sad, and the fire in his eyes burned out.

Sadness took some of the anger from her. "He has doomed you with this gest."

At that moment, he frowned. "What did you say? He would sell me? What do you mean?"

"He will do it. I know, for he sold me. He calls it shrouding, and he betrays Guild members to the Portreeve, although we do not know why. It may be members who have served their purpose in his eyes."

He looked thoughtful for ten or more heartbeats, and a snarl clawed its way to his face. "The Portreeve hanged a friend of mine not a year since. Do you suggest the Guild betrayed him?"

"I imagine so. The Portreeve's men in Zhanghar came for me after Styrrach sold me." Some of the Portreeve's men muttered to one another, and Jorinda realised most of them knew little or nothing of the things they discussed. She became concerned for the man, and for herself. Things might be revealed the Portreeve's men should not be aware of.

Jorinda turned to Pettra. "I must talk to this man further, but not here. May we come into your house? There are things I need to say to him that are for his ears alone." The men around her raised objections and she held up both hands. "You may wait without. He is manacled and is no threat. Not to me or any other."

The man barked out dark laughter. "You may as well hang me now as leave me alone with this one. I will not see tomorrow either way."

"That would not disappoint us." Cruel laughter broke out at the response from one of the Portreeve's men.

Pettra hushed them all. "Of course. Bring him into the house. Jorinda, Deineike, and this man will come in with me. You will wait at the door, and Raolos will know of it if you refuse my command." Some of Raolos's men complained, but they seemed anxious not to offend Pettra and incur Raolos's wrath in the process. One pointed out that Jorinda could be trusted, that she had saved Raolos's life.

Jorinda asked one of the men for his lantern so she could retrieve her dagger. The flowers were in a sorry state, flattened and trampled into the mud, and as she looked around, Deineike led the horses to the edge of the road.

"What do you seek?"

"My dagger. I dropped it while I wrestled with that man." A glint of metal in the lantern light caught her eye, and she bent to the ground. Her dagger lay almost buried in the mud, no more than the last three or four fingers of the blade's length visible. She picked it up, wiped the handle on her trousers, and slipped it into her boot.

Deineike held out her arms, and Jorinda went to her. Deineike held her tight and kissed the side of her head. "I have been so worried."

"All is well, my love. You timed your arrival to perfection. I do not think I could have bested him in the scuffle had the Portreeve's men not arrived when they did. My thanks."

Deineike glanced back along the road. "Those people said they helped you climb a wall, then they put on a distraction. They did not know what turned, but the Portreeve's men told them to stay back."

Jorinda nodded. "That they did. One of them lifted me onto the wall, for I could not reach it alone. I have never had a man's head between my legs."

She laughed, but Deineike looked puzzled. "You told me you and Taro..." Her voice trailed off.

"That we did, but never with his head. Only with his... Not with his head." Jorinda laughed again. "Enough of this. My jest has not landed well, and I must speak more with this man. He holds answers and information, and there is much I do not understand. Raolos has been summoned to Alcmouth and has left."

Deineike gasped in alarm. "Raolos is not here? He is in great peril in Alcmouth. Styrrach will order him killed."

Jorinda lowered her voice to ensure nobody else heard her. "Much must be explained, but I cannot talk of these things before Raolos's men. They must not learn of my past in more detail than I have already let slip. Let us continue this debate in the house."

Deineike glanced toward the man. "Agreed. We must know all we can." She hesitated, then looked deep into Jorinda's eyes. "Pettra's hand lingered long on your cheek."

Jorinda could not meet her gaze, and she kicked at the mud as she considered how best to respond. She had hoped Deineike would not notice the gesture, but that hope proved futile. "That it did. Relief at our return, my guess." She felt a pang of guilt at a lie that further complicated an already tangled situation and would make the truth more difficult if it came out at some point.

Deineike said nothing, but Jorinda could not look her in the eyes. The tall woman drew in a soft breath. "That it was." Relief washed over Jorinda as the awkward moment passed.

They walked up the carriage path to the front door, and the Portreeve's men followed. Pettra walked alongside Jorinda, while the servant hung back behind her employer's wife. At the door, Jorinda took the captive's arm and propelled him into the house while Deineike tied the horses' reins to a rail beneath a large window. With all five of them inside the house, Pettra closed the door and hurried the servant out of the hall about her duties.

THREE
THE INTERROGATION OF SYNNA

In the calm of the house, Jorinda faced the man. "Tell me your name, since you know mine."

"Synna."

She did not recognise the name, but he might still be part of Styrrach's chain of command. "What do you know of shrouding?"

His face became a blank parch. "Shrouding? You have used this word twice. What does it mean? I have not heard it before."

Jorinda studied him but saw no trace of dishonesty in his face. "As I told you, the Guild betrays members to the Portreeve for reasons we do not know. They call it shrouding."

He stared into her eyes, proud but bitter. "Did Balgow betray my friend to the Portreeve?"

Wilash had used the name of the Alcmouth Guildmeister in place of his own when they first met Raolos, and Jorinda winced as she heard it again. "I do not know the circumstances, but that is my guess. It seems Styrrach shrouded me in Zhanghar a year and a bit ago, and I had to flee. That is why Styrrach now seeks me."

"'And a bit?'" He looked perplexed and Jorinda frowned at Deineike, who struggled to stifle a laugh.

Deineike could not resist, it seemed. "She is from Ryl." Deineike and Pettra laughed at the jest.

Jorinda glared at them. "This is a serious matter." Her anxious hiss made them laugh even more.

Synna shook his head. "Styrrach has killed Balgow. Had I known the truth about my friend's death, I would have carried out the gest myself, though it cost me my life." Synna's red face and taut lips portrayed his anger.

It did not surprise Jorinda to learn Styrrach had killed the Alcmouth Guildmeister. "Balgow gave the orders in Alcmouth, but the Guild is part of Styrrach's larger scheme. He enriches himself through the control of prices of goods from the south. He uses the Guild in some way that benefits his operation, and he works with the Portreeve. Many of the gests you have completed will have come to you at the behest of the Portreeve, or even the Bailiff himself."

Synna took a step backward, and Jorinda reached for him, concerned he might fall. "You do rave." His voice dropped, little more than a whisper. "This is unthinkable." He shook his head as if to scatter far from him the things he had heard.

"It is true." Jorinda turned to Pettra. "Why has Raolos gone to Alcmouth?"

Pettra blinked, as though to keep tears from her eyes. "He answered a summons from the Bailiff. He told me no more."

Synna interrupted them. "It *is* true. Raolos answered a call from the Bailiff, true enough. But I carried the Bailiff's letters, at Styrrach's command. I had not linked the two in my mind." He straightened. "Remove my cloak."

Jorinda's heart leapt as her instincts urged caution. This might be some attempt at escape. She reached down for her dagger and held it against his throat. "I will not hesitate to take your life in a heartbeat if you attempt to flee."

He did not turn from her gaze. "I know this. You are Corelle. You are…renowned, if you like the word. Within the Guild, at the least."

Jorinda raised her other hand to his throat and fumbled at the drawstring that held his black cloak fastened. Doubtless he had chosen black with concealment in mind. The cloak had a hood, although it had fallen from his head in the scuffle. As the drawstring came loose, the cloak parted at his chest. Below it, he wore a tunic of bright yellow. "What is this tunic?"

"It is the tunic of a Bailiff's man. The Bailiff's Offices gave me letters to carry to Raolos and this tunic to wear when I delivered them. I planned to use it to gain entry to the house tonight and complete my gest."

Pettra stared at him, her eyes filled with hatred. "It would have done you no good, for I have never seen it before. The Bailiff's men do not deign to visit our house."

Jorinda tried to turn Synna's attention away from Pettra and back to her own questions. "Then you do not doubt me?"

"That I do not." He turned to Pettra. "I apologise for the reason I came here. I will not blame others, for I accepted the gest. You are in great danger, and even if Raolos's men hang me before the sunrise, others will come. Something beyond my comprehension is in play, but Styrrach wants you and your child dead."

Deineike snapped her fingers, and Synna started. "This is the proof." She pointed at the tunic.

Jorinda did not understand Deineike's meaning. "Proof?"

"The tunic proves the Bailiff is involved with the Guild. The Duke cannot ignore the connection."

Jorinda ran the night's events through her mind and tried to form them into some course of action. "It proves nothing unless Synna confirms he carried the letters and wore the tunic under orders from Styrrach." She stared into Synna's eyes.

He gave a derisive laugh. "Raolos has the letters, not I, and this tunic will soon swing from the nearest tree. Several men outside the door will have it no other way."

A silence fell on the hallway. Jorinda's thoughts turned to Raolos, whose life must now be in great danger. Styrrach had sent Synna north to kill Pettra and Raopul, and she guessed he intended to take Raolos's life down in Alcmouth. Once he did so, he would replace the Portreeve with one who owed allegiance to Styrrach, part of the enterprise he and the Bailiff operated.

Jorinda turned to Pettra again. "When did Raolos leave?"

Pettra replied, "Today," at almost the same instant Synna said, "This morning."

Raolos had a day's start on her, but if she left tomorrow, she might still reach him in time and warn him, and he could return to Ort to ensure the safety of him and his family. She exhaled a long, slow breath, her lips pursed. "I will sail to Alcmouth in the morning. I can bring this news to Raolos, and he can return."

Pettra nodded, then drew in a sharp breath. "I forgot. A letter came for you. It arrived at Raolos's office the day after you left. I will bring it." She spun on her heels and ran from the hall. Jorinda looked to Deineike, who raised her eyebrows and shrugged her shoulders.

Pettra returned to the hall with the letter. "Why is a personal letter called a letter, yet a business letter is named letters?" She handed Jorinda the letter.

Jorinda mumbled, distracted as she tore at the seal. "What is scribed, must be." Deineike tutted, and Jorinda remembered her displeasure at the phrase in Syme's tavern so few days ago, though that night now seemed like an eternity past. She glanced up and gave Deineike an apologetic smile before she returned her attention to the letter.

"It is from Wilash. They fare well." She chuckled. "As we imagined, Wilash rated the rowboat an experience never to be repeated." Deineike laughed, the soft tinkle of water as it trickles into an already full tub. "Wilash has found work in a smithy and Klordia works in a small tally house. They have a house and a…" She fell silent.

Deineike's voice took on an impatient tone. "What? Go on."

"Their home has a garden. They grow vegetables."

"Hah." Deineike wore a smug grin on her face.

Jorinda finished the letter and handed it to Deineike.

Synna spoke up, sadness in his tone. "I met Wilash. He seemed a fine man."

"That he is. We believe he had also been chosen for shrouding on the night I killed Cloud."

Synna gave her a wry smile. "Sky."

Jorinda dismissed the correction with a wave of her hand. "Cloud, Sky; he is dead. He would have killed Klordia had I not intervened." She sighed. "That is a story for another time."

Synna nodded. "I am happy they are safe. Where did they go?"

Jorinda became guarded. "That is not yours to know." He lowered his head.

Pettra touched Jorinda on the arm. "We must return to the issue at hand. Raolos is in peril. You offered to sail to his aid. We cannot allow him to be murdered." She gave a small nod as she spoke, as if to confirm her words.

She had the right of it, and Jorinda returned her attention to the matter. She stared at Synna. "Will you assist us?"

He shrugged. "I will not see the sunrise. I am in no position to help you."

If he felt any emotion, he kept it hidden, and Pettra's brow creased. "Do you not fear death?"

He glanced at her. "Those who live by the blade desire nothing more than a quick, painless death when their ruin comes. If that is the fate written for me tonight, I do not fear it."

Pettra turned to Jorinda and whispered in awe. "Is this true?"

Jorinda confirmed Synna's words. "It is true enough, after all else."

Pettra shook her head, and Deineike laid a gentle hand on Pettra's arm. "It is a difficult thing to understand, this life they chose. Do not dwell on it, for it is a puzzle too complex to solve."

Jorinda spoke again. "We might persuade Raolos's men not to put you to death." She voiced her thoughts aloud, uncertain she could calm their blood lust toward the man who had admitted his intention to murder the wife and son of their Portreeve. Nonetheless, the fishmen in Ryl used the expression, *"The small fish may attract the larger,"* and Jorinda decided to roll the dice. She would try to persuade Raolos's men that a greater purpose could be served if Synna lived.

Synna showed curiosity but no fear. "How could you achieve this?"

"They must believe you will act to save Raolos from his ruin. That may cool the heat of their fury." Jorinda looked around but found no encouragement in the faces of the others. "It is worth a try. If not, then I will go alone to Alcmouth and do what I can."

Deineike had other ideas. "You will not go alone."

Jorinda wanted to form objections, but the look on Deineike's face stilled them in her throat. She gave a resigned shake of her head. "We will travel to Alcmouth."

Synna sighed. "If you can persuade the men outside, I will join you and give such aid as I can. As you are no doubt aware, Styrrach will act against us at every turn. The Bailiff also. They will not allow us to live to plead our case to the Duke, I am certain of it, but I may as well be hanged in Alcmouth as Ort." He stopped and looked askance at Jorinda as she and Deineike gave an ironic laugh. "Something amuses you?"

Jorinda replied between her laughter. "That it does not. I spoke similar words in Alcmouth not long ago, nothing more." She composed herself, then continued. "I will ask it of them. You must be kept somewhere tonight, for I will not trust you to stay here with Pettra and her son."

He nodded. "I think I understand why Styrrach hunts you. You are a thorn in his thumb. I understand also why he has failed to catch you. You are formidable."

As her cheeks heated in embarrassment, Jorinda turned to open the door. She did not yet trust Synna, but she recognised his importance to the plan to bring down Styrrach and the Guild. The Portreeve's men looked at her in anticipation as she stepped out, their anger and hunger for justice tangible, as though she could grasp it in her hands. "This man has a part to play in Raolos's safety. He and I must sail to Alcmouth tomorrow and bring important news to Raolos. He will accompany us to the Duke, where we will plead our case. We must strike down an evil that has risen in Dur or our lives may never be the same."

Someone from the rear of the group shouted. "He is a murderer. He must hang."

Another agreed. "That he is, and he came here to kill Pettra. Raolos would place the noose around his neck himself."

Jorinda held up her hands for silence. "That he is. Take him and hang him, and me alongside him, for I am a murderer also."

As she had anticipated, her words shocked the men. Some looked down, others looked away. At length, one spoke. "You are a hero."

The man nearest to Jorinda glared at Synna, who stood behind her. "You saved Raolos. He has not earned such honour. He must die." Murmurs of assent rose from the men.

"You have the right of it. I saved Raolos, but this man wishes to atone for his past and help me to save Raolos again. Will you still judge him with such harshness if we succeed, and he plays a major part in that success? If we fail, we will both die, and Raolos with us, my guess." Nobody replied. "I recall a phrase. *'If you do not stand with me, you stand against me.'*" Jorinda focused on the men, gazed from one to the other. None spoke against her. "You may lock him in the gaol for tonight, but he is under my care. If you drag him to the gallows, return here and drag me there before you send him wherever he travels to afterward. We will hang together."

One of the men stared at her in consternation, and she believed she had lost the bluff. "We have no gaol in which to lock him."

Jorinda looked at him in curiosity. "Then where do you lock criminals?"

"Some spend a night in the stocks. There are no others."

Jorinda tried to unravel his words. "There is no gaol here?"

Another of the men replied. "I do not believe there is a gaol in all Dur."

Jorinda became more puzzled. "What of the heinous crimes? How are they punished?"

The nearest man threw his hands upward. "What heinous crimes?"

She searched her mind for a suitable crime. "Theft?"

"Stocks." He did not embellish his response.

"Violence?"

"There is little violence. Men will sometimes fight one another in a tavern, although the ale throws all the punches, in truth. Stocks."

She floundered for a gaol-worthy crime. "Murder then."

One of the others joined in. "I know two murderers, my guess, and they both stand before me tonight, it seems. The law says a murderer is to be hanged in punishment. Nobody has been hanged in Ort, to my knowledge. Why would anybody murder a person if they would then lose their life on the gallows?"

She stood on safer ground now, for Guild members had been hanged in the past, in Zhanghar at the least. "Where is the gallows, then, if there is no gaol?"

The same man replied. "There are no gallows. It is a phrase; nothing more. A tree would serve, I imagine."

Jorinda stood speechless before them until she recalled something Arella once told her. "Debt. The Debtor's Gaol."

Despite the earlier tension, most of the men roared with laughter as she floundered before them. "There is no Debtor's Gaol. What person would not make good on a debt?" The man who replied wiped at his eyes.

Words failed Jorinda. Did Ort have no crime outside the Guild, or had she been foolish to believe gaols existed? Had Styrrach lied to Wilash all those years ago when he said he would rescue the young lad from the Debtor's Gaol? Jorinda's mother had coerced her to behave with occasional threats of monsters, mythical creatures that feasted on children who disobeyed their parents. Had Styrrach preyed on Wilash's young innocence to drag him into the Guild through the invention of a Debtor's Gaol? Of course he had. Styrrach, the master manipulator, had fooled her and Wilash both. She turned to Deineike for support, but her lover had dissolved into laughter. Synna smiled at her, and even Pettra laughed. It seemed they all found her an amusement even after such a night of stress.

Deineike wiped tears from her eyes and gasped, "She is from Ryl." All present burst into further laughter.

FOUR
ANOTHER RIVER JOURNEY

JORINDA'S CONFUSION ABOUT GAOLS HUMILIATED HER BUT LIFTED THE mood of all gathered around, and she persuaded the Portreeve's men to entrust Synna to her. One even jested that if she allowed him to escape, they would build a gaol so they could imprison her. The jest drew more laughter, curse them all.

Synna slept in a locked office in the Portreeve's Offices, and two men guarded him. A gaol of sorts, Jorinda reasoned. Pettra insisted she would pay for passage to Alcmouth for Jorinda and Deineike, but she would not pay for Synna. He came up with an alternative. Once Jorinda and Deineike were aboard, he would use the token to obtain passage on the same ship and behave as though he travelled alone. The Portreeve's men would hold him at the docks until the women were aboard, then he would follow. From that moment, responsibility for him passed to Jorinda. She hoped she had not misjudged his intent, or she and Deineike might be tipped over the rail one night, their throats cut. She thought it unlikely; he seemed in awe of her skills, and she did not fear him.

When she and Deineike tumbled into a bed in Raolos's house and fell asleep, nightmares came again. She swung from the gallows in the yard of a gaol where the inmates were all victims of her previous gests. Instead of a noose, the gallows had a blade, and it slit her throat as the trap door beneath her feet opened, operated by a lever that whispered, "I love you."

The morning brought relief from the nightmares. Jorinda waited for Deineike to wake, and they rose. Once they had washed, they went down to the parlour. Pettra already sat at a small table laden with breads, meats and fruit.

Pettra gestured to the table as they sat on a couch. "Eat some food before you leave." Jorinda put some food on a small plate, but Deineike seemed reluctant to eat any of it. "Will you not eat?"

Deineike's reply sounded like a complaint. "There seems little point. This morning, I must ride that wooden beast again, and it will separate me from any food at the first opportunity."

Pettra looked confused, so Jorinda explained. "Deineike does not sail well. It does not agree with her stomach."

Pettra insisted Deineike must eat something, and she agreed to take a little fruit. Pettra turned to Jorinda. "I am disappointed I will not be able to wear your dress to the ball, after all else. It would be unthinkable for me to attend alone, and Raolos cannot return in time."

It seemed a minor consideration in the face of the dangers Pettra and her son faced. Those who moved in her social circle must develop a stoicism those of lower status could not grasp. Jorinda searched for a suitable response. "Another opportunity will come. Avoid cake until that day." Pettra laughed, and Deineike looked thoughtful as she chewed on some of the fruit. Jorinda regretted the jest; it alienated Deineike, who had not been a part of it from the start. Worse, Pettra might believe it created some clandestine thread between them.

Deineike broke the awkward silence. "Pettra, you could take Raopul to Dur City and stay with Wilash and Klordia. I am sure you would be safer there."

Jorinda had not considered the idea but thought it had great merit. Pettra, however, shook her head. "I will not leave. Raopul and I will await Raolos's return here. The Portreeve's men will guard the house. We will be safe."

Jorinda doubted the Portreeve's men would be a match for Styrrach's forces, although none might come, and the thread of an idea occurred to her. Synna could return to the Guild in Alcmouth, say he had completed the gest, and buy them some time. It would be risky for Synna, however, since if Styrrach discovered his deception, he would suffer Guild justice and not come by the quick, painless death he had mentioned the previous night. Still, she would propose it to him.

They continued to pressure Pettra to consider the trip to Dur City, but she would have none of it. Jorinda longed to make a start and reach Alcmouth as soon as possible, so she abandoned the notion. Jorinda and Deineike rode their horses to the dock, where they had arranged to meet the Portreeve's men and Synna. The men would return the horses to the stables. Three men stood with Synna on the docks, and the women tied the horses to a rail nearby. They did not acknowledge the men, lest somebody noted the interaction. They took their packs from the horses and walked toward the closest ship.

Jorinda stood at the bottom of the ramp and called up to ask a mariner above her where the ship sailed next. The swarthy man, his olive skin lined as though he spent much time in the sun, did not appear to understand. A dockhand nearby overheard her and said the ship would sail for Zhanghar once resupplied. She thanked him, and they walked on toward another ship. Jorinda looked back at the Portreeve's men and Synna. They had not moved, but they watched the women wander the dock and showed nothing more than mild interest in them.

Deineike's hand stopped Jorinda in her tracks, and she whispered. "Let us pass this vessel by."

Jorinda noticed the name painted on the ship's stern—The Friendship. To her further disappointment, Wilke stood on the rear deck and stared down at her with venom in his eyes.

Deineike pressed a hand against Jorinda's arm and whispered. "Ignore him, my love."

Jorinda did not slow, but she kept her gaze fixed on Wilke, and he returned the stare. They had almost passed him when he yelled down at them. "He is dead, and you killed him."

Deineike kept her voice low and soft. "Who is dead?"

"I know not. He raves."

"Safe travels, jade." Wilke continued to shout as they walked on. "A time will come when I collect the debt owed for his life, you may depend on it."

Jorinda guessed Wilke referred to his friend, the man who had killed Deineike's mother, and wondered how he had died, and why Wilke claimed she had killed him. As they passed alongside the ship, she glanced up again. She spotted a man in a master's coat but did not recognise him. When she glanced back, Wilke had followed them part of the way along the deck, but he stopped and stared after them.

They reached the ramp of the next ship and shouted an enquiry up to a mariner, who told them the vessel would soon depart for Ryl.

Deineike muttered in anger. "Are we fated to find no vessel headed south?" With that, their fates altered. Only two more ships bobbed and tugged at their ropes at the dock, but the first of the two would soon set sail for Alcmouth, and the master sold them cabin space with some glee. Indeed, he seemed so keen, Jorinda wondered whether the carriage of passengers might enrich him alone, that he put the coin into his own pocket rather than pass it to the ship's owner.

He showed them to a small cabin at the rear of the ship. Four bunk-like cots hung against one wall, and four chairs had been placed around a table. Two large trunks sat beneath a round window that looked out behind the ship. The token had never bought Jorinda such a pleasant cabin, and she wondered whether all ships had such cabins aboard against the prospect of passengers who would pay coin for the journey. It seemed an extravagance aboard a vessel that carried cargo for the most part.

Few could afford passage on ships, and the master had demanded a price so exorbitant, their own coin would not have run to it—sixty regals. Jorinda wondered how anybody could ever afford such transportation, no matter how wealthy they might be. She thanked the fates Pettra had given them a hundred regals—an enormous sum of coin. Jorinda had no idea how Pettra had come by it on such short notice, since she had once claimed they kept little coin in the house. Such concerns did not matter, and she did not dwell on it.

Based on Jorinda's recollection of the trip on The Friendship, the voyage between Ort and Alcmouth took four or five days, although Jorinda had been stressed for a large part of that trip and had not counted the days with any care. To ride on horseback would take two tendays or more, she imagined. The river saved a vast amount of time, but at a cost they would never be able to afford without assistance from wealthy patrons such as Raolos and Pettra.

They dropped their packs into one of the trunks, lay on a cot together, and Jorinda stroked Deineike's hair. "I hope the voyage will be kind to you."

"My thanks. My moon cycle is all but done. That will help, I am sure." Deineike turned to Jorinda, and passion blazed in her eyes. "In more ways than one." Jorinda could not understand why

Deineike never allowed any intimate contact during her moon cycle. She burned for lovemaking for much of the pass, but when her moon cycle came upon her, she desired no pleasure herself, though she continued to satisfy Jorinda. For her part, Jorinda felt no such inhibition and remained open to the joy of their sexual activity at any point in the cycles of her life.

Deineike's fingers teased at her and drove the thought from her mind, but she yearned for stimulation from her lover's tongue, so she pressed down on Deineike's head until she slid between her legs. Deineike's tongue delighted Jorinda, who gasped with desire. Her body arched upward as her lover's tongue tantalised her, and Jorinda shook as her passion built into a crescendo inside her. She moaned for more, and Deineike obliged. Jorinda sailed far from Ort even as the ship still bobbed at the dock.

The ship moved out into the river later, and by the midday they headed south to whatever fate was written for them all. They went up onto the deck. The sun held little warmth, and the wind whipped through their clothes to turn the day even colder. As they stood at the rail, Synna came through the door from the cabin area. However things turned, accountability for his actions now rested with Jorinda alone as she had promised the Portreeve's men.

He strolled past them. "Ladies." He gave a slight inclination of his head as he drew close, then continued down the deck, and Jorinda glanced around, as though she took in all the activity on the deck. The master stood on the rear deck with his eyes fixed on them. She could not guess why he might be interested in their interaction with Synna, but she would be cautious.

The wind whipped the river into small, white-capped waves that did not agree with Deineike, and she fetched up soon after Synna had passed them. Jorinda could not imagine how it must feel to be so afflicted whenever she sailed. No words could describe her admiration that Deineike again subjected herself to it in the name of simple loyalty. Synna showed no sign of the difficulty the motion of the ship induced in Deineike as he leaned on the rail near the bow and watched the water slip by beneath the ship.

Jorinda tried to raise Deineike's spirits. "We know more nautical terms than we used to."

"Do you mean shippy terms?"

Jorinda laughed, and Deineike joined in despite her obvious distress. "You know so many words, and often correct me, but you used that strange word."

"I knew the word. It would not come to me. Does this not happen to you?"

Jorinda smiled. "That it does not." A curious look crossed Deineike's face. "What is wrong?" Jorinda reached for her lover, concerned.

"I still have headaches at whiles, and I forget words from time to time." She paused, and Jorinda tried to remain calm, afraid Deineike would pour out some worrisome explanation. Deineike looked into her eyes, a serious expression on her face. "Do you imagine…" She did not complete the question.

Jorinda's heart leapt, and her throat constricted as worry threatened to steal her voice. She forced reassurances from her lips. "It is nothing, my love. You are old, nothing more." She smiled again.

Deineike slapped Jorinda's upper arm, a familiar twinkle in her eyes. "You are a bully."

"Then we are both bullies, for not three days ago, you bullied me in Taro's barn."

Deineike laughed. "That I did."

Despite Jorinda's relief at the laughter, she worried Deineike might have suffered more serious effects after all the blows to her head. "We will find a healer to talk to about these minds of ours. Such a thing must exist in Alcmouth."

Deineike frowned. "Will we stay there long?"

Jorinda could find no simple answer—there were too many parts that moved in the equation. "I will stay only as long as I must.

Styrrach seeks us, we know this. Much will depend on what Raolos wishes to do. Synna might prove unreliable, and we may not be able to persuade the Duke of any connection between the Bailiff and the Guild. How long we stay will depend on how the fates are written. Who can say?"

Deineike's stomach heaved again, and Jorinda rubbed the tall woman's back as she bent over the rail.

Synna moved closer. "She finds the motion unacceptable?" He kept the question conversational.

"That she does." Jorinda offered a hand. "Jorinda."

His firm grip held her hand, but he did not shake it, as many men were wont to do. "Synna." Beyond him, a mariner coiled some ropes on the deck and appeared to pay them no attention. Synna frowned in apparent concentration. "Jorinda. I seem to recall a ship of a similar name. I journeyed north on it two days ago."

The Jorinda must still ply the river. Jorinda had feared somebody would make the connection in time, and Synna, at the least, had. "What a delightful coincidence." She laughed.

He released her hand, and the master strode into view. Synna turned, nodded his head to the master, and walked off toward the cabins.

"Ladies." The master used a conspiratorial whisper. "I urge you to avoid that gentleman. His credentials are disreputable."

Jorinda bit her tongue to suppress a laugh, amused by the formal words the master had used. Synna's credentials were far more disreputable than he could guess. "How dreadful." She feigned horror. "Whatever can he have done to inspire such a caution?"

The master tapped a finger against the side of his nose, although Jorinda had no idea what the gesture implied. "These things are unsuitable for pretty company." Jorinda disliked the expression and wearied of men who used such words.

"We shall be on our guard then. Our thanks for your concern."

Deineike's stomach heaved, and Jorinda focused her attention on her lover rather than the awkward exchange with the Master. To her chagrin, he did not leave. "We have a bread that—"

Jorinda interrupted but did not glance at him. "Oh my. We have eaten this bread, and it is unsuited to our constitutions."

He fell silent for a moment, and Jorinda worried. Had she said something to arouse suspicion? "You have sailed before?"

Jorinda bit at her lower lip. Why would that be unusual? There appeared to be nothing of concern in the comment, but she now yearned to escape the conversation. Deineike continued to retch, in no position to help. "That we have. Our business takes us around Dur. Such a disappointment my business partner suffers so much whenever she sails."

"It is unusual to hear of women who own a business. I find it admirable, I hasten to add."

Jorinda wished she could slice the pretentious smile from his face, but she had tripped herself up. Instead of the usual story they were sisters, she had attracted potential suspicion. "We do not own it, in truth. My father does. He has been ill for some time now, and it has fallen to us to maintain the business. We are the garment makers, so it is not difficult for us to discuss the commissions. We are quite hopeless at the coin side of it, of course, and feel sure we are cheated left and right." She laughed, and he joined in.

He said nothing for a time but did not move away. Jorinda wondered why he did not return to his work, but at last he spoke again. "Perhaps you would join me in my cabin for dinner tonight?" The question took Jorinda by surprise. She did not know how to respond but imagined any who sailed often, as she had claimed, would understand the invitation. She had no wish to be trapped in his cabin, compelled to answer ever more awkward questions.

"Under other circumstances, I would be delighted, but my friend is quite overcome by the movement of the ship, as you can see. Perhaps another night if she recovers." If wishes could write fate, he would walk away, for Jorinda wished him far from her with every bone and sinew in her body.

Deineike's weak voice interrupted the discussion. "Please, I must lie down." Jorinda wanted to kiss her in gratitude.

The master executed a gracious bow. "Then do not let me detain you." Jorinda thanked him, draped one of Deineike's arms around her shoulders, and they staggered across the deck toward the cabin area.

Once in their cabin, Jorinda gushed her thanks. Deineike's feeble reply surprised her. "For what?"

"You saved me from that man."

Deineike lay down on the cot and closed her eyes. "What man?"

"Did you not invent a desire to rest in order to rescue me from the encounter with the master?" Had Deineike intervened by accident?

"What master?" Deineike waved an arm at Jorinda. "I must sleep. Go. Find another to persecute. You give me a headache."

Jorinda did not move for several heartbeats, then she pulled the shutter across the window, kissed Deineike on the cheek, and left the cabin. Deineike's intervention had been a happy coincidence, nothing more. It could scarce have been timed any better, nonetheless.

She wandered into the empty common room and found some bread and cheese laid out on a table, so she ate some of the cheese as she considered their situation. The master and the complications he brought with him should now be avoided at all costs.

Footsteps approached down the corridor, and Synna entered the room. He stood near the open door. "Is your travel companion well?" He sounded casual as he cast a glance out into the corridor.

"She sleeps. My thanks for your concern."

He glanced into the corridor again, then spoke in a whisper, difficult to hear. "He warned me to stay away from you. I imagine he said the same to you."

"That he did, and at great length." She chewed at her lower lip. "I made up a story, but I may have said something suspicious. A sorry turn."

Synna raised his eyebrows. "Indeed. Nothing significant, I hope."

Jorinda sighed. "Time will tell." She did not know how to answer. The master might forget the conversation by morning, or it might gnaw at him until he sought her out to enquire further into the foolish blunder about the operation of the business. "What is scribed, must be."

He checked the corridor again. "You took your name from the ship?"

She looked away. "How do you know of this ship?"

"As I told you, I sailed north to Ort upon it." He hesitated. "You took your name from it?"

Why did he press her? "That I did."

"Dangerous and ill-conceived."

She glared at him. "Please be sure to contact me the next time you are forced to kill the woman you love to escape Guild justice. Let me know what name you have chosen for yourself at that time."

He looked down. "I did not know. I spoke out of turn. Forgive me."

She forced a long breath from her lips, as disappointed in herself as Synna appeared to be with his reaction. "I should not have snapped. It has been a hard year."

"And a bit?" He laughed.

"Be off with you, unless you wish another brawl."

"That I do not." His laughter continued. "You kicked me somewhere it is not pleasant to be kicked."

She raised a hand to her mouth, but not fast enough to stifle the laugh. "I am sorry. I did not realise in the darkness."

"Someone comes." He left, as quick as the blink of an eye, and moments later a mariner entered the room.

The mariner tore off some of the bread and held it before his mouth. "He did not bother you, lady? That man?" He popped the bread into his mouth.

"Not at all. I took no notice of him. He took some cheese I think, then said 'good day' as he left."

The mariner nodded and left. Did they all intend to spy on her every move for the entire voyage? Did Styrrach employ them all, even Synna? Jorinda shook her head. She had not imagined such foolish threats for some time, and she determined to control her thoughts and not succumb to fear. Her mind had little room for further complexities, and she had enough genuine threats to occupy her.

She wandered back to their cabin and peered around the door. Deineike lay in the cot, and her breaths suggested she had fallen asleep. Jorinda did not wish to disturb her, so she went out onto the deck and walked to the bow where she sat cross-legged as the ship ploughed its way down the river toward Alcmouth. Away to her right, the sun dropped below the cloud and shone on her, but it held no warmth and brought no relief to the troubles that beset her. If Deineike continued to be ill for the entire voyage, and Jorinda had to avoid the master and field questions from the crew at every turn, it would be a long and tiresome journey.

It proved long and tiresome indeed. Winter winds whipped the river into a greater frenzy than when they had sailed north, and Deineike either fetched up or slept in exhaustion throughout the journey. Rain arrived on the second day and, like an unwelcome guest, refused to leave. Jorinda spent long periods of time alone in the common room or asleep in their cabin. Most days, she shivered in the bitter wind on the deck as she ensured Deineike did not fall over the rail into the water.

As consolation, they avoided the need to take a meal with the master, although he pressed Jorinda on several occasions. Deineike's care occupied so much of her time, she needed no other excuse. She saw little of Synna, which she judged fortunate, lest contact with him came to the attention of the crew. It disappointed her nonetheless, as she had hoped to discuss what they would do when they arrived in Alcmouth. She wished to sound him out about her idea for him to persuade Styrrach that Pettra and Raopul were dead. No opportunity for that conversation presented itself, to her ever-greater frustration.

On the fourth day, Jorinda opened the door from the cabin area, and to her delight, the rain had stopped. She went onto the deck, grateful for the opportunity to take some fresh air without the bitter, cold wind and rain that soaked her to the bones. Deineike slept on her cot, haggard and unkempt. As she sat at the bow of the ship, and her hair streamed behind her in the chill wind, Jorinda guessed they might need to settle in Alcmouth or take horses back to Ort to avoid further distress for Deineike. A mariner came close, and she asked him when they would arrive in Alcmouth. She tutted in disappointment when he said they had made poor time and would not dock in the capital until the next day.

Darkness fell, and she returned to the cabin. Deineike turned to look at her as she entered. "How much longer?"

"Tomorrow, my love. Only one more night."

"Thank..." Deineike remained silent for a time. "There is nothing to thank. I wish for some vile appellation so I can curse to my heart's content."

Jorinda stroked her forehead. "You sound a little better. I have missed your incessant complaints."

Deineike managed a weak smile, but it vanished as soon as it arrived, and she held out her arms.

Jorinda groaned. "Again?"

"It is worse for me than you, you may believe it."

Jorinda helped her to her feet and out onto the deck, then stood beside Deineike as she retched into the dark night. Nothing came out of her mouth but noise, for she had eaten no more than a few morsels for the entire journey, but her stomach continued to torture her.

They had come to the last night of the voyage, and Jorinda would be glad when it ended. Her last nightmare of the journey proved to be the worst. She dreamt she entered the cabin to find Deineike in her cot with the master, her head between his legs. Jorinda yelled at them. "Rouse yourself. It is time to go onto the deck." They walked out to the deck, where Deineike retched over the rail, then toppled into the water. Jorinda dived in after her and saw her sink to the bottom.

An enormous fish with Arella's face swam up to her. "She is lost to you because she loves you."

As Deineike vanished from her sight, Jorinda opened her mouth to scream, but her lungs filled with water. The fish whipped its tail across her throat and opened a gash from which myriad tiny red fish swam, and they all cried, "I love you."

She woke in a cold sweat, and Deineike's cot lay empty. Jorinda leapt from her own cot in panic and ran out onto the deck. Deineike leaned on the rail, and she reached out a hand to Jorinda as she ran through the door.

Jorinda rushed to her side, her exhaustion forgotten in her concern. "Are you all right?"

"That I am. The river is calmer this morning, and I am not ill. I came out for some fresh air. I did not wish to wake you. The voyage has been hard on you."

Jorinda kissed her. "It has been hard on me? That is your way, to make little of your own troubles." She wrapped her arms around Deineike.

"Are you not concerned somebody might see us?"

"Let them see. I love you." Jorinda's relief that Deineike felt so much better held back her fears over their public displays of affection.

Deineike smiled and pointed down the river. "I think that is Alcmouth ahead."

Jorinda stared forward through the early morning mist. "I think you are right. We may leave this nightmare behind at last. Another begins, however, for we have no certain plan."

Deineike turned to look into the water. "I ate some of the bread before I came out."

Jorinda could not disguise her surprise that Deineike had eaten the vile stuff. "How did it taste?"

Deineike thought for some time before she replied. "Awful."

FIVE
MEETINGS IN ALCMOUTH

JORINDA AND DEINEIKE WALKED DOWN THE RAMP THE MOMENT THE dockhands manoeuvred it into place. Jorinda longed to avoid further awkwardness with the master, and Deineike must have been keen to feel solid ground beneath her feet. Jorinda experienced a moment of difficulty as her legs adapted to the steadiness of the dockside. She had noticed the same effect when she had left ships before and guessed her body had become accustomed to the roll and pitch of the ship across the unpredictable surface of the water.

They moved away from the ship until Jorinda spied a bench. She cast a furtive glance behind her. "We are far enough from the ship. Let us rest here and await Synna." They sat on the bench, and Jorinda looked around for any sign of hidden figures who lay in wait but saw nothing to suggest anyone observed them.

Deineike sat hunched forward, her chin in her hands and her elbows on her knees. "By the fates, what a terrible journey." She sounded as miserable as the day Jorinda told her the horrific story of her past in Torric.

Her laboured breaths and pallid complexion concerned Jorinda. "Are you all right? You look unwell."

"I am well now I am off that wretched thing. My stomach can settle at last."

"When did you last eat?"

"The bread this morning is the only thing I have kept down since we boarded that monstrosity in Ort."

Jorinda urged Deineike to eat as soon as possible. Her strength must have ebbed away to almost naught if she had eaten nothing for five days. Jorinda stared at the ship. She saw no sign of Synna and grew anxious to move away from the docks, but Deineike had not finished her deliberations on the bread. "I wonder how they make it taste as repulsive on one ship as it does on another."

Jorinda turned to look at her, hunched over and battered by sickness for five days, yet still as curious about trifles as ever. "Your mind is a mystery to me. Must you pry into the whys and whats of everything you encounter?" She laughed.

"That I must. Why do we only wear dresses or trousers, for example?"

Jorinda snorted. "You would walk around naked?"

"I would not, in this cold." Deineike's laugh cheered Jorinda, and she hoped the rigours of the voyage receded from her. "Why is there no other arrangement? We could wear a tunic with the skirt of a dress, I think."

Jorinda pondered the concept and wondered why the suggestion had never occurred to her. "That we could. I will make you such a garment. I warn you now; all will stare at you in horror."

"Not as much as if I wandered naked, as you suggest." Deineike gave a small laugh as she answered.

Jorinda felt a tingle in her sex as she visualised Deineike naked. "They would stare even more at your body paraded naked before them. Their desire would be great."

Deineike gave a derisive chuckle. "They would not notice me if you walked alongside me, your breasts displayed to them, and that slender waist. Your bush would guide their eyes to the delicious wine that flows in your garden…" She fell silent, and her cheeks turned bright red. Her voice took on the breathy timbre that always came upon her when aroused.

Jorinda whispered to her. "Are you wet?"

"That I am."

Jorinda imagined Deineike naked on a bed, nostrils flared, pupils dilated, hair dishevelled across a pillow. "Me also." They smiled at each other.

"We could run behind a building and pleasure one another."

Jorinda glanced up at the ship and saw Synna descend the ramp. "Curses. Our new friend ap```````proaches, and we must delay our passion for now." She thought back over the brief moment of excitement. "'The wine that flows in my garden?'" They both laughed at the strange expression.

Deineike sat upright and watched Synna draw near to them. "Do you trust him?"

Jorinda had pondered the question many times on the ship but had reached no firm conclusion. "I know not. I know not what our next move will be, in truth. I would rather Raolos take his family and flee far from here. He is hard-headed, and I fear he will not do so." She sighed. "I cannot decide whether we should trust Synna."

Deineike laid a hand on her thigh. "You will resolve this to the best advantage of all. I do not doubt this. You are remarkable. More, you are magnificent."

She laughed, and Jorinda guessed what caused the amusement as she felt the sting of heat in her cheeks. Synna's shadow fell across them, and she looked up at him.

He squinted at her. "Have you over-exerted yourself?"

Confused, she answered. "That I have not. Why do you ask this?"

"Your face is as red as a beet."

Jorinda slapped at Deineike's thigh as her lover's laughter increased. "Are we observed?" She hoped he would confirm no Guild member espied them.

"I think not, although you must be more certain than I. Your skills are superior to my own."

She tutted, embarrassed further. "Let us move somewhere we can decide our next move."

"I know a tavern not far from here. I am known there and can obtain a private table."

Jorinda hesitated. "A tavern is too public, I think." She did not want to be spotted, but they had things they must discuss, and procrastination would eat into what little time they had.

"It is early. Few will be there, if any. Come, we waste time on this bench." He set off without further discussion, so they rose to follow him. He walked ahead of them and did not look backward. Jorinda looked about as they walked but saw nothing to alarm her. Her concern increased now they walked the streets of Alcmouth again, and she wondered whether they had made the best decision.

The visit to Taro's farm had affected her, changed her attitude, more than she would have guessed, and unleashed such concern for the welfare of Raolos's family, she had felt compelled to return to Ort despite the danger to Deineike. It proved fortunate they did so. The fates were written, and hers had become bound up in the lives of Raolos's family for now. She followed a man who would have been the ruin of Pettra and Raopul but for Jorinda's moment of guilt at Taro's farm, yet now she intended to work with him to bring about the safety of the people Styrrach sent him to kill. The riddle of it defied her comprehension.

Synna glanced back at them as he walked without hesitation

into a tavern a few doors ahead of Jorinda and Deineike. Deineike stopped, and Jorinda turned to her.

Deineike's face had turned pale, and she bit her lower lip. "Are we about to walk into a trap?"

Jorinda thought there might be a good chance of that outcome. "We could walk on and forget Synna."

"The tunic is the proof. Without that, we have little else."

Jorinda rubbed her chin, deep in thought. It would be dangerous to enter the tavern, but Deineike had the right of it. Synna would be of great help to them if he could be trusted. He knew much of how the Guild worked, and she felt sure they could turn that to their benefit if he did not betray them. "I will enter. You will remain without. If I do not return—"

Deineike interrupted her. "Jorinda. Do you speak to some stranger behind me? You know I will not agree to this." She folded her arms before her, an unmistakeable sign of defiance.

Jorinda sighed. She did know it, and well. "So be it. Let us go to whatever fate is written for us." She dropped to one knee as though to straighten the cuff of her trouser leg, slipped her dagger from her boot into the waistband of the trousers beneath her tunic. It would be faster to pull from there, she reasoned, and she might have urgent need of it.

They entered the tavern. There appeared to be no lanterns at all, and the dim light within came from a few candles here and there around the tavernroom. Three grimy windows that looked as though their glass had not been cleaned in some time looked out onto the street, but little could be seen through them. Had they been crystal clear, they might have allowed sunlight in to brighten the tavernroom, but the sun hid itself today. They stopped inside the door for some moments while their eyes adjusted to the low light in the tavern.

The innkeep glanced up at them but made no move to greet them. They walked forward, but he did not speak as he gestured toward the back of the tavernroom. Not a single patron sat in the tavern, and Jorinda saw no reason to keep the door open if he could not sell so much as a groat's worth of ale.

Wary, they moved further into the tavernroom and spotted Synna at a table at the rear. Jorinda sat next to him so she had a clear view of the tavernroom. She did not wish for her and Deineike to be slain by unseen daggers in their backs if things turned awry.

Jorinda explained her idea that Synna should return to Styrrach and say he had completed the gest. He fretted he might be caught in the lie, and Jorinda sympathised with his concerns. He seemed to search for an alternative. "Can we not go to your Portreeve friend and tell him the full tale? We can then obtain an appointment with the Duke and put an end to this sooner."

Pettra had given them the address of the inn where Raolos had taken rooms. They could go straight there and not roll the dice on the plan Jorinda had hatched, but even this simple plan posed difficulties. "His inn will be watched; we can agree on this?"

He gave a nod of confirmation. "There is no question."

Jorinda continued her thoughts. "They will come for us as soon as they may. We may all die, however this turns." She gave a grim laugh, and Synna joined in with a rueful nod. "You may discover useful information if you speak to Styrrach. I still need to understand the shrouding before I go wherever I travel to afterward. It may buy some time for Pettra and Raopul at the least."

"Raopul is her son?"

"That he is, he whom you would have killed in his bed at Styrrach's whim." He bristled, and she laid a hand on his arm. "Still your temper. I do not say it in judgement, though I wonder at my sanity if I trust you. Styrrach scribes all our fates unless we can turn them in a different direction."

His attention switched to Deineike. "You say little of these things. You are not a Guild member, yet you tolerate that Corelle has these skills?"

"Her name is Jorinda, and I love her. I have no other answer, if that one does not please you."

He sat back in his chair. "You love one another? I had thought you a friend or advisor. I heard Styrrach refer to Corelle…Jorinda, I should say, as a deviant. I now understand the reference."

Jorinda fixed him with a cold stare. "Do you share this view?" Deineike had said little enough, but her words could often cast events into turns Jorinda had not foreseen.

He sat in thought for a time. "I have no view. I could not lie with a man, but who am I to judge? I am a hired killer." He spread his hands above the table. "Who am I to judge?"

Jorinda weighed his reply, still uncertain of his trustworthiness. They were committed to this path now. "That will suffice. We do not seek your approval, only your help." A man entered the tavern-room and took a seat at a table near to the door. "We must act. The sand falls in the glass, and precious little time is left to us. What will you do?"

He rose. "I am away to deliver to Styrrach news that will cheer him. I trust the time it buys the woman and boy are well used, as it may be bought with my life."

Before he left, Jorinda ensured they had a plan. "We should meet here again at this time tomorrow. We can update one another and decide our next move at that time." Synna nodded and left without another word. Jorinda waited some moments, then returned her dagger to her boot before they too rose and walked out into the cold, grey morning.

They had no idea how to find the inn where Raolos stayed. They imagined it would be in the wealthy quarter of the city, which lay some way from the square, unlike Ort or Zhanghar. Deineike wondered why all cities did not follow a similar structure, and

Jorinda laughed. "I should have guessed you would ponder this puzzle."

"Do not say, 'What is scribed, must be,' or I shall leave you." Deineike's laugh cheered a sombre mood and a grey day.

"You could not leave me. It is…" Jorinda did not finish the sentence. She did not wish to discover whether Deineike could leave her, lest it turn she could.

Deineike walked alongside her in silence. As they turned a corner and stopped to look around for any familiar sign that might tell them where they were, Deineike said, "You are correct."

"That you cannot leave me?"

Deineike smiled and did not answer. Jorinda noticed a fruit stall and asked for directions. The stallholder did not know the inn but thought he knew the area where it could be found, and he gave them some instructions that might bring them close to it.

As they walked further, the houses became larger, and they entered a wealthier part of the city. Jorinda looked about non-stop and insisted they stop so she could gaze into shop windows and check for any pursuit. They crossed the street, then re-crossed them, and Deineike gazed into more windows while Jorinda checked their surroundings. The precautions added time, and it was close to the midday before they found somebody who knew the inn and gave them directions to Duchy Street, where it could be found.

Jorinda stopped at the corner of Duchy Street and peeked around the wall of a house. The inn stood some way along the street, a large building nestled among many shops and houses, its fresh paint an indication of a proud innkeep. A sign outside proclaimed the inn to be The Duke's Seat. It had seemed an odd name for an inn when Pettra had told it to Jorinda. The Duke's seat would be the Ducal Highhome, as she understood it. The names of inns made little sense to her.

Too many houses stood close to the inn. From the street, it would not be easy to see anybody who watched from any of the myriad windows that looked out from the buildings. She turned to Deineike and explained her anxiety. "Let us see if there is a rear entrance from the next street along."

They walked further, and at the next corner, Jorinda checked the street parallel to Duchy Street. The rear of the inn extended to this street, but as many houses flanked the rear door as the front. A narrow alleyway opened off the street opposite the inn, and a figure lurked in the mouth of the alleyway.

Under different circumstances, the inn would be watched by couriers rather than Guild members. Styrrach would long for a favourable outcome, however, and he might risk Guild members for this task. Nonetheless, a trained Guild member would not skulk in an alleyway rather than hide in a house and watch from a window. The person in the alleyway must either be a Guild courier or some innocent, unconnected with Styrrach's observation of the inn.

Jorinda could not challenge the person in the alleyway with any certainty, and she did not wish to draw attention to an unpleasant scene if the mystery person turned out not to be from the Guild. The two women returned to the corner of Duchy Street, and Jorinda explained they would enter the front door. They would be seen, but they had anticipated as much, and it could not be avoided, in all likelihood. She would ask one of Raolos's men to cross the street at the rear and investigate the figure in the alleyway as a precaution.

When they entered the inn, its size amazed them. A woman stood behind a stained wooden desk in the formal entry lobby. She wore a crisp green dress with "The Duke's Seat" embroidered on it above her left breast. Jorinda had never seen such an opulent inn, and they both stopped and gazed about them in awe at the plush furnishings and elaborate artwork in the lobby.

The woman smiled at them. "Good day, and welcome to The Duke's Seat. How may I help you?" Jorinda had never been spoken to with such respect by a staff member in any inn or tavern in her life.

She walked toward the desk. "We seek a friend from Ort. Raolos."

The woman beamed at her. "May I ask your name?"

"Jorinda."

"Please take a seat, and I will see whether your friend is in the inn." The woman rang a small bell on the counter.

Deineike had already seated herself in a high-backed armed chair near a low table, so Jorinda sat in another close by. Deineike pulled a face that expressed surprise and discomfort at the lavish surroundings. A young lad appeared, and the woman whispered to him before he left, then she smiled at them again.

Deineike leaned close and whispered, "She is quite the smiler."

"That she is. A pretty smile, I think." Deineike slapped at Jorinda's leg, and they looked up at the woman, who smiled at them again.

"Jorinda? What brings you here?" Ibie entered the lobby, immense surprise on his face. They rose and approached him. He did not embrace them, but he nodded his head to each of them.

Jorinda replied in a quiet voice designed not to be overheard. "We cannot discuss that here." She looked to the woman, who smiled yet again.

"Then come. Raolos will be surprised to see you here. We believed you rode off to the west."

Part way up a set of stairs, Jorinda pulled at Ibie's arm to stop him, then whispered in his ear. "There is an alleyway opposite the rear of the inn. I suggest you send a man there. Somebody lingered in the shadows. They might be innocent, but you can be assured your every move here is observed."

He frowned but nodded. "I will arrange it. Come, it appears there is much Raolos will want to hear."

He led them up two flights of stairs. An impressive pair of doors stood at the end of a corridor, and a man in the deep red tunic of the Portreeve stood before them. Ibie opened a door, and they entered a small lobby that led into a parlour, furnished with the same plush furniture as the inn's entrance lobby. At a large desk, Raolos studied a parch. He looked up as they entered, and a look of surprise sprang to his face.

He stood. "Jorinda. Deineike. This is unexpected. I thought you headed west from Ort."

Ibie turned and left the room, and Raolos beckoned to some armed chairs. The women sat in the chairs, and he perched himself on the arm of a couch.

Jorinda explained. "We turned back. We had our reasons, but we will not waste words on explanations. You are in great peril."

"That I am." His voice dripped with sadness. "I am to be impeached from office, and another will be appointed in my stead."

It surprised Jorinda his replacement had been arranged already, and she imagined Styrrach lay behind it. "They waste no time. How do they bring about this outcome so soon?"

He coughed and looked embarrassed. "They claim marital infidelity, which is improper in one such an important position. Women have appeared and sworn complaints against me. I know none of them, of course."

Jorinda frowned. "Then the charges will not stand, will they?"

He rubbed his eyes. He looked tired, his face gaunt and dark circles beneath each eye. "That they will. The dice are loaded, and the Bailiff rolls them to his favour. My fate is written. How they learned, I am unsure."

Jorinda guessed she had missed some part of the conversation. "Learned? Learned what?"

His face flushed. "My apologies. I meant to say I am unsure how they contrived such a tale."

His response lacked sincerity, and for the first time since she had met him, Jorinda's mind entertained the thought that all might not be as it seemed. It mattered little, she reasoned. Pettra and Raopul remained in danger, and Styrrach threatened Deineike. More turned here than whatever sordid tale lay behind Raolos's impeachment. "We have met the man who brought the letters that summoned you here."

A look of surprise crossed his face. "How do you know of him?"

"He wore a Bailiff's tunic, but he carried an assassin's knife. The Guild sent him to lure you here and kill Pettra and Raopul."

He raised a hand to his forehead and tears welled up in his eyes. "My son is dead? Pettra?"

"They live, they live." Jorinda had misspoken, and she rushed to reassure him. The sand fell, but she need not create unnecessary terror in Raolos.

His face took on an inquisitive look. "How do you know these things?"

Deineike answered him. "Jorinda foiled the attempted murder."

His eyes widened. "I owe you a great deal indeed. You have saved my life, and now those of my family. You are a remarkable woman. My thanks."

Jorinda's cheeks burned. "Deineike misspeaks. She brought your men, and they took him into captivity. I played but a small role in the events."

"This Guild wants to kill my family? What monsters are they? I trust the would-be murderer swung from the gallows?" Anger flashed in his eyes, and he balled his hands into fists as though he fought against his temper.

Jorinda imagined he would not enjoy her answer. "That he does not. He travelled here with us and has returned to the Guild—"

"What? You set him free?" Raolos stood and towered over Jorinda, menace in his every movement. Deineike half-rose from the chair and reached her arms toward him.

How could Jorinda explain the bizarre circumstances that had led her here? "Calm yourself, Raolos. He aids us now. He has gone to tell Styrrach your wife and son are dead. He does this at great risk to himself." Now she had come to Alcmouth, face to face with the dangers, her commitment to her original plan wavered. An approach to the Duke seemed too lofty an ambition. Raolos's earlier lie hid something, but she did not know whether it affected their current situation. Styrrach and all who served him might prove too great a force for them to defeat. "It buys time to transport them to safety, but you must return to Ort today and take them elsewhere, somewhere Styrrach cannot find you."

Deineike sat again, and the change of strategy did not seem to sit well with her. "We did not discuss this plan."

Jorinda glanced at her. "That we did not, yet it is the wisest course. I doubt an approach to the Duke can succeed. The Bailiff and Styrrach will pour their energies into its prevention. To flee is the better option. I suggested as much in the first place, before we knew of the tunic. Now I am here, I have changed my mind. I feel the threat of Styrrach in every breath I take."

Raolos gave her a blank stare. "The tunic?"

Deineike took it upon herself to explain. "The man wore the tunic of a Bailiff's man and carried the Bailiff's letters, but he belongs to the Guild. It proves the Bailiff's involvement, which the Duke cannot overlook."

"Will he swear to this, even as he condemns himself?" Raolos's stare pierced Deineike, and even Jorinda felt uncomfortable as she watched on.

"He thought his ruin had come upon him five or six nights ago. Your men yearned to hang him for the attempted murder of your family. Jorinda bought his life when she persuaded them he would help you. He is prepared to swear it." Deineike fell silent and looked at Jorinda.

Dejection swamped Jorinda. "Deineike has the right of it, but the scheme will not succeed, I am sure. Styrrach and the Bailiff have much at stake and will not stand around and do nothing as we bring them down. We have bought some time, but the sand will run out. You must sail to Ort and save your family." Jorinda's frustration at the entire situation grew, and she felt little certainty any outcome could turn out well for them.

Raolos stared at her, anger in his reddened cheeks. "My name would be destroyed by lies, and my family and I would be fugitives who flee from criminals. The cart would draw the horse, would it not? I cannot permit this. Dur cannot be held hostage to the dictates of evil men. Let us discuss an approach to the Duke."

Jorinda bent her head and heaved a sigh. Could nobody else understand they would all die if they tried to fight the forces arrayed against them? They faced the Guild, Styrrach's hatred, the Portreeves of four cities of Dur, and the Bailiff, the second most powerful man in the land. Two women, a hired killer, and one disgraced Portreeve could not defeat such adversaries. It would be madness to believe anything different. Now she had arrived in Alcmouth, the reality struck her, and it frightened her. She feared not for herself, but for Raolos and his family, and above all for Deineike. "It is madness, and I will not take part in it. We will all die."

"We all die." Raolos set his jaw, his eyes cold, hard. "Some can choose when and where, which is the best fate we can hope to be written for us."

Jorinda did not look to Deineike for support, for she knew there would be none. Deineike would not stand by and see injustice done. If she would, then Jorinda's refusal to help Wilash in Alcmouth would have ended their involvement in any of the things that had turned since.

Ibie entered the room, and all heads turned to him. "You guessed right, I think. The man in the alleyway ran off as we crossed the street. We chased him for a time, but I did not care to abandon our post for long with all his presence suggests."

Jorinda turned to Raolos. "Styrrach will know Deineike and I are here within the hour and will plot to kill us. He hates me. You are an inconvenience to his plans, nothing more."

"I will secure a room for you, and one of my men will guard it night and day. You will be safe, I assure you. I will send urgent letters to the Duke. When can this man be expected to accompany us?"

Jorinda shook her head in despair for many heartbeats. Madness; all madness. They had all lost their minds. "This is foolish. We meet with him in the morning, and with luck, we can persuade him to accompany us if you obtain an appointment. In the meantime, our best course is to prepare to return to Ort before we all travel wherever we go to afterward."

Deineike intervened. "One thing I cannot understand in this." It did not surprise Jorinda that Deineike still worried at the thread, but she kept her counsel. "How are Durfolk persuaded to these acts? Raolos's men spoke of the good nature of the people of Dur the other night. How has this Styrrach become so evil? And these others?"

Ibie answered her. "While Dur is peaceful for the most part, men can be persuaded to misdeeds if sufficient coin is offered. As for Styrrach, the explanation is simpler. He is not Durfolk." They all turned to stare at him, aghast.

Jorinda struggled to summon breath from her lungs to form a reply. "What?"

"He gave his place of birth when he obtained the appointment with Raolos. He named a city in Qagrue, a land to the south. I saw the journal."

When they had been asked for their places of birth the clerk had described it as "formalities." Those formalities, at the least, offered some explanation for Styrrach's malice, but something about him still confused Jorinda. "He looks like Durfolk. Others from the south are darker than us, but not Styrrach."

Deineike brooded aloud, it seemed. "He must have lived here many years and become as pallid as we are." Nobody responded.

Raolos interrupted their thoughts. "Ibie, please arrange a room for the ladies and a guard for that room."

"It will be done, though we have few enough men to provide safety for another room. I suspect Jorinda's skills are superior to any our men possess, in truth."

The hotel claimed to have only one room available, on the ground floor at the rear; all the other rooms were occupied. Jorinda thought it would be safer and preferable to a room at a different inn, and when they saw the size of the room, Deineike adored it. It had a large window that looked out onto a small garden planted within the outer wall of the inn.

Ibie assigned Kinpiet, one of Raolos's men, to guard the room for the remainder of the day. They divided the day into two periods, and a replacement guard would take over once he awoke so Kinpiet could sleep. Deineike felt hungry, and the women and Kinpiet went to the tavernroom to order some food. Kinpiet had eaten not long before but sat with them while they ate. They chatted about everything and nothing with him until they had eaten their fill.

Deineike wanted to return to the room, either to fall into the bed or discuss all that had turned in the meeting with Raolos. As Jorinda rose from the table, Deineike summoned the woman who had served them. "Can you send a pitcher of wine to our room please?"

The woman said she would arrange the wine, and they walked back to the room. Jorinda guessed why Deineike had ordered the wine but pressed her to confirm it. "Why do you want wine so early in the day?"

Deineike leaned in and whispered, "It makes you amorous, does it not?"

Jorinda laughed. Wine did indeed make her amorous, but Deineike's flushed face and breathy whisper already had Jorinda on fire for her.

SIX
STYRRACH VISITS THE INN

Styrrach sat in his office and pondered developments. Synna had returned with welcome news—he had killed the woman and child, and Glailam had all but closed the deal that would see Raolos impeached. Women had been found and paid, and they had scribed their mark on parch that claimed marital infidelities via frequent dalliances in inns in Ort. The Bailiff had already held the inquiry where Raolos had pleaded his innocence, as expected, but with so much evidence, even an uncorrupted Bailiff would have had little choice but to impeach Raolos from office. Styrrach had Glailam in his pocket, and the Bailiff would soon deliver the verdict Styrrach demanded. Ort would be his, and with Vjort all but signed, he would have even more outlets for even more goods. He might even search for new lands to deal with, new exotic goods to bring into Dur, if any existed.

A knock came at the door. Styrrach did not speak. Someone opened the door behind him with little delay. "I bring important news."

Excitement in his voice interested Styrrach, who rose and turned to the unfamiliar member. "Speak."

"I have come from The Duke's Seat."

Styrrach held up a hand. "You have abandoned your post?"

Fear and anxiety flitted across the man's face. "That I have, but the news I bring will explain why."

"It must, for you have disobeyed me, and I do not tolerate disobedience." Styrrach sensed the man's exhilaration and could not deny his impatience to learn his news, but he never took his foot from the throat unless great service merited it.

"She is here." The words rushed out, triumphant, breathless. "Corelle is at The Duke's Seat."

Dizziness spun the room, and for a heartbeat, Styrrach feared he might need to reach for the back of the chair so he did not fall. He fought against such a sign of weakness, and his balance returned. She had come here, to Alcmouth? This must be a dream. If true, she had made a terrible mistake, and he now knew her whereabouts. He had her at last.

He had to be certain there had been no mistake. "You know this how?"

"I saw her enter, and the Portreeve's men chased away the courier from the rear entrance soon afterward. She must have noticed him and sent them in pursuit. There can be no other explanation."

"You had a good view of her? There can be no mistake?" For the first time in many years, Styrrach had to battle the excitement he felt. He had no wish to betray the weakness of emotion.

"None. I recognised her. Another travels with her, taller, but Corelle matched your description. There is no doubt. It is her. They entered the inn, and I came here as soon as I could."

"But not until you spent a pleasant time in conversation with your courier friend, I note." The man looked crestfallen. "No matter. Your news pleases me, and your delay is excused." It pleased him, and more. Corelle must be taken without delay. "Send in Gill."

The man ran from the office, and Gill replaced him. "You sent for me."

"Corelle is here, at The Duke's Seat. We will kill her today. Now."

"Why has she come here? It is inconceivable."

"I care not. Doubtless, she..." Styrrach fell silent. He had been about to say she had doubtless come by ship, then recalled Synna, who had also arrived by ship that morning. It would be an inconceivable coincidence for them to arrive so close together, and Styrrach put no faith in even the least hint of coincidence. Something had turned awry, and the jade sought to turn it to her favour. Time for Synna later. Styrrach must act. "That need not concern us for now. Take two men. Kill her. Do not fail me."

Gill turned and went out into the parlour, but Styrrach's own excitement had grown too great. He walked into the parlour and pushed Gill aside.

"I will kill her. Who has skills with herbs?" One of the men raised a hand, awkward and bashful. Styrrach thought it a stupid gesture, but he could not waste time to humiliate the man. "Come with me." He pointed at another "You also." Styrrach walked to the door and did not need to check they followed. They would.

He strode to the inn and explained his plan, which he invented as he walked. Some food would be sent to their room. The food would contain herbs to make them sleep, then he would enter the room and kill them both. It would take but a moment, and Corelle would lie dead under his blade at long last. He did not need to sedate her in truth; she might be good, but none could best him. It had been years since he had carried out gests himself, but he created the Guild and taught those who came after him. They had passed along their skills, *his* skills. He never took chances or gambled on matters of his life, nonetheless. He would sedate her first, kill her, then enjoy the other before he also killed her.

Once they reached the inn, Styrrach approached the desk. A woman behind a counter wore a foolish dress with the name of the inn embroidered upon it, and her smile vanished as he snarled at her. "Innkeep." Nervous, she rang a bell, and a child appeared. Styrrach marched to him, balled the lad's tunic into his fist, then pushed him backward through the door he had emerged from. "Two women stay here?" The lad nodded, terror etched on his face. Styrrach feared the boy might fetch up on him. "Send some broth to their rooms as a gift of the inn."

The boy spluttered. "They…they are in the tavernroom."

A heartbeat's pause at the news, no more. "Show me."

The lad led him into the scullery. Two women laboured at a large stove built around a fire, and another scrubbed at dishes in a basin in a corner.

A younger woman came through a door. She stopped short when she saw Styrrach and his men, the lad's tunic still in Styrrach's grip. The Guildmeister snapped at her. "What?"

She glanced around, but none of the women offered any support, and the lad soiled the front of his trousers. "They wish some wine in their room."

The woman had a tremor in her voice that Styrrach knew well. Fear. "Who do?"

"The two women who arrived earlier."

It seemed too perfect. Styrrach released the lad and pushed his face into hers. "Do you lie to me?"

Her face twisted into abject misery, and tears ran from her eyes. "That I do not."

"Pour it." Styrrach gave his poisoner a look and the man followed the woman as she poured wine from a large cask into a pitcher. Styrrach did not hear their conversation. He did not need to. As long as Corelle died, it did not matter how it came about. Somebody from the inn would summon the Portreeve's men, but Styrrach had the Portreeve in his pocket and would send them away if they arrived before Corelle died.

His man rummaged through a cupboard and came out with a small wooden box. He pushed its contents around, pulled out a pouch, and sniffed its contents. He looked to Styrrach. "Ground valerian. By its diminished smell, I would say it has been stored for some time." Styrrach did not care. He waved at the wine and the man poured some of the powder into it, then stirred it until he seemed satisfied.

Styrrach glowered at the frightened woman. "Take it to them. Do not lock the door when you leave." The woman's sobs deafened him. "You are a disgrace. Compose yourself before you take the wine. They will pity you and draw you into the room elsewise. They are deviants and will use you. You may wish it, my guess." She wiped at her eyes. "Report to me here as soon as the wine is in the room." He stepped back into the lobby. The woman in the green dress still stood at her counter, and she stared open-mouthed at him. He returned to the scullery and addressed the man who had poured the powder into the wine. "How long before it takes effect?"

"An hour, or close to it. Why they have it here, I cannot guess."

Styrrach waved a hand at the man to silence him. He did not care why they had it. He cared more why the man did not carry it if he used herbs in his gests, but he would address that once Corelle lay dead at his feet. He could not wait an hour, however. It would be dangerous to remain here with only two men for that long. Raolos had rooms and guards somewhere in the inn. Styrrach must act.

The woman returned. "They have the wine. Will you hurt them?"

"Would you prefer me to hurt you?" He thrust his face so close to hers, his spittle sprayed her face, and she gave a pathetic shake of her head. "I did not think so."

He beckoned to his men, and they moved to the door. He turned to the woman. "Which room?"

"Near the rear entrance." She continued to sob as she pointed a finger as though to guide him. "A guard stands outside it."

Curse it. Raolos guarded them. No matter. One man against three, and two of Styrrach's were expendable. He liked the odds. "The key." He held out a hand, and she handed it to him. He passed it to one of his men with orders to lock the door behind them when they entered the room, then beckoned for them to follow him. They moved through the door and headed across the tavernroom in the direction the woman had pointed.

The herb would not have had sufficient time to work, and he wondered if he should have assigned the gest to Gill or been in less of a hurry. To admit either now would be an admission of weakness, and he pushed the thought from his head.

He spotted the guard and half turned to his men, looked from one to the other, and inclined his head toward the guard. One of them walked past the guard and turned to speak. The guard turned his head at the words, and the second drove a dagger into his heart. They caught him as he fell and lowered his body to the floor. Styrrach moved forward and tried the door. It had not been locked, so he gestured for the two men to follow as he opened the door, slow, cautious, and silent. "Do not interfere. They are mine to kill." They nodded.

Inside the room, the sound and smell of sex filled his senses. Corelle lay naked on the bed, and the other woman knelt above her, legs either side of her body. Styrrach took two steps, struck the other in the face with the back of his hand, and she hurtled backward off the end of the bed.

SEVEN

A BRUTAL ENCOUNTER

Jorinda thanked Kinpiet for his guard duty and left him at the door as they entered. Deineike closed the door and leaned back against it. She reached for the key.

Jorinda stopped her. "Do not lock it. You have ordered wine."

"That I have." Deineike pushed herself off the door and pulled Jorinda into her arms and kissed her. Jorinda moaned with desire as she pressed herself tight against her lover's muscular body. Deineike's hands ran through Jorinda's hair, and she thrust her tongue into Jorinda's mouth.

They kissed for long moments before Jorinda pulled her head back. "The wine." She took a step backward, breathless with passion. Deineike ran her hands up the inside of her thighs.

"It has been days since you have taken me. I can wait no

longer." She opened her mouth and ran her tongue across her lips. "Take me."

Jorinda held up her hands. "You should not have ordered wine if you desired me so much." She laughed, but she ached for her lover's touch.

Deineike glanced at the door. "I will send Raolos's man to cancel it."

"He guards us. If I am to be driven to wild abandon in this bed, I will feel safer if he is without." Jorinda's resistance crumbled as Deineike's hands slid between her legs.

Somebody knocked at the door and they both turned to look at it. "The wine, my guess."

Jorinda moved to the door and called out. "Who is there?"

"The wine arrives." Jorinda recognised Kinpiet's voice, opened the door enough to peer out, and saw him through the gap. She opened it further, and he glanced down the corridor, so Jorinda leaned forward and followed his gaze. The woman from the tavern-room had almost reached their room, a pitcher in her hands. Her eyes were red, and she sniffed. In truth, she looked afraid.

"Something is amiss?" Although Jorinda felt concern for the woman's apparent condition, she cared more for Deineike's safety.

The woman sniffed again. "The innkeep scolded me and said I had delayed the wine." She pushed past Jorinda and placed the pitcher on the table as Jorinda watched on, surprised by her behaviour. Deineike thanked her, and the woman moved to the door as Jorinda stepped to the table and studied the wine. Behind her, Deineike asked the woman to lock the door if she had a key, and the woman confirmed she did. Jorinda turned as the woman removed the inner key and placed it on the floor. The woman looked up, sad, mournful, then went out and closed the door behind her. A metallic noise rattled from the door, and Jorinda turned to Deineike.

"Strange. Why did she take the key out?"

Deineike raised her eyebrows. "She cannot lock the door with the key still in the lock."

"She seemed frightened."

"That she did." Deineike seemed distracted. "Are there any goblets in the room, I wonder?" A brief search turned up only one cup. "We will share." Deineike took the cup to the table and poured some wine.

Before she could raise it to her mouth, Jorinda reached around her waist and unfastened her trousers. "I need no wine." She kissed Deineike's neck, soft brushes with her lips that brought a deep moan from her lover, who replaced the cup on the table and turned in Jorinda's arms. As they kissed, Deineike unbuttoned Jorinda's trousers. They pulled off each other's tunics and kicked off their boots. Deineike pushed Jorinda backward toward the bed, and they stepped out of their trousers as they moved.

Jorinda lay on her back as Deineike straddled her. The injured knee did not appear to trouble her any longer, and Jorinda gasped as Deineike reached behind herself and touched Jorinda's wetness.

A movement caught her eye, and she turned her head toward the door. Styrrach moved toward them, other figures behind him, and before she could react, he struck Deineike with the back of his hand and sent her backward off the bed.

Jorinda tried to rise from the bed, but Styrrach slapped her face and pushed her back to the pillow. The slap disoriented her, and she blinked as she tried to clear her head. She aimed punches at his head. One connected, but he grabbed at her wrists and held them in his hands. His strength surprised her, and she could not pull her arms free. He climbed onto the bed as she attempted to kick him, but he placed a leg either side of her and straddled her as Deineike had done. She raised her legs and attempted to strike him in the back with her knees, but he shuffled backward, and she could do little damage to him as his weight pinned her to the bed. She writhed from side to side but could not dislodge him. When she looked to the door, two men had closed it and stood against it, excitement evident in their faces.

Styrrach moved his face lower, close to her own, and she snarled up at him as he growled in fury. "At long last, I have you." His spittle hit her face, and she spat up into his own.

She snarled all her hatred at him, her voice guttural. "You will die here."

He laughed. "It is you who will die, and afterward I will show your deviant little friend what it is like to know a man. Then I will slit her throat, and she will join you wherever you travel to afterward. If there is anything afterward, I am sure it will be most unpleasant for degenerates such as you."

Jorinda struggled to pull her arms free, and he pulled her wrists together and held them in one large hand. His other hand fumbled at his belt, pulled it from his trousers, and wrapped it around her wrists as she fought with all her strength to pull her hands free of his grip. How could she be so feeble? She spat at him again and almost tugged one of her hands free, but he wrapped the belt tight around them and slapped her again. Her vision swam, and it seemed as though two Styrrachs knelt above her for a moment.

One of the other men said something, and Deineike swam into Jorinda's view behind Styrrach, who turned to follow Jorinda's eyes. Deineike knelt beside the bed, her face on the blanket. Her arms dangled down the side of the bed out of Jorinda's sight.

Styrrach laughed. "How pitiful. She attempts to rescue you." He gave an evil chuckle, half turned, and grabbed a fistful of Deineike's hair. The other hand still held Jorinda's bound wrists away from his body as he pulled Deineike's head up by her hair while Jorinda thrashed about on the bed and tried to throw him off her.

If he had expected Deineike to cry out in pain, he must have been disappointed. She snarled at him, and her arm came up. She held Jorinda's dagger, which had been in one of the boots they had kicked away before they climbed on the bed. She drove the dagger down into his thigh, and he screamed. He fell forward toward Jorinda, kicked at Deineike, and his foot caught her in the face. She flew backward once again, and he fought to contain Jorinda as she struggled against him with renewed strength. Deineike crashed into the table, and it toppled over. The pitcher and cup both shattered, and the wine spilled across the floor. His weight pressed downward on Jorinda, and she could not force him off, though she bucked and writhed like a wild cat as she tried.

Styrrach slid from the bed and pulled Jorinda upright without ceremony, her arms above her head. She kicked at him and caught him in the shin but hurt her own foot with no apparent damage to him. He pulled back an arm and punched her in the stomach. Her breath whooshed out of her, and her legs buckled. He released her arms, and she fell to her knees with her face to the floor as she tried to gasp air into her lungs. She almost fetched up and fought to control her stomach while she struggled to draw a breath.

Jorinda used the bed as a support and tried to rise to her feet as Styrrach limped over to Deineike, who also struggled to stand. Blood poured from her nose, one of her eyes swollen and closed, the skin around it already a violent purple bloom. As she rose to her knees, he punched her in the face, and she hurtled backward until her head smashed into the wall behind her. She fell to the floor, motionless.

Jorinda howled in torment and anger, and Styrrach glanced back at her. With a grunt of pain, he pulled her dagger from his thigh and threw it toward her, but she dodged to one side, and it missed her, stuck in the wall behind her. Jorinda's lungs screamed for air, and she lost the battle with her stomach, fetched up, then collapsed to her knees. Styrrach picked up Deineike's tunic and tore a strip from it. He tied it around his leg and muttered furious words to himself. Jorinda lurched forward, swung her bound wrists at his back, and struck him hard and low. He gave a yelp and turned to face her.

One of the other men took a step from the door, but Styrrach snapped his head around toward them, and whatever the man saw, he stopped and moved back to his previous post.

Jorinda tried to unfasten the belt with her teeth, but Styrrach cuffed the side of her head, and she fell to the floor. He knelt over her again and clasped one of her breasts with his hand. "I will cut your teats from you before I slit your throat." He pulled his lips back into a snarl and leaned close to her face. He licked her cheek, his eyes ablaze with a madness she could not comprehend. "Then your little playmate will—" Jorinda raised her head and sank her teeth into his cheek above his jawbone. He cried out and pulled his head back, left his blood in her mouth. She spat it toward him.

Shouts and the sounds of men came from outside the room, and he shot a concerned glance toward the door and barked an order. "Prepare yourselves." The men drew their daggers and faced the door, nervous and tense. Styrrach stood and reached behind him as Jorinda struggled to her knees again, determined to fight on. He produced a dagger from the waistband of his trousers as fists pounded on the door. Jorinda could not understand why they knocked on the door while she needed help. He slashed at her with the dagger, but she threw herself backward to the floor, and the blade whistled past her face. The blows on the door grew more intense, and one of the boards splintered above the halfway point.

She heard men shout, "Jorinda. Deineike." The door splintered and fell into the room. Ibie and three other men tried to rush through it, but the two Guild members attacked them. Screams, cries of pain and the clang of metal on metal rang out. One of the Guild men fell backward as blood gushed from a hideous wound across his chest. The other pushed hard at the man he fought and looked at Styrrach.

Styrrach picked up a chair and limped toward the window. He swung it several times until the window glass shattered, its wooden frames and the chair with it. He hobbled through it into the garden beyond while Jorinda tried to rise and reach him, desperate to prevent his escape. The other Guild member turned and ran through the broken window as well. Ibie cried out for his men to the stop the attackers, but Styrrach had gone, his man with him.

Deineike lay naked on her back. Blood covered her face, ran from her ears. Cuts and welts littered her body, and her nose lay askew. One eye had become a purple mass of swollen flesh, and she lay motionless. Ibie tore off his tunic and draped it over her, then turned to one of the other men and barked an order for him to wrap Jorinda in his tunic and free her wrists.

Ibie yelled for one of the other men to pursue the assailant, and the man leapt through the broken window. Jorinda shouted in vain for him not to follow.

Someone wrapped a tunic about her shoulders and pulled the belt free from her wrists as she struggled to reach Deineike, and tears spilled from her eyes. "My love, wake up." Deineike did not move, and Jorinda turned to Ibie. "Fetch help, please. Healers. Please."

The Guild member who lay on the floor gave a low moan of pain, and Jorinda crawled to him and picked up the dagger he had dropped, a poor thing next to Wilash's work. She slashed his throat with it, then drove it downward into his chest with all her strength.

She pushed a bare-chested man aside and knelt beside Deineike. Raolos came into the room and stopped short at what he saw. Other people crowded in; the woman in the green dress from the lobby, and others Jorinda did not recognise. She heard Raolos yell for someone to bring healers to the inn as soon as possible as Ibie knelt beside her.

His concerned voice asked Jorinda the question she most wanted an answer to. "Does she live?"

Jorinda reached for Deineike's neck and found a slow, faint pulsing. "That she does." So little breath remained in her body, she struggled to form the words. Blood stained the chest of Ibie's tunic. "You are hurt."

"A scratch. I wish we had been notified sooner. Your attackers have slain Kinpiet." Jorinda gasped, and fresh tears sprang to her eyes. "They had taken the key from one of the staff and locked the door as they entered to attack you. That slowed us more. I am sorry."

Jorinda turned her attention to Deineike again, who had still not moved. She did not look at Ibie as she replied. "Styrrach. He found us."

Ibie knelt with her beside Deineike for some time, and more people entered the room. Raolos sat on the bed with his head in his hands. A man's voice said, "They have fled. I could not find them."

Gentle hands tried to lift Jorinda, but she fought against them until she heard Ibie's voice. "You must let the healers attend to her. And you also, for you are hurt."

Jorinda allowed the hands to help her stand. "I am unhurt. Help Deineike." Several people gathered around Deineike, lifted her with care, and shooed Raolos from the bed before they placed her on it. The woman in the green dress picked up Deineike's trousers and held them out to Jorinda. Jorinda nodded, and the woman helped her step into them. They were too long, too large in the waist, and they sat low on Jorinda's hips. She tried to reach the bed, but somebody pulled her back and forced her down into a chair where she sat with her hands on her thighs and stared at the ugly red welts on her wrists. Her hands wiped at her tears as others fussed at Deineike, who lay on the bed. She had not moved or made a sound since Styrrach had sent her backward into the wall.

Jorinda looked up at Ibie, who returned her gaze, compassion in his face as she tried to explain some of what had turned in the room. "She saved me. She stabbed him with my dagger, and now he may have killed her." Jorinda fell forward and covered her face with her hands. Violent sobs consumed her, and her body convulsed with agony while the woman in the green dress wrapped her arms around her.

Jorinda lost track of the time as she sat on the chair while despair and hopelessness poured from her eyes in salty tears. She had brought Deineike to this place and held herself responsible for all that turned. *"If she dies, I must die also,"* she thought. "She must not die." She had whispered aloud, and the woman stroked her head.

How had Styrrach overpowered her with such ease? He had been so strong, his hands so big. Without her dagger, she amounted to nothing, as he had proved beyond any doubt. Without Deineike she would be less than nothing. Despair threatened to overwhelm her, and her heart ached in her breast at the thought she might lose the woman she loved.

There were fewer people in the room now, and a man and a woman bent over Deineike as she lay on the bed. The woman wiped at the blood that covered Deineike's face, while the man studied her battered features. They spoke together, so quiet Jorinda could not hear their words, but she had to know whether Deineike would survive the terrible violence she had suffered at Styrrach's hand. "Does she live?"

The man turned to glance at her. "That she does." He turned his attentions back to Deineike.

The woman in the green dress spoke to Jorinda. "You are hurt also."

"It is nothing. Deineike saved me." Jorinda struggled to draw breath into her lungs and could not decide whether the punch to her stomach or her grief made it so difficult to breathe. Her face hurt, and she could taste blood in her mouth. She had bitten

Styrrach's face, and she imagined she could taste his blood, but when she reached up to her face, both her lips were cut. The woman in the green dress laid a gentle hand on her cheek, and Jorinda followed with her own fingers. She found some small cuts, insubstantial, and considered her injuries slight in comparison to Deineike's.

Long ages passed, but at length the man and woman who tended to Deineike stood upright. The woman stretched as the man turned to face Jorinda.

"She has suffered significant injuries. Her nose has been broken. I have set it straight and it should heal, though it may never look as it once did. Her left eye has taken extreme damage, and it is too swollen to investigate for now. The swelling will go down in time, and we may check for damage to the eye itself. I have placed a cold compress on it, which should be changed often. The cold will help the swelling to recede."

"Inflammation." Jorinda recalled the word from the chirurgeon in Torric.

"Indeed. I see you know some medicine. Inflammation should be kept at bay with cold and cleanliness. Flesh is remarkable and will heal itself if decay is kept at bay. We know less about the eye, and I am loath to investigate it until the swelling reduces."

He paused, but Jorinda sensed he had not finished. "There is more?" She feared for him to hear her, lest he answer with words she did not wish to hear.

He nodded, grim-faced. "That there is. Blood has come from her ears, and she has taken severe damage to her head." In her mind, Jorinda saw flashes: the punch to the face, Deineike's head against the wall, the backhanded blow that knocked her backward from the bed, the kick that threw her across the room. "We know little enough of the inside of the head. It is a complex area, one we ignore, to our shame, for there is no way to see what damage is done. It is simpler to deal with the things we can see. The blood from the ears suggests some damage or swelling may have occurred inside her head. I confess I know very little of these things. I have treated patients who have suffered severe blows to the head and the outcomes…"

He fell silent and Jorinda buried her face in her hands. "Will she die?"

He did not answer for many heartbeats, but she could not look at him. "I do not say that. I do not know, in truth. We are powerless to intervene in these injuries. One day, we may learn more about the treatment of such injuries, but we are far from such knowledge yet. She has retreated deep within herself, and I believe this means her body attempts to heal those injuries inside the head we cannot see. I cannot say for certain. If she does not awake, we cannot enquire about her state or do such small tests as are known to us. I am sorry I cannot bring you more hopeful news."

Jorinda nodded but did not remove her hands from her face. His words crushed her. She longed to hold Deineike and awaken her, to cure all her injuries. How unfair that her lover had fought so hard to recover from the devastation wrought on her body by the horse, and now Styrrach had driven her back into those same black depths. Hatred welled up inside Jorinda, and she could not suppress the anguished scream that escaped her lips. A hand rested on the top of her head for a moment: the healer, or the woman in the green dress. Jorinda could not tear her hands from her face to see.

Behind her hands, Jorinda's voice, little more than a breath of air across her lips, might have been too soft for them to hear "I will tend to her. I have tended her before, and I will bring her back to me again." Footsteps receded, and she guessed some of them had left the room, though the woman in the green dress still held her.

The healer had not left yet, at the least. "Jorinda, will you let me treat your injuries before I leave?"

"A scratch." She had no energy for arguments.

He sighed. "Very well. I shall return tomorrow to see how you both fare."

"My thanks." Tears gushed from Jorinda again.

The woman in the green dress spoke again. "Shall we dress you? The men are gone. There is only you and me, and your friend."

Jorinda lowered her hands and looked at Deineike, who lay motionless on the bed, a slight rise and fall of her breasts the only sign she lived. A bandage circled her head across her nose, another across her eyes. Ibie's blood-soaked tunic still lay on her, nothing more.

Jorinda rose. "I must cover her. Will you bring another blanket please?"

"That I will." Before she could leave, Jorinda laid a hand on her arm. "What is your name?"

"Alleece. I will bring a blanket, then we can dress you." She left, and Jorinda sat on the bed next to Deineike.

She stroked Deineike's dark hair. Blood matted it in places, and she resolved to wash it as soon as she could. There were blankets on the bed, but she did not want to move Deineike to pull them out from beneath her. Jorinda leaned down and kissed her forehead. An ugly bruise protruded above the bandage over her left eye. "You look terrible." She gave a sad laugh as a tear dripped onto one of the bandages, and she sniffed and wiped at her eyes.

She thought back to the woman who had brought the wine, how she had cried and seemed upset, even afraid. Styrrach must have been in the inn and sent her to their rooms for some…the wine. They had poisoned it, she guessed. She glanced toward the table, upended on the floor, the broken pieces of pitcher scattered about it like the pieces of her heart, the wine pooled on the floor like the blood from the dead Guild member. Somebody had removed his body; Jorinda had not noticed.

Alleece reappeared with some blankets and placed them on the bed near Deineike's feet. Jorinda held out a hand, and Alleece picked one of them up and handed it to her. Jorinda shook it open, pulled the Portreeve's tunic from Deineike, then draped the blanket over her. Grief swept over her again, and she collapsed with her head on Deineike's stomach. She sobbed, and her body shook from the ferocity of her grief, her thoughts a jumble of sorrow, anger and hatred.

EIGHT

NO ROOM AT THE INN

When Jorinda sat up again, Alleece picked up Jorinda's tunic and fiddled with it, awkward and uncomfortable, her face streaked by the tracks of her own tears. Jorinda stood, took it from her, and slid the tunic Raolos's man had draped around her to the floor before she pulled her own over her head. Alleece wandered to Jorinda's trousers and gathered them up.

"Are these yours?"

"That they are. These are Deineike's." Jorinda looked down at the trouser legs that trailed over her feet and pooled on the floor beyond them. Deineike's legs must be longer than she remembered. She raised one leg, then the other, and pulled the trousers up from her hips to her waist. The legs no longer flowed beyond her, although they still covered her feet. Alleece bent to pick up

Styrrach's belt, but Jorinda snarled and snatched it from her hand. She cast it away into a corner of the room as Alleece took a step back and clutched Jorinda's trousers tight against her stomach.

"I am sorry." Jorinda sniffed back more tears. "The belt is his, the monster who did this." She waved an arm at Deineike as she spoke, and Alleece nodded.

Jorinda sat on the bed again, folded Deineike's arms across her stomach, and took her hands in her own. She gazed in abject misery down on the woman who had endured so much in her life, and she wept again, her grief greater than all she had endured thus far in her life. It could not be borne, but bear it she must, for Deineike's sake.

Alleece cleared her throat. "I will leave you. If you need me, send for me. Two men stand guard outside the room. You can send one of them to summon me."

Jorinda turned to her and frowned in curiosity. "Raolos's men?"

"That they are not, or I do not believe they are. The local Portreeve's men, I think. I do not recognise them."

Terror flooded Jorinda's mind. The Alcmouth Portreeve's men? Jorinda could not trust them. They were in thrall to the creature who had orchestrated the entire murderous encounter. Why were they here? Had Raolos lost his mind? He had entrusted their safety to men who would murder them as soon as Alleece left. They might even be Guild members dressed in the tunics of the Portreeve.

She shot an urgent whisper to Alleece. "Send them away."

Alleece gave her an inquisitive look and waved at the doorway. "There is no door, and until we can arrange a different room, you must be guarded."

Not by them. "Send them away." Jorinda's dagger still protruded from the wall, and she struggled over to it, pulled it loose. "I will guard her. Send them away and fetch Raolos or Ibie.

Do not linger." Jorinda whispered, desperate for the Portreeve's men not to overhear her.

"I do not understand." Alleece spluttered and rubbed one hand with the other before herself.

"They will kill us." Jorinda kept her voice soft even as her anger urged her to scream her frustration and grief. "They are bound up in this and cannot be trusted. Send them away. Do it now." Alleece stared at her as though she had lost her mind. "Send them away or I will kill them both."

Alleece cried again but did not move, and Jorinda tutted. With no other option, she must kill the men before they could kill Deineike. She imagined they would be stationed either side of the door, and she ran a crude plan through her mind. She would take the one on the left first, a slash to his throat from behind, then hope to reverse her dagger and drive it into the throat of the other before he could react. Satisfied the plan would succeed, she padded toward the door.

Jorinda started as Alleece called out. "Wait. I will send them away."

Alleece crossed the room and went through the door. The men claimed the Portreeve himself had ordered them to keep the two women safe, then Jorinda heard Ibie's voice. "What is wrong?" Jorinda did not catch Alleece's reply. Ibie walked into the room and looked at Jorinda, many questions in his eyes.

She hissed an urgent explanation. "The local men cannot be trusted. Have you lost your mind? You would leave them here to kill us at the first opportunity?"

"They are Portreeve's men, sworn to protect the citizens of this land. You are the one who has lost her mind." He glared at her, then softened his face. "Forgive me. You have endured much, and I should not have snapped at you. There is nothing to fear from these men."

"They might be Guild members, not Portreeve's men. I do not trust them. Send them away, or I will kill them."

Ibie's eyes widened, and he looked around. "Do not say these things." He lowered his voice to a whisper. "I am also sworn to protect Dur, and I cannot let you murder these men. You will hang."

Jorinda turned to Alleece, who stood in the door, a hand over her mouth. "Fetch Raolos." Alleece turned and moved out of sight. "Other rooms must be found, where your men can guard us all without the involvement of outsiders. Nobody can be trusted." She pointed a finger toward Deineike. "Does this not tell you I speak the truth?"

He looked unhappy still. "The inn is full."

"Then we must find other accommodation. Deineike lies at death's door, and I will not sit by and allow further attacks on her. I will protect her while there is breath in my body. I failed earlier, but I will not fail again. Do not make any attempt to stand in the way of my resolve." Jorinda would defend Deineike and kill any who tried to stop her. Though she liked Ibie, she would take him if it spared Deineike. She would be his ruin in the blink of an eye, and he should not doubt it.

Ibie shook his head and opened his mouth to respond, but Raolos entered the room and asked what turned.

Jorinda wearied of explanations. She no longer whispered, unconcerned whether the men overheard her. "Those men cannot be trusted. I do not care what words they have sworn, or their loyalty to any office. They are the men of my enemy, whether that be Styrrach, the Portreeve, the Bailiff, or the Duke himself. We must find more secure accommodations."

Raolos stood with his head bowed for a moment, then looked into Jorinda's eyes. "You have the right of it. An error of judgement, made in a fraught moment. Forgive me. Ibie will stand guard, and I will arrange different rooms, where we may feel safer." He spun and left the room. He told the men outside the room they could leave, and his own men would stand guard. They again protested and said the Portreeve had ordered them to stand guard and Raolos's voice rose in anger as he told them he did not care what the local Portreeve had said, his men would stand guard.

In the room, Ibie shook his head and looked confused. Jorinda sat on the bed and laid an arm over Deineike, but she held her dagger in her other hand and kept her eyes on the door. Raolos took longer than she expected, and she grew worried.

Ibie said nothing throughout the wait. Jorinda felt some remorse for her anger at him and thought she should make some amends. None of this had been his fault, and he seemed a decent man to her. "How is your chest?"

He mumbled his reply. "It is not serious. Deineike is our concern. Our own scratches are naught in comparison."

Tears trickled down her cheek despite her best efforts to contain them. "There will be justice." She spoke aloud, then remembered Ibie's words and smiled a weak apology at him. "That is hypothetical." Raolos had used the word in his office, and Jorinda hoped it might allay any contradiction Ibie felt.

"That there will." His reply surprised her. "He will die, by your hand or by the noose. I care not how he dies, as long as he dies. That is justice, as you say, and he deserves it. What he did is inexcusable." His eyes hardened, and his jaw set in fury.

"When did the Portreeve's men come?"

"Not his men alone. He came himself." Jorinda stared at him, open-mouthed, and she forced herself to hide her alarm. "Somebody summoned his men, and he accompanied them. It seemed appropriate. A murder, and two more attempted. He must be seen to act against such violence."

He had the right of it. The Portreeve could not ignore such a heinous crime, even when the man who enriched him had carried it out. The people of Alcmouth would demand action. Their moral indignation would sweep him from office if he did not. The thought worried at her mind, and she tried to link it to all she already knew, but if it would come to full form, it would not do so today. Jorinda could not connect all the threads together. The shrouding wove its way through this, she felt certain. Guild members sold to the Portreeve, while the Portreeve ordered the Guild to murder the citizens. She would unravel it in time. First, Deineike. Once she regained full health, they would tackle the puzzle together.

Jorinda glanced at Deineike, then at Ibie again. "That Portreeve may as well have driven the dagger into your man himself. He is guilty." Her anger, and her hatred of the Bailiff, the Portreeves who worked with Styrrach, and Styrrach himself, threatened to over-whelm her. She must contain it and focus on Deineike's recovery.

Raolos returned at length with his men. "I apologise for the delay. The inn cannot accommodate us. After all that turned here, the innkeep did nothing to assist us. I shall stay at another inn if I ever come to this miserable city again." He gazed into her eyes, mournful. "I digress. I have found a house, where we will all move without delay. I have arranged a cart for Deineike. We will leave as soon as it arrives."

Jorinda acknowledged the arrangements he had made. "My thanks. I will be ready. There is little enough preparation necessary. Our packs are still as they were when we arrived. Your men's tunics are bloodied, but I will clean them once we are in the house."

"That will not be necessary. We will clean them, or new ones will be provided. Deineike is our priority, not a few tunics." Raolos smiled at her. "She will recover, I feel certain of it."

Jorinda returned his smile and hoped he had the right of it. She could not bear to see Deineike so injured, and the thought of her death brought Jorinda to fresh depths of despair and threatened her capacity to draw another breath.

Jorinda gathered up her trousers and Deineike's torn tunic.

Blood spattered the tunic, and since Styrrach had torn a strip from it, the blood must be his. She dropped it to the floor. She would not carry his blood with her. Tunics could be made aplenty, and this one would be left behind. She pushed her trousers into her pack and dropped both packs on the floor beside those Raolos and his men had brought down with them.

It surprised her how many packs Raolos's party had. Most of them appeared to belong to Raolos. She looked at him in amazement. "You do not travel light."

"That I do not." He gave a self-conscious smile. "I have always preferred to be well-dressed, and I own an enormous quantity of clothing, to Pettra's chagrin. She swears I have more clothes than her."

Jorinda recalled the dress she had made for Pettra, and her body shook as her anger rose again. "It grieves me I made that dress for your wife. She insisted on taffeta. That cloth is made from silk from the south. I made a dress for your wife and enriched Styrrach even as he tried to kill the woman I love." She spoke through clenched teeth, furious.

He looked down at the floor, made no reply, but slid his hands into his pockets. His golden rings embarrassed him, Jorinda guessed, for they had also enriched Styrrach, and she suppressed a desire to yell at him in anger about the ill choices he had made that brought this violence to her door.

The rings, the taffeta; they had cost but a tiny part of the coin that rolled into Styrrach's coffers each day, of course. Jorinda had wrought far more violence in her life than Styrrach had brought to the room earlier in the day. Her anger should be directed at herself. She had drawn Styrrach into the room, not Raolos. The Guild did not operate in Ort, and in truth the taffeta may have earned Styrrach nothing. She felt ashamed of her outburst.

She sighed, despondent at herself. "I apologise, Raolos, I spoke out of turn. I am distraught from the attack. Forgive me."

He smiled. "No apology is needed. You have endured much today."

Alleece knocked on the frame of the door. "The cart is here." Unlike earlier, she could not summon a smile. "I am sorry the innkeep would not accommodate you. A disgrace." She looked down and turned from them.

Ibie returned, and the six men pulled the blankets out from beneath the mattress before they folded them over Deineike and bore her up within them. With care, they carried her from the room, and Jorinda followed, morose and saddened by Deineike's helpless state. Jorinda studied the windows across the street, certain their movements were observed, but she spotted no furtive figures watch from any of them. All the packs were gathered up and placed onto the cart, and they set out. Raolos, his men, and Jorinda plodded along behind the cart.

Raolos must have already told the cart driver where to go as no words were exchanged once Deineike had been lain on it. They travelled no more than two streets before the cart stopped outside a house. Raolos produced a key, opened the door, and the men carried Deineike inside. How had Raolos arranged the house and cart so fast in a strange city? The power of coin, Jorinda imagined.

They carried Deineike up a flight of stairs and laid her on a bed. They removed the inn's blankets and covered her with the blankets already on the bed. One of Raolos's men gathered up the inn's blankets and left. All the men were respectful enough to avert their glance from Deineike's naked body as they juggled the blankets. Jorinda imagined the sight of her body would be the least of Deineike's concerns at that moment, but she appreciated their modest gesture.

The men withdrew and left her alone with Deineike and her thoughts. Exhaustion overcame her. They were safe enough for now, and through the window, twilight settled on the city. Jorinda took the dagger from her boot, placed it under a pillow, then kicked the boots from her feet, pulled the blankets back, and took off her clothes. She slid into the bed, wrapped her arms around Deineike with great care, and kissed her.

Jorinda whispered into the motionless woman's ear. "I hope we both awake in the morning, or neither of us, if that is the fate written for us. My love." She closed her eyes and fell asleep within heartbeats.

NINE
STYRRACH LICKS HIS WOUNDS

STYRRACH LIMPED AS FAST AS HE COULD. HE LOOKED BEHIND BUT SAW no sign of pursuit. One of his men caught up to him. The man offered to help, but Styrrach would not show any sign of weakness. "We must separate. Head home. Lay low."

The man looked surprised, but when Styrrach scowled at him, he took off down a different street, and Styrrach continued toward the Guild building. Since the other member had not appeared, Raolos's men must have cut him down.

Styrrach had failed to kill Corelle, although the other woman may have been killed when he slammed her into the wall. He could but hope. The intervention of Raolos's men had come sooner than anticipated. It had taken longer than he had expected to subdue the women. He thought he had knocked the other unconscious when he knocked her from the bed, but the dagger she had thrust into his leg complicated the entire affair. All had turned awry from that moment.

His leg burned with pain, and his face also. He held a hand to his cheek, and blood dripped from it onto the street as he hobbled along. None interfered with his progress, though he imagined he must look like ruin made flesh. He would reach the Guild building and send for a healer to repair his injuries, then plan his next moves, but for now, he forced himself to focus on his escape.

He reached the Guild building and pushed open the door. Gill leapt to his feet as soon as Styrrach entered. Only one other man sat in the parlour, and his mouth dropped open as he gazed on the blood-soaked Guildmeister, who slumped into the nearest chair and barked an order. "Fetch a healer." Gill nodded to the other, who ran from the building without delay.

Gill looked from Styrrach's face to his leg. "What has turned? Has it gone awry?" A dull pain ached in Styrrach's lower back, and he remembered Jorinda had struck him low on his back at one point before she had bitten into his cheek.

He looked up at Gill. "She lives. It went awry. Rescuers came before I could kill them."

"Raolos's men did these things to you?"

"That they did." Styrrach could not admit weakness and reveal the women had injured him. "I escaped with my life, but the others are dead." He lied to make the story sound more dramatic. None would call him out on the lie even if they discovered it.

Gill said nothing, and Styrrach groaned, moved his leg. "Fetch a cloth." Gill scurried off and returned with a tunic. Styrrach snatched it from him and pressed it on the wound where the woman had driven the dagger into his leg. Blood soaked his trousers from the wound downward, and a long trail of blood ran down his tunic from the bite on his cheek.

He must decide on his next moves. He could leave Dur. The day's events must have damaged his organisation. The Portreeve would be obliged to search for those who had carried out such a heinous act in a respectable inn. There were too many witnesses for it to be swept beneath the rug. He had acted without sufficient thought, curse it. His temper, his hatred of the jade had overwhelmed him, and he made poor decisions. He would never admit as much to any other person, but he acknowledged his headstrong response had been inappropriate. He must, however, continue to be strong. His dominance of the entire operation depended upon it.

The situation could be redeemed, but he must lay low for a while, since his description would now be abroad. He could travel to Torric for a time. He would not be hunted there, no more than a cursory investigation, at the least. That would leave Alcmouth in disarray, however, and it remained the most important Guild. These events had all turned because he had misjudged the competence of that imbecile Balgow and left him in charge.

The door opened and a man entered, followed by the member who had gone in search of a healer. The man approached Styrrach, a small leather pack in his hand. "There is little doubt who is the injured one." He laughed, but Styrrach snarled at him, and the man's face whitened. He crouched and lifted Styrrach's hand away so he could investigate the leg wound.

He mumbled, apologetic. "I will need to remove these trousers." Styrrach stood, unbuttoned the trousers, and stepped out of them. The man sucked air across his gums. "A deep wound. A dagger?"

"Are you here to tend my injuries or take notes for a journal on my life story?"

The man coughed. "I will clean and close the wound. You will need to keep it clean, or it will become infected. That is not desirable and could result in the loss of the leg. Do you wish a herb for the pain as I close it?"

"If I could tolerate the pain of the wound, I do not think your efforts in its repair will trouble me, do you?"

"Quite." He worked for some time, washed the wound with water Gill brought for him, then closed the wound. "Now, your face. Let me look."

He peered at Styrrach's cheek for a moment. "A bite?"

Styrrach sighed. "Do you wish a scribing tool brought to you so you may take notes for this journal?"

"Quite. Not a large bite. A child, or a woman. I will clean and close it."

He again cleaned the wound and closed it with the needle and thread. "There. Are there any other injuries?"

"That there are not." The blow to the back had been nothing. Corelle lacked the strength to fight him off, and her punch had hurt but a little. He had grown tired of Quite and wished the man gone. "Gill will give you coin." Styrrach stood, entered his office, and closed the door.

He sat at his desk, consumed by anger and frustration. An hour passed, and a knock came at the door. Gill entered the room and handed letters to Styrrach. "A courier has delivered these."

Styrrach tore the letters from Gill's grasp. "I need trousers." Gill left the office as Styrrach tore open the seal. The letters, from the Bailiff, summoned him to a meeting at The Riverside Tavern that night. The insult infuriated him. Glailam dared summon him, when his tardiness in the removal of the imbecile from Ort delayed Styrrach's business? He balled the letters up and threw them at the wall. He would attend the meeting, but Glailam would feel his wrath.

Gill entered the office again. "I have sent for trousers. None could be found in the building."

"The Bailiff summons me tonight. Who does he reckon himself, to summon me?"

"You cannot go." Gill's face betrayed no emotion even as he

defied the most fearsome man he had ever encountered, whether he knew it or not.

Styrrach balled his fists. "Are you the Guildmeister and I the member?" He kept his voice calm, but fought to control it, so great had his anger become.

"That I am not, but you were seen at the inn and may be recognised. Patrons in the tavern may recognise you from a description. The risks are too great. I know not why you are summoned, but I think it reckless for you to attend."

Styrrach weighed the words and could find no flaw in the logic. The incident had been no more than an hour or two since, and he needed to lay low for some days. To walk into a busy tavern could be dangerous. Gill had the right of it. "You will attend in my stead. You may hear things you do not yet know, and you must handle this information with discretion. It is a test of your initiative and loyalty. I accept nothing less than the highest level of each."

Gill waited for a time before he replied. "What would you have me tell the Bailiff?"

Styrrach turned to face Gill and took his manhood in his hand. "Tell him I will insert this into every orifice in his body if he ever summons me like a common courier again, then tell him to replace that idiot Portreeve in Ort without further delay."

"There is nothing more?"

"That there is not."

The outer door opened and closed, and the other member stood in the office doorway, a pair of simple trousers in his hands. Styrrach took a step forward and took them from him, then stepped into them. They were a poor fit, but there would be time to obtain better from his pack once the others had gone and he could use the passageway into the other building.

Gill turned to leave but Styrrach called him back. "Synna arrived in Alcmouth by ship this morning?"

"That he did, to the best of my knowledge."

"As did the women."

Gill looked pensive for a moment. "You think the two are connected?"

"Summon him. We will see what answer he gives."

"It will be as you say." Gill left the office and closed the door behind him.

TEN
A NEW HOME

THE MORNING SUN THROUGH THE WINDOW WOKE JORINDA, BUT TO HER dismay it did not wake Deineike. Jorinda's sleep had been rife with nightmares as Styrrach threaded through the night and murdered Deineike in numerous gruesome ways while Jorinda pursued him, never able to apprehend him, always slower than him.

Jorinda placed a finger to Deineike's throat and found the same slow pulsing she had found the previous day. She checked the bandages on Deineike's face and replaced the cold cloth over her eye to combat the swelling. Fresh blood had trickled from Deineike's ears in the night, so Jorinda climbed from the bed, dressed, and went down the stairs in search of some cloth and water. Raolos and Ibie sat in the parlour, and they stood as she entered. Raolos asked if Deineike had improved during the night.

"That she has not, but she does not worsen, I think. The same." Jorinda's tiredness made coherent speech difficult.

Ibie looked and sounded concerned. "You look tired. Did you sleep?"

"That I did, but not well. I must attend to Deineike."

Raolos nodded. "Of course. Do not let us delay you any further. When you have a chance, however, there is something we would like to discuss with you."

Jorinda drew a bowl of water from the pump in the yard and returned to the house to search for some cloths. She found some in the small vanity room and took one of them back to the room with the water, then cut the cloth into smaller pieces, soaked one of them, and replaced the dried-out one on Deineike's eye. She checked for any sign of inflammation, happy to detect no smell of decay from the injury, but the eye had swollen even more overnight and turned a bright purple colour.

Deineike's eye horrified Jorinda, and she could not see the eye itself between the swollen lids. She understood why the healer had said he could not investigate it until they reduced the swelling, and despondency pressed down on her. With a sorrowful sigh, she retied the bandage around Deineike's head to hold the wet cloth in place but left the uninjured eye uncovered in case Deineike awoke. Next, she used one of the other cloths to wipe the blood from Deineike's ears and dabbed away other dried blood she noticed around her face at the same time. She feared to touch Deineike's nose, since she did not wish to disrupt the bone repairs the healer had made.

The healer had said he would return this morning, but they had left the inn. Jorinda would need to speak to Raolos about the arrangement. She sat beside Deineike and cleaned the matted blood from her hair, slow and gentle, for around an hour until she had removed the worst of it, then dug in her pack for her comb and worked it with care through Deineike's dark hair until she had tamed it into a measure of tidiness.

Jorinda checked the rest of Deineike's body. She found some small bruises on her arms and legs, but there seemed to be no other significant damage. Jorinda thought it unwise to roll Deineike over onto her stomach, so any potential injury to her back must wait for now. She parted Deineike's lips and dripped water into her mouth. An important step in the process, the Torric chirurgeon had said, and she did not imagine that had changed. In Deineike's pack, she found a tunic, pulled it over Deineike's head with care, then manoeuvred her arms into the sleeves for modesty if any of the men came to the door while the blankets were pulled back.

Jorinda called to Deineike many times but received no response. Throughout the morning, her tears dripped onto the battered body of her lover. She took Deineike's hands in her own and sat beside her for some time and gazed on the broken face, swathed in bandages. Jorinda blamed herself, but she had spoken the truth the previous day. There would be justice, and Styrrach would pay. He had been injured, and she hoped he had bled to death in an alleyway some-where. She doubted it, and in her heart, she reasoned it would be a disappointment, since she would not learn of his death in such circumstances, and she wanted to look into his eyes as he died.

Jorinda could do no more for now, so she went down to the parlour to answer Raolos's earlier request. She filled a cup with some water and took a piece of bread from a loaf on a counter. Deineike's care would be a difficult task, and she must remember to eat and retain her strength.

She sat in an armed chair, exhausted. "Will the healer come now we have moved from the inn?"

Raolos apologised. He had overlooked the healer, called one of his men, and dispatched him to bring the healer at his earliest convenience. He drew a breath and addressed his concerns. "Somebody from the inn brought letters to the house this morning. I have been removed as Portreeve."

Jorinda looked at him, miserable to her core. She wanted to feel more sorrow for his situation, but Deineike's injuries filled her with such sadness she could find no corner of her heart where some sympathy might dwell for Raolos. She forced some words of consolation from her lips, nonetheless.

He thanked her for her concern. "I have the right of appeal, but it is unlikely to succeed. I will avail myself of the right, nonetheless. I will bring all that turned yesterday, and what lay behind it, to the Duke. He may take no notice unless the proof we spoke of can be provided."

Jorinda sighed. She had missed the appointment with Synna, and while she thought it justified, she had no other way to reach him now. "I am sorry Raolos, I have brought that plan undone." She explained the missed meeting, and he wilted, disappointed.

"It cannot be helped. Deineike takes your attention, as it should. I will have my say, nonetheless. I hope you might have some words to say in support of my story."

Jorinda took a sip of the water and stared into the cup, unable to respond. Deineike needed her care, and she could ill afford to be hanged while she tended to her lover. She found no joy in the grim humour.

Raolos pressed on. "Another matter then. Ibie and I have discussed your comments about the dress Pettra requested from you. As soon as my appeal is rejected"—he gave a small laugh, laden with bitterness—"I wish to return to Ort and visit the shop where you bought the taffeta. We may discover something in the owner's tallies that helps us; a name or an address that links to the Guild, anything that helps us discover evidence we can use to press the case further."

Jorinda stared out of the window. She saw so little merit in the plan, she thought it unworthy of consideration. The man must have bought the material from a merchant in Ort, since Styrrach did not operate in the town yet, although that situation would change soon enough now Raolos had been replaced. How could she disavow Raolos of the idea without any hurt to his pride? "You are not the Portreeve. You have no right to look at his ledgers."

"I am, in truth, until my replacement takes office." He gave a bitter smile. "If I leave Alcmouth soon enough, I will still be able to act for a day or more."

She shook her head. "Deineike is in no condition to travel as soon as you suggest. What of us?"

He looked at Ibie, almost for support, it appeared. "We cannot protect you if you remain here. I believe she could be made comfortable aboard a ship. As comfortable as she is here."

Jorinda stared at him in disbelief. "You have never sailed with her. It disagrees with her, and her stomach roils. If she does not regain consciousness, I do not know how that will affect her. If she is conscious, you would add more agony to her on top of all she bears from yesterday."

He looked sad but determined. "There have been attempts on my life, my wife and son's lives, and on yours and Deineike's. I have seen three of my men killed and another suffer serious injury. I cannot let this matter pass, and I must seek answers and retribution in law."

"They will not be your men, soon enough." She cursed herself for the bitterness in her words, although they were true.

"I think if most of them knew of the motives of the new Portreeve, they might remain loyal to me."

Jorinda looked him in the eye and spoke in a firm, unmistakeable tone. "Deineike is unfit for a voyage." She did not care whether Ibie and the others remained loyal to Raolos. She cared about Deineike, and her health precluded a voyage to Ort for some time to come.

"Jorinda, I have limited time. I am sorry. I cannot linger here." He looked again at Ibie, who nodded.

Jorinda heaved a sigh. How could she keep Deineike safe without Raolos's men? They placed her in an impossible situation. Styrrach would learn of the house sooner or later. He might already know. "The idea is madness and would take a terrible toll on Deineike. I cannot protect her, here, alone. They are too many. I might kill every one of the Alcmouth Guild, but they will summon more, from Ryl, Zhanghar, Torric. I cannot fend them off alone. I could not protect her from one man yesterday. How will I keep her safe against…?" Tears burned at her eyes, and she buried her head in her hands.

Amid a desolate silence, one of Raolos's men came into the parlour with the healer from the previous day. "Where is the patient?" The healer's bright tone clashed with the darkness of the mood in the room.

Jorinda looked up and stared at Raolos, but he did not meet her gaze, so she replied. "I will take you to her." She wiped at her tears with the back of a hand and rose from the chair.

The healer followed her up to the bedroom and checked Deineike's injuries. "Her condition remains unchanged. You have replaced the compress, I see." He straightened.

"I had forgotten its name, but I replaced it this morning and dripped water into her mouth."

"You know something of the ways of healers?"

The full extent of how much she knew, and how she knew it, he need not know. "I have tended her before. She fell from a horse."

"The scar on her leg, I presume. It appears to have been a serious wound."

"That it was." It hurt Jorinda to be reminded of those injuries. They had healed such a short time ago, and now Deineike lay at death's door again, and once more the blame sat with Jorinda.

"Did she strike her head in the fall from the horse?"

Tears welled up again. "That she did."

He tutted. "That is ill news. Repeated damage to the head is never a good thing."

Jorinda could not keep the truth from him, though her heart screamed at her to do so. "Another time also. She fainted at…some bad news and struck her head on the floor as she fell."

He shook his head. "You must pay close attention to her when she awakens. Observe her movements, her speech. Do her eyes focus? Is she nauseous?" He looked at Jorinda, and she nodded, dejected. "Did her ears bleed again overnight?"

"That they did, a little. I wiped the blood away, and there has been no more since." She hesitated. "She has suffered from headaches in recent days. They have bothered her."

He shook his head as he spoke. "She should be under more strict medical supervision. Some sickhomes exist, but they are unsuited for the care she requires." He smiled at her. "It falls to you, I fear. I suspect you will do all you can, though you are unqualified. The choices are limited. These injuries are dark arts. We know so little of the how the head works. I can set bone, but I cannot repair what I cannot touch. The inside of the head is beyond our abilities."

"You have done all you can. My thanks. Your words will help me as I tend to her."

"Is she your sister? Or a good friend?"

Jorinda could see no reason for the question. "Does that make a difference?"

"That it does not. Your devotion to her suggests you are related, nothing more. To tend her after the fall and now after this brutal attack. It is remarkable." He smiled at her.

"She is remarkable. She is worthy of the care." Jorinda wiped at her tears.

"Have they apprehended the villain who attacked you?"

"I know not, in truth." The Portreeve of Alcmouth would be

unlikely to apprehend him. *"Only she who stands before you might bring him to justice,"* Jorinda thought, but she did not voice her thoughts.

"Never in my life have I come across such violence. It is unthinkable for a man of Dur to attack a woman in this way." He shook his head and seemed dumbstruck by the idea.

"Not at all unthinkable," Jorinda thought. First Deineike's mother, and now Deineike herself. A sob broke from Jorinda, her legs gave way, and she fell to the floor with a heavy thud. The man grasped for her but could not prevent her fall, and he stood over her and fidgeted, uncertain. Ibie ran up the stairs and cried out, "What has turned?"

The healer placated Ibie while Jorinda's grief shook her entire body. As she fought to control her tears, she resolved anew to kill Styrrach in ways so atrocious, he would beg for Guild justice before she finished.

ELEVEN
GILL MEETS IMPORTANT MEN

GILL LEFT THE GUILD BUILDING AND HEADED FOR THE RIVERSIDE Tavern. Styrrach had lied about the events in the inn; any fool could see it. He claimed the Ort men had inflicted the injuries he sustained, but the healer said a child or woman had inflicted the bite to his face. Styrrach had admitted he had not killed the women. Something had gone awry, and one of the women must have bitten him. If she bit him, she must have also stabbed him. What had turned, and why had Styrrach lied about it?

Since Styrrach had arrived, Gill had been in a constant state of bewilderment. The man behaved like a monster. Gill killed for coin, which made him little better than Styrrach, but no man frightened or revolted him the way Styrrach did. Gill found the Guildmeister's callous disregard for others difficult to believe. He appeared to despise everybody but himself. It defied comprehension. Before

Styrrach arrived, other members would often come to the building to talk about this and that or play at dice or cards. Now they came only when required, if at all. These changes had taken place so soon. Styrrach had been in Alcmouth less than a pass, but his shadow had grown long in so short a time, and Gill did not enjoy the cold of that shadow.

He had walked no more than one street from the building when he saw Synna. He held up a hand in greeting, and Synna stopped before him, curiosity on his face.

"Gill. What is wrong?"

"Why must something be wrong?"

"Your face would turn sweet wine into rancid milk." Synna laughed.

Gill threw caution to the wind. "Look to yourself. Styrrach believes you and Corelle arrived on the same ship. I think he will kill you tonight after all that has turned."

Synna frowned. "What has turned, then?" Gill told him as much of the events at the inn as he knew. In truth, he did know much, but Synna's face turned pale as he listened to the story, and he maundered. "A sorry turn. Our Guild falls apart, I think, and Styrrach is the reason for its demise."

"It is his to destroy, after all else." Gill came to a decision. "I am away to meet the Bailiff at The Riverside Tavern." Synna raised his eyebrows. "Styrrach is injured and must lay low for a time after the day's events, and I am sent in his stead. Meet me at the dog tavern later, and we will talk more." Most ale drinkers knew of the tavern that housed the brutish animal the innkeep kept on a chain near the counter. None but the hardiest or most inebriated would ever start a brawl or press their attentions on the women who worked in that tavern. The dog would rise at a word from the innkeep and drool and growl at all around it. It had always been a mystery to Gill, since few people kept dogs in the city. He knew of few, and this one the evilest of them all.

Synna nodded, and Gill continued on his way. He had always liked Synna and thought the wiry man would have made a better Senior Aide than him. That seemed unlikely now, if Styrrach questioned his loyalty. In truth, Synna had been much changed since his friend had been hanged by the Portreeve, around a year ago. He had become quieter and seemed reluctant to spend as much time at the Guild building.

Something more had changed since he killed the woman and child in Ort. To kill a child would affect anybody, Gill reasoned, as horrific a gest as he could imagine. Synna might not have completed the gest at all, as Styrrach appeared to suspect. Corelle may have persuaded him to help her. By all accounts, she could be formidable, and it must have been her who stabbed and bit Styrrach. Gill resolved to keep Synna out of Styrrach's clutches unless it endangered his own life.

He entered The Riverside Tavern. He had never attended any of the occasional meetings Balgow took here and did not know the correct procedure. He walked toward the innkeep, who stood behind the counter and watched him approach, but he saw some men in the Bailiff's distinctive yellow tunics at the rear of the tavern and changed course. He walked toward them and some of them reached behind their backs. He held up both hands. He had the token in one of them—he had taken it from his pocket as he had entered.

He held it out on the palm of one of his hands, and one of the men stared down at it, then questioned Gill. "Where is Styrrach? I understand he has been summoned."

"He is indisposed." Gill had not noticed at first, but mixed among the Bailiff's men were others in the Portreeve's red tunic.

One of the Portreeve's men scoffed. "I imagine he is."

Another of the Portreeve's men laughed in derision, but the Bailiff's man held up a hand and snapped, "Hold your tongue." He opened a door and ushered Gill inside.

Two men were in the room, but Gill did not recognise either of them. They both stared at him as he entered. The door closed behind him, and one of them asked, "Who are you?"

"I am Gill, Styrrach's Senior Aide. Styrrach regrets he cannot attend the meeting."

The two exchanged a glance, and the one who had spoken shook his head. "He refuses the meeting, who created its necessity. It beggars belief."

The other turned back to Gill. "I am the Portreeve of Alcmouth. This is the Bailiff." Gill nodded. The Bailiff *and* the Portreeve? He had not expected both. "We summoned Styrrach here so he could explain what he did today. He has stirred a nest of snakes, and we must now attempt to keep them in the pit before they poison all we have worked for and bring us to our ruin."

The words baffled Gill. Why were the Portreeve and the Bailiff concerned with Styrrach's actions in the inn, other than to bring him to justice? He had always believed Balgow's meetings were linked to some form of bribery of the Bailiff to ensure the Guild could operate without the scrutiny that might otherwise have fallen on them. Something far larger appeared to be in play, and he did not understand it. If they tested him as Styrrach had suggested, he must tread with discretion. "Styrrach desires the removal of the idiot in Ort." He recalled the message, but he now realised the entire business with the Portreeve from Ort made no sense. Why did Styrrach have any interest in the activities of a Portreeve in a town with no Guild?

The two looked at each other again, and the Bailiff's face turned red with fury. "He demands this of us, after all he has wrought today? His arrogance is beyond the pale. He should be hanged for his actions today, yet he sends a lackey to make demands of us." He emitted a derisive snort.

The Portreeve leaned toward the Bailiff. "The matter of the Ort Portreeve has been attended to, has it not?"

"That it has. He will have the letters tomorrow, and I seek a more suitable candidate for the post as we speak. All will be resolved within a sevenday, I think. Even so, the arrogance…"

The Portreeve turned to Gill. "Tell Styrrach this."

The second message must be delivered to the Bailiff, but Gill's courage failed him. Still, he could not stay silent, for Styrrach might find out somehow, and his life would be forfeit. "I will bring this news to Styrrach. It may calm his temper, for he is vexed you summoned him here in so cursory a manner." That must suffice. He could not mention Styrrach's manhood. The men would call for their guards outside the room, and Gill's own manhood would be cut from him.

The Bailiff's face turned redder at Gill's words, and veins throbbed at his temple, in his neck. Gill feared they would summon their men and cut him down regardless, but the Bailiff replied instead, his words delivered with a fury he made a visible effort to constrain. "Styrrach is out of control, and he threatens all. His actions in the inn today were reckless, and all we have worked for may now be imperilled. Our own positions are endangered by his chaotic deeds earlier. The Duke has demanded to be updated in person on the situation and commands us to bring all involved to justice. You must control Styrrach before we all swing from the gallows. The enterprise that has functioned to bring us all great wealth must not be torn down by the grudge he nurtures for this woman. He should be hanged." Gill did not know what enterprise the Bailiff referred to and could find no connection between the Guild and the wealth the Bailiff had mentioned. The threat to hang Styrrach made more sense, but he could not understand why the Bailiff met with Styrrach if he would rather see him hanged.

The Portreeve fixed Gill with a cold stare. "Raolos's men killed one of those who accompanied Styrrach to the inn, but one escaped. The people of Dur wish to see justice, and it must be so. He will be shrouded. Tell us where we may find him, and I will dispatch my men tonight. He will hang in the morning."

Gill did not understand the word "shrouded," and he stared at the two men. The night had taken a bizarre turn, and here he stood before two of the most powerful men in the land, both of whom spoke in riddles. They wished to hang members of the Guild while they ordered Gill to control the leader of that same Guild and save them all from the gallows. "Shrouded?"

The Bailiff replied, terse, and Gill thought the man had misunderstood his confused repetition of the word. "That he will. We must shroud him. Tell us where we can find him. Do not attempt to buy time to save him. We are all bound up in this, and only his neck may save us. If that alone is enough, I will rejoice, but I fear it will not be unless we can control this feud between Styrrach and the woman."

The Portreeve stared as Gill tried to make sense of the Bailiff's words. Without warning, the Portreeve turned away and let out a small cry of despair. "He does not know of shrouding. Styrrach has kept him at arm's length and wrought our ruin."

The Bailiff glared at Gill. "Is this true? You do not understand the shroudings?"

Gill's mind raced. His life might depend on his next words. They wished to hang the member who had escaped. In truth, he had not realised one of them had escaped, since Styrrach said they had both died. Styrrach had lied about the entire day's events, and it made perfect sense. The Bailiff and Portreeve had described a fiasco of Styrrach's own creation. If Gill admitted he did not understand this "shrouding," they would be sure to call in their men and have him cut down. It would turn to their favour, he could see. A monster, sent to kill them both, slain by their men heartbeats before he could murder them both. He needed to buy some time.

"Styrrach did not tell me one had escaped. Two were sent, and one died, you say. Describe the one who died."

The Portreeve muttered something inaudible, and the Bailiff seemed ready to shatter apart with rage. "He did not tell you one had escaped?" Spittle sprayed from the Bailiff's taut lips. "Has he sent a know-nothing to us, one whom he does not trust with information vital to us if we are to keep ourselves from the noose? It is beyond belief." He also turned away.

Gill agreed with him. Styrrach had told him naught but had sent him here. Why had he done so? To buy time for his own escape? Because he had become unhinged; this seemed more realistic. His actions throughout the day had been irrational and this meeting the ultimate moment of his madness. Gill's life might now be measured in heartbeats and not years, and he mumbled to himself. "He has lost his mind."

The Portreeve heard him and turned to face him again. "Then you must act. He must be brought down, or he must be brought to his senses. We may as well flee south tonight with such coin as we have amassed otherwise. They killed a tall man with an unruly head of hair, greasy and dark. He wore green boots. Green." He gave another derisive laugh.

Gill knew the man with the green boots. He himself had wondered at the boots, for green seemed an impractical colour for boots, but the man had been proud of them for reasons he kept to himself. He wore all mockery of them with that same pride. He had raised his hand when Styrrach asked for an expert in the administration of herbs. The other with Styrrach had been Caiko, a quiet man who used to watch the card games with interest but never played.

Gill guessed if he gave them any information about Caiko, he would condemn him to death. This must be the "shrouding" they had mentioned—to give members to the Portreeve so he might hang them. Could Synna's friend, and others who had been hanged, have been betrayed by Balgow in a similar manner? He struggled with the extraordinary proposition. They had been given up to their ruin by the man who purported to lead them. Gill would need time to consider this development, but unless he now betrayed Caiko, he might expect his time to be short and painful.

He felt sorrowful to his innards. "The other is Caiko." He knew where Caiko had rooms and told them the address, although he also said the man had not been seen since the events at the inn and might not be in his rooms. He saw no reason to tell any lie about the name or the address. Whatever coin had accrued to Styrrach and the two men in the room had not flowed to Gill, and he had no funds to head south as they appeared to. His life depended on his compliance here and, after all else, he did not wish to die.

The Portreeve turned to the Bailiff. "One of the women may die, though the wrong one, I think. She looked sore injured."

Gill had thought himself beyond any further amazement at developments from this day, but he had been wrong. "You went to the inn?" Why had the Portreeve gone there?

The Portreeve seemed surprised Gill had even considered the question. "That I did. How could I not go? The workers at one of Alcmouth's most prestigious inns terrorised, an inn owned by a man who pays vast levies. One of the Ort Portreeve's men killed, and two women guests at the inn beaten in a vicious attack. My position required me to attend, express my horror at the deeds, and assure everyone the perpetrators would soon enough be brought to justice, Styrrach included. We must now decide what we do about him."

Gill tried to find some good news to appease these powerful men. "He can be persuaded to lay low, my guess. He is injured."

"He must leave Alcmouth." The Portreeve sounded insistent. "I cannot be seen to leave any stone unturned in my search for him, but if he has fled the city, I cannot be expected to find him. You must orchestrate this."

Gill pursed his lips and blew out a long slow breath. "You ask much of me, and Styrrach may kill me before the words leave my lips. I will keep him hidden. Your search can avoid the building, can it not? Beyond that, I can make no promise until I speak to him further."

The Bailiff turned again. "This meeting is dangerous to us and has gone on too long. Do what you can. We will attempt to save the situation as best we are able through our own endeavours and will send word if we need to talk again. Do not contact us until the shadow of all that has turned today has been swept away." Gill nodded. "You must control him, or we will all die. All of us." His pointed stare left no ambiguity about his meaning. The Bailiff shook his head and muttered something, but the only words Gill could hear sounded like, "mistake" and, "Raolos."

Gill did not know the niceties of how to leave a meeting with such important dignitaries, so he turned and marched to the door. His mind reeled. He had condemned a man to death, a man with whom he had sat and talked. Styrrach might also take Gill's life when he reported word of the meeting, so unpredictable did the Guildmeister appear. Gill might be hanged along with every member if things turned further awry. The full measure of the destruction Styrrach had wrought through his rash deeds today had not yet been realised.

He walked in a daze to the tavern with the dog. He needed an ale and an ally, both. Could he trust Synna? He should trust nobody but himself, but much of what he had heard in the meeting left him so confused, he needed another's ears to hear it, somebody to help him achieve some comprehension. After all else, Gill needed a plan before he returned to Styrrach. His life hung by a thread, and he could not count all the daggers ready to cut that flimsy string.

He spotted Synna as soon as he entered the tavern, seated far from the counter at which the dog slumbered, harmless in its appearance. At one word from the innkeep, that disguise would disappear, and a ravenous creature hungry to tear out the throat of any it could lay its fangs upon would appear in its stead. Gill skirted the counter by as wide a margin as possible and sat opposite Synna.

The innkeep brought an ale to his table, and he gave the man a groat. Few patrons sat in the tavernroom, and Gill could see no sign of any of the women who worked there. He wondered why no men other than the innkeep ever laboured to serve tavern customers, but he had more urgent things on his mind. He told Synna about the meeting and his concern about members who had been betrayed to the Portreeve, what they had referred to as shrouding. His breath caught in his throat when Synna said Corelle had told him the same thing. Synna confirmed he worked with Corelle; Styrrach had the right of it, after all else. Gill did not mention his betrayal of Caiko; he did not need Synna's judgement on that issue, so he said the Portreeve scoured the city for him, determined to take and hang him before the morning.

He went into more detail about the events at the inn, and Synna appeared shocked and even concerned. Gill thought Synna might be concerned for the women and not Styrrach, but he did not press him on the matter. Synna did not appear to know what to do next, so Gill urged him again not to return to the Guild building, bade him good fortune, and left.

When he returned to the building, Styrrach rested in an armed chair in the parlour. He had changed his trousers, although Gill could not guess where he had obtained the second pair. The Guild-meister may have been asleep, Gill thought, and he looked pale and tired. Given the way the day had played out, that did not surprise Gill, who must handle this situation with some delicacy or Styrrach would not hesitate to strike him down as he had Balgow. No other members remained in the building to aid him, and he thought it unlikely any would have taken his side had they been there, afraid to incur Styrrach's wrath.

Styrrach's eyes opened, but he said nothing, and Gill gave him the news that the Portreeve in Ort had been impeached and would soon be replaced. He made no mention of the Bailiff's suggestion that Gill should control Styrrach and avoided the recommendation for the Guildmeister to leave Alcmouth. Instead, he said they urged him to lay low for now while the winds of time blew the dust of the incident's memory from ordinary folk's minds. Their suggestion infuriated Styrrach, and he stood and smashed a wooden chair into a wall. A large hole bore witness to his anger.

He turned his angry countenance again to Gill. "Watch the inn, night and day. We must find a way to finish the task. Corelle must die."

Gill thought the plan both unworkable and dangerous and strove to find words that would not further enrage Styrrach. "We are short of members, with two lost today and the loss of both Sky and Balgow. It will stretch our resources thin to maintain a vigil."

"No gests will be assigned until this situation is resolved. There is naught else for the members to do. Order it, or I will appoint another as Senior Aide." Styrrach paced the room with a near-comical limp, and his fingers twitched non-stop in some furious trait.

Gill sighed. In truth, he would prefer for somebody else to be appointed, but his own death might come with their promotion. "It will be as you say." Gill paused for thought. How could he frame the matter of Caiko without Styrrach becoming further enraged? "Only one member died at the inn today. The other is shrouded and will hang in the morning."

Styrrach stopped in his tracks and glared at Gill. "How do you know this word?"

"The Portreeve ordered Caiko shrouded. He used the word, and that is how I know of it. I gave him the information he requested. I could warn Caiko if you prefer it. He could flee the city."

Styrrach wore a mask of disinterest. Gill could not fathom how he had composed himself from his frantic fury mere moments ago. "He is shrouded. He is not the first, as you must have guessed. At whiles, it serves us to remove those who have become a threat to us, and now and again one must be sacrificed to appease the demands for law and order the people of this peculiar land so desire."

Gill hoped he kept his face as noncommittal as Styrrach's, although the confirmation that members had been betrayed by the Guild for mere expediency shocked and angered him.

He wondered at the reference to "this peculiar land," but Styrrach interrupted his thoughts. "It is necessary. I warned you hard choices must be made, and now we have come to one such. Are you prepared to shroud others, or does your loyalty turn squeamish at the thought?"

"What is scribed, must be." Gill gave a non-committal shrug. He longed to allay any concerns that might endanger his life. He did not wish to be the next in line for shrouding.

Styrrach stared at him for a time, then nodded. "That it must. What of Synna?"

Did he never forget a detail? Now would be a good time for Gill to lie. "He has gone to ground, and I have been unable to trace him thus far. I can continue to search, if you desire it, although it may detract from our vigil at the inn."

"He has betrayed us then. Why else would he hide himself and not return here? I guess the woman and child are not dead as he claimed. Corelle has won him over to her side or frightened him there. He is marked for Guild justice if we find him. The vigil takes priority, but if he is seen..." Styrrach seated himself in the armed chair again.

Gill wished to leave the building more than he had every wished for anything in his life. "I must rest and will go to my rooms. The vigil will commence at first light. I will pass the word and arrange the details among the members." Styrrach made no reply, so Gill left and headed home. On the way, he knocked on a door and instructed the member who lived in the room to resume observations of The Duke's Seat the next day at the sunrise and remain there until relief arrived. The Guild had secured a room opposite the inn and would continue to use it. He went to his rooms, lay down, and reflected on an evening's events that had taken many strange turns. He must decide on his choices in the morning, but for now he needed sleep. The fates had led him here, and tomorrow decisions must be taken that would lead him toward whatever fates were written for him.

TWELVE
A REUNION WITH SYNNA

THE HEALER'S WORDS SHOCKED JORINDA, AND THE SUGGESTION THAT the recent head injuries Deineike had sustained might complicate her recovery from this latest series of blows shattered her, as though her last hope had been snatched from her. Deineike had become the motivation and strength Jorinda needed to cope with the things that ate at her daily, and she did not have the strength to face a life without her. As the healer spoke, the true horror of Deineike's fates rendered Jorinda unable to stand. The loss of Deineike's mother at such a young age, the horrors she had endured because of her love for Jorinda, and now the threat of the loss of her own life from unthinkable violence. Such a fate ought not to have been written for such a wonderful woman.

Jorinda sat where she had collapsed. Ibie and the healer left, unable to bring any solace to her, as if they felt that to try might shatter whatever remained of her. She could not understand how her body could produce any more tears, yet still they came. She ached with a desolation so complete, she wondered if she had already gone wherever she would travel to afterward, and only her inconsolable grief remained, nothing left behind but sadness in a sack of flesh. She ached for the tears to end so her life might be over at last, and they could place her body into the flames.

Time passed, and a hand knocked at the door, but she had no strength to respond. Ibie's voice came through the door. "Jorinda, a man has come to the house in search of you."

Had Styrrach found them already? Could that be possible? They had only left the inn the previous day, and he had been injured in the fight. Regardless, she could not let him inflict any more injury on Deineike. She reached under the pillow and pulled out her dagger, ready to drive it into his throat once she summoned the will to move.

"Jorinda?" Ibie's soft but insistent voice came through the door again.

Ibie may have believed Jorinda still asleep, but she scrabbled deep within herself and found some strength to reply. "Who is this man?"

"He claims his name is Synna."

"*Synna?*" Jorinda could not recall him. Grief must have driven him from her memory if she had... Wait, she could recall him, after all else. He came from the Guild, a murderer sent to kill Raolos's family. Styrrach must have sent him here to kill her and Deineike. She would send him back to Styrrach in pieces if only she could rise from the floor. Deineike could suffer no more injury at the hands of these killers. Jorinda found some strength deep within her, placed both hands on the bed and struggled to her knees, then climbed to her feet with difficulty, the dagger clutched in her hand.

When she opened the door, Ibie gasped. She could not imagine what he saw, but he reached for her as the room spun before her eyes, and she thought she might collapse again. He gripped her with firm hands, and she focused on his face as she regained some sense of balance.

Jorinda reached for the wooden rail that ran down the staircase. "I will come down and kill him."

"Why do you wish him dead? Has he harmed you? Is he a threat to Deineike, or you?" Ibie sounded angry, and she wondered what had annoyed him. When she concentrated, she realised he must be angry at Synna, and who could blame him?

Jorinda took a tentative step down the stairs. Ibie deserved a reply, but first she needed to pay attention to her descent of the stairs. Ibie's hands gripped each of her shoulders as she strove to move, one stair at a time, toward the hallway below and the outer door of the house.

Ibie questioned her as she continued the laboured descent of the stairs, but she could not focus on the job at hand if she attempted to answer him, and he tutted at each unanswered question. At last, she reached the hallway and moved toward the door. Ibie took a long stride forward and draped an arm around her shoulders, then pulled the door open.

Synna stood outside the door, one of Raolos's men on each side of him, their daggers visible but discreet at their sides. He blinked at the sight of her and swayed backward. "Corelle."

Ibie snapped at him. "What do you wish with her? She is determined to kill you, and we will allow it if we believe it is justified. If you played any part in the events of yesterday, speak now." Ibie grasped Jorinda too tight, and she could not break his grasp to send Styrrach's courier of death wherever he would travel to afterward.

"I played no part in those events. I learned of them last night and have come to warn her. Styrrach lives and still seeks her."

Jorinda stared at him. "We know he lives, and he will never abandon his obsession with me. Has he sent you here to beguile us with pleasant words before you slide your dagger into Deineike's heart?" Fragments of a memory tried to come together in her mind, and confusion grew within her.

"She lives? This is…" He appeared to search for the right words. "This news delights me, for Styrrach hopes he has slain her. He wishes us all dead." His eyes swept across everybody at the door. "He includes me, for he now believes I am a part of a plot designed to bring his ruin."

"You were on the ship." Recollections of Synna's involvement flooded back to Jorinda, and she felt foolish to have forgotten in such a short time. "I asked you to gather information that might help us and come with us to the Duke to lay your story at his feet. Why are you here now? How did you find us?"

Synna gave a short, derogatory laugh. "It proved as easy for me to find you as it will for Styrrach. I went to the inn last night, but they said you had left for other lodgings. I walked the streets for less than an hour this morning before I saw these tunics. Styrrach will soon have the Guild do the same, and you will be found. He will move to kill you. The Bailiff and Portreeve may have already hanged the member who escaped. They have met with Styrrach's Senior Aide and confirmed that which you believed. The shrouding."

Jorinda's senses snapped into focus at the mention of the shrouding, and her confusion vanished. "How do you know this if you are not sent by him?"

He flicked his eyes to Ibie and the other Portreeve's men before he replied. "His Senior Aide revealed these things to me, although whether from some sense of concern for my welfare or from his own guilt, I cannot say. The Portreeve or the Bailiff order the shroudings. Regardless, Styrrach is injured but not dead, and you must all return to Ort. You might defeat his Guild alone, but for reasons I cannot comprehend, he also wields Portreeves and the Bailiff as his weapons. You are not safe here. That is why I came, and now I must flee, or I will be dead. Styrrach made a mistake when he came for you at the inn, which has given you a chance to leave now, while he recovers his health and his influence over the Bailiff. Seize it and leave, I beg you."

Jorinda shook her head as she tried to comprehend his words. "These tunics must be replaced by clothes that will attract less attention, and this conversation must continue inside." She turned, and Ibie relaxed his grip so she could return to the hallway. "Synna, please come in and we will determine what we can do."

She entered the parlour. Raolos stood inside the doorway and had, no doubt, heard all that had been said. Her emotions whirled inside her. Raolos wished to return to Ort, and Synna's words must have hardened his resolve. Jorinda could not protect Deineike alone, and even if she could persuade Synna to stay and help her, the three of them would die. It would not matter if she and Synna cut down many of Styrrach's forces. The Portreeve and the Bailiff would send men to kill them all, if Synna spoke the truth. Portreeves across Dur stood ready to hang Jorinda for multiple murders, and Synna would likewise be betrayed to his ruin by Styrrach. They could not resist the numbers arrayed against them.

As Synna entered the parlour, Raolos's eyes widened. "What in the Five Cities? This is the man who brought me the letters that summoned here. The one you spoke of in the inn."

Jorinda raised a hand toward him. "That he is. He is no threat to you. Styrrach wishes him dead as he does all of us." She turned to Synna. "You said you would flee, but I urge you to aid us further. We must all make choices, and we are all bound up in this."

Synna's face did not betray his thoughts as he stood there. Ibie's hand hovered at his belt, and Jorinda imagined he would strike Synna down at a word from Raolos. Raolos shook his head, and no doubt he grappled with all that had been brought to him in the last day.

Jorinda could never have anticipated Synna's next words. "My heart aches that Deineike has been so hurt. May I see her?"

Ibie replied so fast, Jorinda had no time to take a breath to respond. "I caution you. This is unwise." He stared at her in unmistakeable fury and shook his head.

Jorinda tried to read Synna's face but found it blank, devoid of emotion. "Are you armed?"

He smiled. "Of course, but I will surrender my weapon. I mean her no harm. You have my word, for what that may be worth to you." Unhurried, he raised his tunic, took a dagger from a small leather cover suspended from his belt, and handed it to Ibie.

Ibie took the dagger but continued to shake his head. "Jorinda, this is madness."

Jorinda considered the request. Apprehension gnawed at her, but somewhere in her heart she trusted Synna's claim that he meant Deineike no harm. "This way." Jorinda beckoned for Ibie to remain in the parlour and led Synna up the stairs. She stood in the doorway to the room, Synna behind her. He gazed on Deineike as she lay in the bed but made no move to push past Jorinda, who held her dagger pressed to her side.

He inhaled in surprise as he looked on the injured woman. "He has hurt her more than I expected. Will she live?"

Tears sprang to Jorinda's eyes again. "We do not know. She has not woken since the attack."

After a short silence, he replied. "I will help you. I swear it. What he has done here is…" He appeared to struggle for a word to describe Styrrach's attack on them.

She turned to him, grateful beyond her capacity to explain. "My thanks. Raolos wishes to take ship to Ort, and I believe he would leave us here alone. If you and I attempt to defend her, we will all die

"That we will." He fell silent for moments again. "I have another dagger in my boot."

"I guessed as much. You would have died before you could have drawn it."

"That I would. I do not doubt it."

They looked at each other, a connection between them Ibie and Raolos and all his men could not have understood or shared. They were bound by experiences and fates they had not shared together, but that formed a bond between them, nonetheless.

"These are good men, but they are loyal to Raolos, and he wishes to return to Ort and run off on some fool's errand in search of answers to the riddle he finds himself embroiled in."

Synna returned to the matter at hand. "You do not wish to leave Alcmouth? Can he protect you in Ort?"

"He has been impeached. Some wiles of the Bailiff, or his puppet master Styrrach. He cannot protect us." Jorinda glanced behind her at Deineike. "I do not believe she could survive the voyage."

He smiled. "She did not enjoy the voyage south. If she sleeps as she is now, what will happen aboard a ship?"

"I know not. Her stomach would be thrown about even though she sleeps. She slept often on the journey south but woke at whiles and needed to fetch up. She seemed to find some peace from the problem while she slept, nonetheless. I confess I would rejoice if she woke and urged me to help her to the rail." She sighed. "The journey may kill her. I could not survive…" She fell into the desolation of her thoughts again.

After several heartbeats, Synna posed a difficult question. "Why did that man say you wished to kill me?"

She looked at him and tried to find some words to explain the irrational thought earlier. "Since yesterday, I cannot tell my thoughts from my deeds. My ups are down, and I see threats in everything. I could not recall you, if you can believe that. I believed Styrrach had sent you to kill us."

He laughed, a bitter, mirthless laugh. "Let us return our attention to Deineike. It is as you say. If we remain here, we will all die. If we leave, she may die on the ship, and I fear you would cast yourself into the waters if she did. I would live, my guess. We should leave." He smiled at her, and she appreciated his attempt at the jest, although it brought her no joy. Their choices were no choices at all, it seemed.

She shrugged. "Ibie will be concerned. I think I saw him risk a glance up the stairs. He does not trust you."

"He is right not to. He seeks to protect you, but you could take me before I could draw my weapon. If he trusted me, I do not think you would trust him."

She managed a weak smile. "That I would not."

They returned to the parlour, and she drew in a long breath. "Raolos, we will accompany you to Ort. I hope I do not come to regret this choice. Deineike will require a great deal of assistance and care. I will tend her as best I can, but I will trust your men to arrange such careful transportation to the ship as is possible. Synna will travel with us, and his dagger will be returned to him. We may yet have need of it."

Ibie made no move, but Raolos nodded toward him. He seemed reluctant to hand it back to Synna, and Jorinda laid a hand on his arm. "I know you do not trust him, and you have my thanks for your caution. I believe he means to help us unless his own life is threatened. I place no obligation on him if such danger presents itself, for I would do the same."

Ibie stared at her. "Would you cut me down to save yourself, then?"

She thought for a moment, but he deserved an honest reply. "I might, but I would cut you down without a heartbeat's hesitation if you threatened Deineike."

He glanced away, then handed the dagger to Synna. "I return this to you against my judgement. I return it because you must already know that the words she spoke to me, she also spoke to you."

"That I do." Synna tucked the dagger back into its scabbard. The atmosphere in the room remained fraught. No new friendships had been struck so far.

Raolos gave a cough. "There is other news I have not shared. The Duke sent a courier early this morning. He will come here after the midday to hear my appeal and wishes to see Deineike. His concern for her is genuine, I believe. He says he has ordered his Bailiff to track down and hang all those who are in any way responsible. It is a great honour that he comes here. He need not do so, although I explained we are in danger and told him I did not wish to divide such protection as we have so I could visit his Offices. It would have been easy for him to dismiss my concerns and deny my appeal because I would not visit the Ducal Highhome."

The news did not please Jorinda. "I know you say this in the anticipation Synna and I will pour out our stories to him and bring about the removal of the Bailiff. You wish your appeal approved and your reinstatement, and that is as it should be. Our lives are forfeit if we confess. Deineike might urge me to take the risk in the name of some greater good she could see but few others might, but she cannot do so, and she is in dire need of my aid. I will do nothing to jeopardise her or my care for her. I have already said I will help you, and I will, but I must help Deineike first, for she has paid a terrible price for her love of me in the past year. I imagine that is not what you hoped to hear." She looked away and blinked back tears. "Synna is free to make his own decision."

Synna's decision seemed to have been made. "I am pledged to help Core… Jorinda. I will stand by her while she needs my skills. If she hangs, I will hang beside her, for we both deserve the fate. If she will not speak, then I will not speak. I will not allow my death to break my word to her."

Raolos sighed. "I understand, although I believe we have a chance to remove a pestilence from Dur if we can persuade the Duke. Few know of that pestilence, and we may be able to expunge it with Durfolk none the wiser. I will urge him to consider the amnesty I once spoke of. We will see what fate is written when he arrives, and to brood on it will take us no closer to that fate." He sat in one of the chairs. "He will arrive here soon, in truth. The day has taken many turns and has slipped by us."

Synna turned to Ibie. "Styrrach will have the inn watched, and when he does not see you come and go, he will investigate. If the house is not already watched, it soon will be. Your men should be prepared at a moment's notice for any moves he may make against you. The Portreeve acts out of some expediency he sees in the severity of..."

He fell silent, and Jorinda turned to stare at him. He squinted as though he tried to identify an object that lay on some far horizon. Jorinda prompted him to tell them what bothered him. "What is it?"

He muttered, distracted, almost to himself. "The shroudings. Guild members betrayed to the Portreeve. We do not know why. Gill told me the Portreeve came to the inn yesterday, after Styrrach's attack, and said he would bring the attackers to justice. He is Styrrach's toy, so he says these empty words from some obligation to the vows of his office. Is that why they sold members to him? Have our colleagues died to save the face of the Portreeve?"

Jorinda considered his words. She could not believe anybody would order the death of those who served them for such a vile and selfish purpose. Styrrach must be an animal if he traded lives for political appearances. She shook the thought from her head. "We must focus on what we know at this point. All may be revealed in time, and you may be right. For now, we should concentrate on how to bring Deineike to Ort alive."

Synna frowned as he appeared to ponder the situation. "If Styrrach does not already know we are here, he will as soon as the Duke arrives, for that will attract the attention of most of the neighbourhood. The Duke's men will swarm the area in those ridiculous yellow tunics, and Styrrach could follow them to our door in the blackest night. We should prepare to leave tonight, or tomorrow at the latest."

Ibie nodded. "I will make arrangements." He glanced at Raolos, who gave him a curt nod, and Ibie continued. "I can spare a man to attend to these matters now Synna is here." Synna nodded, and Ibie left the parlour and went to the rear of the house. Not long afterward, one of Raolos's men walked through the room and out of the house. Ibie returned and ordered the rest of his men to remove their tunics and don less conspicuous clothing before they resumed their posts outside the house.

THIRTEEN
A VISIT FROM THE DUKE

RAOLOS SAT IN THE CHAIR WITH SADNESS ON HIS FACE. "IF WE MUST leave so soon, how can we arrange a Pyre for Kinpiet?"

Ibie let loose a long, miserable sigh. "The Pyre would be risky under any circumstance. They might see an opportunity to strike at us while we mourned."

Raolos placed a hand on the top of his head, ran it through his hair. "What evil is this, that we cannot hold a Pyre for our fallen? This must end. Normality must be restored to our lives, our land." He could not disguise the despair in his voice.

Jorinda tried to find some comfort she could impart. "A Pyre can be arranged, even though we are not in attendance." Jorinda's guilt that there had been no Pyre or Sending for Arella or Taro consumed her.

Raolos gave a sad shake of his head. "A Pyre with no Sending. It is a disgrace."

Jorinda decided to leave him to his disappointment over the loss of his man and the fact he could not attend the Pyre, and she climbed the stairs to check on Deineike. As she closed the door, she noticed Synna seated on a stair near the hallway. He stared at his dagger as he turned it over in his hands time and again. There had been no change in Deineike's condition, but Jorinda replaced the compress and wiped away some blood from an ear. Deineike's eye did not appear to have changed in appearance, and Jorinda imagined it would be some time before it would improve.

She kissed Deineike's forehead. "We must move you soon, my love. We are not safe here, and we return to Ort, where I hope we may find more help for you and keep you safer. I confess I do not know what fates are written for us. Raolos has been impeached, and I am unsure what forces he can summon to protect us all. I will die before I permit further harm to befall you, I swear it. Please come back to me, I ask no more of you." Jorinda kissed Deineike again, sat on the bed beside her, held one of Deineike's hands, and shed despondent tears.

Sounds of commotion drifted up the stairs an hour later, but she did not open the door. She guessed the Duke had arrived but had resolved to say nothing to him unless he assured her no consequences would arise from her confession.

The light faded outside the window when she heard footsteps climb the stairs and a knock at the door. Raolos's soft voice came from the other side. "Jorinda, the Duke wishes to see Deineike and speak with you."

Jorinda imagined it would be an immeasurable honour for most Durfolk to speak with the Duke. They would spend many hours in preparation and would wear their finest clothes, brush their hair, and douse themselves in the sweetest fragrance they could afford.

In comparison, Jorinda guessed she looked a mess. She still wore her bloodied tunic, her hair had been neglected since the fight and doubtless straggled like a bird's nest on her head, and she wore no boots. With a resigned sigh, she rose from the bed and opened the door.

Below Raolos, Synna stood in the hallway and gazed up at her. She whispered so as not to wake Deineike. "She is not some sculpture or picture for people to gaze upon at will. She is injured, and she should not be disturbed any more than is necessary to tend to her."

"I know this, but the Duke insists. Will you deny him? I do not have the courage to do so."

She sighed. "What of your appeal? How does he rule?"

He looked down. "He sees no grounds to overturn the Bailiff's decision. He wishes to investigate my claims about the corruption in his service, but he needs proof if he is to do so. He would not agree to an amnesty for any who confessed to any involvement in my allegations. He said he could not pardon someone who had been convicted of no crime. I remained circumspect and stopped short of any accusation that the Bailiff himself played a direct role in this corruption. Without the amnesty, I reasoned you would say naught, and I cannot provide proof unless I work further to expose the operation." He shrugged and looked downcast, but Jorinda's position remained steadfast. Deineike must be protected and tended, and Jorinda would not entrust that task to anybody but herself.

"I am sorry, Raolos." His abject misery touched something inside her, and she laid a hand on his shoulder. "Bring the Duke upstairs for a brief visit with Deineike. His self-importance might amuse her, and she will awaken to tease him. She does not suffer arrogance with good humour."

He smiled at her in gratitude and returned down the stairs. He reappeared not long afterward and gestured. A man whom Jorinda guessed must be the Duke came from the parlour and climbed the stairs toward her.

He stood not more than a span above her own height and had a stocky build, twice her age at the least, more even. He sported a neat, trimmed beard that tapered to a point close to the collar of his tunic. Jorinda had never seen clothes of such a high standard as those he wore, nor making of such spectacular quality. Instead of the usual wool or spun yarn most clothes in Dur were made of, his tunic had been crafted from brocade, a material created from silk and so expensive, it would be far beyond the coin of even a person as wealthy as Raolos. More coin for Styrrach, she thought in fury. His trousers appeared to be velvet. His tunic sported golden buttons polished until they gleamed as bright as the summer sun, and he wore a long cloak fastened to two epaulettes on the shoulders of his tunic. His trousers were tucked inside calf length brown leather boots, buffed to a high gloss.

Two men followed him, dressed in the bright yellow of the Duke's Offices. Their clothes also sported the golden buttons, and they each carried a short sword in a scabbard at their hip. Hats that resembled a pie gone awry, collapsed into itself, perched atop each of their heads, though they seemed ready to fall off at any moment. Few Durfolk wore hats, and with good reason if these represented the best of Dur. Jorinda thought them the most ridiculous hats she had ever seen. Raolos, Ibie and one of his men followed while Synna loitered at the bottom of the staircase.

Two steps from the top of the stairs, the Duke appeared to notice her for the first time. If her dishevelled appearance shocked him, he did not show it. He held out a hand toward her, a large golden ring with some lavish precious stone set into it on one finger. She did not know what he intended her to do. Did he invite her to link arms, as at Raolos's house after the attack in the

Portreeve's Offices? Should she take his hand? He might need help to climb the final stairs—he did not look like a man much used to physical exercise.

Awkward heartbeats passed. Behind the Duke, Raolos raised his hand to his mouth in an exaggerated gesture. Did he expect her to kiss the Duke's hand? She could find no rational explanation for such a bizarre gesture, did not know how to break the predicament, and did not know how to address a Duke.

Raolos laughed. "My Duke, forgive her. She is from Ryl."

The Duke laughed with him, but Jorinda shot Raolos a scornful glance. How dare he use Deineike's jest even as she lay injured in the room? The comment kindled her ire.

"A fine city." The Duke withdrew his hand, and a concerned look crossed his face. "Such a terrible atrocity occurred to you and your friend yesterday. I have instructed my Bailiff to spare no resource in the hunt for the vicious fiend who perpetrated this unimaginable violence. Two of them have already gone wherever they travel to afterward, one at the hands of Ibie and his men, the other hanged by the Portreeve this very morning. The third remains at large, but we cast a net that will reel in this fish, and he will pay with his life."

He had used a great many words, none of which interested Jorinda. She did not wish for his net to catch Styrrach. She wanted to watch the life leave his eyes, not hear that he swung from a tree somewhere many days distant from her. She did not reply.

"Are you injured? I hear your friend suffered terrible hurt." The Duke persisted with the conversation and did not appear to have noticed her continued silence.

Jorinda replied at last, still unhappy she must make small talk with this wordy man. "I am hurt but a little. A scratch. Deineike has grievous wounds and has not awoken since the attack. She suffered several blows to her head, and we fear they may have caused her some injury that can neither be seen nor mended by any skills the healers possess."

"A tragedy." His voice sounded like the purr of a cat and held neither conviction nor falsehood. Men of such great import as the Duke must find it easy to use words filled with little sincerity. Synna had shown more concern than this man, in truth. "Is there anything I can do to help you?"

"You could hang your Bailiff, whose complicity in the attack sickens me." Jorinda could not contain her fury at the Duke's pretence of concern while his senior servant plotted with Styrrach to kill them. She considered the Bailiff as culpable as the Guildmeister. At the least, he had his hand in Styrrach's glove. Meanwhile, this pompous man stood before her, preened himself, and mouthed empty absurdities at her.

The collective gasps of astonishment at her words deafened her in the heartbeat that followed. "You misspeak in your anger, I am sure." The Duke measured each word as though he fought against a fury as powerful as Jorinda's own. What right did he have to become angry at her for her words? How much more did she have the right to anger? His most senior official played some part in the grave injuries Deineike had suffered.

"That I do not. He is bound up with killers and miscreants, and if you will not bring him to justice, then you are complicit with him."

"Jorinda." Raolos's horrified voice yelled from behind the Duke.

The Duke snarled, his attempts to contain his anger swept away. "I remind you to whom you speak, young woman. With but a word from me, my men would cut you down, and your impertinence would justify it. I am the Duke of all Dur. I feel genuine sorrow for the position you find yourself in, but my patience for your insolence is thin."

Jorinda sneered at his ludicrous threat. "Your men would die before those clumsy steel encumbrances they call weapons could clear their scabbards, were they to try." More gasps.

"You threaten my men and me?"

"I do not threaten, ever. Rather, I tell you the consequences if you attack me. You refuse to hear the truth about your Bailiff, who consorts with murderers. You condone the removal of this decent man"—she pointed toward Raolos—"from his office on fraudulent accusations confirmed by paid performers. Is this how a Duke acts? I do not think much of it, in truth."

"You speak of things you know nothing about. An investigation into Raolos's infidelities found against him. Your opinion of the charges is of no consequence." His face had turned bright red, and his eyes flashed with a rage he seemed to struggle to contain.

Jorinda could see no point in further argument, and she took time to slow her heart and cool her temper before she spoke again. "You should leave. Take these buffoons in their stupid hats with you. Your presence here does not help Deineike, and I tire of you."

Behind the Duke, Raolos and Ibie stood open-mouthed. The two guards had their hands on the hilts of their swords, and below them Synna had climbed several stairs to stand behind Ibie, a hand at his belt beneath his tunic.

The Duke's fury must have been immense. He wheeled on Raolos. "This is the gratitude your people show me when I visit you in this difficult time?" Spittle flew from his lips, and he turned back to Jorinda. "Good day to you. I wish your friend well. It is as well she could not hear your words. I feel sure she would be ashamed of them."

"You know nothing about her, and she is my lover, not my friend. Do not tarnish her character with your ill-conceived assumptions about what she might or might not approve of." She turned, walked into the room and slammed the door behind her. She leaned against it, slid to the floor, raised her hands to her face, and wept bitter, angry tears.

Darkness fell outside and nobody came up the stairs. Would Deineike have been ashamed of her? She might have been, in truth. Without question, she would be disappointed at Jorinda's rudeness, although she would not care that it had been directed at the Duke any more than if it had been somebody employed to empty a chamber pot. She would be angry at the injustice, and although she might be critical of Jorinda's words, she would support the defence of Raolos and the criticism of the Bailiff.

The knock she had expected came after she had sat, thoughtful and tearful, against the door for some hours, and Synna's soft words drifted through the door. "Jorinda. How do you fare?"

"Not well." She pulled herself to her feet and opened the door. Light spilled in from candles on the landing, and Synna stood bathed in their warm glow.

He raised his eyebrows. "Quite the speech."

"Did I go too far?"

"I imagine you could have spoken with less honesty. He is the Duke, after all else. His ego is bruised, but Deineike suffers more. I feel no sympathy for him."

"Is Raolos angry with me?"

He laughed. "That he is not. He is livid. Ibie also."

Jorinda sighed. She owed them an apology, she guessed. If there had been any chance the Duke might have been persuaded to change his opinion on Raolos's appeal, her outburst must have destroyed it. Yet another example of a temper she could no longer trust not to erupt in a heartbeat. "Will they leave us here now and sail back to Ort?"

"Ibie suggested it." He gave another short laugh. "Raolos is a good man, my guess. He said Deineike played no part in your outburst and did not warrant the fate that would be written for her if they left her here. He arranges a cart for her, and a ship. We leave in an hour. I have come to tell you to prepare for our departure."

She nodded and glanced at Deineike. "I hope she will bear the journey."

"As do I."

He half turned, but she laid a hand on his arm. "I saw you, while I spat out my grief and fury at the Duke. You stood ready. My thanks."

"You had the right of it. You would have cut them down. If they had managed to draw those clumsy ornaments from their scabbards, they could not have wielded them in these narrow confines." He jerked a thumb behind him to indicate the stairway. "I only wished to ensure Ibie did not strike you down as you took them."

The answer saddened her. "Are we monsters, Synna? We would kill good men without a second thought in our rage?"

"I did not say I would kill him." His eyes twinkled in the candlelight. "I would have ensured he did not kill you, which is not the same thing. We would have died in any event. The Duke had twenty men at the least in those laughable clothes outside, and two more in the parlour. It would have made a good end to a life lived to little consequence, my guess."

She had no response. He had not answered her question, and it had not needed an answer. They were monsters, and Deineike lay immobile because of the creature Jorinda had become. "My thanks. I will ready us for the cart." She smiled at him. "You called me Jorinda."

He gave a self-conscious shrug. "It is your name, after all else, and what they all call you. I felt like a mutton in a pen of milk cows whenever I said 'Corelle.'"

"What do you know of muttons and milk cows?"

He poked his tongue out at her, turned, but hesitated at the top of the stairs. "You may not have made an enemy, but you have lost a friend. The Duke raved for some time about your words, but the threat to kill his men rankled him. He intends to instruct the Bailiff to hang you if he can find any proof you have murdered anybody."

He glanced back at her and smiled. "One more noose; nothing to concern you. I ceased to count them some time ago." He went down the stairs, and she closed the door. Darkness embraced the room, and she re-opened the door a crack to allow some light in.

Jorinda pulled her boots on and slid the dagger into them. She had taken nothing from their packs, so she picked them up, carried them out of the room and down the stairs, and dropped them in the parlour. Raolos sat in an armed chair with a hand against the side of his head. He turned to observe her as she entered, but he did not speak.

Head lowered, hands clasped before her, Jorinda spoke in a quiet, humble voice. "Raolos. I apologise. I spoke harsh words."

He gazed on her. "That you did, although few could argue you spoke anything but the truth. The threat to his guards angered him the most, nonetheless, and the fates are written. You defended me in your tirade, and I appreciate it, although I wish you had done so in a more constructive way. What is scribed, must be. We have decided to leave straight away. Synna believes the Guild will now know with absolute certainty where we are since Durfolk filled the street. They poured out to catch a glimpse of the Duke between our door and his carriage."

"That turn owes nothing to my words, at the least. Such attention was guaranteed when he decided to come here."

Misery crossed his face. "I doubt I would have come alive to his Highhome. The Bailiff would have seen to it, so I entertained the prospect of the visit, caught between doubt and uncertainty. I should not have agreed to allow him to speak to you. You are a forthright woman, and I made a bad decision. He is the Duke, and he insisted. I did not feel I could refuse him."

"We cannot rewrite the fates. I am afraid Deineike may not survive the voyage. I do not care about the Duke."

"My men have arranged a carriage and a cabin with a comfortable bed for her. I have hired a healer to voyage with us in case her condition worsens. He will return once we have her comfortable in my home."

Jorinda's eyes watered again. He had arranged such care for Deineike despite the outburst. Few would have done so. "My thanks. How can you lavish such coin on her now you are not the Portreeve? I can never hope to repay you."

"You will never have to. I have my own successful business interests, and at present, Deineike has great need of the comforts my coin can buy."

"Did you arrange a Pyre for Kinpiet?"

"That I did. A Pyre has been arranged, though the Sending will not be heartfelt." He again looked sad, and Jorinda had no words to bring him comfort.

Ibie came into the house. "The carriage is here." He ignored Jorinda, spoke to Raolos.

Raolos nodded and turned to Jorinda. "Is Deineike ready to travel?"

So much complexity wove through such a simple question. Jorinda would not resist, but she deemed it reckless to move Deineike. The injured woman could be brought to the carriage, but her readiness could not be ascertained. Deineike could not describe how she felt, and nobody understood how she might react to the journey. Jorinda shrugged. "I hope so."

While Jorinda took the packs out, the men went up the stairs and carried Deineike down, wrapped in a blanket from the bed. An enclosed carriage with two benches opposite one another across its width stood outside the house, two horses in line either side of the shaft. The men laid Deineike on one of the benches, and Raolos sat on the other. Jorinda did not know whether she would be welcome in the carriage, so she dropped her packs on the floor and closed the door. Synna raised his eyebrows at her, and she shrugged her uncertainty.

They set off toward the docks. Jorinda, ever cautious, checked every alleyway or street they passed and looked for unusual movement in any window along the way but saw nothing untoward, and they reached the docks without incident. As the carriage approached the ramp of a ship, Synna sidled up to her.

"That is a large tally house." He kept the conversation casual as he inclined his head toward one of the darkened buildings along the docks. Some of the tally houses spilled light onto the dock as they handled cargoes from the ships at the dock, but many stood silent and black. Jorinda half-turned toward the building Synna had indicated. A figure crouched in the shadows and watched Raolos's men carry the packs onto the ship.

She pursed her lips. "Should we take him?"

Synna shook his head. "We are watched, as we knew we would be. There can be little doubt we are watched by more than one member. If we kill this one, we kill a man who is not responsible for all that has turned, and Styrrach will still know we have left. Let them report we have left Alcmouth. The wheels turn as they will, and we will deal with the consequences as they arise."

Jorinda nodded, deep in thought. He had the right of it about the Guild members, who were pawns in Styrrach's game and watched at Styrrach's order. Their life need not be spent in payment of the Guildmeister's debt to her.

The ship sailed north in the dark, and Jorinda sat in a chair next to Deineike's bed. Raolos's healer studied Deineike with meticulous attention and decided they had made her as comfortable as they could. He felt Jorinda had not forced enough water past her lips, and she must do better. When Jorinda told him Deineike fetched up aboard any ship, he suggested they lie her on her side so she could fetch up and not choke, even if she did not wake.

Jorinda questioned him about the consequences of large quantities of water, but he said she must find a way to resolve it. Jorinda did not believe she could position Deineike on a chamber pot while she remained unconscious, so she gathered up as much cloth as she could find and placed it beneath Deineike.

Jorinda fell asleep in the chair next to the bed and awoke from a nightmare, stiff and cold. Darkness still surrounded the ship outside the cabin window, so she climbed with great care into the bed, wrapped an arm around Deineike from behind, and whispered, "I love you." She kissed Deineike's back and fell into another troubled sleep.

FOURTEEN
RAOLOS INVESTIGATES

THEY SAILED NORTH BENEATH COLD GREY SKIES THAT POURED RAIN down onto the ship most days as the wet season soaked the land. For the first two days, Deineike neither moved nor woke, and Jorinda changed the compress, cleaned her, and removed the soiled cloths as instructed by the healers. It broke her heart to wash Deineike's intimate areas when she would rather pleasure her lover to the limits of her sanity and beyond. The ship rolled in the waves, and occasional bile would spill from Deineike's mouth. Jorinda wiped it from the floor and sheets and cleaned Deineike's face. To Jorinda's disappointment, Deineike did not wake when she fetched up.

On the third day, Jorinda sat on the bed as she combed Deineike's hair, and her lips moved. Jorinda's heart leapt in her breast. She leaned close and whispered, "Deineike, can you hear me?" Nothing indicated Deineike had woken, but Jorinda embraced her and told her she loved her, encouraged she might one day return from wherever she had withdrawn to.

When the healer came to the cabin to check on the patient, Jorinda told him about the movement of the lips. He thought it might have been some involuntary motion but did concede it might also be a hopeful sign. He cautioned Jorinda not to raise her hopes too high; it had been such a small sign and might mean nothing.

Synna, Raolos, and Ibie often came to the cabin to check on Deineike and sit with her for a time so Jorinda could go out onto the deck and take some fresh air. Nobody mentioned the argument with the Duke. The journey did not seem to have any adverse effect on Deineike's health, but she showed no sign of improvement either, and Jorinda's concern grew each day her lover did not awaken.

With only a day of the voyage left, Jorinda sat in a chair next to the bed and watched over Deineike, when to Jorinda's delight, Deineike's less damaged eye opened, though no more than a slit. Jorinda jumped up and sat on the bed next to her. "Deineike? Can you hear me?"

Deineike managed a weak smile, and Jorinda's tears poured from her. "Jorinda." Deineike's voice sounded frail, little more than a feeble croak. Jorinda leaned closer so she could hear, but the eye closed again and Deineike did not speak further, so Jorinda ran to the cabin door and shouted for someone to bring the healer. He seemed pleased there had been some sign of progress at last. Synna ran in and said he heard something had turned awry. Excited, Jorinda told him what had turned, swept him into her arms, and cavorted around the cabin while he followed her with a wide grin on his face. Raolos and Ibie also appeared and laughed as Jorinda refused to release Synna from her ecstatic dance.

Deineike did not awaken again before they reached Ort. As dockhands unloaded the ship's cargo, Ibie went ashore to arrange transportation while the others remained aboard the ship. He returned with the cart Jorinda had ridden in before. They laid Deineike in a second cart, smaller and flat, and they set off to Raolos's home. Jorinda choked when she saw the tender care the men gave to the injured woman, as though she might be a loved relative of their own.

The men carried Deineike upstairs into a large room and laid her in the bed. The healer checked her for some time and said he saw no ill effect from the voyage. Despite Jorinda's relief, she yearned for Deineike to wake and speak again. Raolos thanked the healer who had travelled north with them, and Jorinda embraced the embarrassed man as she gushed her thanks. Pettra embraced her, too long for Jorinda's comfort, and even Raopul seemed glad to see her again.

They sat in a parlour to discuss their next moves. Raolos wanted to visit the garment maker as soon as possible, before the replacement Portreeve arrived, and he lost his official position.

With little enthusiasm, Jorinda nodded. Now she had returned to Ort, she had no enthusiasm for the idea and no desire to be involved. "I think you run into a blind alleyway. I am certain there will be no information to learn from this man. Styrrach has no operation in Ort, and I am sure the garment maker bought the material from a merchant at a fair price. That merchant may have bought it from another and so on. It could be long trail before you find someone who works for Styrrach, and that person will not be in Ort. It is fruitless."

Raolos tutted. "That it may be, but the alternative is to sit here on my hands and do naught until I am replaced, and the Guild comes to kill us all. Would you prefer me to take this course?"

She ran the palm of a hand across the top of her head in frustration. "That is not my intent. If you believe you will gain some intelligence from it, then go to the garment maker. I have already given you his address. I must tend to Deineike."

"I have sent for the best healers in Ort to tend her and would appreciate it if you would accompany us to this shop. You may hear or see some vital thing we might miss."

Jorinda continued to rub her head as she contemplated the situation, and she pressed a fingernail into her scalp. To her surprise, she found the pain welcome, and it served to focus her thoughts. While she did not wish to leave Deineike alone, she felt obligated to deliver some token assistance, if only to assuage her guilt at the vast amount of coin Raolos had lavished on them in the name of Deineike's care. "Very well. I will visit the shop with you, though I have no confidence we will discover anything to our advantage. I will spend some moments to make sure Deineike is comfortable, then please be ready to leave. The sooner I return to her, the happier I will be."

Jorinda ran up to the room where Deineike lay in a large bed, an ornate cover spread over her. The cloths beneath the injured woman did not need to be replaced, so Jorinda dripped some water into her mouth, then went downstairs, a tight, heavy sensation in her heart.

Ibie, Synna and Raolos stood near the outer door, ready to leave. Raolos walked at a brisk pace to the store where Jorinda had bought the taffeta, tucked away in a quiet corner of the commercial quarter. Ibie and Synna walked beside the Portreeve, but Jorinda fell some way behind, her thoughts occupied by Deineike. Raolos strode with purpose into the store, and Jorinda trudged in some moments after the others, miserable and with no confidence in the plan. She wished with all her heart to return to the house in case Deineike woke again.

The shop owner did not recognise Raolos and needed an explanation of his position as Portreeve. Raolos pointed to Jorinda as he told the story of the taffeta purchase. The man remembered the transaction and the difficulties he had encountered when he dyed the material. Raolos asked to see the man's tallies, and a heated debate followed about the rights and wrongs of the Portreeve's right to investigate the business matters of one who had committed no crime. Jorinda thought the man would refuse, but when Raolos told the story of the attack on Deineike and how it might be linked to trade in goods from the south, the shopkeeper relented and brought his tally ledgers out to the counter of the shop.

To Jorinda's irritation, Raolos had again used Deineike as part of the conversation without permission. Deineike might have had no objection, but Jorinda did not find it easy to overlook the casual way Raolos turned her terrible injuries to his own advantage. She tried to convince herself she over-reacted, and she fought down her anger.

The man flicked through the ledger until he found the purchase information for the taffeta, and he turned the ledger so Raolos could see the entry. Raolos's face turned red, and his head slumped.

Ibie stepped closer to Raolos. "What is wrong?"

"The material passed through a tally house here in Ort, and they sold it to this man for a large sum."

It did not surprise Jorinda; the man had no involvement with Styrrach's enterprise, but Raolos seemed more deflated by the discovery than he ought to have been. His next step must be to visit the tally house to determine whether the owner belonged to the operation, although no doubt he had bought the material from a southern ship or had it brought to Ort by a merchant from another town or city, where Raolos would have no power to investigate further.

They thanked the man and left the shop. Once they were clear of the street, Raolos stopped and leaned on a wall. He cursed to himself, and Jorinda stepped away and left him to his anger for a time, though it seemed excessive. Had she not warned him he would learn the man played no part in the schemes of Styrrach and the Bailiff?

She could contain her impatience with his annoyance no longer.

"I predicted this outcome and said you wasted time on the pursuit of a wild bird. Why are you so irritated I am right?"

He glared at her, sullen and resentful. "Because the tally house he bought the material from is known to me. It should be, for I own it."

Jorinda stared at him, stupefied. His own tally house belonged to Styrrach's organisation? That made no sense. His tally house must have bought the material from another at a fair price, then.

He tutted. "The tally house does not bear my name, for it might seem inappropriate for the Portreeve's tally house to operate under his own name. Because of my position, merchants and ship's masters would prefer to deal with my business, which would be unfair to the other houses. I can investigate the tallies in my own house, of course, but they will lead to another who sold us the material. You had the right of it. The trail will grow cold here in Ort, and any answers must lie elsewhere."

Jorinda said nothing more of how she had always expected this outcome. It would not improve the situation, and they trudged back to Raolos's house in despondent silence. They had not been away long, in truth, but she longed to check on Deineike.

Pettra sat in the main parlour when they returned, and as they passed through the parlour, she asked whether they had learned anything helpful. Raolos explained what had turned, and she appeared disappointed. "What will you do next?"

Raolos sighed. "I will check the tallies and discover where the material arrived from. No doubt it came in by ship from another city, and there will be little more I can do here in Ort, my guess."

Pettra frowned. "Why do you not buy the materials yourself from the ships? Would that not cut off the supply to the other cities? You will either sell the goods at a more reasonable price and close Styrrach's business or anger him so much he takes some action against you that will allow you gain proof." They all stared at her, dumbfounded, and her face turned red. "What? Have I misunderstood the concept?"

Raolos gave her a weak smile. "That you have, I am afraid."

An idea took shape in Jorinda's mind, and she turned to Raolos. "Pettra has found the answer, nonetheless."

Raolos's confusion stared back at her. "How?"

"The goods you buy direct from the southerners are bought at the same price as Styrrach pays, I would guess. The difference comes when you sell them onward to Ort's merchants at lower prices than Styrrach does in the cities he controls. That is why he eyes Ort for his scheme, so he can sell them on at a higher price and take his profit from the sales."

Raolos shrugged, and Synna stared at Jorinda with a blank look of incomprehension. Ibie frowned and asked, "Where is the answer in this?"

"It is so simple. I cannot believe we have not come to this idea before." Jorinda's excitement for the idea Pettra had sparked grew. "You must pay more for the goods you buy, as must all tally houses in Ort."

Raolos stared at her as though she had lost her mind. "You ask me to pay more for goods I can already buy at a lower price? Is your plan for me to become insolvent?"

"That it is not." Words rushed from Jorinda as she struggled to contain her enthusiasm for her idea. "Why would merchants sail their ships past Ort when you will pay them more for their cargoes? Why would they not sail past Alcmouth to sell them for a higher profit here in Ort?"

Raolos's eyes widened. "Why indeed? You seek to disrupt Styrrach's plan and drive his customers to Ort."

"That I do. He will be outraged."

Synna sounded doubtful. "Why would he not match the new price?"

Jorinda gave an excited shake of her head. "He could, but he will not. He will act against Raolos. Remember, he will have a Portreeve here soon, and the Guild will arrive not long afterward."

"Hold." Pettra reached toward her husband. "You ask Raolos to increase his price so Styrrach will kill him? That is madness."

Jorinda turned to her. "He will kill Raolos either way if he can, and he is already furious after the failed attempt to kill me. He tried to kill you once and failed. He smarts from the pain of those failures. He will come for Raolos whatever we do."

Ibie still seemed perplexed. "Then how does this new scheme help us?

Jorinda sighed, out of patience with the explanations for something she visualised with such clarity. "Raolos has been replaced as Portreeve. Styrrach has suffered numerous setbacks, and he needs time to rebuild. His fury when he hears of Raolos's trade arrangement will be great, and he will act at once. He will order the new Portreeve to intervene. Ort's tally houses must be brought into his scheme, and he needs the Guild to accomplish that, but he cannot establish a Guild here straight away, while we can offer higher prices tomorrow. He must act, and the new Portreeve is the sole tool he has at his disposal here. The Portreeve will be told to send his men to arrest Raolos, but on what grounds? Ortfolk will be outraged, and the Portreeve will be forced to back down, or be deposed by the will of the people, who will press the Bailiff to replace him, and the Duke will learn of it."

"A nest of snakes." A smug grin spread across Raolos's face. "They will not wish such exposure, and by the time the Portreeve receives his orders, our new arrangement will be well established."

Synna pointed out a complication. "He may send Guild members."

Jorinda sneered. "I hope he does. We will apprehend them and hand them to the Portreeve, who will be forced to hang them and bring their confession to the Bailiff."

Raolos laughed, a grim, ironic laugh. "Styrrach will not like this turn."

Jorinda agreed. "His finances will be impacted, or he will be hanged. One way or the other, we will bring him down." Jorinda smiled at Pettra, whose words had sparked the thought in the first place. Pettra returned the smile, and the sparkle in her eyes left Jorinda uncomfortable. She regretted the impulse.

As he spoke, Raolos shook his head, and concern creased the corners of his eyes. "The other houses must join me. I cannot sustain the higher prices for long if I must sell at the same price as them."

Jorinda acknowledged the potential issue. "You will not need to, my guess. Styrrach will be livid, and he will act as soon as he can. If his scheme does arrive here, the sale prices will rise. That is how it operates, so you will earn more even if we fail."

Raolos looked deep into her eyes and brooded in silence for a time, then said, "We will do it." Everybody broke into relieved smiles.

Jorinda knew Styrrach, knew he would be infuriated if they tried to take part of his coin and take advantage of his own idea. He would act, though it might take time. He ran the operation with a firm grip, and most ships' masters would be petrified to trade with them and incur Styrrach's wrath, but that did not matter. Word of the offers would come to Styrrach and would be sufficient to bring his blood to the boil. "*Boiling water scalds, and boiling blood scalds the more,*" the old Ryl phrase went. Styrrach's blood would boil so hot he must attempt to stop the threat to his coin, and he would scald himself in the process.

Pettra's mistaken remark had provided them with a chance to shut down Styrrach. If he did nothing, his threats would be seen as bluster, and more merchants and ship's masters would trade with Raolos, at a fairer price to them. If all the ships defected to Raolos, the Dur market would obtain the goods at a fair price, and Styrrach could no longer pocket the enormous profits. There could be no loss for anybody but the Guildmeister. They had the perfect plan.

Ibie's serious words broke Jorinda's thoughts. "I will start the operation in the morning."

Raolos gazed on him with sadness. "That you will not. The Portreeve's Offices cannot be embroiled in this. The operation will be run from my tally house, with no opportunity for any to cry 'Corruption.' We must not become the evil we seek to destroy."

Ibie seemed stunned, then he smiled. "You have the right of it, but after all else, I cannot work for a Portreeve who is the puppet of this Styrrach." His eyes sparkled with excitement. "I resign my position."

Raolos smiled back at him. "I accept your resignation. But now you find yourself without work, I fear you will fall upon hard times. I offer you a position as my representative in an enterprise I am about to commence. The wage will—"

"I accept." Ibie laughed and turned to Jorinda. "I know you wish to tend to Deineike, but I beseech you to aid me for a day or two at the least as I start this enterprise."

Jorinda did not have the heart to dampen the joyful spirit that had come over them. They had all enjoyed little enough happiness in recent days. "I will help you tomorrow, at the least. I feel certain Synna might be persuaded to work for you, though he should be rewarded for his efforts."

Pettra turned her head toward Synna, then appeared to decide something and drew in a sharp breath. "He arrived in Ort determined to kill Raopul and me, but he now seems committed to better outcomes. Jorinda has the right of it. If he will help, he must be compensated."

Raolos stared at his wife and seemed ready to argue the point, but he sighed and looked away. "So be it. If Ibie will have him."

Ibie nodded and extended a hand to Synna. "If Jorinda recommends you, there can be no reason not to hire you." Synna shrugged and took his hand, though he seemed uncomfortable as Ibie pumped it up and down.

Jorinda wanted to check on Deineike. "We three will visit the docks tomorrow and board every ship that carries a name from beyond Dur. That will sow the seed."

Raolos stopped her as she turned to leave. "My thanks. You have served us well in a short time, and though the Duke's feathers were ruffled, I am grateful for all you have done. Tomorrow I must return to my office and prepare for my departure, but the downfall of this man seems possible at the least, and in no small part thanks to you."

Jorinda felt the heat burn her face, and she nodded before she scampered from the parlour to run up the stairs and into the room. Deineike lay as she had before they left for the garment maker's shop, and the fact Jorinda had not missed any time while Deineike might have been awake did not assuage her disappointment that she still lay unconscious. She changed the compress and checked the cloths, which did not need to be changed, then dripped some water into Deineike's mouth and checked her ears, relieved to see no indication of fresh blood.

She sat on the bed and talked about the incidents of the day to Deineike, even though she guessed she spoke to herself. The familiar sound of her voice might help bring Deineike back from wherever she had gone, and Jorinda would do whatever it took to bring that about. She could not bear to believe she might lose this woman and pushed any hint of despair from her mind even as her heart lay heavy in her breast. Sadness weighed on her, threatened to crush her. She must remain hopeful, as she knew Deineike would if their situations were reversed.

It had grown dark outside, and she closed the shutters, then picked up the pitcher and dripped more water into Deineike's mouth. Her throat rippled as though she had swallowed the water, and Jorinda gasped as Deineike's eye sprang open, and she gazed up at the ceiling.

"Deineike, my love." Jorinda took one of her hands. "Come back to me. I miss you."

Deineike's lips moved, but Jorinda could not hear her. She lowered her head close to Deineike's lips and thought she heard her rasp, "I am thirsty." Jorinda sat up, dripped more water into Deineike's mouth, and she swallowed it. Tears gushed from Jorinda's eyes and ran down her face onto the bed cover. "I cannot see. A bright light." Deineike's voice sounded gruff and cracked, almost inaudible. "My head aches."

Jorinda stroked the dark hair back from her forehead. "You are injured, but do not fret. I will care for you, my love."

Deineike managed a weak smile, and her eye closed again. Jorinda fussed at Deineike's hair for a time, but she did not reawaken. Relief had washed over Jorinda when Deineike spoke, and it brightened her mood. The improvement had been immeasurable—from the depths of an unbreakable sleep to speech—and ecstasy flooded Jorinda. Deineike would come back to her soon, and things could be as before. They would leave and head somewhere safe, where they would live out a life of quiet solitude, unconcerned by the affairs of the great and the good, or the evil. They could have their vegetable garden, after all else, and Jorinda would spend as much time in it with Deineike as her lover desired. She would never leave her side again once she recovered.

Jorinda slid into the bed and wrapped Deineike in her arms. Somebody knocked on the door, but she ignored it. Doubtless it would be Raolos or Pettra, come to check on Deineike. For tonight, she would not share with anybody that Deineike had spoken. She would hoard it to herself. Sleep swallowed her up, and the nightmares stayed away.

FIFTEEN
SOMETHING PRECIOUS IS LOST

THE SOUNDS OF THE HOUSE WOKE JORINDA, AND SHE OPENED THE shutters. A grey, miserable day greeted her, the sky full of low clouds, unable or unwilling to hold onto the vast quantities of water that somehow gathered inside them, and they drenched the land with rain. The window looked onto the rear of the house, and Jorinda studied the garden below. Hedges and grass, all trimmed to perfection, with some small trees she did not recognise here and there. Two large plots held a few vegetables, but she guessed many others would only grow when the warmth of spring coaxed them from the soil. Jorinda smiled. Once Deineike returned to full health, they would grow old together and become experts on the growth cycles of vegetables. She had never imagined it until the attack that rendered Deineike so helpless, but now she craved it. She did not care for vegetables overmuch and ate them as little as possible, but the vision of her and Deineike in their garden brought a flutter to her heart.

Jorinda turned to Deineike, desperate for her to open her eyes again, but she saw no sign of consciousness, so she performed all her checks and replaced some soiled cloths. No blood had seeped from Deineike's ears overnight, and Jorinda applied a fresh compress. The damaged eye appeared less swollen this morning. She leaned forward to place a tender kiss on Deineike's lips and went down the stairs.

Ibie and Synna sat at the huge dining table, where a meal of sliced hog, bread and cheese had been laid out. Jorinda ate some of the food, more from a desire to maintain her strength for Deineike's care than hunger. Once they had finished their meal, they stood in the doorway and stared out at the rain, reluctant for the soaking they would endure.

Ibie sighed and held out a hand into the rain, no enthusiasm visible. "We have picked a fine day to start our new venture."

"That we have." Synna hunched his shoulders against the elements even though he had not left the house.

"Let us go." Irritated, Jorinda pulled her cloak about her, and they set out. The sooner they began, the sooner they would finish. In truth, she now regretted she had agreed to help, since she wished to be in the room in case Deineike woke again.

They trudged through the rain to the docks. Despite their cloaks, the rain had soaked them all to the skin by the time they reached a building Ibie declared to be Raolos's tally house. They sheltered inside the tally house for a time as a large pool of water at their feet grew drip by drip, fed by their cloaks. The tally master appeared from the rear of the building, and Ibie introduced him to Synna and Jorinda before he gave the man a cursory overview of what might change if the volume of business through the tally house increased after the plan. The tally master asked Ibie one or two questions, then left them to their business.

Jorinda badgered them to leave the tally house, and they wandered along the docks. A large three-masted ship stood at the southern end. The crew carried fresh supplies aboard, and with a glance among themselves, Ibie led Jorinda and Synna up the ramp. Dark-skinned mariners bustled about on the deck and spoke to one another in a language Jorinda did not recognise. The three found the master on the aft deck, and to their relief he could speak their language.

Ibie introduced them, then asked the master where he headed.

"I sail for Zhanghar, then home."

"What cargo do you carry north?"

The master gazed into Ibie's eyes, stony-faced. "That should not concern you, I think."

Jorinda turned to Synna and asked him to show the master the token. Fear crossed the man's eyes as Synna held the token in the palm of his hand, and Jorinda took over from Ibie. "This token will be swept from the land. In future, we will buy your goods from you here in Ort at a fairer price than you are paid today. None will board your ship under this token again once we establish our operation. You need not fear us."

The man blinked, doubt on his face. "I know not the price paid, as you speak. I carry goods for those who pay me for space in hold of ship, is all."

Although he might be little more than a transportation provider, Jorinda wanted to be sure the message got back both to Styrrach and those who paid the master. "Soon enough, Styrrach will not be the person you carry these goods for. We mean to drive him out of business. Please tell those who pay you to carry their goods we will pay a fairer price and will not use threats of violence to enforce our business arrangement. Any who travel aboard your ship will pay for their passage when our plan is realised. No token. You understand my words?"

He nodded, but the fear did not leave his eyes. "Understand

your words. You understand fish will clean your bones if you run afoul of the one you name?"

Jorinda leaned in close and whispered in his ear. "I do not fear him, for he will be dead, hanged by a new Bailiff, or fallen to my blade, which I would prefer."

The man looked taken aback, but he regathered his dignity. "I will tell your words in Qanti when I return. What will be outcome and if it will sit well with those who hire my ship, the time will reveal."

Jorinda believed he had agreed to pass on the message, although his grasp of the Dur language fell some way short of perfect. She, however, could not have spoken a word of his language, and she respected his ability to converse so well in two languages.

Ibie seemed anxious to get off the ship. "We are grateful for your time."

They walked further along the docks, but no other ships from beyond Dur could be seen. They called into the Master's Offices and requested information on any southern ships due to dock through the day. He told them no precise schedule existed, since it depended on winds and tides, and ships from the south often arrived unannounced. Ships might arrive on the next high tide in a little over an hour.

The news frustrated Jorinda. The idea had seemed so simple last night, but it might take them a year or more to intercept every ship that called into Ort. They would miss every ship that went only to Alcmouth, Zhanghar, or Torric. Their foolproof idea had made fools of them, in truth. Ibie made a half-hearted attempt at encouragement, and they called into a tavern where Ibie and Synna drank a tankard of ale while Jorinda stared at the table as dejected thoughts of Deineike swam through her head.

Two hours later, they wandered out into the rain again and returned to the dock. They stared south through the rain, and

Synna said he thought he saw sails. The wind had strengthened, and it whipped the bitter, cold rain against their faces as they squinted through the downpour. Long moments passed, and at last Jorinda spotted white sails against the grey sky. She hoped it would be a southern ship and not The Jorinda, The Friendship or one of the other Dur ships that plied their trade up and down the river.

As the ship drew closer, they saw the three masts that marked it as a southern ship, better suited to longer voyages than the smaller two-masters that worked the river and coasts of Dur. They retreated to Raolos's tally house to shelter from the rain while they waited for it to dock. Jorinda thought the time had crept well past the midday, but she could not see the sun and could do no more than guess its position in the sky.

Jorinda had all but lost her patience, and she urged the men to board the ship and deliver the message before she returned to the house. They splashed along the dock, reached the ship, and boarded it. Ibie again introduced them and explained their purpose to the master. Once more, the master needed sight of the token before he would listen to their tale of how trade with Dur would soon enough be a different experience to the current one.

"No different for me, I think. Different for the merchants."

Jorinda replied. "The merchants?"

He nodded. "Merchant aboard might wish words with you over this."

Ibie sounded excited. "There is a merchant aboard the ship?"

"Yes, he is aboard."

Jorinda had never heard anybody confirm something by the use of the word "Yes," and it surprised her the master had not used the familiar "That he is." Something had been lost in the translation between the languages, she guessed. "May we speak with him?"

"Yes, you should speak with him." The master did not move.

Ibie sounded terse, as though tired of the misunderstandings. "Will you take us to him?" The master seemed to grasp what Ibie had asked him, turned to a nearby mariner, and barked a command in words that meant nothing to Jorinda. The mariner set off toward the main deck but stopped to look back at them, and Jorinda guessed they should follow him.

He led them inside the cabin area beneath the aft deck and knocked on a door. He spoke through the door in his own language, and the door opened. A man stood before them, dressed in a dark red tunic and black trousers, both well made from good quality linen. Tall but robust, he grew a small tuft of hair below his lower lip that seemed absurd to Jorinda on an otherwise clean-shaven face.

"How can I help you?" He had almost no trace of the accent the master had spoken with.

Ibie introduced himself and explained the proposal once more. The man did not appear afraid as the two masters had been, paid close attention to their words, but did not invite them into his cabin. The mariner lingered nearby, although Jorinda guessed he could not understand their conversation.

The merchant leaned on the frame of the door once Ibie had finished. "Styrrach has a competitor, this is what you imply?"

As before, Jorinda took over. "That he does, for it is our operation."

"A woman may speak for your organisation?" The man asked Ibie the question and raised his eyebrows.

With a nod, Ibie replied. "Many things will change in Dur as the passes turn." Jorinda noted his non-committal response but wished he had stressed the weight her opinions and words carried.

The merchant made an unusual facial gesture, and his pursed lips moved from side to side. Jorinda imagined the movement of his lips meant he pondered all he had heard. Some time passed before he continued. "Styrrach knows of this?"

Ibie nodded again. "That he will, soon enough."

The man raised his eyebrows. "I have a deal with Styrrach. You would have me break my word to him and trade with you?"

Jorinda grew tired of the man. "Styrrach's hold over these trades is ended." The man's eyes tracked to her, unhurried, as though he had no real interest in what she said, and a faint smirk came to his lips. She continued as anger crept into her voice at the thought of the Guildmeister. "He is a murderer and will answer for those crimes to authorities, official or otherwise."

The man pursed his lips again. "You think yourself the 'otherwise' of which you speak? A woman would kill Styrrach." He gave a short laugh. "I think not."

Synna's dagger flashed, and he held it against the man's throat. The mariner moved, but Ibie held up a hand toward him. Synna's lips drew back in a snarl. "Do you believe I could now kill you?"

The man showed no fear. "It would appear so."

Synna slid the dagger into the scabbard at his belt and pointed to Jorinda. "Fear her. She would have struck me down before my dagger could reach her neck."

The man nodded to Jorinda. "Then I am impressed."

Jorinda sighed, tugged Synna's sleeve, and pulled him away from the man. The demonstration had been over dramatic and unnecessary. She turned to the merchant again. "We have offered you a price fairer than Styrrach will pay. He will rage and rail and tell you he will cast us all down when you break your contract with him, but I will cast *him* down. You may make your choice. Further words are pointless unless we are so fond of our own voices, we must make noise for the sake of our own vanity."

He laughed and wagged a finger at her. "I like you, though you are but a woman. Tell me, will you honour me with your name?"

"My name is Jorinda. You may tell Styrrach you spoke with Corelle. He will be more familiar with that name." The success of the plan required Styrrach to know Corelle worked with Raolos to steal his business.

The man bowed his head to her. "Rakulaj, my name. Respect is due. We have exchanged names. This is a great honour in my land. You people of Dur throw your names away at any excuse." He laughed. "Your friend handed me his as his first words. There is no respect in this. I will bide my time before I share mine with your other friend, for his dagger suggests a lack of respect."

Jorinda hesitated, unsure she had followed his convoluted thread. Strange customs must exist in his land, and she thought about his words and searched for an appropriate response. "Respect is due."

He laughed. "If all the women of this land were like you, Corelle of Dur, your friend's words would be true. Your women would hold a stronger voice in your lives, I think. Come; I have heard your words. I do not know whether there is sincerity in them or whether they are barbs for Styrrach's temper. When next I send a shipment to Dur, I may instruct my master to visit your tally house, or I may instruct him to sail onward to Zhanghar, where my prices are guaranteed, at the least." He smiled at Jorinda. "I will pass your message to Styrrach. I will not deliver it myself. My wife would be distressed if I returned to her in small pieces." He laughed loud and long.

Ibie spoke, but Rakulaj did not glance at him. "Our words are sincere, I assure you."

The merchant smiled. "Then we shall see what your fates have written for you. Respect is due." He stared at Jorinda as he spoke, and he bowed to her. She returned the bow in the belief it must be some sign of courtesy in his culture. "Good day to you all." He closed the door, and they turned to the mariner, his face a picture of confusion.

Back on the dock, Jorinda said the meeting with Rakulaj ensured Styrrach would learn of their plans, although it might take some time if the ship sailed home first. The others agreed, and Jorinda, anxious to return to Deineike, said she would return to the house. Ibie wished to remain on the docks lest another ship arrived, and Synna offered to wait with him. They both wished Deineike well, and Jorinda headed back to Raolos's house.

The rain had not eased, and by the time she arrived at the house it had soaked her all over again. She shook her cloak outside the door to rid it of some of the water, although her clothes were so wet the effort seemed futile. She knocked on the door, and the servant who answered it said Pettra sat with Deineike. Jorinda asked for some cloths with which she could make some effort to dry herself before she crossed the carpets, since she felt certain they must have cost a great sum.

Jorinda did the best she could to dry herself and climbed the stairs to the room. Pettra sat in the window and read from a parch, but she looked up as Jorinda entered. She wore a fitted dress, and the room smelled of her usual scent. Jorinda went to the bed and leaned over Deineike to kiss her temple. "How has she been?"

"She woke once, earlier." Despite her joy that Deineike had awoken again, Jorinda choked on disappointment; she had not been here. "She called your name but soon fell asleep again." Pettra smiled up at her. "How were your endeavours at the docks?"

"Successful, I think. I am certain word of our scheme will come to Styrrach. I fear the plan will have limited success if we restrict ourselves only to Ort, but Styrrach may be so enraged he will bring himself undone."

Pettra rose from the chair. "I will leave you with her. You must have missed her today." Jorinda flashed her a grateful smile, and Pettra laid a hand on her arm as she passed. "Join us for dinner, please. Raopul asks after you, and it would please Raolos. It would please me also."

Pettra gave her a coy smile, which convinced Jorinda she could not join them. "I will if I can. Deineike may have need of me." She looked down at the woman in the bed before she returned her gaze to Pettra and lifted the hand from her arm with gentle fingers, anxious not to offend. "My thanks for the time you spent with her."

Pettra gazed into her eyes long enough for Jorinda to feel uncomfortable, then purred, "My pleasure."

Jorinda let out a long sigh as Pettra left. They should move to an inn. Pettra's unwelcome attentions seemed both innocent and suggestive at once, and Jorinda could not deny a sense of jealousy that Pettra had enjoyed another moment of Deineike's consciousness rather than her. She pulled the chair near to the bed and sat as Deineike slept on. Jorinda checked for a pulsing, found it much as she remembered it from previous days. She changed the compress, but the cloths beneath Deineike needed no attention. Pettra must have attended to them, or Deineike had drunk insufficient water. Jorinda dripped some into her mouth, anxious not to let her body lack water after the concerned words of the healer aboard the ship.

Noises came from outside the room, and Jorinda imagined Raolos had returned, or Ibie and Synna. The evening wore on, and she watched for any flutter of Deineike's eyelid as she combed Deineike's hair and washed her. The sounds of meal preparation and conversation drifted up from downstairs.

She sat on the bed and ran her fingers through Deineike's hair as she whispered in desperation. "Please come back to me my love."

At the words, Deineike's eye sprang open. She stretched an arm toward the end of the bed and a warm smile spread across her lips. "Arella." Her voice, little more than a croak, did not match the joy in the smile. Jorinda glanced to her left even though she knew Arella could not be there, then looked back and smiled. Deineike moved her outstretched arm toward Jorinda and caressed her cheek. Jorinda raised her own hand and stroked the back of Deineike's, tender, affectionate touches on the soft skin. Deineike looked up at her and Jorinda could no longer hold back her tears. They spilled down her face and over their hands as Deineike's feeble voice spoke again. "Do not cry, my love. Arella has need of me."

Her eye closed, and she let out a strange, harsh breath. Her arm went limp, though Jorinda still held it to her cheek. Concerned, Jorinda lowered Deineike's arm to the bed cover. "Deineike?" She gasped and reached toward Deineike's neck but could not find any pulsing. She cried out again, louder. "Deineike." She placed her cheek close to Deineike's mouth but could feel no breath.

She pulled back the cover and blankets and pressed on Deineike's stomach, down and release, down and release, hopeful it would draw breath into Deineike's lungs. *Breath.* Deineike needed breath, and Jorinda bent, pulled downward on Deineike's chin to hold her mouth open, then blew into it as hard as she could. She repeated the breath several times, but when she reached for Deineike's neck, she still could not detect a pulsing.

Jorinda screamed as tears poured from her. "Deineike. My love." She pulled Deineike up into her arms, and Deineike's arms flopped to her sides. Jorinda held the dark-haired head to her breast and let out an anguished howl laden with all her grief. Behind her, the bedroom door opened, and footsteps entered the room.

Pettra cried out in alarm. "What has turned? Jorinda?" Raolos let out a strangled cry.

Somebody yelled; Synna, Jorinda thought. "Fetch a healer."

Jorinda rocked back and forth, Deineike's head cradled in her arms. Tears streamed from her chin into Deineike's hair. "Deineike, my love. Do not leave me." Deineike lay still in her arms and would not reply. Jorinda's heart shattered in her breast. "I cannot live without you. Come back to me."

People shuffled behind her, but she did not turn to look at them. She continued to rock Deineike backward and forward and spoke soft words, urged her to say something. Sobs filled the air, but she could not tell if they came from her own agony or that of others.

Pettra spoke after some time. "Jorinda. A healer is here. Can he look at her?"

They wanted to take Deineike from her. Jorinda whipped her head around and screamed. "That he cannot." Pettra started. "She is mine. You will not touch her. None of you will touch her. Get out. Get out." Nobody moved, and their tears and the compassion in their faces became too much for her. Jorinda picked up the comb from beside the bed and hurled it at them. It struck Raolos in the arm and bounced to the floor. "Get out."

She kissed Deineike's temple and cradled her to herself again as she whispered into her beautiful black hair. "My love, I am sorry I shouted." Feet crossed the carpet, and the door closed. Jorinda did not know how long she sat with Deineike clutched to her breast as she wept, beyond any consolation. The woman Jorinda loved more than life itself had gone. Styrrach had killed her. She let out a long, guttural cry of agony, then shushed herself and whispered, "I am sorry my love. I failed you." Worse, she had killed Deineike. The thought burned in her mind, and her tears intensified.

Hours passed, and darkness fell outside the window, but Jorinda still sat on the bed and whispered occasional words of love to Deineike. She ignored a knock on the door. The door opened for a heartbeat, then closed again. Jorinda lay Deineike down, retrieved the comb, then combed Deineike's black hair for some time. She arranged it around the beautiful face that would never smile at her again. Her fingers dropped the comb to the floor, and she lay in the bed beside Deineike, one arm across her stomach, a leg thrown over Deineike's own, nuzzled into Deineike's neck and apologised again, then kissed her cheek. The bandages still covered Deineike's face, and Jorinda sat up and removed the compress from her eye, the bandage from across her nose. Deineike's crooked, purple nose did not make her any less beautiful. Jorinda screamed again, her agony unbearable.

The door opened again. "Jorinda? Are you all right?" Pettra's soft voice sounded tearful and concerned.

"Get out. Leave us." Jorinda strove to keep her voice quiet, so she did not disturb Deineike.

The door closed, and she nuzzled closer into Deineike's neck. "I am sorry Deineike. I have brought your ruin to you. It is all my fault. Please forgive me." At that, she remembered she had not told Deineike the truth, either about the incident with Pettra when she had measured her for the dress, or when Pettra's hand had lingered over-long on her cheek on the night they foiled Synna's attempt to kill Pettra and Raopul. Jorinda took her arm from across Deineike's body and ran it through her own hair. Guilt penetrated every part of her, and she dug her fingernails into her head, clenched her teeth as she pressed her nails into herself with all her strength, and ignored the pain as she told herself it could not compare to the pain she had brought to Deineike.

To her alarm, Deineike had grown cold. "My love, you shiver." Jorinda pulled the blankets tighter around them and noticed blood on her hand as she took it from her head. The night dragged on, and she slept from time to time. Nightmares more horrific than any she had ever experienced filled her restless moments of sleep. Whenever she woke, she held Deineike or pressed her fingernails into her own head as she berated herself for the loss of the woman she loved more than life.

Light crept through the window, and still she wept and held the woman she loved. Deineike's cold skin had lost its colour, she felt stiff, and when Jorinda tried to move her hand to her own cheek, the entire arm raised and would not bend.

Another knock came at the door, but still Jorinda did not answer. She had no energy for speech. Her agony had drained her, and she had slept little. The door opened and feet moved around the bed. She saw Pettra but did not look up into her eyes.

"Jorinda." Pettra's soft voice, broken by sobs, betrayed her misery. "We must take her and prepare her. There must be a Pyre. I know you wish to hold her longer, but we must take her or take you to another room. I am so sorry." She wept louder, and Jorinda looked up at her. Pettra looked terrible, her eyes and nostrils red and her hair dishevelled.

Pity for Pettra's plight flooded Jorinda. "Do not cry. She will be back soon."

Pettra sighed. "Jorinda." She sat on the bed and placed a hand on the cover over Jorinda's arm. "Will you let us prepare her? We must arrange her Pyre."

"I will not." Jorinda screamed as her anger drove away her momentary concern for Pettra's sadness. "She needs no Pyre. She is asleep." Her body shook with each sob that broke from her. She kissed Deineike's cold cheek. "She is asleep."

"Please Jorinda." Pettra sobbed as loud as Jorinda. "She has gone. Our hearts break for her and for you. Please let us take her and prepare her."

"She is asleep." Jorinda's resolve weakened as her momentary outburst of anger receded. She reached up and pressed her finger-nails into her scalp again.

"Jorinda, do not do that. There is blood in your hair." Pettra pulled at Jorinda's arm.

"Out. Get out." Jorinda's rage flashed inside her again as Pettra tried to take Deineike from her.

Pettra sat on the bed in tears, but she released Jorinda's arm. After some time, she stood and moved from sight. The door did not close, but Jorinda heard her feet skip down the stairs. Soon enough, heavier footsteps climbed the stairs, and somebody stood behind her.

Raolos sounded miserable. "Jorinda, please let us take her." Jorinda pressed her nails into her head again, but Raolos pulled her arm free. She fought against him, attempted to tear her arm from his grasp, but he held her arm pressed against his stomach, and she gave up the fight.

Deineike had gone. She had died; she had not fallen asleep. Jorinda could no longer deny it. *"I am dead also. I do not wish to live without her. They want to arrange a Pyre. They will burn her, and only memories will remain. I cannot survive on memories alone. They may as well cast me into the Pyre with her. I am lost without her."* What had Deineike once said? "Without Jorinda, there is no Deineike." She had the right of it. They were two or they were none.

She did not look at Raolos as she whispered. "Take her. Send Synna to me."

Raolos released her arm, and she pressed her fingernails into her scalp. He tutted but left. A short time later, footsteps entered the room once more, and Jorinda closed her eyes as she felt Deineike lifted from the bed. Sobs wrenched her apart, and her body spasmed, uncontrollable, as they carried away everything she cared for.

Synna's voice interrupted her grief. "Jorinda?"

She did not open her eyes. "Kill me. I cannot live any longer. Kill me."

He sounded as though he had choked on something. "Jorinda..." She waited for him to agree. Long moments passed, and he neither spoke nor slew her. "I cannot do it. You know I cannot. I am sorry for all you suffer, but your death will not atone. I am sorry." He left the room—left her alive. He had betrayed her, and she cursed him.

She heard feet behind her again. Would they never leave her alone? A strong hand pulled at her arm, and she could not fight it. Raolos's angry voice once more rang out in the desolate room. "You must not do this to yourself. There is blood. I must get Pettra or one of the servants to clean the blood from your head. Please do not continue to hurt yourself. I beg you. You hurt us all, and our hurt is already more than we can bear." He sniffed. "Will you say her Sending?"

How could he ask it of her? How could she watch everything she loved placed into the flames, then find words to capture all Deineike meant to her? Jorinda would rather fall into the fire herself. She could not say the Sending. If she did, Deineike would never come back. Jorinda would have no words she might survive in that moment. "I cannot." Less than a whisper, those words, all she could muster.

"She must have a Sending."

"I cannot." She had no other response. Why did he press her?

He sighed. "We will make some arrangement. We will hold the Pyre tomorrow. Today, we must prepare her. You must find some strength by tomorrow. You must go to her Pyre."

"How can I go? I cannot breathe without her."

"You must. She would not wish you to abandon life—"

Jorinda sprang upright, furious at his words. Her lips contorted into a furious snarl. "You did not know her. Do not presume to imagine you know what she would or would not wish. We are two. Do you understand? We are two or we are none. Leave me." Drained, she fell back into the bed and wept.

"If I leave, will you promise not to hurt yourself any further?"

"That I will not." Jorinda sobbed and draped her free arm across her eyes. "I should die for all I wrought in her life. I must be punished, and since that faithless traitor will not kill me, I will inflict such pain on myself as I can." At that, she remembered her dagger. Long ago, after she killed Arella, she vowed she would end her own life. The time had come to honour that vow. She had no reason to live any longer. "Very well. I promise." She would not keep the promise, but she needed to rid herself of Raolos.

"You promise?"

She could not hold back the anger that flooded her answer. "I have promised, have I not? Begone. I wish to sleep." He sighed but did not leave straight away. At length, he released her arm. She slid the arm beneath the blankets. She mumbled, resentful. "You see? I keep my word."

"Sleep for a time. I will send a servant to clean the blood from your hair later." He left but did not close the door behind him, and Jorinda lay still for a time. If one of them stood near the door and listened, they would tire of the vigil in time and believe she had fallen asleep. She controlled her breaths, soft, rhythmical, as if she had fallen asleep.

After some time, she risked a swift glance at the doorway. Nobody in sight, and she heard nothing. The trained assassin had outlasted them, as she had always known she would. She slid from the bed, ran to her boots and reached inside, but found no dagger. Synna. He had taken it when she had asked him to kill her. His treachery knew no bounds.

She fell to the floor and screamed again.

SIXTEEN
THE PYRE

Jorinda lay on the floor of the room and sobbed, consumed by immeasurable, irredeemable loss. The fates had stripped her of everything she had ever been and left only her grief behind, a grief greater than the sum of all that had been taken. Her tears soaked the carpet and still more came. Deineike had gone—everything that had mattered in her life. Arella's death had torn Jorinda to pieces, and she had feared she might never again be complete. Deineike had saved her and helped her to rebuild herself; less than before, but more by far than she would have become without Deineike. Now Deineike lay dead, and nothing could ever replace her, even if Jorinda lived until time itself died.

Jorinda did not move from the floor as the day crawled on. At whiles, one or other of them ascended the stairs and peered into the room, but she did not look up. She pressed her nails into her scalp ever harder. Her blood soaked into the carpet, and still she pressed, curled up into a ball, knees drawn up to her chest. When she looked at her hands, her fingers were bloody, hair and pieces of flesh trapped beneath her fingernails. She placed her fingers in her mouth and sucked off the blood and flesh, then swallowed it all before she dug her fingers into her scalp again. Without the pain, her hatred for herself could not be borne. Her head throbbed from the pain, but she could not stop. Her blood must atone for what she had done to Deineike. Nothing less would suffice.

Others had harmed Deineike also, and now they must pay. Styrrach and the Bailiff must die. They would scream in terror as they died while the artist of their demise laughed in their faces. She longed to carve them into pieces before one another. Deineike deserved no less. Once Jorinda killed them, she would die also. If she travelled somewhere afterward, she might hear Deineike's laughter again.

Footsteps approached, and she opened her eyes. Pettra gazed down on her, and tears ran down her face. "You promised."

Jorinda sneered at her. "I lied. I am a monster. What did he expect?"

Pettra crouched beside her and pulled at the hand that dug into her scalp. "Please stop Jorinda. You break my heart anew."

Bitter, black words spat from Jorinda's throat—a throat raw from her sobs. "You are fortunate. My heart is shattered beyond repair. I will never be whole again. I have lost everything."

"That is not true. Others here care for you, and we grieve for Deineike also. You must find strength to attend her Pyre. You cannot hide here while she is sent."

"I cannot speak the Sending. Do not ask me to." Jorinda dug at her head again, though Pettra pulled at her hand and tried to prevent it.

"You need not speak. Khittie—the singer we spoke of once

before—lives in Ort and does not travel far during the wet season. She will attend and sing a Sending song.

"She knows nothing of Deineike, nor me." Jorinda had no strength for anger at this news, but it seemed inappropriate for a stranger to speak or sing Deineike's Sending.

"You cannot speak, and none of us believe we could find words. Although we loved her, we did not know her as you did, and not well enough for a Sending."

"You did not love her."

"That we did, in our way. A remarkable woman. I knew her for such a short time, but I could see that. Even Synna saw it, and he knew her for even less time."

"Do not mention that traitor's name in the same breath as my Deineike."

Pettra's soft voice held no recrimination. "Do not be harsh on him. He told us what you asked of him. He could not carry out your request. You will come to see that in time." Pettra waited some moments, but Jorinda did not reply. Synna had betrayed her, the truth of it. He called himself a killer, but he would not kill her. Worse, he had taken her dagger so she could not kill herself. Pettra spoke, softer than before. "You must let me wash your hair. It is thick with blood."

"He took my dagger."

"That he did not. I took it, the first time I saw you hurt yourself. I feared what you might do."

"You made the right decision, for I would have killed myself many hours since." Pettra's confession did not absolve Synna of his other crime. He had refused to kill her.

Pettra sobbed aloud. "Jorinda, Jorinda. You break my heart. Your grief is unbearable to me, and yet I must bear my own grief also." She continued to pull at Jorinda's arm, but she did not have Raolos's strength. "May we wash you?"

"Do what you will. I am destroyed. Only leave me in peace

afterward, I beg you." The conversation with Pettra exhausted her. Did the woman not realise Jorinda had shattered into myriad pieces when Deineike died? Deineike would never return to reassemble those pieces, and whatever Jorinda had been before, she could never be again.

Pettra left but soon returned, and not alone. Stronger hands than Pettra's pulled Jorinda's fingers away from her head before Ibie, Synna and another man lifted her and sat her on the bed. Pettra had a bowl filled with water, and some cloths floated in it with which she mopped at Jorinda's face. Raolos held her arm above her head so she could not press her fingernails into her scalp, and she could not fight his strength.

She surrendered. "You need not hold my arm. I will not hurt myself."

Raolos sounded angry. "You promised as much earlier, but you did not keep that promise."

"Something at which I am without peer." Jorinda heaved a desperate sigh. "Nonetheless, for Deineike's sake, I swear it. I will not hurt myself again." *"For now."*

Pettra had finished with her face, it seemed, and turned her attention to Jorinda's hair, and she muttered as she did so, anger threaded through every word. "So much blood. This must stop. Jorinda, do you hear me? You must not continue to hurt yourself in this way."

Jorinda loosed a sad sigh, but she nodded. She would spill all the blood in her body for one more hour with Deineike. One more chance to tell her she loved her, and to hear her laugh. She would spend all the blood in Dur for those few moments.

Pettra sounded almost casual as she focused on her task. "I have arranged a dress for you for tomorrow. It may not be a perfect fit, but you must wear black. It is a Pyre."

Jorinda did not care for the tradition, did not care for any traditions. She cared for Deineike, who would never come back. Jorinda could go to the Pyre naked; it mattered not to her. "I would rather wear her clothes."

Raolos released her arm, and she let it fall into her lap. "You must choose what Deineike will wear to her Pyre."

Jorinda's tears flowed without end. Could there be no limit to how much a person might weep? "The dress I made for her when you first met her. It is in her pack. It caught her love for life. It captured Deineike."

Pettra agreed. "That it did."

Ibie picked up Jorinda's pack, but Jorinda stopped him. "That is my pack. The other is hers."

He dropped her pack, picked up Deineike's, and carried it from the room.

Pettra combed through Jorinda's hair with her fingers and sighed. "Such a mess. You must stop this. I cannot bear to see you hurt yourself so. As fast as I clean the blood, more gushes out of all these holes you have dug in yourself."

"Deineike's death dug a greater hole in me." Jorinda covered her face with her hands and wept even louder. Her body shook again as pain tore through it.

Pettra held a strand of Jorinda's hair in her hand as she spoke. "If we leave you to sleep, will you hurt yourself again?"

Jorinda thought it inconceivable she would not. Her punishment for all she had done to Deineike had not even begun, and it could not end until she killed Styrrach and the Bailiff. She gave one miserable nod of her head, and Pettra sighed again.

Raolos spoke again after a few heartbeats. "We will stay with you through the night. We will take watches over you, so we each get some sleep at the least. We cannot allow you to hurt yourself more. I will stay first."

Would they never leave her alone? Did they not believe her? Why did they fuss and preen when she wished nothing more than to kill Styrrach and the Bailiff, then herself? What did it matter to them if she hurt herself? They had no right to feel guilt over it. They had made arrangements she had taken no part in, and they would not leave her to grieve in peace. She hated them. "Do what you will. I do not care. I no longer have anything to care for."

"That is not true." Pettra spat out the words, compassion forgotten for the moment. "You must care for yourself, as we do. Do you think Deineike would be happy to see you this way?"

Jorinda's lips peeled back from her teeth in anger. "That she may. I killed her. She might believe I must be punished for that crime."

Raolos spoke kinder words than his wife. "You did not kill her. Styrrach did."

Jorinda scoffed at his words, a pathetic attempt to make her feel better about herself. There were not enough words in Dur to succeed in that endeavour. "I placed her where he could attack her. I placed her where Hiw could knock her from her horse. I killed her." She threw herself face down on the bed, and tears poured from her again. She raised a hand to her head, but somebody pulled it away and pressed it to her side.

They covered her with a blanket, put out the lantern in the room, and closed the shutter on the window. The darkness surprised her—she must have lain on the floor for many hours. They left the door open, and light flowed in from the landing. Each time she reached for her head, strong hands prevented her. She slept for brief periods, restless and fitful. At whiles, she heard soft voices next to the bed, and they brought new hands that pulled her own away from her head through the long night.

The morning brought them all into the room again, Pettra with a black dress in her arms. Jorinda dreaded the day. How could she stand and watch the woman she loved placed into the flames? It would be too much to bear. How had anybody throughout all the history of the land ever borne it? There could be no event worse to behold.

Pettra fussed at Jorinda's hair again. "There is no new blood, thank the fates." The men have paid a hard price, but they have done their job. I must wash your hair again, then we will get you into this dress. Will you again swear you will not hurt yourself if the men leave while you dress?"

"You ask much of me. I will swear it. You need not stay. I will dress myself and I will not hurt myself." Jorinda did not wish Pettra to dress her. She had not told Deineike about the previous incident and could not bear the guilt if the older woman admired her naked body.

Pettra tutted. "You have sworn. I will wash your hair, and you will dress. Then we will await the carriage." A servant carried another bowl of water in, and Pettra again washed the blood from Jorinda's hair before she combed it into some semblance of normality, Jorinda guessed. She did not care to look at herself in a reflecting glass.

At last, they all left the room and closed the door. Jorinda sat on the bed and buried her face in her hands. As if by instinct, her hand crept to the top of her head, and she dug her fingernails into her flesh, but she pulled them away, mindful of her pledge for now. She must attend Deineike's Pyre, and though she doubted she could get through it, she would do all she could to ensure the Sending went without flaw, for Deineike's sake. After that, her compliance with their wishes would not be promised.

Pettra had brought a plain dress of good quality making. They had asked about Deineike's favourite colour so they could all wear something in that colour. More traditions, and she had not known the answer, in truth. She had said vermilion since they were bound by spilt blood in so many ways. The dress did not fit her well, but she did not care whether she might win any awards for the stylishness of her clothing.

She called out. "I am dressed." Pettra came into the room to tie Jorinda's hair back from her face with a red ribbon. It looked familiar, like the one Klordia had worn in one of her nightmares. Pettra also wore a plain black dress, although hers fitted better than Jorinda's, better, in truth, than might be appropriate at a Pyre. A red shawl draped about her shoulders represented Deineike's colour, and her favourite scent wafted through the air ahead of and around her.

Raolos came in and offered her his arm as he had done the first time she had visited the house. At the least, she knew what to do, and since her legs were unsteady, she linked her arm through his and allowed him to help her down the stairs. A light rain fell outside as the front door opened, and Ibie offered her a cloak.

"My thanks, I will brave the rain. Deineike will be soaked by it, and so will I." Pettra took a cloak and wrapped it around herself. All the men wore black trousers and cloaks. A coach waited outside, a grand, enclosed carriage with red velvet seats that faced one another. Ibie and Raolos helped Jorinda into it, and Pettra followed her. Raolos climbed in with them, but Ibie and Synna took up station on each side of it. Other men stood behind it, but she did not recognise them. She imagined they were Raolos's employees. The servants also came out of the house, dressed in black and ready to follow the coach, or so it seemed.

Another cart stood some way ahead of the coach, and she guessed it carried Deineike. Jorinda looked across at Raolos. "Will I have a chance to say goodbye to her before the Pyre?" She sobbed so hard she struggled to form the words.

"Of course, if that is what you desire."

Pettra held a delicate kerchief to her face and blew her nose on it often. Raolos reached into a pocket, produced a larger one, and handed it to Jorinda. Mucus ran from her nose into her mouth as tears streamed down her face. She pressed the kerchief to her face and cried into it. This must be the worst day of her life.

The coach set off. She gazed in sorrow at the rain and at Synna as he walked along beside them. He glanced around often, and she guessed he found it difficult to cease his vigilance. Guild training might never leave either of them.

As they turned corners, glimpses of Deineike on the cart, surrounded by flowers, and in her cream dress, ripped Jorinda apart. Deineike's dark hair had been styled into a bun, but the rain seemed determined to turn it into a frizzy mess.

Jorinda touched Raolos's knee. "I wish to walk beside her." He nodded, opened a small hatch high at the front of the coach, and whispered something. The coach came to a halt, though the horses still moved in the traces. Jorinda reached for the handle, but Synna pulled the door open before she could turn it. He looked up, curious, and she explained. "I will walk next to her cart." He kicked out the small step from beneath the door and held up a hand toward her. She took his hand and climbed from the coach.

The cart ahead of them had continued a short distance before the driver realised the coach had stopped, it seemed. She had further to walk than she had guessed, in truth, but Synna walked with her. The bruises on Deineike's face seemed more prevalent now her skin had turned pale and lifeless. Some attempt to colour it must have been made, but the rain had washed it away.

Jorinda walked behind the cart to have the best view of Deineike as they moved on. It took half of an hour to reach the area of the city where the wealthy held their Pyres. But for Raolos and his coin, Deineike would have had her Pyre in the common area, since Jorinda could not have afforded the coin for the ornate surrounds of this place. She guessed Raolos had paid for everything.

The Pyre took place in a small lawned area, surrounded by a beautiful sandstone wall, taller than Jorinda. They passed through a decorative metal gate, and Jorinda stumbled as she saw the Pyre itself, a collection of wood stacked in neat rows around a low plinth. Many people had gathered already, and she imagined Pyre workers and the singer would be among them. Who the others might be, she did not know. Friends of Raolos and Pettra, she guessed. As the cart came to a halt, she thought some of the men sported the red tunic of the Portreeve beneath their cloaks. Raolos might no longer be the Portreeve, but it seemed some of his men had come to the Pyre.

Many hands lifted Deineike from the cart with care and placed her, reverential, on the plinth. Jorinda swayed, and Synna reached to steady her. She gave him a grateful smile. Raolos, Pettra and Ibie joined them, and Raolos indicated she should approach the plinth. Jorinda gazed down on the body of the woman whose love had sustained her through the darkest nights and whose ruin she had brought about. Her head swam, and her vision blurred. She reached out with both hands and steadied herself against the plinth, unsure whether she could trust her legs to hold her upright as grief wracked her body.

She leaned forward and kissed Deineike's lips. They were cold and did not return the kiss, and for many moments Jorinda could not control her grief. Tears poured from her and mingled with the rainwater on Deineike's face. Her anguished sobs stole all her breath, and she struggled to compose herself. She kissed Deineike again. "Goodbye, my love. I do not know how I will go on without you." When she tried to take a step back, she almost fell, and Raolos and Ibie each took one of her arms to guide her a step backward.

A man in sombre clothing and no cloak stepped toward her. "Who will speak the Sending?"

Jorinda did not know how to respond and looked to Pettra, but a woman who stood nearby stepped forward and lowered the hood of her cloak. Jorinda recognised the singer from Vjort, Khittie; tall, slender and some years older than Jorinda, but beautiful, with long straight blonde hair that soon became saturated.

"I will sing the Sending." The man nodded at her. In Vjort, she had been accompanied by other musicians, but she appeared to be alone today.

She turned to face Deineike and began to sing. She had a flawless voice, as clear as a stream in spring. It soared into the rain and told a tale of loss and love that drew tears from all present. Jorinda grew breathless with grief as the melancholic melody of the refrain washed over her.

> *"I remember you, and all you saw me through.*
> *The fun, the rain, the joy, the pain, I hold onto."*

The words echoed in Jorinda's mind, and Deineike's smile swam before her eyes. Her legs would no longer support her, and even as Raolos and others nearby reached for her, she pitched forward onto her knees, then collapsed back onto her haunches. She covered her face with Raolos's kerchief and screamed into it. A head rested on her shoulder, and an arm slid around her shoulders. The scent told her Pettra held her, but Jorinda kept the kerchief pressed tight to her face.

The song ended, but long moments passed before Jorinda could compose herself again, there on the wet grass with Pettra's head on her shoulder. Nobody spoke as she knelt in abject misery before the Pyre and strove to gather herself. Deineike must have a Pyre and Jorinda must be strong, as she knew Deineike would have been had the Pyre been her own. She lowered the kerchief and nodded up at the man who had asked about the Sending. Those present stepped forward and picked up pitchers of scented oil from around the base of the Pyre, then sprinkled them over Deineike's body.

Raolos knelt beside her and whispered in her ear. "Will you light the Pyre?" She turned to look at him, but her despair robbed her of any words. She shook her head in anguish, and he nodded. "I will attend to it, if you will allow it."

Jorinda nodded once, and he stood, took a lighted torch from a man who stood to one side, and placed it into the wood piled around Deineike. Despite the rain, the flames soon took hold and consumed the woman Jorinda loved. Jorinda could take no more; the grass raced up to meet her, and blackness came over her as she felt the devastation of her loss no more.

When she opened her eyes, she lay on the grass. The rain still fell, and she had no idea how long she had been gone. Someone had draped a cloak over her. People stood or crouched beside her; Raolos, Pettra, Ibie, Synna, and others whom she did not know. She wanted to smile, to let them know she lived, but had no joy within her she could force to her lips.

Pettra tried to smile, failed. "Are you all right?" Jorinda could not push words of denial from her throat, so she shook her head.

Raolos held out a hand. "Can you sit?" She took his hand, but she lacked the strength to grip it. Some of the people around her placed gentle hands beneath her head and on her shoulders and raised her until she sat slouched forward, an empty, barren shell. She no longer held the kerchief, so she wiped at her eyes with a hand. "You had us worried."

Jorinda drew in a breath and managed to gasp, "I am sorry," before despair overwhelmed her again and she fell back against whoever stood behind her, her face to the sky, and she howled her heartbreak into the rain.

Somebody said they should take her back to the house, and they raised her to her feet as many hands supported her. The singer stood close by with a concerned look on her face.

She stepped forward, placed a hand on Jorinda's arm, and whispered in her ear. "I am sorry. Loss is a terrible thing to bear."

Jorinda's voice failed her again, trapped somewhere deep within the pain that flooded her body, and Pettra spoke for her. "Our thanks for the beautiful song. Your voice is extraordinary."

Khittie smiled. "My thanks." She turned to Jorinda again. "I hope time may heal some of your pain. Words mean so little, but you have my condolences." She turned and walked away as those around Jorinda half walked, half carried her back to the coach and helped her into it.

Jorinda lay on one of the benches, Pettra and Raolos opposite her. A thought entered her head, and she fought to force the words from herself. "She is gone?"

Pettra nodded and tears streamed down her face. "You fainted and lay unconscious for so long we became frightened. She is gone. I am sorry." She turned to look out of the window as the carriage moved off, and Jorinda let out another cry of anguish.

SEVENTEEN
A DARK MOURNING

N ОВODY SPOKE AS THE COACH BUMPED ALONG THE STREETS TOWARD the house. Jorinda had no sense of time, but at length, it stopped, and the door opened. Raolos and Ibie helped her out of the coach and into the house. Pettra and one of the women servants took her up to the room and brought cloths to dry her with. The rain had soaked the dress, and blades of grass patterned the otherwise sombre cloth. Jorinda's knees were muddy, her hair plastered to her head. The ribbon had disappeared, and her only pair of shoes had become saturated. She ought to have worn her boots, but she had little enough energy to consider such petty matters.

The dress and shoes removed, Jorinda wearied of the two women who pushed her body around as they dried her with the cloths, so she shoved them aside and fell onto the bed. They pulled the blankets and bed cover over her, then the servant left. Pettra closed the shutters even though Jorinda believed it could not be long past the midday.

Pettra sat on the bed for a time before she bent down and kissed Jorinda on the cheek. "Try to sleep."

Jorinda sighed with remorse. The woman she loved now slept for all time, and Jorinda wished to close her own eyes forever and travel to wherever Deineike had gone.

Pettra rose and left the room, but she did not close the door. Jorinda dug the nails of both hands into the flesh of her scalp as hard she could and hoped the pain would make the terrible memory of the day recede. It did not, and her tears did not relent either. She lay motionless in the bed, her fingers pressed hard into her head, and Khittie's song played over and over in her mind. It had been a Sending song, intended for any who mourned the loss of a loved one, but the refrain had spoken to her as though it had been composed for her.

Raolos or Pettra peered around the door from time to time. Raolos entered the room once and pulled her hands from her head, but she dug her nails into herself again as soon as he left. The day wore on, but Jorinda had no concept of the passage of time. She heard voices at whiles, but other than Raolos and Pettra, she did not see anybody else look into the room.

After several hours, sleep took away the agony of grief as her body shut down after the traumatic events of the Pyre. She dreamt of Deineike, of her smile, her laughter and her blue eyes. She saw Deineike and Arella side by side. They stood hand in hand and smiled at her, then both spoke at the same time. "I love you." They disappeared. Only Deineike's voice remained, and it repeated, "Do not cry, my love. Arella has need of me."

Jorinda awoke with a start. An eerie silence wrapped the darkened house in its embrace, and Deineike did not lie beside her to comfort her and tell her it had only been a dream. Her life was fated to be this way from now forward. How could she survive without the one thing that had made her life bearable? The question had no answer, but Jorinda must complete vital tasks before she could go wherever she would travel to afterward. Styrrach and the Bailiff must pay the ultimate price for Deineike's death.

Styrrach. His name sickened her. She must travel to Alcmouth and hunt him down. She would do so as soon as the agony eased, if it ever did. He had brought about Deineike's death, but she could not ignore her own part in it. If she and Deineike had not met that night at Taro's farm, Deineike might be alive today and not gone into the flames. Three lives would pay for Deineike's. Jorinda's would follow once the other two fell to her blade. She tried to recall the word for a three-sided shape. Triangle, she had it. Who would help her now with all these words she struggled to form? It did not matter. Once all three sides of the bloody vermilion triangle that brought Deineike's ruin had been torn down, Jorinda would feel this pain no more.

She must recover her dagger. As soon as she saw Pettra later, Jorinda would demand its return. Wilash's keen blade would slice the life from Styrrach and the Bailiff and could then claim Jorinda's own. She hoped there would be something afterward, so she might be reunited with Deineike.

Sleep came again until the noises of the house woke her. She lay in the bed with no strength to rise. The night had not lifted her grief from her, and she missed Deineike. Nothing remained for her in this life; all she had lived for had been taken from her. She reminded herself three lives, not one, must be the price. That would sustain her for now.

Pettra entered the room. "Did you sleep?"

"A little."

Pettra opened the shutters. Rain still fell outside the window. "A grey day." Pettra mumbled the words to herself, it seemed. "Will you eat something?"

Jorinda shook her head. She had no appetite for anything other than vengeance followed by death. Food played no part in her plan.

"You must eat something. You cannot lie there and neither eat nor drink. It is unhealthy."

Jorinda gave a derisive snort. "What do I care for health? I have no health. It burned on the Pyre yesterday." Tears came again, and she wiped at them in anger. Would they never cease?

"Jorinda, please eat something, or at least drink a little water. When did you last eat or drink?"

Jorinda shrugged. She did not know, in truth. She did not feel hungry and guessed she might not keep any food or water down. To her relief, Pettra tutted and left her alone.

A servant brought a small pitcher of water and a cup later in the morning, poured some of the water into the cup, and offered it to Jorinda, who waved it away. The woman placed the cup on the small table beside the bed and left.

Why did people need servants? Were they so idle or inept they could do nothing for themselves? It had never occurred to her before, but now she considered it, it angered her that people expected others to perform all their menial tasks for them. Deineike would not have approved of servants, even if she had possessed all the coin in the Duke's vault.

Pettra came and went throughout the day. She urged Jorinda to drink or eat, and she pulled Jorinda's hands away from her head as she dug at her scalp. Pettra had devised a technique of her own that allowed her to pull Jorinda's arm away, but she could not keep one or the other from Jorinda's scalp for long. Jorinda dug at herself not for the pain alone. It comforted her and distracted her from the incessant memories of Deineike that swamped every heartbeat.

Night fell, and another day of hopelessness and despair had passed her by. She reasoned she must rise from the bed at some point if she meant to kill Styrrach but had neither the strength nor desire for it yet. It would wait another day or two. She must eat again to perform the gests she had assigned herself. At one point in the darkness, she tutted at herself. She had forgotten to demand the return of her dagger. Tomorrow, she told herself. She must not forget again.

Another day passed, and Jorinda lay in the bed in tears, consumed with grief. She dug her nails into her head for much of the day. Raolos and Pettra appeared at whiles and urged her to stop. They held her arms away from her, but as soon as they left the room, she resumed the pain and comfort. Night brought no relief, and the days blurred into each other as she struggled to understand why she had been left so alone and bereft.

Pettra brought some bread into the room as another morning arrived, and Jorinda decided to eat some of it and hope she could keep it down. The pain of her grief remained as potent as the day Deineike died, and she could not reckon how long her every heartbeat would be filled with the unbearable anguish of her memories of Deineike. She took some of the bread, and Pettra moved the pillows about to support her as she sat up in the bed.

Jorinda nibbled at the bread while Pettra tutted because she had not drunk any of the water. "Your face grows thin, I think. You must eat." She smoothed Jorinda's hair back from her face, but Jorinda turned her head away from the gesture. "Your hair is matted with blood. I must wash you, and you must cease to hurt yourself. I will send for a healer today. He could have some advice that will help us."

"There is no 'us.' You need not declare yourself my baby-watcher."

Pettra took hold of the hand Jorinda raised to her scalp. "Jorinda, you grieve, I know this. More than grief afflicts you though. You are unwell, and we must find some way to return you to your former self."

Anger burned in Jorinda's words. "I will never again be the

person I have been. Styrrach ensured that when he stole from me the only joyful moment I have ever known."

Pettra sat in silence for a time, and Jorinda handed the bread back to her. She had managed a few bites, but it tasted worse than the bread aboard the ships. Despite Pettra's disconsolate look at how little she had eaten, Jorinda could face no more. Pettra fussed at the pillows and took two away. "These must be cleaned or burned. They are covered in your blood. I wish you would stop this hurt you do to yourself. It breaks all our hearts."

Jorinda lay back and wished Pettra would leave. She did not care about pillows, she wanted Deineike, but Deineike would not come back, and Jorinda missed her so much, a physical ache that hurt more than when she dug her nails into her head. She wept again, and Pettra touched her hand before she took the bread and pillows away.

An hour or more passed, and she heard footsteps on the staircase. Pettra led a man into the room whom Jorinda did not recognise and introduced him as a healer. Jorinda said nothing to him; she had no need of a healer, only somebody who could return Deineike to her.

"May I look at your head?" He kept his voice soft and low, and he made no move to approach the bed. "Pettra tells me you have injured yourself."

Jorinda said nothing, and he took a tentative step forward and bent to look at her. He sucked a sharp breath across his lips and reached toward the top of her head. She did not move to stop him, so he pushed her hair about. He leaned closer and peered at her scalp for a time until he straightened and studied her face for a time. "It is as Pettra says. You have injured yourself a great deal. None of the wounds are large, but they are plentiful. Why do you do this to yourself?"

She clenched her teeth and glared at him. "That does not concern you."

"That it does. It concerns me very much. Pettra tells me you grieve for your lover. These damages you inflict upon yourself will not bring him back."

"Her." She glowered at him, furious. How dare he presume she loved a man?

"I apologise. If you continue this damage, she will not be returned to you, even if you tear all the flesh from your scalp. You have also eaten and drunk nothing, I hear. You need to do so, for the body cannot sustain itself without nourishment."

"That is good then. I will join Deineike." She turned to glare out of the window. Pettra had told him a great deal, it seemed. Did the woman have no respect for Jorinda's private matters? Would she shout them from the roof of her house next, for all Ort to hear? It infuriated her.

He sighed. "I would still be interested to know why you do these things to yourself."

She waved an arm at him but did not turn to face him. "Why did she die?"

"We all die. She died because we are mortal. Everybody dies."

She faced him again and raised herself up from the bed on her elbows. "What killed her? She had been attacked, but she lived for days, then she died with no warning. I can make no sense of it. It should not have turned as it did."

"Can you describe the nature of the attack? Violence is unknown—"

"I know. Violence is not common in Dur. Believe me, I have heard those words many times, but I tell you it is more common than you might believe. She had been struck in the head many times over recent passes."

He nodded and looked downcast. "Head injuries are a mystery to us. When a loved one goes wherever they travel to afterward, those they leave behind insist on a Pyre when we would be better served if they allowed us to investigate the situation within the skull. Thus, we learn nothing. We believe the brain may swell or bleed, and blood will sometimes come from the ears in these cases." Jorinda nodded in misery. "In her case also, I take it. Beyond that, we are left to guess. Some die as soon as they are injured, others carry on for some time." He threw his hands up. "We do not know. I wish I could tell you more."

He had told her nothing. It sickened Jorinda to think he might have cut Deineike's head open to prod and peer inside it. He had the right of it, nonetheless, for unless such practices were permitted before the Pyre, how could the mystery of the brain be understood?

The healer turned to Pettra and spoke to her. "If you can, I recommend you clean the blood from her hair and find some way to prevent her from further injury. I suspect she uses the pain to distract herself from her loss. You must find a way to distract her so she causes herself fewer injuries. Also, she needs a bath and, of course, she must eat. There is little more I can do for her, but do not hesitate to call on me if there is some way I can assist you." He bade Jorinda farewell and left. Jorinda thought Pettra had spent coin on nothing, since everything he mentioned, Pettra had already said. Pettra must have hoped something beyond her own knowledge could be achieved.

They left her alone again, and some hours passed before Pettra returned with a bowl of water and some cloths. "Will you allow me to wash you? Your hair is filled with blood, and you smell, the truth of it. You must bathe." Jorinda had been half asleep when Pettra reappeared, and as she tried to focus her senses on Pettra's request, thirst nagged at her. She reached for the cup, but Pettra picked it up and handed it to her. She sipped some of it while Pettra studied her.

Jorinda returned the cup to Pettra. "There. I have drunk some of your water. I trust you are satisfied."

"I wish for you to remain well. Nothing more."

The sadness in Pettra's voice stirred regret in Jorinda for the way she had spoken to her over the past days. Pettra had not been responsible for Deineike's death and had striven to help Jorinda through the darkness that had fallen upon her. Jorinda had been harsh and rude in response, and Deineike would not have approved.

"My thanks." Jorinda wished she could say more, but the words would not form in her mind, and she could not release the pain that drove her unfair treatment of Pettra. To be without that pain might suggest she had forgotten all Deineike had meant to her. There might come a day when the agony lessened, but not today.

Pettra broke an awkward silence. "Shall I bring you some bread?"

"I will try to eat some later."

Jorinda lay back in the bed and closed her eyes. If she feigned sleep and did not dig at her head, she hoped Pettra would leave, but the older woman hovered nearby for a time before she spoke again. "I will wash you." Jorinda did not reply.

The warm water stung Jorinda's wounds as Pettra placed a cloth under her head, then washed her head and hair. Pettra tutted and sighed as she worked. Jorinda's head must have a great many marks from the countless injuries her nails had inflicted, but the pain satisfied her as a punishment. It had taken such a short time to become a comfort, like a familiar article carried around as reassurance against distress.

Pettra fussed at the injured scalp for some time, then turned her attention to Jorinda's face. As the gentle strokes of the cloth and the warmth of the water soothed her, Jorinda's thoughts drifted to Deineike. She found it difficult to focus on the happier times, and her mind returned time and again to her hatred of Styrrach. Bitterness ate at her even as she strove to keep it at bay, fearful of a day she could no longer bring Deineike's face to mind through the fog of her self-hatred and the white-hot lust for vengeance that burned inside her and threatened to leave behind nothing but a barren, malicious husk.

She imagined Deineike's laughter and let it run loose through her mind, where it shone a light into her inner darkness as it always had. Though she tried to resist him, Styrrach soon imposed himself into her reverie, drove out all light, all joy. Her entire body tensed, and she imagined her dagger as it slashed across his throat, and she watched in glee as the life fled from his eyes, Deineike avenged.

She shook her head to scatter her thoughts, Styrrach with them, and gasped in surprise as she realised Pettra had a hand on one of Jorinda's breasts, caressed it and rubbed at the nipple, which hardened in response. Jorinda opened her eyes in horror, and Pettra had her other hand between her own legs, her face red and her nostrils flared.

Jorinda grabbed at Pettra's wrist, pulled it away from her breast. "What in the Five Cities are you about?" Her fury at Styrrach turned its attention to Pettra, intense and untrammelled.

Pettra stared at her through narrowed eyes. "You are beautiful. From the first time I saw you—"

Rage consumed Jorinda. "I love Deineike. You know this."

"Deineike is gone." The petulance in Pettra's voice stoked the fires of Jorinda's anger, and they sprang up, hotter, as Pettra continued. "I am here, flesh before you, and have needs you could fulfil."

Her words sickened Jorinda. "Your needs are not my concern. You are mistaken if you think I seek an alternative to Deineike. None such exist—not you; not anybody."

"You need to be distracted from this hurt you do to yourself. Distract yourself with me. I wish it with all I am."

Jorinda glanced toward the window and huffed out a heavy breath as she tried to calm the furious beast of her temper before she did something she might come to regret. "Pettra, this cannot be. I mourn the woman I love. I doubt I will ever love again, and I doubt I will ever wish to. You have a husband. He must attend to your desires."

Pettra snorted. "I wish to lie with a woman. I have long desired it."

Jorinda raised a hand to her forehead as she struggled to comprehend Pettra's words. It proved easy to slide her hand to the top of her head, and her fingernails began their work. No sooner had the nails dug in than Pettra pulled at her arm to prevent it.

As she pulled at Jorinda's arm, Pettra cried out. "Stop that." Anger replaced arousal. "I curse myself if my desires lead you to hurt yourself. You must do this no longer."

They fought against one another, but the incident had drained Jorinda of any resolve that might once have dwelt within her. Angry, she shook Pettra's hand from her arm, turned onto her side, and stared out of the window in sullen wretchedness. "You should leave." Pettra sat motionless for a moment, then gathered the cloths together and left, with a promise to send some bread to the room and an exhortation for Jorinda to eat some of it.

Jorinda stared out at the rain as the day turned from grey to greyer and twilight drew its pre-dark veil across the land. Another incident with Pettra. She must find a way to curb Pettra's fascination with her, before Deineike could learn of it. Guilt swathed her; she had betrayed Deineike, and for a heartbeat, she had forgotten Deineike had died. Jorinda had not asked for the dagger to be returned, and Pettra might not come to the room again, embarrassed to have been caught as she caressed Jorinda and pleasured herself.

Footsteps on the staircase interrupted her thoughts, and Raolos peered around the doorframe. "How do you fare? I have brought some bread. Pettra says you must eat some of it, and I am not permitted to leave until you have done so."

Jorinda could not face him after the incident with his wife. He would read it in her eyes and might even kill her. She had no dagger to defend herself with and doubted she possessed the strength or the will to resist him if he attacked her.

Raolos stood next to the bed. "You must leave the house." His words shocked her. He must have already learned of his wife's fascination with her, and he threw her into the street. She turned to face him, but he did not appear angry—rather, he showed admirable control. "The new Portreeve has taken office. He has had some complications with his men." He chuckled to himself. "Many of them have left his employ, and I find myself beset by requests for employment in my business. It will be so, of course. I will have more guards than him, I think." He smiled, but Jorinda did not return it.

What did he mean? She could not understand him any more than she had been able to understand the strange language of mariners on the southern ships. He had not finished, and Jorinda hoped his meaning would become clearer. "He will find others anxious to work for him, my guess. Some of the men who left his employment tell me he has asked about you. He knows you as both Corelle and Jorinda. I fear your new name will not disguise you any longer. He will send his men here, since he knows we travelled together, and you fought against Styrrach in my office. You are in danger here and cannot stay."

Like a lantern light springs to life in a darkened room, under-standing dawned. He urged Jorinda to leave not because of the incident with his wife. Styrrach had instructed his lackey, the new Portreeve in Ort, to find her and either hang her or send her south to rougher justice. How could she leave the house? It had been days since she had even risen from the bed for more than a few moments, and she could not imagine how she would leave, nor where she would go. She squinted at him in indecision.

The tale had not ended, not yet. "You must go to the house you stayed in when first we met. He will learn of it sooner or later, but we will buy ourselves some time to make other arrangements. He will look here first, since this house is mine, and he will know of it. The other is Pettra's, and it may take him some time to discover it. You must dress and ready yourself." He hesitated. "You have not risen from the bed for days now other than to relieve yourself, as I understand it. You must leave it now. Your safety depends on it."

"Let him come for me," she thought. She wearied of life; it had lost its sparkle. Some of the Portreeve's men would die with her, if she remembered to demand the return of her dagger. Others might be hurt though. Raolos, Pettra, Raopul, the servants—blood she must not have on her conscience. She would be alone at the other house, where only her own life need concern her. Pettra would not be there either, so there would be no more awkward incidents.

"It shall be as you say." Jorinda dragged herself upright in the bed and pushed the blankets from her. "I will leave now."

He looked away. "You cannot leave now. I did not mean this moment. Tomorrow will suffice. You are naked." He seemed flustered. "You cannot leave before you are dressed. Arrangements will be made tomorrow."

How could his wife be so consumed with her, but he would not gaze at her naked body? She had not intended to arouse him, but the contradiction puzzled her. Her mind blurred, and she found it hard to concentrate on a thought for more than a heartbeat before another insisted on her attention. She fell back in the bed and tugged the cover over herself. "Tomorrow then." The two words sapped her strength, carried on what little breath she could summon from her body.

He left, and she nibbled at the bread. Once she left Raolos's house, she could take the opportunity to travel to Alcmouth and kill Styrrach. She would be out of the bed that held so many painful memories, which might spur her to action. Tomorrow. She closed her eyes and fell into another restless sleep.

EIGHTEEN
REVELATIONS AND ANOTHER NEW HOME

Styrrach stared at letters from Rakulaj, a merchant from Vyrrmod, to the south. The letters claimed Corelle had approached Rakulaj and proposed an alternative trade arrangement with Ort. Styrrach should have ensured the jade never left Alcmouth while he had the chance. Now Rakulaj suggested they revisit their contract since prices appeared to have become fluid in Dur.

Styrrach would arrange for Rakulaj to be killed as soon as possible for his arrogance, but there would be time enough for him later. The Bailiff had sent the new Portreeve to Ort, and Styrrach's impatience to get to the bottom of this new development had him anxious to send orders for the new Portreeve to step up his efforts to track down Corelle. He must also consider how to establish a Guild in the town. The time had come for his business to commence operations in Ort.

He shouted for Gill, and the Senior Aide opened the door to his office. Styrrach held out the letters to him and watched Gill read them. The man showed no reaction, though he knew little about the particulars of the organisation yet. Gill handed the letters back to him and waited in silence.

Styrrach tried to determine Gill's loyalty, but the man proved difficult to read. "I cannot allow this man to further disrupt my business enterprises. Raolos and Corelle must be killed. Raolos is no longer the Portreeve, and his death will attract less attention now. Send members north today who will see it done. Other members must meet southern ships at the docks to remind the masters of those vessels where their loyalties lie. This plot to take our business must be thwarted. I will not stand for it. The masters are to be reminded to deal with the tally houses in the cities we control, such as Parulo and Elger's houses here, and they will no longer deal with those in Ort until we advise them to."

Gill shuffled his feet. "I fear we have insufficient members to undertake all these tasks. We have suffered grievous losses to our numbers, more than Sky and Balgow. Synna is lost to us, and two more fell because of the attack in The Duke's Seat. A further two have not been seen in days, and their rooms are vacated. I estimate we have seven or eight we can count on."

Styrrach wiggled a finger at Gill to indicate he should follow him as he left the office and entered the parlour. Gill needed a reminder of his place in the organisation, and Styrrach's frustration boiled. He picked up a wooden chair and smashed it against the wall. It disintegrated and left only the crosspiece from the highest point of the chair's back in his hands. He threw the piece of wood at Gill, who raised an arm to deflect the wood away across the parlour.

"I do not ask your opinion on these things. I have told you what I need done. Do not question me. Ever." He ran a hand through his hair and fought to restrain an urge to kill Gill where he stood.

"Send two men north to Ort. If they are unsuccessful, tell them they need not return south. They must kill Corelle first, for they may not both survive that encounter. I will give them letters to guarantee help from the new Portreeve. Any others who are available will begin to canvas the ships today. Is this clear?"

"That it is."

"Do they think they can best me?" Styrrach spat on the floor. "They will learn it is not an easy thing to gain an advantage over me."

"That they will."

Styrrach beckoned for Gill to wait in the parlour and returned to his office. He sprang open the passageway, hurried into the next building, and retrieved some coin from a pouch buried deep in the pack he had left there. He returned to his office and summoned Gill again. "This coin will cover expenses and gest fees for the two who sail north. The remainder is for you. I do not buy loyalty; it is given without cost, or the consequences are catastrophic. I reward good service. You may consider this a payment in advance of the tasks I charge you with now. Do not fail me. Should you do so, you will have no need of coin where I will send you."

"My thanks."

"Bring the two who will sail to Ort here before the night is over, and I will have the letters prepared."

Gill headed out of the building and Styrrach reread the letters from Rakulaj. Insolence. Such an affront. Styrrach had worked to create the enterprise, and Corelle and Raolos sought to enrich themselves on the fruits of his labours. He resolved to ensure the members sent to kill them scattered their remains far and wide. Raolos and Corelle would enjoy no Pyre. Their endeavours against him had earned them only the cold solitude of death, and they would learn he could not be bested. Furious, he kicked his chair across the office, and it lay askew against the wall. The act reminded him of the kick he had delivered to the face of Corelle's deviant accomplice, and his manhood hardened. In his mind, he relived the violence he had perpetrated on them, and he pleasured himself.

Jorinda rose and dressed herself. The hour was early, and she did not know when Raolos might expect her to relocate to the other house, but she wanted to be ready. Last night, she had imagined the move as the first step in her plot to wreak vengeance on Styrrach, but this morning she felt lethargic and indifferent. The tears no longer streamed from her eyes without respite, but the hollowness within her had not lessened, and neither had her fury at Styrrach.

What should she do with Deineike's clothes? She had no reason to keep them, since they would be an extra burden to carry south to Alcmouth when she sailed there to kill Styrrach, so she sat cross-legged on the floor and opened Deineike's pack. It held some tunics and trousers, most of them Jorinda's making. She shook each of them out and stared at them before she placed them in two piles. Deineike had only owned one dress, and she had worn it to her Pyre. Jorinda took the last tunic out of the pack and pressed it against her face. Deineike's smell lingered on it, and tears came again as memories of her flooded back, borne on the scent of her body from the tunic. Jorinda would keep this tunic, she decided. Her tears had soaked it, but she placed it into her own pack

Beneath the clothes she found a small pouch with a few coins and another with some hygiene items and jewellery. She placed both pouches into her pack. At the bottom of the pack lay all the sketches Deineike had done in Torric. The hobby had been abandoned once they fled Torric. There had been little enough opportunity, in truth. Miserable, Jorinda took the sketches from the pack and studied them one by one. Most were of her, but Deineike had possessed so little skill, most of the figures in them did not resemble a person. The person who appeared most often in the sketches had large breasts, Deineike's representation of Jorinda.

There were a few sketches of flowers and one other Jorinda recalled well, as she had needed to ask Deineike about it. Jorinda had believed it to be a picture of a tuber from which making pins protruded, roped to a broken wine cask, but Deineike had assured her it was a horse that pulled a cart. The sketch had small holes in each corner, as did some of the others. Jorinda had felt compelled to pin the horse sketch to the wall because Deineike had been so proud of it. Jorinda planned to pin all the sketches to the wall of her bedroom once she settled in the new house, and she pushed them into her pack as tears streamed from her eyes.

Jorinda lifted the pack onto the bed and sat beside it to await whoever would take her to the house. She dug at her scalp as the time flowed by, and nobody came. After some time, she picked up the pack and walked down the stairs to seek an answer on when she would move. Raolos sat in an armed chair in the parlour, and he stood as she entered.

"You have risen. I did not wish to disturb you early, but it cheers me to see you out of bed at last." Without fuss, he reached up and pulled her arm away from her head. She had not realised she dug at herself. "Pettra has gone ahead of us to prepare the house."

Jorinda hoped her instinctive grimace had been quashed before it had reached her face. She had hoped the move to the other house would remove the conundrum of Pettra from her life. After Jorinda moved in, with luck, Pettra would not visit the house alone.

Raolos went to the outer door and smiled at her to join him. Synna waited outside, and a small cart stood near the door. They helped her into the cart and Raolos climbed in alongside her. The driver cracked the reins over the back of the horse and the cart lurched forward as Synna strode alongside.

Jorinda called down to him. "Will you not ride with us?"

"That I will not. I prefer to be on foot, ready for all eventualities." No doubt he meant any threat to them.

They reached the house without incident and left the cart and its driver outside. Pettra hummed a tune from somewhere in the rear of the house; the scullery, Jorinda thought. She hummed the Sending song Khittie had sung at Deineike's Pyre, and the melody brought Jorinda's tears once more. Raolos strode through the parlour, and Pettra fell silent.

The pair entered the hall from the parlour. Pettra embraced Jorinda and kissed her cheek. Uncomfortable, Jorinda endured the embrace, certain Raolos would produce a dagger at any moment and strike her down where she stood from his jealousy.

"Which bedroom will you occupy?" Pettra's bright, conversational tone must have been an attempt to cheer Jorinda. "I will bring bedsheets and blankets. The large one on the upper floor?"

Jorinda could not face that room, much less sleep in the bed for even a heartbeat. Too many memories of passion with Deineike lay there. At the mention of it, she recalled Deineike's happiness as she had claimed the room over Wilash and Klordia, and she again wiped away tears. "I will take one of the rooms on the lower landing, I think. The other is too large for one person."

Pettra took her hand, and since Jorinda did not wish to create a fuss, she tolerated it. "Come, pick one and we will prepare it." Pettra laughed as she pulled Jorinda toward the stair.

Raolos smiled, doubtless relieved to hand Jorinda over to Pettra's care. "We will leave you to your fun. We have business to attend to."

"Can you not stay a while?" Jorinda almost begged him, desperate for them to stay. "I have not seen Synna in many days, and I would like to learn how things go with the southern ships."

She could think of no better excuse at that moment, and she hoped it would work to keep them both at the house until Pettra felt ready to leave.

Raolos smiled at her. "I imagine our business can wait, if you wish us to stay a little longer."

A frown crossed Pettra's face that Jorinda hoped her husband had not noticed as she allowed the older woman to pull her up the stairs. Raolos and Synna followed, although they appeared uncertain as to whether they should.

Pettra again asked which room Jorinda would choose, and she picked the room that overlooked the front of the house, reluctant to sleep in the one Wilash and Klordia had occupied. She must scribe them a letter to tell them of Deineike's death. They would be distraught, but she should let them know. Pettra ran from the room, returned with some bedding, and spread it over the bed. She refused to allow Jorinda to help, and Jorinda could not understand why the woman kept servants to attend to her every whim when she could undertake these small domestic chores herself. Jorinda would never understand the wealthy and the motivations that drove them.

Pettra wanted to unpack Jorinda's belongings, but Jorinda did not wish her to touch Deineike's sketches, so she insisted they all return to the parlour to hear about the southern ships. Raolos told her they continued to board any ship from the south as it docked in Ort. They had met with a variety of responses, and the first day seemed to have been the most successful. Some masters had refused to hear them out, and Jorinda agreed with his theory; the fear of Styrrach lay behind the refusals. One master did not rent his ship out to merchants but bought and sold the goods himself, and he had expressed some interest in further discussion but felt he should let Styrrach know in the name of fairness. This outcome did not disappoint them since the main objective of the exercise had always been to infuriate Styrrach.

Jorinda could not detain the two men overlong in case they became suspicious, and they wished to go about their business after all else. She persuaded Synna to return that night for a meal, but she could do nothing more to detain them and avoid excessive time alone with Pettra.

Once the men had gone, Pettra said she would prepare some food for them. She disappeared into the scullery, and while she fussed with food she had brought to the house, Jorinda wandered into the second, smaller parlour. They had not used it when they had lived in the house the first time, although the furnishings and wall coverings were of the same quality as the larger room. As she walked back to the hallway, she noticed a door set in the enclosed underside of the staircase she had not noticed before, and she opened it, curious. She could make out nothing in its dark interior, and she decided to bring a lantern, but as she turned from the small room, she started. Pettra stood close by and gazed at her.

Jorinda tried to cover her surprise. "I have never noticed this door before. What is within it? Do you know?"

Pettra shrugged. "It is a storage cupboard, nothing more. I doubt there is anything within. Come, I have prepared some food and water for us." She held out a hand.

Jorinda sighed in frustration. "Pettra…"

"It is good to see you out of the bed." Pettra beamed at her. "We are all pleased. We hope you will soon find some measure of peace. The loss of Deineike crushed us all."

Jorinda lacked the strength to resist, so she allowed Pettra to lead her back to the parlour, hopeful there would be no repeat of yesterday's incident. Meats, cheeses, bread and fruit had been laid out on platters, and a large water pitcher stood with them on a table near the armed chairs. Jorinda sat in one of the armed chairs rather than the couch so Pettra could not sit next to her.

Jorinda nibbled at the cheese, more to avoid unpleasantness than from hunger. She sipped at some water, and Pettra's eyes followed her every move. It might have been a part of her apparent obsession with Jorinda, or it might have been anxiety about her health. Jorinda could not decide which.

Jorinda tried to distract Pettra with some mundane conversation. "Raolos tells me this house is yours. How do you come to own a property?"

Pettra laughed. "It belonged to my parents. They died some years ago. The fevers took them." A look of sadness crossed her face. "They gifted it to me rather than Raolos. It rankled him at the time, I think. Unlike most Durfolk, he holds different views these days and believes it should be easier for women to have more stature in our society. I do not think he would now have it reassigned."

"He is a good man. I am sorry to hear of your parents' deaths."

"We all die." Pettra sighed. "They were too young. Those we love are sometimes taken from us before we are ready."

"That they are." Jorinda wiped at her eyes. "When Deineike was but a few years, somebody killed her mother." She did not confide the full story to Pettra. Too much pain lay in that tale.

Compassion flooded Pettra's face. "That is terrible. Such a hard thing for a child, I imagine."

They were silent for a time, a heavy, morose silence that weighed on Jorinda like a solid length of timber. She brooded on the murder of Deineike's mother. Wilke had claimed the murderer had died. There might be some justice in that in truth, although she would like to learn why he claimed she had been responsible.

At once, Pettra stood. "I must away. I have chores." Jorinda imagined she had few chores other than to gaze at herself in a reflecting glass, then felt guilty at the thought. Pettra had been more than kind to her, and Jorinda had cast her in an unfavourable light only in response to the unwanted advances. It had been unfair, but she been unable to resist the thought.

She escorted Pettra to the door and waved her off. It seemed strange Pettra would walk when her wealth provided carts and men at her beck and call. As Jorinda returned to the parlour, she cursed herself—she had again forgotten to insist on the return of her dagger.

She gathered up the remnants of the food. Neither of them had eaten much, despite Pettra's exhortations for Jorinda to eat. She covered the food with a cloth. It would serve for Synna later that day if he came. She poured some more water into a cup and carried it up to the bedroom, pinned all Deineike's sketches on the wall with her making pins, but left all the clothes in the pack. She did not know how long she would remain in the house but doubted she would be there for long.

She returned to the parlour and lit a lantern, determined to investigate the cupboard beneath the stairs, but Pettra had been correct. It held nothing, and she could not explain her sense of disappointment. The rest of the day she spent in the parlour, consumed by memories of Deineike. She forced herself to drink a cup of the water and could not resist the temptation to press her nails into her scalp.

Synna came to the house as darkness fell. They chatted about this and that, and he ate most of the food. He had taken rooms some streets away and seemed pleased to have better accommodations than he had enjoyed at any time before. It seemed Raolos paid him well enough for him to lavish some coin on better quality rooms. He became guarded when Jorinda asked him what work he did for Raolos, and she did not press him.

He left, and as he disappeared into the darkness, she closed the door but could not lock it. She searched the house but could not find the door's key. Nothing frightened her in Ort, not yet, so she went to her room, took off her clothes and climbed into the bed. It had not yet grown late, but the day had wearied her. She had not been out of bed for such a long time in many days, and it had been a challenge. Her motivation to engage with people had faded to nothing soon after she stepped outside Raolos's house. She would spend longer in bed tomorrow since the demands on her would be less strenuous.

Jorinda must eat more in the future to build up her strength and kill Styrrach. She spent her days consumed by thoughts of his death, and of Deineike. Since Deineike's death, the nightmares had not been as frequent nor as vivid, and she had no explanation other than her abject grief. Much of the time she felt a wretched desolation, but when she thought of Styrrach, a white-hot hatred replaced the despondency for a time. She could not break the cycle and could not imagine how she might do so.

NINETEEN
DEINEIKE IS BETRAYED

Jorinda fell into a deep sleep and did not awaken until daylight entered the room. She had not closed the shutters, and although rain fell from a grey sky outside, the night had fled. She lay in bed and watched the clouds scurry across the sky as the rain beat against the window glass. A numb sadness descended upon her, and she closed her eyes. Her eyelids could not constrain the salty tears that trickled down to the pillow. She missed Deineike so much, she wished she could die, that the pain would cease. Somebody sat on the bed and startled her, and when she opened her eyes, she saw Pettra.

Pettra held up a placatory hand. "Did I frighten you? I am sorry, I did not intend to."

"I could not find the key to the door last night." Jorinda guessed she sounded petulant, but Pettra's presence on the bed made her want to squirm away, uncomfortable.

"Raolos's idea. He said we needed to keep watch on you. I am sorry."

Pettra's apologetic smile did nothing to ease Jorinda's irritation, and anger welled up inside her about the key. She was twenty-two years and no longer a child, and she resented their arrogance as they made decisions on her behalf without any consultation. She maintained a churlish silence.

Pettra gazed around at the sketches, and her smile changed to one of entertainment. "You have decorated."

"Deineike."

"They are lovely. So different." Of all the descriptions of the sketches a stranger could come up with, "different" must surely be the kindest. "They are of you, that is obvious. She loved you very much, I think."

"That she did, though I do not know why."

Pettra stared at the horse and cart sketch for some time. "This is a large coin that is taken from a chest?"

Jorinda gave a tearful laugh. "That it is not. It is a horse and cart. So she said."

Pettra tilted her head to one side and stared at the sketch. "I see it, I think. Is it an early work?"

Jorinda laughed again. "She had no talent, but she spent her days trapped inside by a broken leg and took pleasure from it. I would give all I am to have her sketch me another tuber tethered to a wine cask." She covered her face with her hands and wept, her body torn asunder by each sob.

Pettra did not speak as Jorinda cried for a fate that could never be unwritten and had robbed her of Deineike. As the intensity of her sobs decreased, Pettra laid a hand on Jorinda's arm. "You cannot lie in bed for the rest of your life, Jorinda. It serves no purpose and does you no favours. Will you come down to the parlour with me and eat something?"

Jorinda gazed through painful eyes at Pettra. No rain dripped from the woman's hair or her clothes. "How did you arrive here this morning?"

"A coach. The rain pours down outside. I would prefer to walk, but I would have been drowned by the time I arrived."

Jorinda did not think Pettra would have drowned, no matter how hard it rained, but her fatigued mind could not unravel the puzzle. "The coach waits without?" An elaborate coach in the street might attract unwelcome attention, and the thought worried at Jorinda's mind.

"That it does not. I sent it away. It will return later if the rain persists. I suspect it will. It is the wet season, after all else."

Jorinda sighed. It seemed Pettra meant to stay at the house for some time, and it would be cruel to send her away in such rain. How ironic—a woman who would take a life for a few regals hesitated to send a woman into a rain that might do no more than make a mess of her hair.

Pettra stood, her voice bright and cheery. "Come. I will wash and brush the catastrophe atop your head, and we will enjoy some food downstairs. I have brought more, since I am certain you have done as instructed and eaten all that remained yesterday."

Pettra's spirit could not be quelled any more than Deineike's, it seemed. Jorinda could never best Deineike's optimism even at her strongest, and she felt far from strong now. She let out a resigned sigh. "Very well."

Pettra busied herself in the privy. "You must light fires. The house is cold, and so is the water. I will light them later, but you must maintain them." Jorinda poked her tongue out toward the sound of Pettra's voice. The woman seemed determined to pester her to death. The instrument of Jorinda's torture carried a bowl of water into the room. "This will be cold, I warn you." She laughed as she squeezed excess water from a cloth.

Pettra had the right of it. The water made Jorinda gasp as Pettra washed the blood from her hair. With a second cloth, she dried her hair with such vigour, Jorinda thought she might shake her head from her shoulders. Pettra had brought no brush or comb, so Jorinda pointed to her pack where a comb lay in her vanity pouch. Pettra walked round the bed, sat behind Jorinda, and combed the tangles from the brown hair. She sighed and held a hand before Jorinda's face, voluminous strands of Jorinda's hair clutched between her fingers.

"Your hair falls out in clumps. I am certain something is awry with your body. Wretched healer. Such a charlatan. I will bring another." Jorinda paid scant attention and believed Pettra might have spoken to herself, in truth.

Pettra continued to comb the hair, and Jorinda closed her eyes. Pettra wore her usual scent, and it filled Jorinda's nostrils. Deineike had never worn a scent, and Jorinda did not like to smell anything that hid a woman's true odour, even though she found the scent pleasant enough.

Pettra dropped the comb and wrapped both arms around Jorinda's waist. "That looks better, although I am unhappy your hair falls out so much." Jorinda lay back against her, lost in her thoughts of the scent. Pettra's hands slid upwards to cradle her breasts, and she nuzzled into Jorinda's neck at the same time.

Jorinda heard Pettra's breaths become heavier as she fondled her full breasts. She should resist. How could she betray Deineike's memory so? She must resist, but Pettra appeared determined to avail herself of Jorinda's affection, and there might be no way to stop her. Jorinda lived in the woman's house, and to reject her might create complications. Her best hope would be to leave the house and sail south as soon as she could.

Jorinda's voice caught in her throat, which surprised her, and her sex tingled. "What of the food you mentioned?"

"I hunger for different food." Pettra's voice took on a husky tone, and her breaths became heavy and more rapid. She seemed aroused and slid a hand down toward Jorinda's sex.

This had gone too far. Jorinda grasped Pettra's slender wrist and pulled the arm away from her intimate area. "Pettra, this obsession you have with me must end. You are married, and you have a son."

"He is not my son." Pettra breathed into Jorinda's ear, and her warm breath threatened to overwhelm Jorinda's resistance as she continued to press her hand downward despite Jorinda's attempts to prevent it.

Jorinda turned in Pettra's embrace as far as she could. "What?"

A long sigh escaped Pettra's lips. "Raopul is not my son."

Jorinda reflected on all the interactions between Raopul and Pettra. She had shown such affection for the boy. How could he not be hers? "How is this possible?"

Pettra sighed again and paused the struggle to reach Jorinda's sex. "Raolos lay with one of our servants. It began many years ago. He thought I knew nothing of his dalliance, but I knew, and I tolerated it. I had grown tired of his attentions, in truth, if I had ever enjoyed them. I craved other fruit. Ten years ago, she became with child, and the scandal would have destroyed him. He had not been Portreeve long, and he begged me to help him. He would give her a home and an allowance if I would say nothing."

She sighed again, a long, sad breath of misery-laden air. "Something went awry. The baby had not positioned itself as it should have. The birthwife wished to cut her and remove the baby. Her screams…" She hesitated. "It broke my heart to hear her. Then she screamed no more. She"—she shrugged—"fell silent. I had waited downstairs, and Raolos came down in tears. The baby had lived, but she had not." A lone tear trickled down her cheek, dripped onto the bed from her chin.

Jorinda paid rapt attention, horrified by the tale. The woman must have died in agony. "You kept the baby?"

"I agreed to raise him as our own. He knows nothing of his real mother. He ought to, for he resembles her and his father. There is nothing of me in his face, but he seems not to guess." Pettra wiped at her eyes, then pinched the bridge of her nose between a finger and thumb.

Jorinda could scarce believe the horrific tale. "When the Bailiff impeached him for marital infidelity, Raolos asked me how they had learned. It seemed like a slip of the tongue, and I did not know what to make of the comment at the time. Now I understand." She released Pettra's hand and touched her cheek. "It must have been a difficult time for you."

Pettra snorted. "That it was. I endured unspeakable torture. After all else, I held the baby innocent of blame, and me account-able, for I had turned a blind eye to the dalliance. It suited me to avoid Raolos's attentions, dream of women, and pleasure myself while he sweated and grunted with her." She paused, a far-away look in her eyes. "What did you say once? Something about anguish, when one woman must hide her love for another for the sake of societal acceptance. I found myself in that situation. Married well to a successful, charismatic man. The only problem—I wished to feel a love different from the one society dictated for me."

Her hand dropped between Jorinda's legs. Jorinda had been enthralled by the tale, but she cried in surprise as Pettra's finger caressed her, and she pulled at Pettra's arm again. "I spoke those words, and I know the pain you feel. You are compelled to live as you do rather than as you wish. But Pettra, the person you seek cannot be me. I love Deineike."

They struggled against one another again, as they had at Raolos's house. Pettra seemed aroused, her mouth open and her nostrils flared, eyes half closed. She licked her lips at whiles, and

Jorinda grew angrier that Pettra would not relent from her attempts to press her attentions on her. Jorinda released Pettra's arm and attempted to push her away, but Pettra still had an arm tight about her waist, and she could not dislodge her. With horror, Jorinda realised Pettra might be close to the peak of her satisfaction, and fury surged in her breast as Pettra took pleasure from her despite her love for Deineike. Her rage peaked at the betrayal of Deineike's memory, and as she lost all control of her temper, she slapped Pettra's cheek.

As the flat of her hand contacted Pettra's face, Pettra let out a loud groan and her body shook. The turn of events disgusted Jorinda, and when the arm around her waist relaxed, Jorinda pushed Pettra away. She fell onto her back but wore a lascivious smile and ran her tongue around her lips, her eyes closed as she moaned, "Hit me again."

Jorinda shuffled back on the bed and stared in disbelief at Pettra, the hair she kept coifed to perfection much of the time dishevelled around her face. Her cheek sported an ugly red blotch from Jorinda's palm, and she had a hand between her legs. The sight revolted Jorinda. "Have you lost your mind?"

Pettra made no reply other than to reach between Jorinda's legs again, but Jorinda snatched her arm away. Pettra ran a tongue around her lips. "Make me come again. I have pleasured myself for too long."

The use of the word baffled Jorinda. "'Come?'"

"It is a word Raolos used in his passion when we lay together. As he finished, he would cry, 'I have come to my excitement.' Often, he would only say, 'come.'"

"I have never heard the word used in this way."

"Be that as it may, make me come again." Pettra held her arms out towards Jorinda. "I beg you."

Jorinda looked at her in disdain and snarled. "You sicken me."

Pettra moaned again. "Use me."

Jorinda shook her head as unfamiliar emotions chased each other through her mind. Pettra raised her arms toward her, and her fingers clenched and unclenched in a clear exhortation for Jorinda to fall on her. An animal lust took hold within Jorinda, and she collapsed forward onto Pettra. Their tongues thrashed in each other's mouths, and Pettra's fingers dived inside Jorinda's wetness even as Jorinda's eyes gushed the wetness of shame down her cheeks.

When Gill left Styrrach after the meeting, he left a man whom he believed had teetered too long on the edge of madness until he tumbled down into its grip. He visited the home of two of the members and told them Styrrach had gests for them and would give them letters at the Guild building. They both expressed concern at recent events, and Gill could not disagree. He decided to delay the order to board all the southern ships until the next day and called into a tavern to drink a tankard of ale, then another, before he wandered home in shock. The madness that had gripped Styrrach as he smashed furniture and ordered deaths in towns far away while the events in The Duke's Seat still hung over him had both frightened and worried Gill.

Gill's life had become bound up in Styrrach's fates, and there could be no easy escape. He had little enough coin and would not know where to go if he did attempt to run. Nightmares had sailed down the Alc into his life on the day Styrrach arrived, and they had brought him to the door of his ruin. The next morning found him tired and irritable after a fitful sleep.

He tracked down two members and gave them their assignment. They asked whether Styrrach intended to disband the Guild since he appeared bent on its destruction, but Gill could not answer the question. In truth, he did not know Styrrach's intentions, other than his fixation on Corelle's ruin and the destruction of the Portreeve in Ort. He did not know what lay behind the obsession, but Gill believed Styrrach had passed beyond reason. A killer must remain calm and be adaptable to whatever turned. Guild training had taught Gill no complication could not be redeemed, that panic served no purpose, so he resolved to see what he could find in the situation to improve it in his favour.

The moment Gill entered the building, Styrrach came out of his office. When he saw Gill, he beckoned him into the office. No other members were in the building, and Gill reasoned they could talk in the parlour, with no need for such dramatic covertness. None-theless, he followed Styrrach into the office. Styrrach wore a smile on his lips, although Gill saw no joy in those cold, devious eyes. The Guildmeister fidgeted from one foot to the other, as if some-thing had him excited.

Gill hoped his expeditious discharge of Styrrach's orders lay behind the Guildmeister's joy, but Styrrach disavowed him of that notion when he snatched up letters and handed them to his Senior Aide.

They were from the new Portreeve in Ort, and they referred in mournful, respectful terms to the death of a beloved citizen of Ort whose Pyre had taken place on the day the man had taken up his new office. The person who had gone wherever they travelled to afterward had been… He paused, careful not to look up at Styrrach as he read the next words. Small wonder Styrrach had become so delighted. The dead person had been Corelle's closest friend, it turned.

Gill did not know Corelle, nor did he know the woman she trav-elled with, but it seemed the injuries Styrrach inflicted on her in The Duke's Seat had been sufficient to kill her, though it had taken her some time to die. Styrrach radiated joy, but Gill stared at the letters and gave no indication he had finished. He felt no pleasure at the news, in truth. He suspected the two men who sailed for Ort might pass Corelle somewhere on their journey, for she must now head south to exact vengeance for the death of her friend. In truth, rumour had it she had been more than a friend. Their lives were all in jeopardy; Corelle's reputation spoke of a killer almost without peer, even though she had not bested Styrrach. She might be in Alcmouth already—

"Do you read so slow you have not read the news yet?" Styrrach yelled, his voice raised with excitement in a way Gill had never heard it raised in anger.

Gill looked up and could scarce believe Styrrach could betray so little of what he felt through those emotionless eyes even as the rest of his body exuded exultation. He made a cautious reply, careful to betray no feelings. "She is dead, Corelle's lover."

"One less deviant in the land." Gill did not correct "less" to "fewer," and Styrrach gave a cold, mirthless laugh. "It is my fervent hope the jade will be devastated. How I wish I could see her and lick the tears of grief from her face."

Gill did not feel the same satisfaction. No stranger to death himself, he had murdered many men, but never a woman. He thought himself immune to the horrors of death, but a small part of him considered this woman's death wrong. She had done little enough to the Guild and nothing at all to him. It seemed inappropriate to celebrate her death.

Styrrach's laughter died in his throat. "You do not share my joy at this news?"

Gill shrugged. "She posed little enough threat, my guess."

"Her death is a blow to Corelle, and Corelle is a great threat to you, no matter that you might think yourself her equal. The death of her deviant companion is worthy of celebration for the pain it will bring her. Is the role of Senior Aide no longer to your taste?"

Gill had had his fill of the bully who stood before him. "You are the Guildmeister. You are free to replace me if you wish. The parlour is doubtless filled with eager replacements."

Styrrach stared at Gill, and the fingers of one hand twitched. He turned pale, and Gill could not remember the lines on the Guildmeister's face when he had first arrived, no more than a pass ago. The Bailiff had urged Gill to control Styrrach, but it seemed no such fate could be written. "I gave you tasks last night. One, at least, I know you fulfilled, for I sent letters with the men you chose. The other?" The Guildmeister had switched from joyous child to manipulative man with so little effort. How did he change his skin with such ease?

"Men are at the docks and will pass your message to all ships from the south that come there. I will visit any others I can trace and arrange for the work to continue until you declare otherwise."

Styrrach turned his back, and Gill did not wait to be dismissed. He left the building and walked to the tavern with the dog, his every step dogged by the anticipation of Corelle's dagger between his ribs. He sat at the counter beside the dog in the hope it might save his life if she tried to kill him while he drank. One tankard became four, then more, and by the end of the night his legs would scarce carry him through the door. He fell many times and bolted the door of his room as soon as he passed through it. He collapsed before he could reach his cot and slept where he lay.

TWENTY
IRRESISTIBLE TEMPTATIONS

JORINDA LAY ON THE BED BESIDE PETTRA, THE OLDER WOMAN'S ARMS wrapped tight around her. Jorinda had said, "You sicken me," but had fallen on Pettra like an animal and betrayed Deineike to such an extent she felt she could no longer bear to draw another breath. Pettra had begged her over and over to pleasure her with greater ferocity and to strike her again. Jorinda had been unable to hit her a second time; it seemed wrong, and she could not repeat the violence.

They were spent, and Jorinda wallowed in her self-disgust. She could not blame Pettra. Although the woman begged and cajoled her, Jorinda had succumbed to her desire, and only Jorinda could be held accountable. Deineike's Pyre had been only a few days earlier, she guessed, and Jorinda had already betrayed her memory and lain with another. It could not be excused, another in a litany of unforgivable crimes Jorinda had committed.

Pettra stirred, and Jorinda pulled herself free of the entanglement of the older woman's arms, climbed from the bed, and reached for her clothes as Pettra opened her eyes to look up at her. "Where are you headed?"

"I am hungry." Jorinda lied to Pettra to get out of the bedroom and think. There must be no repeat of what had taken place this morning, no further dalliances to deepen her treachery. Jorinda's mind might break if she piled more guilt on all she bore already. Deineike had told her she would be destroyed if they became separated. Jorinda longed to leave and sail to Alcmouth, settle scores in that city, but first she must restore her strength, and for that she would need food. She would eat whatever food Pettra had brought. She had not lied, after all else.

Jorinda left Pettra in sleepy lethargy and went down to the scullery. Pettra had brought bread and cheese, so Jorinda tore off a piece of each and filled a cup of water from a pitcher that stood on the counter, then sat in the parlour to eat it. Pettra had the right of it; the house felt cold, and Jorinda must light the fires later.

The food proved difficult to eat, and Jorinda guessed her stomach had become unused to such quantities, but she ate as much as she could and drained the cup. Pettra came into the parlour, sat on a chair next to her, and laid a hand on Jorinda's arm. "Never have I felt such satisfaction. I did not dare dream it could be so sublime. My thanks."

"Why do you give me your thanks? I do not deserve them."

"That you do, for you awoke a woman I have hidden for too long."

Jorinda blew out a short breath. She could never tolerate praise, and today more than ever. "You awoke that woman, not me. I betrayed the woman I love." She dug at her scalp.

"Jorinda, do not berate yourself for your desires. Deineike has gone, and I cannot believe she would wish you to experience no joy again in your life, ever. Nor would she be content to see you hurt yourself so. Please stop."

Jorinda gave a bitter laugh. "It gave me no joy, you may be assured."

Pettra slid from the chair and knelt before her, an arm across Jorinda's knees. "You may take more joy if we go upstairs again and explore more of these sensations you bring to my body."

"You should leave." Jorinda could not meet Pettra's eyes. Shame threatened to shatter her into myriad pieces. "Will Raolos not wonder where you are?"

"He knows where I am. His concern for you is as great as mine."

Jorinda said nothing, mired in her guilt. Pettra stood, collected a small bag Jorinda had not noticed, and knelt on her haunches before her. "I have something for you." She pulled Jorinda's dagger from the bag, and her hands trembled as she held it out.

Jorinda snatched it from her. "I will have need of this and had meant to demand its return. If the Portreeve comes for me, I may now at least take some of his men with me before they kill me."

Pettra chewed at the inside of her mouth. "Do you think they will come?"

Jorinda did not know, although she imagined they would if she remained in the house for long enough. "That they will, my guess."

Pettra reached into the bag again. "I think Raolos's concern for your health is no longer as important as your safety from others. I wish to give you the key, but I seek a promise from you first."

Jorinda gave a short, ironic laugh. The paths of her life were littered with the remnants of broken promises. "I will promise. You must judge whether I will keep that promise, for I do not promise to do so."

"You do not know yet what promise I seek. How can you agree to make the promise?"

Jorinda repeated the same laugh, a bitterness in her heart. "Because I have made many promises, all in good faith, and have shattered every one of them without hesitation. I need not know what I swear to, for it is unlikely I will keep any promises my tongue will beguile you with. My word is as worthless as my life."

Pettra smiled. "Your tongue should not be scolded in this way. It is remarkable." Her hand slid along Jorinda's thigh.

"Deineike was remarkable. I am a monster." Jorinda grabbed the hand and stopped its movement toward her sex.

Pettra gazed at her for a time before she continued. "If you swear in Deineike's name, I think you would honour your word."

Jorinda's anger burned bright within her. "You would use her against me when I have betrayed her here today? I am not the only monster in this room."

"I do not use her. My point is, you are too harsh on yourself." Pettra's expression might have been sadness or anger. Her face proved difficult to read.

"Your point is not well made, and you are wrong. I am too easy on myself. I am a hideous creature."

Pettra's smile returned. "Deineike did not think so. I do not think so either."

Jorinda waved an arm in dismissal. "You are like her in this regard. I despair of this ability to see good in the worst situation. It baffles me."

Pettra rose on her knees and wrapped her arms around Jorinda. "There is good in you, but you bury it deep in yourself, I think."

"Deineike thought so also. You both delude yourself. Whatever good you think you see in me is a deception. I am like a stone on a hot, sunny day, warm to the touch but flipped over to find the underside is cold; as cold as death itself. I am death."

Pettra stoked Jorinda's hair, as tender as Deineike had once been. "I know you despise yourself. I suspect Deineike knew also.

You will not permit yourself any joy, and this is why you find no peace in this life."

"She brought me joy." The argument brought Jorinda no joy, and she wished Pettra would give her the key and leave.

Pettra's voice dropped to a soft whisper. "As can I, if you will allow it."

All question of whether Jorinda could feel even more miserable were swept away. The conversation with Pettra exhausted her and so darkened her mood, she wanted nothing more than to lie on the floor until she died. She abandoned the argument. "What is this promise you would have me break?"

"If I give you the key, will you swear to allow me into the house tomorrow?"

Jorinda gave a sharp, loud laugh as the irony of all that had been said became clear. "You ask me, by my love for Deineike, to swear to open your own door to you so I can betray her and lie with you again? I had the right of it. You *are* a monster."

"I am afraid to leave here with the door unlocked. The Portreeve may come. I am afraid to leave here with the door locked, for I might never taste again what I have tasted today."

Pettra did not move, and Jorinda guessed she had the key in the small bag. "I could take the key. You could not stop me. If you resisted, I could kill you. Your death would not lie on my conscience in the least if it served me." As she spoke of death, calmness descended on her, her Guild training not forgotten.

"You have the skills to kill me. I do not think you could." Pettra's earnest eyes bored into Jorinda's.

Jorinda's head slumped forward. Pettra had the right of it; she could not kill her. She already had the blood of two women on her hands, and she did not wish to add to that count. "I will open the door tomorrow. Give me the key." The words condemned her, and she fell into the abyss, as Deineike had always said she would.

Pettra took the key from the bag and laid it on the floor, then reached up and kissed Jorinda's forehead. She placed her hands around the back of Jorinda's head and ran her fingers through her brown hair. She sank down a little and brushed her lips against Jorinda's, then her tongue insisted its way into Jorinda's mouth. With a resigned sigh, Jorinda pushed Pettra backward and slid a hand between the older woman's parted legs.

Afterward, Jorinda lay in despair on the floor of the parlour as Pettra went upstairs to attend to her appearance. When she came down the stairs again, she had tidied her hair, and she had recovered her breath. Her cheeks were bright red, and she mumbled about it. "The mark has not subsided. I have pinched the other cheek to bring colour to it. It is not noticeable, I hope."

Jorinda thought Pettra looked as though she had exerted herself, but her despair at her weakness had crushed any inclination to debate inanity. "That it is not."

"The carriage should return before too long. The rain has not ceased all day." Pettra had switched back into her role as the wife of an important public figure, at ease with small talk. Jorinda took no pleasure from the chit chat, had no desire to indulge in it.

She could not fathom the need for pain that seemed to excite Pettra, who had again begged Jorinda to hurt her as they writhed together on the parlour floor. Jorinda had again refused. It felt abhorrent to her. Lovemaking ought to be tender, not violent. What Pettra asked for might resemble the comfort Jorinda took when she dug her fingernails into her scalp. Pettra might punish herself for some perceived transgression, mayhap related to the death of Raopul's mother. Who knew? Pettra alone, but Jorinda lacked the strength to raise the issue and feared if she did, it might only serve to arouse Pettra again.

Fingers rapped at the door, and Pettra knelt beside her. "I will see you tomorrow. You will open the door?" Jorinda waved a hand in the air but did not speak, and Pettra kissed her lips, a kiss that lingered overlong, then stood. "Lock the door after I am gone. Stay safe, and please do not harm yourself tonight."

She left and closed the door. Jorinda lay on the floor as night turned the sky black outside the window. "I am sorry." She whispered to Deineike, though she doubted her lover could hear her. "I am sorry." She cried so hard and so long, sleep took her before her agony could subside.

The wind woke her as it howled outside, and Jorinda had no idea how late the hour had grown. Darkness wrapped the house in its discomforting embrace, with either little moon outside or heavy cloud the moon could not pierce. She felt around for the key, locked the door, and dragged her weary body up the stairs to collapse into the bed. Outside, the wind called out all her failures and accused her of innumerable evils. "Guilty," she whispered, and fell again into a troubled sleep.

She lay in bed for some time after she woke. The rain had stopped, but the wind remained, and it battered at the window glass as leaves skittered past and clouds raced across the sky. With luck, the wind would persuade Pettra to stay home today. Jorinda yearned to stay in bed all day, but she must leave Ort as soon as possible and must return to some semblance of normal food and drink intake if she wished to do so.

She dressed in the same tunic and trousers as yesterday, found the dagger she had dropped on the bedroom floor in the darkness, and slid it into her boot. She ate the remains of the bread and cheese from the scullery, washed down with some water, but she now had no food in the house and pondered whether she should venture out to buy some more.

The knock at the door startled her, and she crept to the window to peer out. Pettra stood outside the house, her cloak pulled tight about her, and Jorinda folded forward in disappointment, her hands on her thighs. She sighed but turned the key in the lock before she returned to the chair in the parlour.

Pettra's windswept hair straggled around her bright red cheeks. Had the redness from the slap yesterday lingered overlong? Pettra chattered as she closed the outer door, as though she thought Jorinda might not have noticed the weather. "It is windy outside. I walked. It animated me." She carried the same bag as yesterday and waved it in Jorinda's vague direction as she passed her on the way to the scullery. "I brought you more food. I see you have eaten all that remained. That is good." Her voice drifted from the scullery and Jorinda wanted to yell her thanks for the food so the older woman would leave. That seemed unlikely, in truth. Pettra reappeared and chewed at a small piece of bread, distracted.

"Animated?" Jorinda's curiosity about the word matched her anxiety to talk rather than fall into bed with Pettra.

"You do not know this word?" Jorinda shrugged. "Exhilarated or refreshed. Those are close. Do you know these words?"

"That I do."

"Did you sleep well?" Jorinda nodded, unhappy but drained of the stamina to describe the torment of the restless night. "As did I. You exhausted me." Pettra sounded as though she wore a smile, but Jorinda did not look up at her. Pettra knelt before her and peered into her face. "All is well?" She did not wait for an answer but raised herself up and pushed the hair on top of Jorinda's head about. "I see." She muttered the words but did not elaborate on what she had seen. "I will wash your hair later. I wish other fun before that though." She stood and held out a hand.

"Pettra…" Jorinda longed to resist but lacked the resolve to argue or resist despite her assertion to herself there could be no repeat of the betrayals of yesterday. She had fallen, in thrall to the betrayal she despised, incapable of resistance even as she detested herself for her weakness. Pettra pulled her to her feet and led her from the parlour up the stairs.

Pettra fumbled at the fasteners of her cloak and swept it from herself with dramatic flair. Beneath it, she wore the taffeta dress

Jorinda had made for her. Jorinda gazed at her, disconsolate, weary beyond surprise. The low neckline showed the cleavage Jorinda still thought too bold for the social occasions the dress had been designed for, and the fitted bodice and skirt accentuated Pettra's slender waist, the flare of her hips. She looked sensational in the dress, as Deineike had observed when they delivered it to her.

"I have had no opportunity to wear it until today. How do I look?"

Pettra looked like Jorinda's destruction, but Jorinda could force no breath from her lungs to form the words, could only nod once. Pettra pulled her toward the bed and kissed her, passionate and urgent. Her tongue danced around inside Jorinda's mouth and a hand caressed Jorinda's breast. Pettra moaned with desire the moment she touched Jorinda as her other hand thrust between Jorinda's legs and rubbed at her.

Jorinda pulled her head back and stared into the eyes of a wild animal. Pettra's nostrils flared, and her lips parted as her breath gasped from her. Jorinda whispered. "Why? Why me?"

"You are beautiful, and violence and danger are all about you." Pettra sighed into Jorinda's ear as she flicked Jorinda's nipple to hardness. "That is why."

Jorinda pushed her, and Pettra fell backward onto the bed. Her legs moved as though she wanted to open them, but the fitted skirt held them no more than a span apart. She held out her arms, and her fingers again clenched and unclenched to beseech Jorinda to come to her. When Jorinda swatted her hands away, Pettra gasped and held her arms out again.

Jorinda's disgust for herself drove her into a rage. What turned here, other than the betrayal of Deineike and Jorinda's surrender to Pettra's base desire and carnal passion? She knelt on the bed and straddled Pettra. Pettra reached up and scrabbled at her hair to pull her head down toward her lips. She pulled so hard she hurt Jorinda, who swatted her arms away again in anger.

Pettra reached up for Jorinda's arms and ran her hands up them toward her shoulders, but Jorinda pulled them loose and held them before her as Pettra panted. "Bind them."

"What? Have you lost your mind?"

"I cannot keep my hands from you otherwise." Pettra fought to reach for Jorinda's hair.

Pettra's strange attraction for violence, the betrayal of Deineike and Raolos, her grief and guilt; Jorinda found herself in an unreal situation, and it broke her. She could tolerate no more of the guilt and shame. She cried aloud and fell to one side of Pettra. The moment Jorinda released her hands, Pettra fumbled at the buttons of Jorinda's trousers and tore them open. She pushed her hand between Jorinda's legs and rubbed at her as she breathed into Jorinda's ear, "Touch me."

Jorinda's despair and hatred of herself welled up in her, and she cried. She tried to formulate some words of resistance, but Synna's unexpected voice cut her thoughts off.

"What are you about?"

TWENTY-ONE

FRIENDSHIP IS TESTED

Jorinda's head snapped to one side, and Synna stood in the bedroom doorway. Pettra ceased to rub at her, though she left her hand inside Jorinda's trousers, brushed her hair back from her face with her other hand.

Confusion, shame, and embarrassment flooded Jorinda. "How did you get in?"

"The door is unlocked." Synna glanced to one side in alarm and held up a hand, but too late to stop Raolos, who peered around the door frame.

Jorinda closed her eyes and heard Pettra say, "Raolos." Jorinda had no words for any of them. How had things turned so awry since she and Deineike had sailed south from Ort to Alcmouth such a short time ago? Jorinda could sink no lower than this. She had fallen to the floor of the abyss and could never climb out again.

Why had the men come here? Why had she or Pettra not thought to lock the door? Valid questions, but a more significant one lay unasked. Why had she betrayed Deineike and brought herself to this dreadful place, to be caught in bed with the wife of someone who had done so much for her and Deineike? The ultimate betrayal of everything good in her life. Her complete devastation, pieces of her cast into the wind and blown to all parts of the land.

She opened her eyes and stared into Synna's. "Kill me."

"I need not, for others are in Ort bent on that task already. We came to warn you. I curse that we did. You are unworthy of our concern."

Raolos had said nothing, and he stared at what lay before him. How could he comprehend what he saw—his wife with her hand inside the trousers of the woman who had saved his life and for whose lover he had arranged the Pyre? Jorinda could not imagine what emotions must tear at him. Synna's anger paled into insignificance next to the treachery she had wrought on Raolos.

Jorinda broke the heavy silence. "How do you know this?"

"Two members from Alcmouth left a ship today, here in Ort. They are here to kill you, my guess. I wish I had told them where to find you."

Disturbed by the news, Jorinda sat up. "Raolos. You are in danger. They will not be here to kill me alone. They will kill you, Raopul, and Pettra also. Styrrach has acted sooner than we anticipated. The merchant must have stopped in Alcmouth and told him, as he said he would." She pulled Pettra's hand out of her trousers. "We must act. I must, at the least, since I now doubt you will aid me, and I cannot blame you for it. I must kill them before they come for you, which I believe they will do as soon as they can. They do not know how to find me, but it will not take them long to discover you."

Raolos spoke at last. "You lie with my wife? After all I have done for you? This is friendship to you?"

There were so many threads to the tale, but Jorinda could spare no time to explain. "The least of my life's misdeeds, I assure you. Believe me, I have visited more evil than this on those who have crossed my path."

Pettra leapt to Jorinda's defence. "I brought this about. She is here at my request."

Jorinda buttoned her trousers, ignored Pettra, and spoke to Synna and Raolos. "Go down to the parlour. I will join you there in a moment, and we will discuss all that has turned." Raolos turned away without hesitation and might even have left the house. Synna shook his head and followed him.

Pettra reached for Jorinda's hair, but Jorinda stood and held up a hand. "Wait here. I will resolve this, and your presence will do naught but stoke the fires."

"Come back to me as soon as you can. I still burn for you."

Jorinda shook her head. How had it come about, this mess she found herself mired in? She saw no resolution as she trudged down the stairs, lost in her misery. Raolos and Synna sat in the smaller parlour, and she joined them. "Raolos, I am sorry—"

He cut her off. "I imagine you are, but sweet words will not atone for what you have done here. You have betrayed me."

His anger flowed from him like flames that threatened to burn Jorinda to ash. Despite her contrition, Jorinda felt compelled to remind Raolos of his predicament. "That I have, and Deineike with you. We find ourselves here nonetheless, and you are in danger."

"My men will protect me. You must now fend for yourself."

How could she blame him for his response? "That is reasonable. I do not ask for your help, and I do not expect it." She turned to Synna. "Tell me of these men you saw."

He stared at her, his jaw set in anger. "I saw them leave a ship as

I came out of the tally house. I recognised them as Alcmouth members, so I followed them."

Jorinda shook her head, irritated with his choice. "Reckless. They might have marked you."

"What you do here is reckless. I followed them and trusted my own abilities to avoid detection. They took rooms in an inn near the docks. They will doubtless seek information already."

There could only be one course of action for Jorinda to take. "I will go to their rooms tonight and kill them."

Synna shook his head. "They are two, and they are trained. It will not be easy to best them."

Jorinda did not care. "Then they will kill me. That is possible, and I am certain some would not mourn my death."

The vitriol in Raolos's voice could not be missed. "You refer to me? I do not wish you dead, if that brings you any comfort, but I do not wish my family dead either, despite this betrayal."

Jorinda turned to him. "I will kill them, or I will die. If I die, look to Synna and yourself to protect your family. If I live, I will sail to Alcmouth and kill Styrrach and the Bailiff."

Raolos stared at her open mouthed. "I now see why you lie with my wife. You have lost your mind, doubtless with grief for Deineike. You will kill the Bailiff? Those might be the most foolish words I have ever heard."

Jorinda tutted, annoyed by his dismissal of her plan. "Styrrach then. He must pay for Deineike's death. The three of us are bound together, another terrible triangle linked by blood. He has damaged it, but I must destroy it."

"You have joined three others in your fates now. You, Pettra, and me. You have broken my marriage as Styrrach has broken this connection you see between the three of you."

Anger flared in Jorinda. "I have lain with her, and I am ashamed of that. You broke your own marriage when you lay with your servant and put a child in her." She grimaced and looked away, ashamed of her words as soon as she uttered them, then looked back, past Synna's look of horror to Raolos's hurt expression. "Raolos, forgive me. Those words were uncalled for. You have the right of it. I have undone all, as I have always done."

The anger fell from Raolos's voice, his words now laden with dejection. "You have the right of it, though Pettra had no right to tell you about it. Not a day goes by I do not regret what turned with Hylsie, Raopul's mother, but I love him, and I could not imagine life without him, despite the circumstances."

Synna held up a hand and shot Jorinda a purposeful look. "We digress. If they kill you, they remain a threat to Raolos. We cannot allow that. I will help you kill these two."

Raolos stared at him, his eyes wide with apparent disbelief. "You will aid her? She lies with my wife beneath my own roof, and you will help her?"

"It is her roof." Jorinda again blamed her anger for words she regretted the moment she said them.

Synna held up a hand again as his own temper reddened his face. "Raolos, you employ me to keep you safe, but you see this the wrong way. I came to Ort to kill your wife and child, and Jorinda prevented it. She bested me. If these two can kill her, they can kill me. I do not help her. She helps me."

Raolos stood and clenched his fists. "I have my men. I do not rely on you alone."

Synna sighed. "Your men do not have the skills to match the Guild. You are a businessman, and a successful one. We are killers" —he waved his arm between himself and Jorinda—"and are trained to succeed. We must take them before they can reach your family."

Raolos looked deflated. "A sorry profession. So be it. Do what you will. I will attempt to save my marriage while you attempt to save our lives." He turned to Jorinda and spat out furious words. "I owe you a debt, but you should have let Styrrach's man kill me in my office, for you have brought darkness into my life. I hope I never see you again." He strode up the stairs on enraged feet, and Jorinda moved further into the parlour to sit in one of the chairs, her head in her hands.

Synna's taut lips and angry tone left his feelings in no doubt. "A sorry turn. I do not understand what has turned here, in truth. What of Deineike? Have you forgotten her already?"

"I betrayed her, and Raolos." Jorinda looked up at him. "I betray all who come close to me. You should have killed me in Raolos's house, as I begged you to."

Raised voices flowed down the stairs, and Synna shook his head and repeated himself. "A sorry turn. Will you sail for Alcmouth as you say?"

"I mean to kill Styrrach. The Bailiff too, if I can. I have little left but my hatred for them, and for myself. Styrrach is my first mark. Twice I have been close to him with a chance to kill him, but he fled both times. There cannot be a third time. Afterward, I imagine I will kill myself, since none will do this for me, though I plead with them."

Raolos came down, stomped from the house, and slammed the door behind him. Synna hesitated, and Jorinda inclined her head to the door. "You must go with him, for they may watch him by now. Tell me the name of the inn, and I will meet you there at the sundown. You must make sure Raolos's family are safe before you come."

Synna nodded, told her the location of The Dockside Inn, where the men stayed, then left. Jorinda feared to return to the bedroom. Pettra had not left with Raolos, and Jorinda had no desire to learn why. She sat in the chair as time passed, but Pettra did not come down, and she wondered whether he might have hurt her. She doubted it but could not drive the thought from her mind, so she ascended the staircase, reluctant but concerned.

Pettra lay on the bed and appeared not to have moved since the two men interrupted them. She lay in silence, but Jorinda could see her breasts rise and fall as she breathed. "Pettra?"

Pettra turned her head to look at her. "Come to me. I yearn for your touch."

Jorinda sighed. "You should leave." How could this be? Her husband had caught her in a dalliance, yet she still desired fruit that might spoil her marriage forever?

"Raolos said as much, but I am still here."

"That you are. It is your house, and I imagine you may stay for as long as you wish. Tonight, Synna and I will attend to the two who have come here to kill us all. Afterward, I will sail to Alcmouth and settle my score with Styrrach."

Pettra sat upright. "You cannot leave me."

"I do not leave you. We are nothing. I lay with you yesterday, that is all. You will find others."

"I want no others." Jorinda remembered how she had said those same words in the barn at Taro's farm, not so long ago, and she sighed. Pettra pulled the skirt of her dress up to her knees. "Touch me. Take me. Then go about your business tonight. I will be here when you return."

Jorinda sighed in exasperation. "You will be with your husband and a boy who thinks of you as his mother, who has need of you. You will not be safe here once I leave. If they kill Synna and me, they will come for you."

"Do not say that. They will not kill you."

"That they may. I do not know what fate is written for me tonight."

Pettra stared at her and pulled the dress higher. "Then if you must die, do not die unfulfilled." She held her arms out toward Jorinda, who turned and went back down the stairs, and Pettra did not call to her.

Jorinda stood at the outer door and turned the day's events over in her mind. It would be too early to visit the tavern yet. She planned to arrive there earlier than she had told Synna, but the Alcmouth men would not be the easy marks she had gathered intelligence on for her gests in Zhanghar. The longer she loitered there, the greater the risk they would see her. With a heavy sigh, she turned the key in the lock and went back to the bedroom.

Pettra had pulled the dress up to her waist, and she rubbed at herself. She reached a hand toward Jorinda, and Jorinda went to her. "I want you to touch me."

"You must go home afterward. It is not safe for you here."

"If I can walk, I will go home, I swear it. If I am unable to walk, then you will have done all I desire, and I am prepared to die." She raised both arms toward Jorinda. "I do not wish to walk."

TWENTY-TWO
DEATH VISITS A TAVERN

JORINDA AND PETTRA LAY NAKED ON THE BED AS THE LIGHT DWINDLED outside. Despite her inexperience with other women, Pettra had been a competent lover who demanded ferocious satisfaction, and it tired Jorinda to pleasure her. She appeared insatiable and begged for more touches even as Jorinda lay exhausted beside her. Jorinda must leave for the inn, and she pulled Pettra's hand from her.

With a breath of self-hatred, Jorinda spoke. "It is time. I must leave, as must you. I wish you had arranged a cart, but I will walk to your gate with you to see you are safe."

"My legs may not support me." Pettra laughed. "You have drained me."

"Then you must crawl. I cannot carry you, and you cannot remain here. Rise. Dress yourself and go to your husband. You have a marriage to save." Jorinda stood and pulled her clothes on, but

Pettra made no move to dress. "Pettra, you must go. I cannot protect you. If I fall…"

Tears trickled from Pettra's eyes. "Must you go?"

Jorinda picked the dress up and pulled Pettra upright. "I must." She tried to pull the dress over Pettra's head.

Pettra laughed, wiped at her eyes, and sniffed. "You made the dress, but you forget the skirt is fitted, and I must step into it."

"Then step into it, before the Alcmouth men kill us all."

Pettra stepped into the dress and pulled it up. She did look spectacular in the dress, and Jorinda felt a twinge of desire again. Pettra found the comb and attended to her hair while Jorinda took down Deineike's sketches and pushed them into her pack.

As she looked up, Pettra stared down her in dismay. "You do intend to leave?"

"That I do. I have said as much."

Pettra sniffed again and wiped at her eyes. "Take me with you."

Jorinda's patience had worn as thin as parch. "I cannot take you with me. I go to my death, in all likelihood. I will be killed for certain if I must look after you in your ballgown. You cannot come with me."

"I do not wish to remain without you. I cannot remain without you."

Jorinda clenched her fists at her side. "How can I make this any clearer? I leave here to die, tonight or some days from now. I deserve it. You have a husband and a son who need you. You cannot come with me."

Pettra ran to her and threw her arms around her, her head buried in Jorinda's neck. "Do not leave me, please. I love you."

Jorinda held her at arm's length. "You do not know me. You are infatuated at best. To speak of love is a delusion." She rose and went down the stairs, her pack in her hand. Pettra tugged at her all the way, but Jorinda would not be dissuaded now. She unlocked the door and left the house. Pettra followed her and cried as Jorinda locked the door and handed over the key. Pettra had not picked up the bag of food, but Jorinda imagined she would collect it some other day. They set off toward Raolos's house as Pettra pleaded beside her and begged her to turn back and live with her in her house. Jorinda could not grasp the attachment Pettra had made to her after so short a time, but she must focus on the task at hand. They had already left the house later than she intended, and her impatience to reach the tavern drove her at a brisk pace toward Raolos's house four streets away.

When they reached the house, Jorinda pushed Pettra through the gate, gentle but firm. As she turned, Pettra ran to her again and clutched at her arms. Jorinda almost dragged her to the door of the house and instructed the servants to take her inside and ensure she did not follow. They appeared surprised but did as instructed, and the door closed as Pettra screamed at Jorinda to come back. It had been one of the more unreal moments in a life lived on the edge of credibility ever since the day Jorinda met Arella.

As she walked toward the inn, Jorinda wondered how Arella would feel about all that had turned in the previous two days. She had seldom given Arella a thought in recent days, but she hoped that if Deineike and Arella had travelled anywhere afterward, they had met again. She did not deserve either of them and could no longer bear to consider she might have to face them again and explain her inexplicable behaviour.

How had the two men from Alcmouth come to Ort so soon? She had lost track of the days since Deineike had died, but it seemed inconceivable they could be here so soon unless both ships, the merchant's and the one they sailed north on, had made excellent time. The days must number more than she recalled; there could be no other explanation. It seemed but three or four days to her since the Pyre, but the grief-stricken days in bed in Raolos's house must have numbered more than she remembered. Styrrach wasted no time, after all else. The plan had succeeded, better than they had anticipated.

Cautious, she glided through the shadows outside the inn. She spotted Synna even though he had chosen an excellent place to hide. She would have hidden in the same place, had she arrived first. Her training guided her eye to the spot and revealed him to her. Their marks had the same training, of course, so they could not guarantee they were not already observed.

Even as she slid down behind the low wall that lay in darkness across from the inn, Synna whispered to her. "I have not seen them come out." He paused. "You are late."

"Complications."

Synna handed her a pouch. A substantial amount of coin jingled inside it. "A gift from Raolos. He does not wish you to remain in Ort for lack of funds." As she pushed the pouch into her pack, Synna smiled. "Will you fight them with your pack in your hand?" He gave a soft laugh.

"That I will not. I will leave it here."

He glanced at the inn. "Little remains unaccomplished in my life that can be completed behind this wall."

She smiled at the jest, admired his courage in the face of an unknown fate. "Then let us be about our business." They ran across the road and entered the inn. Only a few patrons sat scattered around the tavernroom, but Synna grasped her arm as they entered and pulled her behind a wall where they had no view of the tavernroom.

He hissed a sound of frustration, then spoke, his voice no more than a soft breath in the noise of the tavern. "They are in the tavern-room. I do not think they saw us enter, but this complicates our task."

Jorinda risked a hurried peek around the door of the tavern-room. There could be no doubt about the two Guild men. They sat side by side on a long settle at the rear of the tavernroom, and

Jorinda could not imagine how the men had not seen them enter. They had an air of cautious menace and wore dark clothes. A tankard sat before each of them. She turned to Synna. "That is a disappointment."

He stifled a laugh. "That it is." He gazed at her for a moment. "I wish I could have known you better. Deineike too. A sorry mess drives us to separate after tonight. Have you lost your mind? Why did you lie with Pettra?"

Jorinda clutched for the thoughts that whirled around inside her head. "In truth, since Deineike died, it is as though I have been elsewhere, as though I have watched myself, unable to influence my own thoughts and actions. It began before Styrrach and Porl came to Raolos's office. One night I woke in the house and wandered around naked. I could not explain what turned then, and I cannot account for it now. Something snapped in my mind, and I could not control myself."

Synna looked earnest. "Can you control yourself now? I do not wish to die because you become a player in some delusional festival."

"That I can. When Raolos arrived in the house this morning, I think whatever had become unsnapped snapped back. I have told you I cannot explain. Do not press me. I wish to kill these two, but I will kill you as well if you do not drop this matter."

Synna stifled another laugh. "Do you have a plan?"

Jorinda held out a hand toward him. "Your cloak." Synna's cloak had a hood, and he passed it to her. She put it on and raised the hood. "They do not know me for certain and may not recognise me beneath the hood. They will be cautious, nonetheless, and will watch as I pass them. You will run to them. Sit on the closest side of them. Once you make your move, I will sit on the other side. Then we will see what unfolds."

Synna's silence stretched out for ten heartbeats or more. "That is your plan?"

"If you have a better one, feel free to reveal it."

He shook his head but took his dagger from its scabbard and held it low against his thigh before he gave an urgent whisper. "Go."

Jorinda reached down, pulled out her own dagger, and concealed it in the folds of the cloak before she pulled the hood lower over her face and stepped into the tavernroom. As she had suspected, the two members fixed their gaze on her as she approached them. As she drew level with the first one, one of them glanced away from her. *Synna must be on the move.*

Jorinda took one quick step next to the closest one. His arm moved, and the other faced Synna, who had already sidled up to him on the settle. At that moment, an idea came to her, and she threw herself onto the lap of the one nearest to her, raised her dagger to his throat, and leaned into him so it would not be seen by other patrons. She brought her head close to his and hissed into his ear. "Do not reach for your dagger or you will die."

To her left, Synna leaned against the other man, whose face turned pale. The man whose lap she sat on whispered back, "You would not dare, in so public a place."

"That I would. Styrrach has taken everything I cared for from me, and I would be happy to strike you down and take my chances with the noose."

His hand loitered near his belt, but he did not reach for the dagger she guessed lay there. "Corelle." He spat out the word as though he had only now realised who sat on his lap.

"The same. Your name?"

"Adijon." He moved his head back as though to escape the tip of her dagger, but she wrapped an arm around his neck as a lover might and held his head in her firm grip.

She whispered again. "Styrrach sent you here to kill Raolos and me?"

"That he did."

Synna and the other man also spoke in hushed whispers, and she shot Synna an inquisitive glance. He nodded, and she reasoned he had cowed his mark. It seemed she need not worry a dagger might strike from her left. "We will rise and leave in a moment. Draw no attention to yourself, or I will take your breath. Do you understand?"

"Curse you. I know your reputation. You will kill me here or once we leave the inn. I will not go with you. I will take my chances in this room, where other eyes may see what turns."

Jorinda glanced at Synna again and inclined her head toward the door. He tugged at the sleeve of the other man, and they both rose. As they walked, close together, toward the door, Synna laughed out loud, and the other patrons looked toward him as he yelled to the innkeep. "My friends have taken more ale than is good for them. This one must fetch up, and a matrimonial storm brews between those two I wish no part of." The tavernroom erupted in laughter at this. A wry smile sprang to Jorinda's lips. Synna had played a perfect hand.

Adijon may have believed her distracted by Synna's jest, and he raised a hand toward her dagger. Without hesitation, she drove it deep into his throat. His eyes widened, and he gurgled as blood gushed from the wound. She pressed on his other hand with all the strength she could muster as he scrabbled for his dagger in his death throes. His blood spurted out into her face and down her clothing, but she kept her body pressed against him as she pulled her dagger from his throat, slashed at the side of his neck, and opened his artery. As the life faded from his eyes, she pulled his dagger out of his belt and swiped its blade through his blood, then dropped it on the settle near his lifeless hand before she slipped her own dagger into her boot.

His death had come about in no more than a few heartbeats, and now his blood ran down toward the floor. She cried out in alarm. "Help me. I beg you." She leapt backward and crashed into the table behind her. The tankards of ale skittered to the floor. "He has opened his own throat." She kept the hood over her head as far as possible to obscure her face and hair.

Patrons leapt up and rushed over to him as she backed away. A man grabbed at her, yelled into her face. "What has turned? Are you hurt?"

"Help him." Jorinda screamed at the man as she pointed to the dead Guild member, and he turned toward her victim. All eyes were on the dead man, who had slumped to the floor at the foot of the settle in a pool of blood and ale. She turned, ran from the tavernroom, and leapt the wall across the road where Synna and the other man crouched.

Synna hissed at her. "What has—"

"Flee." Jorinda grabbed up her pack, and all three ran as hard as they could. When she glanced back, people ran from the inn and cast about them. When she looked ahead again, Synna had turned a corner, and the other with him. She followed them. "Let us hope we have not been seen." The two men panted and leaned against the wall of a building. "Go. We are not safe yet."

Synna stopped three streets away and turned to face Jorinda. "You cannot walk the streets." He gasped the words out, short of breath. "You are covered in blood. To Raolos's tally house, as quick as we can. You may clean up and change your clothes there." He set off again.

The other man followed him, and Jorinda wondered what had turned between them. She had no time to consider the development, needed to reach the tally house away from suspicious eyes as soon as she could. She followed them. Her training and instincts told her not to run, but she disregarded them as the prospect of a noose filled her thoughts.

Ahead of her, Synna had reached Raolos's tally house. Light shone from a window high in the frontage, but the closed doors presented an unwelcome face. Synna fumbled in a pocket, produced a key, and unlocked a small door set into the larger doors of the tally house. He pushed the door open, and the three of them tumbled through. He closed it behind them, and Jorinda dropped her pack and bent forward, her hands on her thighs. Her entire body shook, and she sucked enormous breaths into lungs that burned from the exertion. Her stomach cramped, and she battled the urge to fetch up.

Breathless, Synna gasped, "What turned?"

"He resisted." Jorinda saw movement from the corner of her eye, and she snapped upright. Ibie appeared from somewhere in the back of the tally house. He stopped when he saw them, and he stared in horror at Jorinda. He said nothing but moved toward them and reached for his belt. Synna held up a hand and Ibie stopped.

Jorinda wanted to know why the other Guild man appeared so pliant. "What of this one?"

The man looked at her in fear. "You have killed Adijon?"

"That I have. Must I kill you also?" She glared at the man, and he took half a step backward.

Synna spoke in a calm voice. "He is not a threat."

Ibie joined the conversation, doubtless confused. "What has turned?"

Synna explained. "The threat is neutralised. One is dead, and this one wants to sail away and turn from the Guild."

Jorinda glowered at the man. "How convenient. Faced with your ruin, you abandon your duty and your service to Styrrach?"

"I have never served him." The man spat on the hard dirt floor. "I joined the Guild before he came to Alcmouth. I dislike him, and he murdered Balgow before my eyes, for no reason I could determine. Since he arrived, the Guild is all but destroyed." Synna nodded as the man spoke, and the man turned to him. "Synna, tell her I speak the—"

Jorinda interrupted him. "You would rather Styrrach hunts you, as he hunts me?"

"That I would not. I fear him. I will leave Dur."

Jorinda found the story difficult to believe, and Ibie's presence needed explanation. She turned to Raolos's man. "Why are you here at this hour?"

He addressed his reply to Synna, not her. "I returned from the three-master tied to the dock a short time ago. I spoke with her master. Our proposition did not impress him, but I must speak to them all as I see them arrive."

The Guild member turned to him. "Does the ship sail north or south?"

Ibie shrugged. "South, I think, since it arrived earlier from the north."

"I can obtain passage on it with the token. Wherever it heads, that is where I will travel. It will be preferable to where she may send me to." He inclined his head toward Jorinda but continued to address Ibie. "You will find few favourable responses to your suggestions. I hear Styrrach threatens all the masters anew. Gill tells me your scheme has infuriated Styrrach." Jorinda smiled. The idea had succeeded so far.

Ibie's reply seemed to have no connection to the man's words. "Do you have a trade?"

"I used to be a mariner, the truth of it. I tired of the life and met Sky in a tavern in Alcmouth one day. He persuaded me to this course. I regret it, but I am bound up in it now." He looked miserable as he spoke, and he turned to Jorinda. "You killed Sky?"

Jorinda confirmed it. "That I did."

The man sighed and looked downcast. "He also tired of the Guild and turned to the drink because of his unhappiness. A pity you slew him."

"He would have killed us, had I not done so, although you claim he tired of the Guild."

"Once you are in, to leave is…" He fell silent.

Ibie shook his head. "You cannot use the token. I told the master the token will not be used under our trade arrangement, not an hour since."

Synna frowned. "Give him some coin and see him away, then."

"That I will not." Ibie's face grew stern, and he looked at Jorinda for the first time as he spoke. "I will not fund those who came here to kill Raolos. I urged him not to give you coin, but he desires you gone with every breath he takes."

"Give him the coin, man." Jorinda wished the man could play some part in the exposure of Styrrach's schemes, but his testimony would be no more valuable than Synna's or her own. "Which would you rather spend it on, to speed him on his way, or on three Pyres for Raolos and his family? Those are your choices."

The Guild member muttered. "I cannot comprehend what has turned here."

Ibie stared at Jorinda, and contempt blazed in his eyes. "Very well. I will fund his voyage, and I will stand on the dock until the ship has gone from sight. It would be well if he never returned here."

The man answered. "I shall not." Ibie wheeled and stomped off to the rear of the building.

Jorinda turned again to the man. "The ship is unlikely to dock in Alcmouth, but if it does, stay out of sight. The docks will be watched, and you must not be seen. Beyond that, your fates are written, and good luck to you. I sail to Alcmouth. Styrrach's fate is written also, and my blade will end him." The man gasped, but Jorinda picked up her pack and asked Synna where she might find a vanity bowl.

Behind the door he pointed to, she found a bowl, some cloths and soaps, and a privy. Jorinda tore off her clothes and pumped some water into the bowl, then scrubbed at herself until she had removed most of the blood. She pulled on some clean trousers and a tunic, threw the bloodied cloths to the floor along with her own clothes. It went against her instincts to abandon the clothes, but she would have no need of them once Styrrach and the Bailiff were dead, and she reached her ultimate destination.

Jorinda gazed at herself in the reflecting glass. For a moment, Deineike's face appeared in the glass behind her, and she turned in shock but saw nothing there. She shook her head to clear her thoughts and faced her reflection again before she spoke aloud, her mind filled with her vow in Torric, after she had slain the wrong man. "The vow is shattered once more. I have killed again and will kill more before this is done. I am sorry my love." More words spoken in the room in Torric came to her, memories of the time she had told Deineike her birth name, Corelle. "*I will never call you that. I will always call you Jorinda,*" Deineike had said. Jorinda spoke to her reflection in the glass. "You will never call me Jorinda again." Tears stung Jorinda's eyes. "Nobody will." She picked up her pack and returned to the tally floor.

Ibie and the man had left, but Synna still stood there. "How did you kill him in so public a place and still escape?"

"Luck." Jorinda pulled open the door. "Farewell Synna." She stepped out into the night.

TWENTY-THREE
RUIN SAILS SOUTH

CORELLE HAD WALKED NO MORE THAN A FEW STEPS WHEN SYNNA called to her. "Jorinda. Wait a moment."

She turned to face him. "Corelle."

He looked perplexed. "What?"

"My name is Corelle. Corelle became a killer, while Jorinda tried to avoid death but failed. I will abandon Jorinda and be Corelle the killer once again." Klordia had preferred Corelle and had found Jorinda more of a killer's name, but she had it backward, after all else.

Synna shook his head. "You are a mystery." He told her about his conversation with Gill after the attack on her and Deineike and gave her a description. "You will not mistake him. The upper part of his left ear is missing, the result of some gest that turned awry. Seek him out. He may be sympathetic."

"My thanks." Corelle set off again in search of a ship that would sail for Alcmouth. She ignored the three masted ship Ibie had mentioned. He stood near the ramp, the Guild member by the rail, doubtless some arrangement Ibie had insisted on to ensure the man sailed south and took his threat with him. Jorinda would not seek passage on that ship. She imagined it would head south to whichever land it came from, as Ibie had told them it had arrived from Zhanghar. It re-supplied in Ort before the voyage home, she reasoned. Two other ships bobbed at the dock, both two-masters, little activity around either of them. She walked up the ramp of the nearest ship and asked for the master, who had retired to his cabin, so she waited for him to be summoned. The ship sailed to Alcmouth but would not leave until the morning; something to do with a delayed cargo. Corelle wanted to leave sooner, so she said she would enquire aboard the other vessel.

That ship also sailed for Alcmouth and would depart in an hour, when the tide changed in their favour, so she paid for passage. A crew member showed her to a small cabin with two bunks, two chairs at a table, and a small, round window that faced across the darkness of the Alc toward the Eastlands. She had not sent the letter to Wilash as intended, so she resolved to scribe it as she sailed south and deliver it to a courier in Alcmouth before she set about her deadly business.

Corelle left her pack in the cabin and went out onto the deck to stand at the bow and watch the docks for signs of Portreeve's men. No doubt they would be summoned to the tavern, and her story that the man had ended his own life would not stand up to much scrutiny. It had served in the frantic moments as shocked patrons attempted to understand what turned, but the story had only a short life, and she would now be sought.

The hour dragged by, but dockhands appeared at last. They stretched and yawned as they set about their work and exchanged banter among themselves. They threw ropes aboard, pulled the ramp clear, and the ship moved out into the current. The three-master sailed ahead of them, and as both ships piled on sail, the larger ship pulled away. Corelle had left Ort behind, and revenge and death lay ahead of her.

Corelle slept well the first night, rocked by the motion of the ship, no doubt. She awoke refreshed but miserable. She had dreamt of Deineike and Arella, who reprimanded her for all her broken vows and would not accept any of the excuses she attempted to beguile them with. They stared at her with sad eyes as she tried to explain. "I love you. Both of you." They shrugged, and the recriminations began again. The dream did not distress her as the nightmares did, but she woke with Deineike's face in her mind and guilt in her heart.

She rose and found some bread and cold meats in the common room. Three mariners bade her good morning as she entered, and they watched her take some of the meat to a table, a curious amusement on their faces. One of them asked, "You do not eat the bread?"

She gave a terse response. "It is muck." They stared at her with blank expressions. The jest made her even more miserable, as it reminded her of the conversation with Deineike about the bread aboard The Friendship. How could a jest make a person miserable? It must be one of life's mysteries, and she settled for a better explanation. "I do not suffer from the motion of the ship. I have no need of it." They raised their eyebrows as if they understood and spoke no more to her. The unfamiliar word, "muck," might have unsettled them or persuaded them she must be simple. She did not care to engage in idle tittle tattle with them in truth, and it did not disappoint her when they did not pursue the conversation.

As she ate, a random thought entered her mind, as they often did. The ship sailed, but nobody called its crew sailers. Mariners sailed the ship. There appeared to be no logic to it. Why did sailers not sail the ship, while mariners marin… Corelle could find no word for what mariners might do, and the thought had made her even more miserable as it opened an old wound. She thought back to the time Deineike had questioned Syme about why tavernrooms existed in both inns and taverns, and she sighed and blinked away tears. Would this be the fate written for the remainder of her life, to be reminded of Deineike at every turn?

Out on the deck, Corelle found a man in an officer's coat near the wheel. When she enquired about parch and scribing tools, he promised to have some sent to her cabin. She sat at the bow and became even more morose as she thought back over the voyages she had taken with Deineike. Even though the motion of the ship did not disturb her, the journey would be painful if she found Deineike in every corner of the vessel.

Death held no fear for her now she stood so close to it, and she longed for it, in truth. Corelle had been an awkward child with few friends but had not been the creature she had now become. She deserved death for all the dreadful things she had done since she decided to join the Guild. Those who had loved her lay scattered in her footprints, dead or destroyed. She wondered about Pettra and how things would turn in her marriage.

The stiff breeze turned a cold day colder. Corelle did not understand how ships could sail regardless of the direction of the wind. At whiles, they sailed straight forward, while at other times, they appeared to meander from side to side. Although she imagined some art known to the mariners captured the wind in the sails from wherever it blew, it mystified her. The conversation with Deineike where the word "nautical" had eluded her sprang to Corelle's mind. She slapped a hand on the deck in anger and hoped she would never have cause to sail on a ship again. They had become nothing more than a bothersome pit of miserable memories with no escape.

With some difficulty, she turned her thoughts to the task ahead of her. She would track down Styrrach's new Senior Aide, Gill, the man Synna had described. Corelle hoped he would be as sympathetic as Synna had implied. If not, she might have to kill him. With luck, she could find some valuable information from him about Styrrach's movements. It would be difficult to kill Styrrach—the hardest gest of her life. It might prove impossible to kill the Bailiff, more so if he learned she had killed Styrrach, but she would attempt it, nonetheless. If it brought her own ruin, it would not be a terrible outcome, but she hoped to kill him first.

All Guild members knew the locations of the Guild buildings in each city, the names of Guildmeisters, and even some members. Regardless, it would not be simple to kill Styrrach. Corelle could not walk through the door and slay him with the ease of one of her gests in Zhanghar. He would be surrounded by Guild members and would have his own skills, so she must create a situation where she could take him alone and by surprise. Many men who had not expected her blade had fallen to it, and Corelle had felt no qualms. She would not hesitate to kill Styrrach in his sleep or from behind. She longed to watch his life leave him, and that would suffice. His death would not bring Deineike back to her, but it would be some small measure of payment for the deaths of both Deineike and Arella.

To kill the Bailiff would not only require a foolproof plan, but a vast amount of luck. She pushed the thought from her mind for now and focused on Styrrach first and foremost. Once he lay dead at her feet, there would be time enough to consider the Bailiff.

The day wore on, and she grew cold, so she returned to the common room to find more food, which she took back to her cabin to eat. The officer had made good on his promise, and she found parch and scribing tools on the table. She had not locked the cabin, and no trunk had been provided, but her pack lay undisturbed where she dropped it, the coin pouch still wrapped in Deineike's tunic. The lantern spluttered into life against the gloom of the cabin, and Corelle sat down at the table to compose the letter to Wilash.

It seemed appropriate to dispense with frivolous details and tell him of the tragedy behind the letter. *"I send this letter to let you know my beloved Deineike is dead, killed by Styrrach."* She stared at the sentence for a time before she struck through the word "my" and scribed "our" above it. It seemed an abrupt start to a letter, but she did not want to deceive him with insignificant titbits about her life, then reveal the death of Deineike as an afterthought. Content with the sentence, she gazed at the parch and wondered what more she could add after such stark news. She pondered the letter for some time before she settled for, *"I travel to Alcmouth to avenge her."*

Tears stung her eyes, and she leaned back in the chair so they did not drop onto the parch. She wiped the sleeve of her tunic across her eyes and waited until she felt the tears had paused for a time before she bent to the task again. *"I doubt I will survive the encounter. I wish you and Klordia happiness."* The words did not cover one quarter of the parch but she could find nothing more to add. She signed the letter, *"Corelle,"* and laid the scribing tool on the table.

She had said nothing of her part in the death of Deineike and had blamed Styrrach alone, but she could not bear to begin the letter again. She imagined Wilash would know she held herself to blame, and if he did not, then he would not learn it. She had scribed the letter but had no seal for it, so she folded it and searched deep inside her pack until she came up with the letter from Wilash Pettra had handed to her when she had returned to Ort. As she choked back fresh tears, she scribed his address on her succinct letter. She would ask the master to place his seal on it tomorrow.

Corelle lay on one of the bunks and stared in dejection at the one above her. She wished it would move as Deineike turned in her sleep, but it swayed with the motion of the ship and nothing more. Sleep took her, and she dreamt Deineike and Arella harangued her for her abandoned promises again.

The voyage passed with painful familiarity. Corelle rose, ate, sat at the bow, ate, slept. She avoided conversations with the mariners as much as possible, and once she obtained his seal on her letter, she did not see the master at all. The day before they were due to dock in Alcmouth, she asked one of the mariners if they kept a whetstone aboard. She followed him to the common room and waited as he searched for one in a cabinet and handed it to her. She took it to her cabin and passed close to an hour as she stroked it up and down the blade of her dagger. Thanks to Wilash's skills, the edge had lost little of its keenness. Nonetheless, she considered it time well spent to hone it to optimum sharpness ahead of her tasks in Alcmouth.

Satisfied, she returned the whetstone to the cabinet where the mariner had found it. One of the mariners in the common room made a half-hearted attempt to persuade her to join him for a drink in a tavern when they docked, but she rejected his clumsy advances, relieved none of the others had made any attempt to press her for a dalliance. None would do so if they knew the nature of the beast they tried to lie with, beautiful to behold but ruinous to love.

Alcmouth came into view the next day as she sat again at the bow. Buildings on the bank became more prevalent as they sailed on, and close to the midday, she saw the docks ahead of them, ran back to the cabin, gathered up her pack, and stood in the doorway to the deck. She hid as far back in the passageway as she could while the ship came alongside. She hoped nobody would see her as the mariners cast ropes down to the dock and the ship tied up. Dockhands pushed the ramp up to the deck, and the mariners made it fast. Without delay, the ship's crew set about their work to offload the cargo.

Corelle stood in the doorway for long moments and scoured the docks for any person who lurked in shadow or climbed the ramp onto the ship. She saw nothing untoward but did not doubt

Styrrach's men watched the docks from some vantage point. Her cloak had no hood, and she had left Synna's blood-soaked one back in Ort. She strolled down the ramp behind a mariner who struggled with a crate and stayed as close to him as she could, careful not to impede him in his work. He placed the crate near several others on the dock, and she slipped between them, then crouched down to her pack as though she searched for something within it. She saw nothing to alarm her as she swept the dockside with surreptitious eyes, but it only increased her anxiety. Guild members must be somewhere, and while she could not see them, they may have seen her.

A noisy gaggle of men approached the crates—the crew of another ship headed to a tavern, she thought, and she fell in alongside them. One of them turned to her, and she flashed him a sweet smile. He slid an arm around her waist, and she did not resist, though she slipped around to his other side so she walked between the taller men. The man draped his other arm around her shoulder and pulled her close, and she bit down on the snarl that rose to her throat as his hand came to rest on her breast. The men all stood taller than her, and she hoped she would not attract any attention— nothing but a courtesan among a crew long on both coin and desire at the end of their voyage.

The men made for a tavern at one end of the dock, but she could not allow herself to become cornered inside an unfamiliar building. As they drew close to the door, she pulled away from the man whose arm hung about her shoulder. He grabbed at her, but she ducked under his arm and ran down an alleyway alongside the tavern. Raucous laughter broke out behind her, but she did not look back until she reached the end of the alleyway. Nobody had followed her, and the man whose prospects had turned from mundanity to promise, then disappointment in so short a time must have given up on her.

Corelle did not recognise the street the alleyway opened onto, but that mattered little at this point. She set out in a random direction, made many unpredictable turns and stops, and doubled back several times. She entered the occasional shop and stood far in the rear while she appeared to study some item. She checked every face in the shop and observed any who followed her in.

She came to an inn called The Common Inn, and the play on words appealed to her, so she entered, sought a room on an upper floor, and paid in advance for four nights. The room, on the third floor, lay toward the front of the inn, well away from the staircase. A window looked out onto the busy street, and she stood some way back from the window glass to watch the city folk scurry about below her. She felt certain nobody had followed her, but at some point, she must have been observed. The outcome seemed as favourable as might have been expected, and she dropped her pack onto the bed.

Delay would achieve nothing, so she locked the door and slipped the key into a trouser pocket as she sought a rear exit from the inn. She invested some time to establish her location in the city and discovered the inn stood only a few streets from the cottage she had shared with Deineike. Once she established her whereabouts, she headed for the Guild building without further hesitation.

She needed directions twice, but in time she found Water Street, where the Guild building stood, and lingered in the doorway of a house some way from it. The building resembled all the others she had seen, a plain house in a terrace of ten or more, more houses and a small shop that sold foodstuffs opposite it. She wandered further and turned into the street parallel to Water Street.

No alleyway ran between the two rows of houses, which did not surprise her, since the house would have been chosen to have but one entrance. The parallel street looked the same as Water Street, a long row of houses, most in poor repair. No rear exit from the Guild building existed, as she had anticipated. One door is easier to guard than two, and escape would be no concern if danger called. Anyone who entered the Guild building uninvited would die under many skilled blades and would pose little threat to those within the house.

Corelle returned to Water Street and made herself comfortable on the doorstep of a house across the street, near the corner. She sat with her head bowed to obscure her face from any casual observer, but not so low she could not spot any movement from the house or the street. After an hour, to her disappointment, the door opened behind her. She did not look round as a young boy spoke. "What are you about?"

"I am tired."

The child paused before he replied. "This is my house."

"That it is. Are you on your way out or have you come to talk to me?" Corelle kept her attention on the Guild building, frustrated the child had spotted her.

"My mother will be home soon."

The woman might arrive at any moment, or not for an hour or more. As Corelle weighed the risks of a confrontation with the mother that might attract unwelcome attention, her fortune changed. A man came out of the house, and he matched the description of Gill so well, she had no doubt it must be him. He looked around, wary, and his left ear confirmed his identity. The top had been sliced away, it seemed, a neat cut from a sharp blade. Corelle shuffled backward through the open door into the shadows inside the house. The boy sounded surprised. "Hey." He did not elaborate on his opinion of the development.

Gill stood outside the building for a time, then crossed the street. He walked four paces and re-crossed the street. He may have suspected somebody watched, or he might always move with such caution, but neither suited Corelle. His alertness would make him harder to follow without a high risk of detection. Gill crossed the street at a brisker pace and turned in her direction. She pulled the boy inside the house and closed the door until Gill's footsteps passed the house, then opened the door a crack. His back receded down the street, but as she leaned further out, he turned and walked back toward her. She whipped her head back, and when she looked again, he had gone, so she walked from the house without a backward glance at the boy.

She peered around the first corner in time to see Gill enter an alleyway on the opposite side of the street. He must have doubled back for no purpose other than to flush out anybody who followed him. She doubted he would double back again, so she ran along the street to the next corner and turned. When she reached the alleyway, she risked a furtive glance down it and saw a figure stride toward her, silhouetted against the light from the far end. She guessed it to be Gill as he continued along the alleyways, but the shadows hid any details, so she entered the alleyway and hoped her own silhouette would also be indistinguishable. The figure had almost reached her as she closed the gap between them, but they stopped and half-turned. Gill, without a doubt. He must have decided to head back the way he had come, so she pulled her dagger from her boot and ran toward him.

As she broke into a run, he ran away from her. No doubt he tried to flee because he saw her as a threat. She had a momentary advantage, for she had already been on the move as he turned, and she reached him before he could gain any speed. Corelle grabbed for his tunic and hissed at him. "Stand or die." He swatted behind himself at her arm, but the gesture cost him as he lost some balance from the effort, and she raised her dagger to his throat.

He came to a halt and stood motionless. "Corelle. You have found me at last."

"How do you know I come for you?"

He laughed. "A tenday ago, Styrrach received letters. They advised us of the death of your companion. I have expected you ever since."

"You have had a long wait, but now I have come."

"That you have. Before you kill me, I took no joy from the news. He did, but not me."

His words washed over her like the spray from the water as she sat at the front of the ship, a trifle to be ignored. "I am here to kill him and take vengeance for Deineike. Synna tells me you may be sympathetic and might assist me."

He drew in a sharp breath before he replied. "Is Synna with you?"

She supplied a cautious answer. He need not know everything. "That is not for you to know. Does he speak the truth?"

He laughed. "You cannot kill Styrrach. You had your chance, at the inn. You missed him then, and he is cornered, an injured animal now. He is more dangerous than ever. The Bailiff and Portreeve are in his pocket, and there are but two of you."

"I intend to feed them to the flames alongside him. I know of their involvement in his scheme, and I will take all their tomorrows also."

A few moments passed before he spoke again. "You rave. You might take Styrrach. The Bailiff is untouchable."

"We shall see. You can choose whether you live to see the outcome or not, but I plan to destroy his empire and him. It has already begun."

"Letters from a merchant mentioned your efforts to undermine his business, and he sent men to Ort in response. Your friends there lie dead under their blades already, my guess."

Corelle laughed, a bitter, ironic sound that echoed from the walls of the alleyway. "Do you mean Adijon and his companion? Adijon has gone wherever he travels to afterward, and the other has fled Dur thanks to my mercy."

She did not need to wonder whether her news surprised him; his wide eyes and open mouth confirmed it. "You are as capable as the rumours suggest. I see my ruin is upon me. Afterward, you should seek tally house owners at the docks. Parulo and Elger are two I have heard of, but there will be others. They are bound up in it somehow. They may have information to help you to kill Styrrach. It will not be easy, and the docks are watched, but you may be good enough—I am caught between doubt and uncertainty." He paused for a heartbeat. "Make it quick."

Corelle considered the information he had provided and wrestled with herself to determine his fate. "How many are in the building?"

"One. Styrrach is not there. I know not where he is."

Could she believe him? He seemed to know a little of Styrrach's scheme, but not enough to suggest Styrrach held him in close confidence. "You will live for now. I am sworn to kill him, but I sense you are not yet a significant part of his enterprise. You came to your position after I killed Sun, I guess, and Styrrach does not yet entrust you with all his secrets."

"Sky."

The correction irritated her. "I do not care about his name. I have changed it to 'Dead,' and I plan to rename more before my vengeance is satisfied. Do not alert Styrrach to our conversation unless you wish to be among their number."

He snorted. "If he learns you had me under your knife and allowed me to live, but I ran in terror, he will kill me where I stand. He will not learn of our conversation from me."

"Leave Alcmouth then and tell any whose lives you wish to save. I will burn all before me, and those who choose to remain will not be spared." She pushed him away from her. "Go."

He hesitated a moment, then turned and ran down the alleyway. Corelle returned the dagger to her boot and turned the conversation over in her mind. He had claimed only one member was inside the Guild building, but she could not trust that information. Styrrach must be there; he must know of her arrival in Alcmouth by now and would not be so reckless with his life as to have only one guard.

Gill had mentioned tally houses. Styrrach must use them to receive the goods he bought and sold. He might be at one of the houses, but if not, she could kill one of the owners, outrage Styrrach and flush him out so she could take him. The owners deserved it for their complicity in Styrrach's actions, after all else. She would weaken his enterprise in the process and send a message to the masters and merchants Ibie spoke with in Ort. It might serve to persuade some of them to Raolos's favour, which could be no bad thing. Her mind made up, she set off toward the docks.

As she walked, she reflected on gests she had carried out or heard about. Many of them had been tally masters—the one who had recognised Arella came to mind. That man had mentioned something about arguments over coin. Corelle and Arella had thought he meant the levies, but she now guessed he meant the share of Styrrach's coin he received. No doubt he had asked for more and had been killed for it. The two Gill had mentioned would be a blow to Styrrach's business if they lay dead at her feet. He would need to find replacements. Any disruption she brought to his enterprise must infuriate him more. He would make a mistake somewhere, and she would have him.

Twilight cloaked the docks by the time she arrived. Corelle had been more careful than usual after the contact with Gill. She did not know how he might react, but she could not trust him. He had given her some morsels of information, but he had not been the sympathetic ally Synna had become.

Both tally house owners proclaimed their vanity from their tally houses with large, bold signage that advertised their ownership. Corelle moved across the docks, worried she might be seen, then sat between some bales of cloth on the docks where she could monitor the doors of each. As darkness closed around her, a well-dressed man emerged from one of the tally houses. As he moved away, someone shouted to him. "Greetings, Elger."

The man laughed, waved at another behind her somewhere, and cried out in response. "Will you take a tankard?"

"That I will." Corelle tutted. An innocent must not die, and now she needed to decide whether to follow them and hope for an opportunity or wait for the other, Parulo. The old Ryl expression, *"Better the caged bird than two that fly free,"* seemed appropriate, and she decided to follow Elger.

Her mark joined his friend, and as they walked off together, they laughed at some jest one or the other had shared. The shadows of the darkened buildings aided Corelle as she stole along behind them, but her senses tingled, since those same shadows also served anybody who might seek to thrust their dagger into her. The men entered a tavern on the docks, and she paused. They had richer tastes than the mariners earlier in the day. This tavern had the look of wealthier patronage, with fresh paint and an elaborate sign outside. A burly man stood at the door, some form of guard, she reasoned. The noise from the tavern suggested many patrons enjoyed a drink at the end of their day.

When she ran around the next building, the tavern had a rear exit that posed a further problem; she could not watch both doors, but neither could she enter the tavernroom and risk discovery. If she had Synna with her, they could watch both exits, but she shook the futile thought from her head. She must roll the dice, so she gambled Elger would return to the tally house after he had taken his ale. She found a vantage point from where she could watch the front door.

They had been inside for an hour at the least when the other man came out of the tavern alone. He walked off in the direction of the docks, and Corelle cursed. Had her mark remained within to take more drinks with other friends, or had he slipped away through the rear exit? She debated within herself and resolved to run to the rear exit, but she had taken no more than two steps when movement at the door caught her eye, and Elger came out. He might have relieved himself after his friend left or had finished some conversation before he departed. Corelle slowed to a walk, crossed the street, and melted into the shadowy doorway of a chandlery near the tavern.

She pretended to study the window as Elger strode past her away from the docks. He appeared not to notice her, and as she followed him at a distance, she wondered why he walked rather than ride in a carriage, an idle thought to occupy her mind as she followed him. He did not deviate from his course and did not glance around as he walked, a man unworried that death dogged his footsteps.

Corelle closed behind him as he turned a corner into a different street. She checked her surroundings and saw nobody. In a soft, suggestive voice, she called his name, and he turned. When she came out of the shadows close to him, a smile formed on his lips.

Lantern light spilled from a nearby house, flashed on the blade of her dagger, and Elger smiled no more. He fell to the ground and clutched at the vermilion ribbon across his throat. Corelle did not break her stride as she crossed the street and slipped away into the shadows.

TWENTY-FOUR

STYRRACH RECEIVES SOME BAD NEWS

STYRRACH LAY ON THE COT IN THE HOUSE NEXT TO THE GUILD building for many hours as he reflected on all the developments since The Duke's Seat. Letters had arrived that morning from Ort. There had been no mention of the men he had sent north, but the letters said the new Portreeve had not yet located Corelle. Of more interest had been the news that a letter addressed to her had arrived at the Portreeve's Offices, and when the Portreeve had opened it, it revealed the address of Wilash and another, Klordia. Klordia must be the one Balgow's ineptitude had failed to kill, the one who had worked for Glailam's Senior Tally Master.

They now lived in Dur City. Styrrach had no contact there but would instruct Gill to send death north-east for them both, nonetheless. Gill would no doubt carp about insufficient numbers of members. He complained too much and had been a poor choice as

Senior Tally Master. His ability to scribe and understand numbers had been his sole useful characteristic, it turned.

Styrrach rose from the cot and passed through the passageway into his office. He opened the door to the parlour, where only one member sat at a low table. He played a solo card game and glanced up as Styrrach entered the parlour. "Has Gill been seen?"

The man appeared confused. "He emerged from your office earlier. Did you not see him there?"

Styrrach lied and hid all trace of surprise from his face. Gill must have been in the office while the Guildmeister rested in the adjacent house. "That I did, but I seek him again now, not hours since."

The man looked as though he now understood Styrrach's question. "He left. He did not say where he went."

Styrrach considered the man. Few of the members came to the building, and none of them sat there and played at cards. "Do you scribe?"

The man flicked his eyes to one side, as though he needed time to consider the changed direction of the conversation. "That I do."

Styrrach wondered whether he should replace Gill with this fellow, but at that moment, a red-faced man blustered in from the street. As Styrrach turned toward him, the man came to an abrupt halt and gasped. "News." Styrrach waited in silence, and the man appeared unsure whether to continue for long heartbeats. "Elger is dead, his throat cut this evening, near the docks."

Styrrach's fury burned within him. Corelle had arrived in Alcmouth and tried to undermine his operation further. She planned to kill his tally house owners. What other explanation could there be? No other Guild member would dare to kill without a gest from him. She had slit his throat, her signature, designed to send him a message. Styrrach had killed her degenerate plaything, and now Corelle had come here, bent on his downfall. She would not succeed.

He covered his rage with an outward calm. He could afford no show of weakness. "Summon all the members here without delay."

The man, a courier, Styrrach imagined, swallowed hard. "It is late."

"That it is." Styrrach waited as the man stood before him in confusion. "You are still here." The man turned and fled, and Styrrach sat at the table opposite the open-mouthed member. "Let us play."

An hour passed, and Styrrach thanked the fates they had not played for coin. Either the man must be Dur's most gifted card player or a cheat of unparalleled ability, for Styrrach had scarce won a hand. He should have been angry, should have killed the man where he sat, but it fascinated him, in truth. He contemplated a request to the man to reveal whatever ploy he used to ensure victory but refrained. Such skill should not be tainted by so ugly an accusation.

Two other members had arrived, and at last Gill entered the building. Nobody spoke. The three stood huddled together and watched the card game with interest that appeared to border on the morbid, as though they expected Styrrach to erupt in a fit of temper. Styrrach did not glance up from his cards. "How many do we wait for?"

Gill mumbled a miserable reply. "Two, if they come."

They did, although one of them came almost half of an hour later, by Styrrach's estimation. "Well played." He smiled at his opponent, who inclined his head in acknowledgment.

Styrrach stood. The red-faced man who had brought the news had not returned. Styrrach must have been correct, as usual; nothing but a courier. The Guildmeister looked from one to the other. Six members. No more remained? "Before the death of the Senior Aide, how many members did Balgow have?"

Gill looked upward and appeared to calculate. "Sixteen or so, my guess."

Styrrach could account for eleven of them. Balgow and Sky, Synna, the two sent to Ort and these six before him. "Five have not answered the call?"

"They have not been seen since…" Gill hesitated. "For some time."

Styrrach fixed him with a cold stare. "You have all heard the news tonight, I am sure. A trusted colleague has been slain by the jade, Corelle. She is to be hunted down. The honour gest is rescinded. Bring her before me, dead or alive. That is now the gest. One hundred regals the reward. Dead or alive." The members drifted out, silent, but Gill remained when all were gone. "You are still here."

"You will be alone if I leave. She might watch the building."

Styrrach laughed, a scornful laugh Gill must think had been directed at him. "Let her come. I almost killed her once, and I will succeed if she challenges me again. I am her equal and more, and now she is alone, without the help of her companion and the intervention of Raolos's men, I do not fear her." Gill stayed silent. "Do you fear her?"

"I fear her reputation."

"That disappoints me. Your tenure as Senior Aide is ended. I need no coward at my side." Styrrach turned, walked into the office, and closed the door. He would not give Gill the satisfaction of any sign of his fervent anger, lest the man mistake it for some weakness Corelle had unlocked. Gill had failed him and admitted he feared Corelle, a woman, which Styrrach could not tolerate in a Senior Aide. Once he heard the outer door close, he returned to the parlour, placed a hand on the chair the member who had played cards had been seated in, snatched it up, and smashed it over and over against the table. He demolished both and scattered the cards across the parlour.

Furious, Styrrach went through the passageway into the building next door. Time to leave. The death of Elger would send the Bailiff off into yet another round of recriminations and self-concerned anxiety. The Guild had been reduced to a handful of members, Raolos worked to undermine his business, and Corelle had arrived in Alcmouth to kill his partners in that business. Without Styrrach, the enterprise would collapse, and the Bailiff and Portreeve might be exposed and hanged.

Styrrach's neck would not wear the noose. He would gather his coin, and within a day or two he could sail away from this tragic land. He could return south to Qagrue, a land where the sun shone for more than a few days each year, the citizens were not spoon-fed innocents with more righteous indignation than spine, and he would be a rich and well-respected member of society.

His parents had always described Dur as strait-laced and uneventful. They had moved to Qagrue before he had been born but talked of their homeland all the time. As the years passed and he listened to their stories, he sensed a weakness in Dur ripe for the exploitation. He persuaded a merchant to sell him a ship's hold of goods; goods his parents told him could not be found in Dur. The purchase of the goods and the rental of the ship's hold had taken all the coin he possessed and some extra he stole from his parents, but he planned to sell them at an exorbitant price in the little land of his ancestry and grow rich. The scheme became more successful than he had dared to hope, so he expanded it and recruited Krage, then others, to share in his enterprise as it grew too large for him to manage alone. He controlled it still, but others carried out the day-to-day work.

A competitor once attempted to approach one of the southern merchants, as Raolos now did, and Styrrach knew only one way to remove the competitive threat. The ordinary people of Dur would be horrified by murder, so Styrrach had formed the Guild. He soon found men who were undaunted by the prospect of murder for a few regals, and there had been no real threats to his expansion from that day forward.

Until now. Corelle threatened his success, and against all the odds and his own endeavours, she had become a credible risk. He had sufficient coin, and he no longer needed more, in truth. The signs all pointed south. He would see her dead, nonetheless. She had become an irritant, and he yearned to flush her from the land before he left. He craved that more than all his coin. In Zhanghar, she had been nothing more than a deviant member whose resolve had wavered. He had selected her to be shrouded to remove her degenerate tendencies from the Guild, but she had become so much more now.

He hated her. Why would he not hate her? She had almost destroyed his organisation, but he would see her dead within a day, two at most, then he would leave. He lay on the cot and found he had become aroused by the thought of Corelle's death, and he laughed to himself. She would be horrified by a man who became aroused at the thought of her. He pleasured himself as he imagined her mutilation, and as blood spurted from her sex in his mind, his passion shot from his manhood into his trousers.

TWENTY-FIVE
THE DESTRUCTION OF THE TRIANGLE

WITH ELGER DEAD, CORELLE MADE HER WAY BACK TO WATER STREET. She stayed on the opposite side of the street and used the darkness to cover her cautious approach to within four houses of the Guild building. A low hedge gave her a good view of the Guild's door, so she lay on her stomach behind it. She would be difficult to see as she lay in near darkness. It seemed the best location to wait and see what fell out of the cage she had rattled.

Little more than an hour passed before footsteps echoed down the street. Not a Guild member; the person made too much noise for that, but the feet ran with an urgency that must mean they came with news of Elger's death. She had the right of it. The feet ran into the Guild building and carried a slim man inside with them. He panted, his breath whistled in his chest, and she guessed he either did not often exert himself or had run a substantial distance.

Within a few moments, he came out of the building and ran off again. Corelle wondered whether she should follow him but decided to await developments. Gill had claimed Styrrach had not been in the house earlier, and if he had told the truth, she must wait for the Guildmeister to arrive. When he did, she might see an opportunity to take him in the street before anybody inside the building could aid him.

Still as a stone, Corelle lay with her dagger covered by her arm, protection against any treacherous glimmer of light that might betray her position with a flash from the steel of its blade.

Within an hour, two men arrived together. They spoke in hushed tones, and she could not hear what they said, but they entered the building. Not long afterward, Gill also entered. Styrrach must have returned before she arrived, and the slim man had brought him the news of her handiwork. The Guildmeister had summoned all his members to him, she reasoned, but to what end? Did he surround himself with a wall of daggers she could not penetrate?

After half of an hour, two more appeared and entered the building. She had counted five, plus Styrrach. Insurmountable odds. She could not kill them all, since Styrrach would sacrifice all five before he would risk harm to himself. She could not succeed tonight. There must be more members in Alcmouth, but none arrived. More might already have been inside before she arrived. Some may have fled—Synna and the one in Ort had abandoned the Guild, and she had told Gill to leave and warn others. Still, she could contrive of no workable plan to kill Styrrach with so many members in the building. She would leave and begin again tomorrow.

Corelle sighed in frustration. Had her plan been so perfect she had driven Styrrach to ground and brought herself undone? She had killed Elger, which seemed the ideal way to spark Styrrach's temper and flush him into the open, but it might now have had the opposite effect to the one she desired. Curse it, she must return to her room.

She pushed herself up onto her elbows, ready to crawl backward and abandon her hideout, but the door to the building opened, and several men emerged. She froze, half raised from the ground, fearful one of them might spot any hint of movement from the corner of an eye. Five men emerged, but Gill did not come out with them. Her muscles screamed in protest as she held the uncomfortable position, and the men talked among themselves in hushed voices, but she did not dare to move.

At last, they moved away, and she lowered herself to the ground again with a sigh of relief. Gill remained inside, and others too, for all she knew. At least one more had come out than had gone in. Five went in, and five had come out, but Gill made six. She did not know what task the five had been dispatched to perform but guessed they had been sent to find and kill her. How to proceed now? If only Styrrach and Gill remained within, she could take them both with surprise and some luck, but she had no idea of the building's layout or of where the two men might be, and there may well be others. Better to remain hidden and await further developments for a time.

Once again, she did not have long to wait. Gill followed the others out into the street, and he did not check his surroundings as he had done earlier in the day. He appeared dejected. He had not taken her advice to flee, and he served as Styrrach's Senior Aide, so he must have told the Guildmeister of his meeting with Corelle. Styrrach would not have shown him any kindness once he learned Gill had missed an opportunity to kill her. That might explain his miserable demeanour. Doubtless, Styrrach had belittled him in some way. Corelle knew the Guildmeister and his barbed tongue, knew the wounds it could inflict even as it left no visible trace.

Corelle decided to follow him to see if she could learn more about what had turned. If Styrrach had stayed inside, alone, she should enter and kill him, there could be no doubt, but if he held back members for his own protection, and he must have done so, it would be a fatal mistake to blunder into the building alone. She followed Gill at a distance, out of sight, and he turned at the corner. He walked past the alleyway, and once he reached a dark stretch of the street, she called to him.

He turned to seek her, and she stepped out from the shadow before him. He seemed uncertain; afraid. She hissed into his face. "You did not take my advice. I warned you of the consequences if you ignored it."

He looked at the ground, then back up to her face. "Where would I go? I have little coin, and if Styrrach did not hunt me down and slay me, you would."

"He is in the building?"

"That he is."

Corelle had guessed as much but needed more information before she made her decision. "I saw six leave, if I count you. How many remain?"

"No others. Styrrach alone."

Could she trust him? The thought enticed her, but she must not follow her heart. A cool head makes better decisions than a passionate heart, after all else. "Describe the building."

"The outer door opens into a parlour. His office door sits in one wall. There is a staircase and a small pantry at the back of the parlour. There are two bedrooms up the stairs, and a small privy."

It sounded much like the Zhanghar building. Styrrach would be in his office; he liked to intimidate and manipulate the members in the smaller room. She could slip inside unheard and open the office door. He would sit or stand with his back to the door, as he always did. He might have no time to react before she took him. If Gill had told her the truth, of course. "Do you lie to me?"

"That I do not. He asked me if I fear you, and I told him I do. I am removed as Senior Aide. The members seek you—one hundred regals the reward. Dead or alive—his words."

Corelle glanced around at this development, irritated. She had overlooked a dangerous possibility. The members all sought her death for a vast reward, and Gill might be the bait in a perfect trap. They might converge on her now, intent on her ruin and the reward. "Have you betrayed me?"

"Betrayed you? How?"

"Do others come here now to save you? Are you the bait to lure me out?" She glanced around again but saw nothing suspicious.

He paused, then laughed, a reaction she had not anticipated. "That would have been a fine plan. You have greater guile than him, however, and he has not considered this possibility." He shook his head and let out a huff of breath from his nose.

She could not trust him, and she must act, whatever fates were written. "Have you warned him I am here to kill him?"

He blinked. "That I have not."

She gazed into his eyes and saw no lie, but she made up her mind as Deineike's battered face swam before her. What had turned at the inn could not be forgiven. Her lips curled back from her clenched teeth. "You should have sent somebody to warn us as he descended upon us at The Duke's Seat."

He looked puzzled. "Why would I have done so?"

She transformed her snarl into a cold, contemptuous smile. "Why? Because had you done so, Deineike would still be alive, and I would not be your ruin." Her hand flashed upward, and her dagger opened his throat from one side to the other. He stared at her for a heartbeat, wide-eyed, then fell sideways into the street. She turned and walked away before his lifeless body struck the ground.

Corelle had killed Gill out of spite. It had been an act of temper unlike any gest she had ever carried out in her life. It had not been the vengeance Deineike's life demanded—that required other deaths, but some small part of that price had been paid.

She returned to Water Street. Much now depended on the truth of Gill's words. If Styrrach did remain in the house alone, she had her chance to kill him. If two or more members guarded him, she doubted she could succeed. Gill said he had been removed as Senior Aide, so he may have told the truth out of bitterness. That might also have been an elaborate fabrication, of course. On balance, she wanted to believe him, but her fates rested on her next decision.

Corelle stood across from the building. No light shone from inside, but heavy shutters would cover the upstairs and downstairs windows. The Guild would permit no curious eyes to peer through the window and see things they should not. She had not attempted to disguise her approach, but nobody had confronted her. The others had gone in search of her. One of them, however, might return if they guessed her intentions.

As the memory of Deineike's devastated face in the inn came to her mind, she made her decision, and she snarled again. It must be now, or it might be never. Without hesitation, she strode to the door and tried the handle. As she had anticipated, the door had not been locked. The handle gave a small metallic squeak as she turned it, but she had passed the point at which she could turn back. If the noise from the door betrayed her, she must hope Styrrach believed one of the members returned with news that would make the Guildmeister a hundred regals poorer.

She turned the handle further, stepped through the door, and closed it behind her, the dagger before her in readiness. As Gill had described, the door opened straight into a parlour. A few chairs occupied the room, along with the remnants of more scattered around among some playing cards. Unless the remains of a table lay among the broken chairs, none could be seen. Corelle hoped she lay behind the destruction of the furniture, that

Styrrach had burst into a rage when he heard she had killed Elger.

Gill told her the closed door to one side of the parlour led to Styrrach's office. She skipped past it and peered up the staircase. No light shone upstairs, and a lantern on a cupboard against the wall opposite Styrrach's office illuminated the parlour. When she returned to the office door and listened against it, she heard no sound, but she waited, patient. If the squeak from the handle had been overheard, curiosity would lead somebody to come out of the office to investigate it in time. Styrrach loved to humiliate and intimidate, and he stood with his back to the door, silent and motionless, to enhance his menace. His patience would only be tested so far though, and if his office door did not open, curiosity must require him to investigate.

Long moments passed, nobody emerged, and Corelle heard nothing through the door. No breaths, no slight cough, no foot shuffled or chair creaked. She did not move, silent as a blade of grass as it grows, her breaths slow, rhythmical, and through her nose. She could listen at the door all night, but it would achieve nothing, so she reached up in one smooth motion and took a firm grip that did not disturb the handle. She slowed her breaths even more and concentrated on the handle. No room now for anxiety, excitement, or nervousness to bring her undone. Jorinda stood on the brink of the most important gest in her life, and she did not wish it to turn awry. At that moment, she recalled Arella's voice in The Ship's Yard on some occasion or another, heard her say, "*I never fail.*" Corelle did not share Arella's blind faith in her abilities. She weighed all possibilities and gambled only on the probability of a successful outcome.

Corelle turned the handle and pushed the door open, then stepped through as it opened. She moved to one side, crouched low. Nobody. She held her position for a moment, then straightened and allowed herself a long, slow breath as she gazed around the office. The anticipated chair and table stood there, unbroken, but little else other than a few pieces of parch on the table. Styrrach was not here. Either Gill had lied or Styrrach had left while she questioned the former Senior Aide.

Corelle cursed herself for the decision to follow Gill, a decision that appeared to have cost her the chance to kill Styrrach tonight. She took a step forward into the room, and to her surprise, as she stood deep in thought about her next move, the wall opposite her moved. It opened inward and Styrrach stood in a narrow passageway behind it, his eyes wide with surprise as he saw her.

Styrrach broke the lengthy silence that ensued. "You. How have you come here?" His voice, familiar, unpleasant, stirred her hatred like a breeze blows dust from the street. It rose around her, surrounded her, consumed her.

"I used the door." Corelle did not laugh at her own jest. She stared at his thin face with its sunken cheekbones, his shoulder length dark hair and his wiry frame. She loathed him, but she fought to control emotions that wanted to shake her to pieces and urged her to leap forward, driven by blind hatred rather than the cunning of an experienced killer.

He gave a terse laugh. "What do you think you will do here?"

"That which I have done to your tally house puppet and your Senior Aide already. I am here to kill you in payment for the death of Deineike."

"Gill is dead?"

"That he is, unless he can survive without blood in his veins."

He nodded. "A weak, easy mark, filled with fear of you, and Elger nothing but a tally house owner. You now face the best, and your fate is written." He sneered, but his eyes did not change, emotionless and barren, a parch filled with scribing nobody could read.

She needed one more answer before she allowed her blade to

perform its deadly work. "Before I send you wherever you travel to afterward, I wish to know why you shrouded me."

His bitter laughter laid waste to the silent emptiness of the building. "I shrouded you for the same reason I shrouded the others. These weak Durfolk cannot stand to see death in their streets. Somebody's neck must pay the price for the deaths, or the Portreeve might lose face, and a Portreeve who is out of favour is no use to me. I chose Guild members to pay that price. You had lost interest in your work, and if I needed another reason, I could not tolerate a deviant in our midst. The choice required no consideration, in truth."

"You sacrificed members for no reason?"

Corelle jumped as he barked out a short, scornful laugh. "I sacrificed them for the best reason there is—coin. As long as everything continued to accrue to my favour, the lives of a few members mattered not at all." A malicious grin split his face.

He had not moved throughout the conversation, but at once he grasped at the chair near him and hurled it at her. He had tried to catch her unawares, but his eyes had flicked to the chair a heartbeat before he reached for it. Corelle stepped to one side as he threw it, and it hit the wall where she had stood a heartbeat before. She crouched and raised her dagger as some fragments of the chair struck her but caused no injury. Styrrach pulled his dagger from his belt, and they faced one another across the room.

Corelle gave him a cold smile. "You will now go to join Hiw, Porl, Sky and Gill."

He laughed again. His malignant chuckle that might have cowed lesser adversaries, and it sent cold chills through Jorinda's body. "I have a higher hand. What did you call her? Deineike?"

"Never would I have believed her name could sound as ugly as it does when it spills from your lips." She kept her eyes locked on his as she watched for some hint if he moved to attack.

"I imagine any deviant's name sounds ugly enough."

Corelle resorted to the ruse that had brought Hiw's companion undone, and she straightened. "I cannot live without her, in truth. Send me to her." She lowered her dagger, but her eyes did not leave his.

He took a step forward. "A feeble attempt at deception. Is this your strongest hand? I would not be taken in by any word you spoke, jade. You are a deviant, and your words are as repugnant as your desires."

He took another tentative step toward her, and she slashed her dagger up from her side, as fast as the crack of a whip. He stepped back, but her dagger nicked his leg and cut his trousers. Blood appeared from the cut, and she taunted him. "Is that the same leg Deineike stabbed you in?"

He smiled, cold and vicious. "Your blade is keen."

"It should be, for Wilash made it."

Anger flickered across his eyes, and he mumbled. "Another traitor I must deal with before I leave." She wondered if he had spoken to her or reminded himself of some promise

He had bested her, after all else. He had distracted her with his words, and while she considered them, Styrrach lunged forward and thrust his dagger toward her heart. The attack caught her unawares, and Corelle reacted too late. She could not avoid injury, but she might yet cheat death. She stepped to one side and turned away from him, too late to avoid the dagger, as she had known it would be. The blade pierced her left arm high up, close to the shoulder, and his momentum drove it deep into her. Agony coursed through her, and blood sprayed out of the wound onto Styrrach and the floor around her. She could not suppress a scream of pain as the dagger embedded itself deep in her.

He reached up with his other hand, grabbed a handful of her hair, and wrenched it downward. Corelle screamed again, and agony burned through her scalp. He tried to pull her off balance, but his body twisted sideways as he tugged at her hair. She brought her left fist up into his groin, and he in turn cried in agony as her punch crushed his stones. He tried to step back, released her hair, and squinted as tears sprang to his eye. Floods of pain washed through her body, but Corelle clenched her teeth against them and brought her dagger up across his stomach. With a savage howl, she slashed it across the width of his body with all the strength of her pent-up hatred and fury. Her blade opened a deep cut across his stomach, a gash so brutal and deep, the dagger struck his ribcage. The impact jarred it from her grip, and it flew across the room.

He looked down as his lifeblood gushed out of his stomach, and he brought both hands together over the horrendous wound across his entire stomach. He looked up at her with a quizzical expression and took a step back. "I trained you well." He gave one last bitter laugh.

"You did not train me." Blood gushed out of him, and much of it soaked her. Her trousers had turned red from his blood, and he gave a small, strangled cry as he collapsed to his knees.

Corelle clenched her teeth and pulled his dagger free of her arm with another scream of agony. Blood poured down her arm and ran from her fingers onto the floor like a waterfall. Styrrach reached for the table as he swayed, his skin pale. His face twisted in anger, and she drove his own dagger into his left eye. She did not take her gaze from his as she watched the last remnants of life leave him, and he pitched forward. The blade of his dagger snapped as his face hit the floor and the handle clattered across the room.

TWENTY-SIX
RICHES BEYOND THE DREAMS OF AVARICE

Styrrach lay dead at Corelle's feet, but she heard her own ruin call her name. Her legs trembled, and she almost fell backward. She must stop the blood that poured from her arm, so she crossed the room, picked up her dagger, and cut strips from her bloodied tunic. She wrapped one strip around her arm above the wound, held one end in her teeth, formed a knot, and pulled it tight with her other hand. She wadded another up and used a third to tie the wadded cloth on top of the wound in her arm.

Out of some habit, Corelle bent and felt at Styrrach's neck but found no pulsing. At once, tears leapt to her eyes, and she slumped to the floor next to his body. She cried in part from the pain that coursed through her, but above all, she cried for Deineike, whose vengeance she had visited on Styrrach, but who had not returned to her in exchange for the Guildmeister's life. The sand fell as she sat and sobbed in a pool of blood that spread across the floor all around her.

Her makeshift bandage had already become soaked in blood, and if she did not receive some attention for her wound, she would bleed to death. She would welcome death once the Bailiff had answered for his part in Deineike's death, but that price had not yet been paid, and she must make some effort to collect the debt, at the least.

Waves of pain tore through her as she dragged herself to her feet and bent again to wipe the blade of her dagger on Styrrach's back. His dead fingers clutched a sizeable tuft of her hair. On an instinct, she raised a hand to her head, and it came away bloodied, but she could not tell whether the blood came from her head or had already covered her hands from the fight.

She gazed in wonder at the passage behind the wall he had appeared from, but before she could decide whether to investigate or leave and seek help, the handle of the outer door squeaked. She crouched, then turned to face the open door as footsteps approached it from the parlour, her dagger held ahead of her body.

A man's face peered around the door, and his mouth dropped open as he beheld the carnage of the office. "What..." His question died in his throat as he met Corelle's eyes.

"Styrrach is dead. You need not join him, but I will kill you if I must."

"Corelle?"

She did not recognise him, and she laughed. "You will not now collect your hundred regals. You will not be sold to the Portreeve for a fraction of that amount either, for he has fallen to me."

"Sold? You rave. Your injury weakens your mind."

"My mind had been weakened long before this injury, but all that turned between him and me began when he sold me to the Portreeve. He has sold colleagues and friends of yours; I have no doubt of it. Synna had a friend whom the Portreeve hanged some passes ago. All Styrrach's endeavour." She sighed, dizzy and faint. "You may believe me or not, I care not. If you attack me, you may kill me. If you stand here and discuss Styrrach with me, I will bleed to death anyway. Attack me or stand aside, those are your choices, and I must press you for an urgent decision."

He flicked his gaze to her arm. "I had no love for him, and now he is gone, and Gill too, the Guild is no more, my guess."

"You know of Gill's death?"

"He lies in the street not far from here. The Portreeve's men are there, called by a local. I came past there moments ago. You killed him?"

She wiped at her eyes, filled with a sudden regret for that impulse. "That I did. I have done worse things, but I could have let him live. Anger and grief drove me. There you have it. What is scribed, must be. What is your decision?"

"You need help, or you will bleed to death, as you have said. Come, I will run for a healer. Sit down and try to move as little as possible. You cannot walk the streets dressed in the blood of Styrrach." He turned, ran from the building, and left Corelle to decide what he intended.

He might bring others, afraid to challenge her alone even in her weakened state. He might disappear and abandon her to bleed to death, or he might bring the healer he had promised. He had the right of it about her clothes. Blood covered her, and her shortened tunic exposed her stomach. She turned, placed her dagger on the table, and retied the bandages tighter. She inspected the passageway and pulled the wall to but did not close it lest she could not open it afterward. She hoped the man had not noticed it, but she could not be certain.

She picked up her dagger from the table, slid into it her boot, closed the office door, and sat on a chair in the parlour. Her head swam, her sight blurred as dizziness threatened to overwhelm her, and it seemed she might not live to kill the Bailiff after all else. The door handle squeaked again, and the man returned with another who carried a small leather satchel. That man looked aghast at the sight of her and rushed to untie her bandages. As he tugged at the sleeve of her tunic, Corelle pulled her dagger from her boot and cut the sleeve away above the wound.

He wiped at the wound with the cast-off sleeve and sighed. "A bad incision. There is a risk of damage to the muscle, but the bigger risk is loss of blood. I must close the wound and stop the bleeding. You have been fortunate indeed. The knife missed the artery here. Had that been cut, you might already be dead."

Corelle glanced up at the Guild member, who looked on in curiosity, before she replied. "Do what you must."

"Quite." The healer opened his satchel and turned to the other. "Is there water?"

The Guild man nodded and went to the rear of the house, where he reached into an alcove Corelle had not noticed and picked up a bowl. He carried it back and placed it on the floor next to her. Some water sloshed about in the bowl, and the healer dipped the discarded sleeve of her tunic into it, then wiped the wound with it. He adjusted the bandage above the wound and tied it tight. He took a needle from his satchel, not unlike one of her own making needles, and pushed a thread through its eye.

"This will hurt." Corelle laughed. How could it hurt more than the blade that caused the injury? He pushed the needle through her arm, and she groaned in pain as he wove it back and forth across the wound until he had closed the wound. He pulled clean cloth from his satchel, formed a wad, and tied it around her arm. He seemed satisfied, and the wound no longer gushed blood.

"You will need to take care of the wound and replace this pad at whiles. Do not allow infection into the wound."

"Inflammation." She felt tired, faint, and struggled to concentrate on his words.

He looked up at her and smiled. "Quite." He stood and seemed to notice her head for the first time. He tutted and wiped her head with the damp sleeve from her tunic. "These injuries…"

"It is better you do not ask."

He stood, hesitated, then turned to the Guild member. "Do I perform this work as a favour?"

With a struggle, Corelle reached into her pocket, pulled out a pouch, and waved it at the healer. "I have coin."

He took it, reached inside, and took some coins. "My thanks." He turned and left.

Corelle looked up at the Guild member. "My thanks also. You need not have helped me, after all that has turned. What will you do now?"

He waved a hand at her and laughed. "I must find another trade, it seems. My deadly skills may no longer be in demand here unless you intend to become the new Guildmeister."

She could not subdue a weak laugh at his jest. "That I do not."

"Farewell Corelle. What has turned this last year, I cannot guess. Your name has come to my ears many times, and now I see you are all that has been rumoured, and more. If you see Synna again, greet him for me and remind him he owes me six groats."

Corelle laughed, her mood lifted by their camaraderie. "Take the groats from my pouch. I will clear his debt and his dishonour."

He smiled. "I do not think I will insist on repayment. My thanks. Fass is my name." He offered her a hand, and she gave it a weak shake before he left Corelle to sit in silence and consider her next move. Styrrach lay dead, but the Bailiff still lived. Fass had the right of it, she thought. She could not walk the street covered in so much blood, more so if the Portreeve's men were abroad in the quarter in pursuit of Gill's killer.

Corelle wondered about the staircase, so she washed her hands and arms in the bloodied water, picked up the lantern, and went to the rear of the house. The pantry lay empty, and she climbed the stairs, slow and steady as she tested each one before she trusted her weight to it. Her left arm hung stiff at her side, and every movement of her body sent shock waves of pain through her from the wound.

At the top of the stairs, she found two bedrooms off a short landing, as Gill had said. A layer of dust covered the floor, unmarked by footprints. She walked into the first room and shone the lantern about. It surprised her to find no cots in the room, and the same when she checked the other bedroom. Two cloaks hung from a wooden peg on the back of the second room, and she picked one from the peg to examine it. Made from wool, dark grey and with a hood, it stank, but it would serve to disguise her bloody clothes when she left the building.

Corelle carried the lantern back down the stairs, the cloak slung over her shoulder, and returned to the office. She marvelled at the mysterious wall and checked the other three walls. She pushed on them, but none opened as the one that had admitted Styrrach earlier. She scooped up the parch and letters from the table before she pushed open the wall and exposed the passageway. Scratches in the floorboards and a pattern in the dust indicated where the panel had opened and closed, and she admired the ingenious feature of the building. She could see no way to open it from the Guildmeister's office; no latch or keyhole could be found, but inside the passageway she found a latch. She pushed the door closed with a metallic click. She used the latch to open it again and studied the office side of the panel around the area of the latch. Above the door, marks high up on the panel suggested there might be a hidden device that opened it.

Curiosity nagged at her to explore what lay beyond the passageway, so she did not want to close the door and lock herself in Styrrach's office. She stepped through into the passageway, closed the door behind her, wandered forward, and emerged into a parlour like the one in the Guild building. She must be in the house next door, but the passageway mystified her, since she would have expected the buildings to be separated only by a wall without room for a passageway.

A cot stood in the room, a pack next to it. She opened the pack and found some men's clothes along with more letters and parch. A pouch with a substantial amount of coin lay wrapped in a tunic at the bottom of the pack. Corelle dropped the pouch, the cloak, and the parch onto the cot and continued to explore the second house, upstairs and downstairs. Other than the cot and pack, it appeared to be empty and unused.

She sat on the cot and read the letters, curious to learn what they concerned. The Portreeve in Ort had opened a letter addressed to her and sent Wilash's address to Styrrach. Chills ran down her spine. Corelle had still not sent her letter to Wilash, and now she must open it to add a caution, since the Guild may already have been dispatched to find him. She read the account of Deineike's death and Pyre and wiped her eyes with the back of a hand as the memory stung her.

There were letters from the Bailiff and some of the Portreeves around Dur. Most were cryptic, summonses for meetings and the like. One suggested the Portreeve of Vjort might be ready to join Styrrach's scheme. In another, the Portreeve of Zhanghar said a killer must be found and hanged as several prominent citizens had complained about the death of a local man. Corelle remembered the gest, although it had not been assigned to her or Arella. As she read the letter again, she realised it held proof that tied the Portreeve to the Guild, and she scrabbled among the letters for any from the Bailiff addressed to Styrrach. She found a reference to a meeting at "RT," whatever that meant, some time ago, but no others had been sent direct to the Guildmeister. It would be enough, and she slapped a hand on the cot in elation. She had found proof the Bailiff and the Portreeves did business with Styrrach.

Corelle paused, her smile frozen in place. She could prove they did business. If she wished to paint Styrrach as a killer, she must give evidence of the things he had ordered her to do. He had attacked her and Deineike in The Duke's Seat, and had killed a man in Raolos's office, but those things did not link the Bailiff to his organisation. The letter in Zhanghar had been worded to suggest nothing more than a cry for justice to a prominent businessman of the city. If she gave the evidence that provided the link, she would be hanged and would not see the Bailiff die. Worse, only one person would act on the letters and her evidence—the Duke, and she could not expect an audience with him since she had threatened him and his men.

Corelle paced the room. She would need Raolos's help, but he had made it clear he wished her gone from his life. Despite Raolos's desire never to see her again, the continued corruption of Portreeves throughout the land must convince him. He must see her if she could bring proof to him, proof he could present to the Duke and bring down those Portreeves, and the Bailiff with them, but what if he still refused to see her and ordered her run out of Ort on sight? The puzzle needed further thought.

As the word "puzzle" passed through her mind, she decided to investigate the strange panel again. She pressed her ear against the inside of the panel, heard no sound from beyond, pulled the latch, and opened the door. She reached up toward the marks she had noticed earlier, though she had to raise herself onto her toes to reach it. When she struck the panel near the marks, she heard a click from the latch. That must be how the doorway opened from the office side. An ingenious escape route for one paranoid about their own safety, she decided. She stepped through and shone the lantern around in the passageway, still uncertain why it existed, and gazed at both side walls for some time. High up on one side, the wall appeared warped, and she reached up and struck it, as she had in Styrrach's office. She returned to Styrrach's office, picked up his chair, and carried it back to the passageway. She closed the panel behind her.

When she stood on the chair, she could reach all the way to the ceiling, and when she struck the wall where it joined the ceiling, she heard another metallic click. The side wall moved inwards, so she moved the chair and pushed on the wall. It resisted her, and she grunted as she pushed at it with her right shoulder. It would not move far, but she created a gap wide enough to squeeze through. Her left shoulder rubbed against the door, and she doubled up in agony as she clutched at the wound and gritted her teeth. Her vision swam before her, and she feared she would faint from the pain. Tears streamed down her cheek as she cried in despair at the unbearable ache in her arm.

The pain subsided at last, and Corelle found herself in a space between the two walls, a large trunk on the floor, covered in a thick layer of dust. As she tried to open the trunk, she disturbed the dust and sneezed often. Sweat dripped from her face, and she grunted and heaved, but she could not open the lid and did not wish to risk her dagger on an attempt to pick the lock with only one useful arm, so she went back to the pack where she had found Styrrach's letters. She inspected every part of it and tipped all its contents onto the floor.

Corelle could not find a key but felt sure it must be somewhere in the house. If the trunk belonged to Styrrach, he would have kept the key near him even when he had left Alcmouth, so it must be in the pack. Impatient, she tore at some of the seams of the pack, then drew a deep breath and paid them greater attention. At length, thanks to her making abilities, she spotted a piece of stitching that looked different from the rest of the pack. Most eyes would not have marked the slight difference at all, but to Corelle the pattern stood out, a subtle difference, as her own stitches might have been from her mother's.

When she unpicked the stitches, she found several small keys in a hidden flap beneath. She congratulated herself on her cleverness and returned to the trunk. She tried some of the keys in the lock until, with a delightful click, it opened, and she pulled the lid up. She coughed and sneezed anew as the disturbed dust filled her mouth and surrounded her, and she wafted at it with her good arm. Countless pouches had been stacked inside the trunk, and when she pulled one open, she gasped at the sight of a vast quantity of coin. The coin weighed so much, she struggled to lift the pouch from the trunk. If all the pouches weighed the same, the trunk would require two or more strong men to lift and could only be carried any distance on a cart.

Corelle took every pouch out of the trunk. The vast wealth Klordia had alluded to lay around her feet, and she slapped a hand to her forehead and shook her head in disbelief. The dust suggested this trunk had lain here unopened for years. How much more had Styrrach hidden away in other places? Some of the pouches held precious stones rather than coin, and she recognised some of the stones the wealthy folk of Ryl liked to have attached to their finest gowns, knew how much they cost. Diamonds, rubies, and amethyst she recognised, but some she did not; a pale green stone, another a dark orange, and a blue stone that dazzled in its intensity and reminded her of Deineike's eyes, or Arella's.

Corelle piled most of the pouches back into the trunk. She kept two pouches of the stones and one of coin, although the coins weighed too much to carry with any comfort, so she poured some of them back into the trunk. Only once she had tipped half of the pouch's contents into the trunk could she carry it. She locked the trunk and dropped the key into a trouser pocket, relieved she had not picked the lock and risked any damage to it.

She struggled to pull the wall closed and cursed her left hand, all but useless in the task. Whenever she moved the arm, it sent unbearable spasms of pain through her body. She closed the panel at last as sweat ran down from her brow to sting her eyes, and she put the letters and the pouches into Styrrach's pack. By the time she added the pouch she had left on the cot, the pack had become so heavy, she grunted with effort as she raised it to her shoulder. Although the outer door had been locked, the key had been left in the lock, and she opened it enough to peer out. Night still lay on the city, but the dawn could not be far away. She pulled the cloak about her, the smell of decay and dampness disgusting in her nostrils, but it hid her bloodied clothes, and she wrapped it tight about herself, hoisted the pack onto her shoulder, then had to drop it again to lock the door.

At last, the door locked, the keys in the pack, and the pack across her shoulder, she set off. She walked at a steady pace away from the street where she had killed Gill and took a circuitous route to The Common Inn, latched the door, placed her dagger under the pillow, and fell into a heavy sleep.

Some hours later, she woke as light crept around the edges of the window shutters, and when she opened them the bustle of city life filled the street outside. It must already be after the midday, so she exchanged her bloodied clothes for fresh ones, slipped her dagger into her boot, and transferred the letters, keys and pouches into her own pack, hoisted it onto her shoulder and set off for the dock.

As she walked, she realised she might now be the wealthiest person in all Dur, far richer than the women she had been so contemptuous of when she made dresses for them in her father's shop in Ryl. She laughed at the thought, heedless of what people around her thought. She turned a street corner and saw the watery sunlight dance on the surface of the River Alc ahead of her.

TWENTY-SEVEN
CORELLE SAILS NORTH

PETTRA DABBED THE LACE-TRIMMED KERCHIEF AT HER EYES. SHE AND Raolos argued again, and as ever, they argued round and round but never reached a conclusion. Jorinda had left a tenday or more ago, and every day since, Raolos and Pettra had revisited the worn-out arguments about their respective sexual infidelities. Pettra had moved out of their bedroom into one of her own, but he came and went whenever he felt the need to antagonise her.

Fury consumed Pettra every time Raolos professed his hurt because she had lain with Jorinda despite his own dalliance with Hylsie, a dalliance that produced a child. Pettra had raised Raopul as her own despite the true nature of his parenthood; the boy could not be blamed in truth, but it had taken all Pettra's resolve to accept the situation and save face for her husband in the decent society in which they moved. That society's expectations had locked her into a marriage with a man even as the desire to lie with a woman burned within her for most of her adult life. Jorinda had set loose those desires, and now Raolos punished her for it every day.

Anger turned Raolos's face scarlet, and his eyes were wet with tears as he again berated her. Pettra lost her temper, as she almost always did, and his voice rose to a yell. "You do not understand how it frustrates me. You mope around the house and sulk over a woman you will never see again. She is dead, I imagine."

She screamed at him, furious. "You monster. Do not say such things. Jorinda will come back for me once Deineike is avenged." Fresh tears streamed from her eyes.

"Deineike cannot be avenged. Jorinda betrayed her as much as she did me. I hope never to see that creature again. She has destroyed our life together, and you cannot see past your infatuation to accept it."

"I am not infatuated. I love her. You know nothing of love."

He sighed. "Pettra, you do not love her. You are infatuated, nothing more." The anger left his eyes, and a terrible sadness flooded them. "Did you ever love me?"

She sniffed and threw the saturated kerchief at him, then snatched another from the open dresser drawer beside her. Had she ever loved him? He had been a kind suitor, and both sets of parents had believed it a good match. He had been funny, amiable and attentive, but desires within her had given rise to doubts even as they stood before the Portreeve to celebrate their marriage. They had not been married long when Raolos himself became the Portreeve, and their life turned into a whirl of social functions as he worked countless hours to better both their situation and that of the town. "You are a good man, but the dalliance with Hylsie damaged any trust between us." She looked down and pressed the kerchief to her eyes. "That I did not. I do not believe I ever loved you." He choked and gasped, but she could not look at him. "I craved different fruit. At every ball, I watched couples dance, and I longed to be in the arms of somebody's wife. Jorinda permitted me a taste of that fruit. I cannot go back. I love her."

He yelled again. How easy it had been for him to become angry once more. "You do not love her. You do not even know her. I know more of her than you do. She is an animal, a murderer who killed her own lover."

The lie inflamed Pettra's own anger, and she twisted her face into a mask of animosity. "That she did not. Styrrach killed Deineike. You try to cast the death of that sweet woman in your favour."

He gave a sad sigh. "I do not mean Deineike. Another, before her. Jorinda hinted at it the day Styrrach came to my office, so I asked Synna, and he told me the tale. The other, Arella, belonged to the Guild also, a killer like her. Jorinda killed her to spare her own skin and fled. That is why this Styrrach pursues her with such fervour."

She glared at him in disbelief. He sought to beguile her with falsehoods for his own ends. "You lie. Synna lies. He…" She fought for breath, indignant, and she wiped fresh tears from her eyes. "He is a killer you keep about yourself for some reason that eludes my comprehension. I do not believe his words."

"Pettra, they are cut from the same cloth, those two. They are killers. I fear she would as soon thrust her dagger into you as allow her own life to be compromised."

"You lie. You are jealous, and out of envy you make up these… horrible lies about the woman I love. I despise you. You revolt me. Get out." He did not move. "Get out." She screamed with all the breath she could summon, and he started.

Pettra crossed the room and beat at him with her fists, but he caught her wrists in his hands and held her at arm's length. He shook his head, and she blazed with rage. She kicked at him and connected with his shin. Anger crossed his face, he yelped, and he pushed her backward. She fell onto her bed as he turned and stormed from the room. She leapt to her feet and ran after him.

He strode down the stairs and yelled backward at her. "I must go to work. If you do not wish to be here when I return, that might be for the best."

She screamed as she followed him down the stairs. "I will not be. You may depend upon it."

Pettra continued to scream insults at his back until Raolos reached the door and pulled it open. He did not leave the house; he stood motionless and stared out onto the carriage path. Pettra ran up behind him and pushed him, pummelled her fists against his back, and he turned toward her. At once, she covered her mouth with her hands as tears of anger changed to tears of joy. There at the door, a confused look on her face, stood Jorinda.

The voyage north brought the return of the nightmares. In one, Corelle slit the throat of Styrrach, then watched in horror as Deineike and Arella fell on his body and tore off lumps of his flesh with their teeth. They glanced up at her, blood smeared across their faces and an animal rage in their eyes. Each of them said, "I love you." Their mouths filled with his flesh, Corelle found their words difficult to understand. Arella produced a fan, and a blade sprang from it. She severed his erect manhood and held it aloft, and she and Deineike fought for possession of it as each attempted to wrestle it from the other. They cackled like mad women as they rolled together on the floor and clutched at Styrrach's manhood, which remained erect even after they cut it from his body.

Corelle woke in a cold sweat, hopeful the ship would dock in Ort today. Rain had fallen without end since she left Alcmouth, and all her new-found wealth could not buy a glimmer of sunshine in the sky or in her mood. She sat at the bow every day, soaked to the bones, and wept for the satisfaction Styrrach's death had not brought her. She had torn up her letter to Wilash and composed a new one in which she told him of Deineike's death, her vengeance on Styrrach, and warned him of the threat to his and Klordia's life even though she had killed the Guildmeister. She did not mention the coin or precious stones, nor the letters she hoped would see the Bailiff hanged, and her alongside him.

The ship did reach Ort later that day, and after she left the ship, Corelle sought out a courier business, delivered the letter to them, and paid for its delivery. She took rooms at an inn in the wealthy quarter, bought a lockable trunk, and arranged for it to be delivered to her rooms. With her pack over her shoulder, she wandered to Syme's tavern and ordered a goblet of wine. He seemed delighted to see her, and when he asked after Deineike, she told him of her death. The news devastated him, and they wept together for a time. It seemed he had not exaggerated his fondness for them, after all else. She called in at the cake shop and bought two pieces of Deineike's favourite pastry, then sat on the wall and ate them both.

As night fell, she returned to the inn, where the trunk had been delivered. Corelle locked all the keys, coin, and stones in it, then secured the key on a string around her neck. She passed a disrupted night, the nightmares incessant, and awoke exhausted early on another rainswept morning.

Corelle rose and dressed. She saw no advantage in further delay, so she gathered all the letters into her pack and set off for Raolos's house. The rain had saturated her by the time she walked up the path toward the door. No guards stood outside the house, which seemed reckless with all they knew of Styrrach's threat.

A commotion within gave her pause as she went to rap on the door. Pettra screamed, and Corelle wondered whether she argued with Raolos. She decided to leave them to it, but the door opened, and Raolos stood there, his mouth open as he stared at her in disbelief. Movement came from behind him, and he stumbled forward before he half turned. Beyond him, Corelle saw Pettra, her eyes red-rimmed, her nostrils flared, and her fists clenched. As she spotted Corelle, Pettra covered her mouth with her hands.

Pettra pushed past Raolos and ran toward Corelle, her arms extended as her fingers clenched and unclenched in the familiar gesture. She wore a nightgown, and in no time, the steady rain soaked it as she threw her arms around Corelle's neck and showered her face with kisses. In the doorway, Raolos's head fell forward, and he slumped back against the door.

Corelle attempted to pull Pettra's arms from her neck, but already encumbered by the pack, she could not do so with only one useful hand. She gave up and stepped forward with some difficulty. Raolos looked up, and Corelle could not imagine his pain as he observed his wife draped around the woman he had hoped never to see again.

Raolos's voice dripped with misery, and Corelle felt sorry for him. "Why are you here again? Did I not give you sufficient coin?"

"That you did, although I will repay you every one. I have news that has an impact on your family's safety, and I have a question for you. If you can stand to hear me, I will tell you what I have to say, and you may decide what you do with my words, if anything."

Pettra whispered in Corelle's ear and begged her to come up to her bedroom and ravish her. Raolos glanced at the spectacle before him, and a tear ran down his face. He gave a slight, sad nod and held out an arm to indicate Corelle should enter the house. He did not move from the door, so what she had to say, she must say in the hallway.

She drew in a breath. "Please, Pettra, I need to speak to Raolos."

"Afterward." Pettra smothered her with kisses, her voice breathy with desire. "He can wait. I have missed your touch."

Miserable, Corelle looked at Raolos, and he wiped at his eyes. Despite Pettra's attentions, she told her tale. "Styrrach is dead. I have killed him. I found letters that link him to the Bailiff and Portreeves. If you still wish to put an end to the corruption of these would-be servants of the citizens of Dur, you may have them and take them to the Duke."

Her words stopped Pettra's amorous attentions, and Raolos stared at her. His sadness gave way to tangible excitement. Pettra laid a hand on Corelle's left arm, who winced with pain as it came to rest over her wound. Pettra gasped. "You are hurt. Is it a bad wound?"

"A scratch." A lie.

"Come into the parlour and show me these letters." Raolos led them into the parlour. Pettra fussed about Corelle's arm and wanted to bring a healer to the house straight away. Corelle handed over the letters, and Raolos read each one with deliberate care.

Corelle asked Pettra to arrange a healer, hopeful it would distract her, and she ran from the parlour and called for one of the servants.

Raolos looked up from the letters. "I do not understand. Are they scribed in some code?"

"That they are. Most call for meetings with Balgow, Styrrach's appointed Guildmeister in Alcmouth. One calls for the death of a Guild member from Zhanghar. They link the Bailiff and the Portreeves with Styrrach."

Raolos nodded. He had seen the same issue she had, she guessed. "The letters link the Bailiff and Portreeves to the Guild. Most are addressed to others, not Styrrach. Even the ones that do are businesslike. They seem like letters any Portreeve would send to a successful businessman who paid large levies."

"Styrrach did not run an honest business. He ordered Guild members to kill, or other Guildmeisters did so on his behalf, which elevates any association with him to a murderous one. Any Guild member can translate the cryptic Zhanghar language. A Guild member who is prepared to testify that Styrrach ordered them to kill people in exchange for coin can confirm the connection that damns the Bailiff, and other Portreeves."

Raolos sounded cautious, his eyes non-committal. "That they could. A Guild member who testified these things, however, would be a murderer by their own confession and would be hanged."

A short silence ensued before Corelle sat straight in her chair and replied. "That she would."

From the corner of her eye, Corelle noticed Pettra in the door-way. How much had she heard? Corelle glanced at her, and Raolos followed her eyes. Pettra stood with her hands pressed to her temples as tears streamed down her face. "Please. I beg you. You cannot do it, Jorinda. Raolos, do not permit it. The Duke will hang her."

Jorinda replied, soft and gentle. "I am a killer, Pettra. I deserve whatever fate is written for me."

"You have killed. You are not a killer. You are an affectionate, tender woman." Pettra rushed to kneel before Corelle, wrapped her arms around her waist.

Jorinda sighed. "Deineike said much the same, but you are both wrong. I am irredeemable. There is no way for me to bring any justice to these holders of high office for their involvement in Deineike's death unless I pay my debt for the loss of her life also." Corelle turned her gaze to Raolos. "Will you take the letters to the Duke?"

He sat and stared at the letters in silence as he seemed to wrestle with his conscience. He looked up. "Is there no other way?"

Corelle shook her head in denial. "Synna might testify in my place, but his connections are to Balgow. I killed for Styrrach in Zhanghar, and my word gives the connection between the Guild and the high offices more credibility."

He sighed. "What of Pettra?"

"She is your wife. She is yours to attend to afterward."

Pettra screamed. "Jorinda. I will not permit this. I will not let this despicable wretch drag you to Alcmouth, to stand and watch as you swing from the gallows. I will not permit it."

Raolos looked into Corelle's eyes. "I have misjudged your character."

"That you have not." Corelle loosed a miserable sigh. "I have found Styrrach's coin, or a large stash of it at the least. I have keys that will give you access to it. I know you will use it well to improve the lot of the Durfolk, the street urchins above all. Deineike grew up on the street; I would like the urchins helped in her name."

He nodded but seemed lost for words. Pettra sobbed aloud and would not release Corelle from her grasp as Corelle continued. "We will sail tomorrow if you are can arrange your affairs. The next day if not. There is naught to be gained from a delay."

Pettra sobbed. "There is all to be gained. I will not let you go."

Raolos found his voice again. "Where do you stay?"

"I have taken rooms at The Ort. As strange a name for an inn as I have ever encountered."

He smiled. "Did some of Styrrach's coin find its way into your pack? The Ort is the best inn in the town."

"That it did." She laughed. "I am not above a little petty thievery."

"Styrrach is dead, you say. Do you find any peace over Deineike's murder from this?"

Corelle shook her head. "More must be paid, and that debt will still not be settled." She had been angry aboard The Friendship when she overheard Deineike say the death of the man she had believed killed her mother had brought her no peace, but Corelle now understood.

"I will stay with you at The Ort." Pettra's unhappy voice broke as she spoke through sobs. "I will gather some clothes, and we will leave. I wish to spend every moment with you until you leave."

"Your husband doubtless has a different opinion about this arrangement." Corelle reached out and took Pettra's chin in her fingertips.

"I care not what he thinks about the arrangement." Pettra clambered to her feet. "I will return soon."

As she ran from the room, Raolos called to her. "Pettra, put some clothes on. Do not walk the street in your nightgown." He looked at Corelle, and an awkward silence passed between them.

Corelle tried to spare him further pain. "I can leave now, before she returns."

"She will follow you. I cannot prevent her, or I will destroy her. If things turn as I expect them to, she will be destroyed anyway. Let us not hasten that agony."

Corelle nodded. They were brave words, and she respected him for them. Whatever drove him into the arms of his servant did not concern her, but he appeared to be a decent man for all that. He had, in truth, had the misfortune to marry a woman whose desires did not suit the arrangement.

He sat deep in thought, then spoke again. "It does not frighten you, the thought of your death?"

"That it does not. I have earned it by my actions, and the only thing I desired to live for has been taken from me. What purpose my long life could serve is hidden from me. Somebody once told me my fates were muddied waters, and I tire of it."

He stood. "I will arrange our travel. I will pay your fare, although you are now as wealthy as the Duke himself, it appears." She inclined her head toward him, a small acknowledgement of his offer. It might seem churlish to reject it. He went on. "I will do as you ask with Styrrach's coin. I hope I will find somebody to assist me in this, for I confess I do not know where to begin."

"My thanks. I trust you will carry out the request to the best of your abilities. You are a good man, I think."

"I will send word of our travel details when they are secured." He left the house.

TWENTY-EIGHT

TO ALCMOUTH AGAIN

CORELLE WAITED FOR PETTRA, WHO TOOK AN INTERMINABLE LENGTH OF time to reappear. No healer appeared, and Corelle guessed it had fled Petra's mind when she heard Corelle offer to sail to Alcmouth with Raolos. When Pettra did come into the parlour, she wore a blue satin dress of quality making, and a servant followed her with a trunk. Corelle laughed. "Do you leave forever?"

"I have brought some necessities, no more." Pettra pouted. "Come, I need a cloak, and I have arranged a cart for my trunk. We can ride it, or we can walk in the rain."

"We will walk, I think. I am already saturated and can become no wetter."

"How romantic." Pettra sighed, a sparkle in her eyes. "Jorinda, I am so glad you are back. I will persuade you not to follow through on this madness you and Raolos spoke of." A coy smile played at her lips.

"My name is Corelle again. I have abandoned the other."

She wrinkled her nose. "I do not like this name. I prefer Jorinda."

"My name is not yours to choose. You may like it or not, that is your choice, but it is Corelle."

"Did Deineike like this name?"

"That she did not. She would not call me Corelle, but in truth, I travelled as Jorinda at the time."

"What served as sweet wine for Deineike will serve as sweet wine for me. I shall call you Jorinda."

Corelle sighed. "I cannot force you to call me Corelle. You may call me Raolos if you wish. I might not, however, respond to a name other than my own. That is my right."

Pettra wrinkled her nose again. "Raolos? I hope never to hear that name again when we leave this house."

Corelle mumbled a response as dark as it was pointed. "I fear you will be disappointed." Pettra had pulled on her cloak, and her trunk had been taken out to the cart, so they may as well leave for the inn.

They wandered along behind the cart. Pettra's beautiful, coifed hair soon resembled rats' tails that hung down the side of her face, but she would not be downcast by the weather. She took Corelle's hand as they strolled, and despite her first instinct, Corelle tolerated it, did not snatch her own hand away, although she became despondent as she remembered she had passed up the opportunity to hold Deineike's hand in public. Her life had been littered with disappointments, but her time with Deineike had not been one of them. For however long she still lived, she determined to have more positive thoughts about the time she had been granted as Deineike's lover.

How Deineike would feel about Pettra's infatuation with her

could not be guessed. Corelle would have preferred to have spent the rest of her time in Ort alone, but she could not fault Raolos's argument that his wife should enjoy some moments of joy before Corelle once more sailed south toward her fate.

They reached the inn, where two enthusiastic young lads carried Pettra's trunk up to Corelle's rooms. The boys' eyes widened as Corelle gave them each a regal for their efforts. As soon as they left, Pettra slid the latch across the door, dropped her cloak onto the floor, leaned back against the door, and ran her hands up her body to caress her own breasts. The wet dress clung to her body and accentuated every curve of her figure. Her nipples stood upright and pressed against the dress, her face flushed, and her lips parted, and Corelle felt a twinge of desire. After all else, Pettra must be entitled to a few moments of joy, she thought as she pulled her into her arms, and Pettra enjoyed a great many moments of joy.

Afterward, Corelle lay awake and listened to Pettra sleep. She had again begged Corelle to strike her, but Corelle could not oblige, could not bring herself to hit Pettra despite desperate exhortations to do so. Corelle enjoyed the responsive, passionate lovemaking Pettra brought to her bed but knew she could never give in to the demands for pain Pettra seemed bent upon. Corelle had never encountered it before, and it baffled her.

Pettra woke late in the day, and the moment she awoke, she dived between Corelle's legs, where her tongue carried Corelle beyond her concerns about the violence Pettra craved. Late in the day, Corelle suggested they should visit the tavernroom to eat a meal, but Pettra insisted they should eat at an establishment near the square she often frequented. Corelle had not realised establishments existed like the one to which Pettra took her. Unlike the tavernroom of an inn, its sole purpose appeared to be the provision of meals. Corelle could not understand the list of foods on the parch a staff member handed her, and Pettra had to guide her and explain almost every item.

The meal cost an exorbitant price, but Corelle's new wealth meant she could afford to pay. The polite staff attended to their every need to the point of reverence, and Corelle felt some discomfort at the experience. She found the food too rich for her tastes but did not doubt it must be of the highest standard. They shared a pitcher of wine, the cost of which would have fed Deineike and Corelle for a sevenday as they had ridden south toward Torric. She guessed Pettra had chosen a good wine, and Corelle imagined that to those with the taste to determine such things, it might have been of the highest quality. She, however, could not discern between a wine that cost a few groats for a cask and one that cost a hundred regals. Her experience and taste were too simple.

Pettra thrived in the establishment, which she called a cenacle, though Corelle confessed she had never encountered the word before. She smiled as she recalled all the words Deineike had introduced her to. If felt good to find a memory of Deineike that uplifted rather than depressed her.

They walked back to the inn hand in hand. Pettra seemed comfortable with the gesture, as Deineike had been, and Corelle wondered whether her own concern for it in public might be a fault of her own creation, as nobody seemed perturbed by it as they walked. Styrrach's contemptuous words about her relationship with Deineike seemed vulgar in comparison to the easy, natural way Pettra seemed prepared to demonstrate her affection before everybody else. Styrrach would say no more words, vulgar or otherwise, and Corelle smiled in grim satisfaction.

As they lay in each other's arms in bed, Pettra used every argument she could come up with to dissuade Corelle from the journey south to her ruin. She swore herself to Corelle for as long as she lived and promised they would move together into the house she owned if she would but stay in Ort. Corelle asked if the Portreeve's wife would abandon the requests for violence in their lovemaking if she stayed, and Pettra promised to make every effort to do so.

Corelle had said it only as a jest, but Pettra took encouragement from the question, and Corelle had no choice but to shatter her illusion that the request had been serious.

It seemed hard for Pettra to accept the comment as nothing but a jest, and she cried again. Corelle tried to comfort her, but she became more and more morose. At one point, she wiped at her eyes and stared into Corelle's own. "Did you kill your lover so you could escape from Styrrach?"

Corelle sighed. All her secrets laid bare at every turn. It beggared belief. "How did you hear this tale?"

"Raolos claims it. He says Synna told it to him." Corelle remained silent for a time as she thought back to Arella's death. "Jorinda? Say it is untrue."

"It is true, Pettra. I killed Arella. There is blood on my hands, and I cannot excuse myself for my actions."

"There must have been no other alternative. You would not do this. You will not even strike me, though I beg you to do so."

It did appear to be a contradiction. Corelle would not slap Pettra, who longed to be hurt, but she had killed Arella. She could not resolve such mysteries. "The alternative would have been a death more painful than the one I gave her. That is what I told myself, at the least. The truth is simpler. I feared for myself."

"What did you fear?"

"They came to kill me." Corelle's dejection grew with every word of the story.

"Yet tomorrow you would sail with Raolos to your death."

Tears sprang to Corelle's eyes. "I do not understand. Please, let us talk no more of this. I cannot fathom what I have become. Do not try to comprehend me."

Pettra nuzzled her neck and draped an arm across Corelle, but she struck the left arm where Styrrach's dagger wound lay, and Corelle yelped in pain. "Tomorrow we must get a healer to look at your arm." Pettra fussed at the dressings as she apologised.

"There seems little point."

"That there is. I refuse to believe you will not come back to me. You have left me twice, but once you return, there will be no third."

Corelle recalled a similar phrase she had used for her encounters with Styrrach. She had said it to Synna, and her prediction had proved correct when she killed Styrrach at the third attempt, but she doubted Pettra's would be. "We will visit a healer." Corelle relented, anxious to avoid any further back and forth about trifles.

Pettra refused to sleep without further pleasure, and Corelle obliged, then watched sleep take Pettra afterward. Pettra's complex nature puzzled Corelle. Deineike had been simpler to understand. She had lacked Pettra's societal graces, but the differences between them ran to more than that. Pettra was around twice Corelle's years, but like Deineike, she appeared never to have outgrown an intense need to cling to another. The similarities ended there. Pettra had suppressed her most basic instincts for the pleasure Raolos's wealth and status brought to her. Although she shared Deineike's irrepressible optimism, Pettra suffered from a sense of desperation for events to always turn in her favour. She appeared afraid of unhappiness, unprepared or unable to accept the harsh truth that life could not always be ballgowns and fancy meals, and she thrived on attention, appeared obsessed by a desire for others to find her attractive. Her sexual appetite seemed insatiable but ran to pleasures Corelle could not accept as healthy.

The morning found her wrapped in Pettra's arms and tears in Pettra's eyes. Corelle wiped them with tender strokes. "What is wrong?"

"Nothing. I watched you sleep. You are beautiful. I cry from happiness because you came back to me. I beg you not to sail south with Raolos."

"Pettra, I did not come back to you. I came back to persuade Raolos to sail south with me. That is the truth of it."

Pettra gave a tearful laugh. "You say you did not come back to me, yet here you are, in bed with me. You refuse to make me come again, but you lie with me."

Corelle laughed. "I had not realised you wished further pleasure." The insatiable desire Corelle had contemplated last night appeared already, and they had woken no more than moments before.

Pettra's nostrils flared, and she climbed on top of Corelle. "I am awake, am I not?"

Pettra proved difficult to sate, and the midday had all but arrived before Corelle could climb from the bed. She dressed in her customary trousers and tunic while Pettra fussed her way into another fitted dress that accentuated the slimness of her waist and the roundness of her hips. Raolos's wife manipulated her breasts in the low-cut bodice to reveal her cleavage to its best advantage and smiled when she looked up at Corelle, who watched the performance with amused detachment.

They went in search of a healer, and Pettra claimed to know of the best in Ort. Corelle felt sure the best healer in Ort would have a list of patients so long, no appointment could be secured for many passes, but he agreed to see her that day as an apparent favour to Pettra. They had time to wait, and Corelle persuaded Pettra a stroll would be as beneficial as a return to bed. They wandered the streets under grey skies that threatened rain, the smell of the impending downpour musky in Corelle's nostrils, but the day stayed dry. They chatted as they strolled, bought lunch at a small bakery Pettra claimed as the best in Ort. The cakes might have been of a higher quality, but they lacked the memories of the ones from the shop near Syme's tavern, and without those memories, any cake would taste like ash and dust to Corelle.

They returned to the healer's rooms late in the day. He removed the bandage and studied the wound. The closing work did not impress him, and Corelle laughed, agreed with him, and suggested she might have done a neater job herself. Nonetheless, he advised they did not undo the closing, since the flesh had begun to knit after several days, but he cautioned her the scar would be unattractive. He applied a herb that stung, and he told her it would draw off infection. For once, Corelle resisted the temptation to reveal her knowledge of the word "inflammation," and he bandaged the arm with more skill than the Guild healer. When he examined her head, he said some flesh had been torn away with the hair, but he expressed more concern with how the other scars had come about.

Corelle convinced him there would be no repeat of the injuries; she no longer hurt herself since she had killed Styrrach. He did not ask how she had come by the stab wound. His work appeared superior to the Guild healer, but he charged an outrageous sum, and Corelle could never have afforded his fees before she stumbled on Styrrach's hidden wealth.

The women returned to the inn. Letters had been delivered for Corelle. Raolos had secured passage the next day and asked her to be at his tally house an hour after the sunrise. The news devastated Pettra, and despite Corelle's attempts to drive the sadness from her with vigorous lovemaking, she could not be consoled. She cried and held Corelle tight long after they had made love until her misery and the exertion wore her down, and she slept.

The next day, Pettra would not allow Corelle to walk to the tally house alone and trudged along beside her from the inn, her misery clear in her face, her body, the way she hung her head. The large front doors of the tally house stood open when they arrived. Ibie stood in the storage area, and he nodded at Corelle as she approached.

He pointed to the rear of the tally house. "Greetings. Raolos and Synna are in the office, at the rear."

Corelle acknowledged him with a brief smile. "My thanks. Pettra will need to return home soon if you can arrange it."

Ibie turned his eyes to the tearful, distraught wife of his employer, and he sighed. "It will be as you say." At once, he embraced Corelle. "You do a brave thing today. I do not approve of all you have done, but the land will be much improved once this scourge is removed. My thanks."

Corelle squirmed in his embrace but forced herself to pat his back with her hands. "That scourge is already much removed, and you have played a great part in it." Corelle felt the usual heat in her face and turned to Pettra. "You should return home now."

Pettra shook her head from side to side, a violent refusal, and her eyes shone with tears that threatened to flow from them at the least encouragement. "I will return once the ship has left the dock. I will not leave a heartbeat before I must."

Ibie shook his head at the outburst, but Corelle could neither insist Pettra return to her home or that Ibie take her there. Raolos and Synna emerged from the rear of the tally house and asked if she had prepared to depart. They both carried packs.

Corelle had not expected Synna to sail with them. "Synna travels with us?"

Synna gave Corelle an affectionate smile. "That I do. I understand you have become the wealthiest woman in Dur and reason you will require protection."

She laughed. "I am not so wealthy I could repay your debt to Fass."

He joined in the laughter. "Then I must have heard a lie, since I only owe him five groats."

"Six, he reckoned." Corelle smiled, and the jest lightened her mood for the moment.

They walked onto the dock and approached a ship. They boarded, and Pettra trudged, miserable, behind them. The master himself escorted them to their cabins. Corelle had a comfortable cabin with a bed, some chairs, a table, a trunk and even some space where a dress or two might hang. Pettra clung to her in tears, and Corelle pressed the key to her rooms at The Ort into her hand, along with the key from around her neck. "In the room is a trunk with some coin and precious stones in it. This key opens it. Have the best maker in Ort fashion you a dress that will show off your figure to its fullest. A fitted bodice, my suggestion. Wear it with pride at the next ball." Corelle had a pouch of coin and some of the stones in her pack but had left the rest in the rooms. She would not need them where she would travel.

Pettra cried, inconsolable, but took the key. "I will wear the dress on the first night you and I attend a dance together, after you return. I love you."

They kissed, and Corelle ushered Pettra from the cabin and into Ibie's care. Pettra stood on the dock and watched as the ship made ready to sail, and Corelle waved to her from the deck as the ship moved out into the river. She watched Pettra and Ibie become smaller and smaller until she could no longer make them out, then heaved a sigh, went to the bow, and sat down to begin yet another dull trip down the river.

Synna joined Corelle at the bow of the ship most days as they sailed south. They talked little, occasional stories about Guild life or tales of things that had turned while Corelle had been in Alcmouth earlier in the pass. On the second day he asked about the death of Styrrach, and Corelle felt she owed him an explanation about Gill's death also. It appeared to sadden him, but he voiced no judgement. The story of the passageway amazed him. No rumour of the passageway had ever been mentioned among the Guild members. Corelle wondered whether even Balgow had known of its existence.

When they reached Alcmouth, Raolos took rooms at an inn, but as threatened, The Duke's Seat had lost his patronage. Once they were settled, they walked to the house next to the Guild building. Synna and Corelle remained vigilant but noticed nothing on the street to concern them, and they entered the house. The lantern Corelle had left behind still stood there, but she could find no flint. She listened at the wall to the Guildmeister's office but heard nothing, so she pulled the latch and opened the door. Styrrach's body had gone, and the blood on the floor had dried to a deep reddish-brown colour. She took a flint from the parlour and lit the lantern before she closed the panel again behind her and opened the one in the passageway. With three of them, they found it easier to open the inner wall, and she unlocked the trunk. Synna let out a low whistle, and even Raolos gasped.

Raolos whispered and seemed overwhelmed by the wealth before him. "There is so much coin here, your vision for the street urchins might be expanded to give a generous sum to every child in the land."

"What do I care? Do good with it, as Deineike would have wished."

Raolos suggested they leave the trunk in the house until the Duke came to a decision, but Corelle preferred to arrange for it to be moved to Raolos's rooms in the inn, so they set off again to find carters who could undertake the task.

It took four men to lift the trunk onto a cart, and they could not carry it, so they dragged it from the house. At the inn, they were forced to move most of the pouches up to Raolos's rooms one by one before they brought the almost-empty trunk into the rooms. Darkness shrouded the city before they had finished, and Corelle paid them two regals each for their labours.

The next day, they decided to dispense with any formality and present themselves at the Ducal Highhome to request an audience. The longer they left it, the less time there would be to act before all involved fled justice. To send letters through the normal channels might take many days, so they decided to arrive unannounced and continue to do so until they gained an audience.

Heavy rain fell from a blanket of ill-tempered clouds as they set off in a coach, and Corelle's mood spiralled downward as they rumbled through the wet streets. She could not turn back now; the dice had been cast, and she had rolled ones. She hoped her fate would help Raolos roll a high score, and she contented herself with that. Unlike his normal demeanour, Synna stayed quiet in the coach, and Raolos's eyes alternated between glum stares out of the window and sorrowful glances at her. Corelle tried to smile but could summon no warmth to it and abandoned the effort.

The coach turned onto the Duke's Highway, and tears welled up in Corelle's eyes as she remembered the song Deineike had sung as they rode south a year ago. It had been an extension of the song Arella had sung years before. Deineike had added a line about two highways and told Corelle, or Jorinda as she had called her, she would build Jorinda's Highway and come to her on that highway as Jorinda lay in her bed. Deineike had become embarrassed by the foolish story, but now as Corelle thought back on the moment a sad smile flickered on lips reluctant to agree to any sign of joy.

The coach drew to a halt. The moment had arrived, and Corelle's fate was about to be written.

TWENTY-NINE

AN AUDIENCE WITH THE DUKE

They stepped out of the coach before the Ducal Highhome, and Corelle gazed in wonder on the magnificent building. It oozed wealth and authority, and the coin in Styrrach's trunk might not even pay for someone to clean the window glass. Rumour had it there was a window glass in the Ducal Highhome for every light in the night sky, and she did not doubt it now she stood before the building.

The building had been built from deep red stone, cut into small rectangular blocks, laid upon each other with meticulous attention to detail. A pair of enormous Ortwood doors, so large the coach could have passed through them with room to spare, led beyond the exterior wall of the building. Guards in the distinctive yellow uniform of the Duke and his Bailiff stood either side of the doors, each with one of the ridiculous hats perched atop his head, and each armed with long poles with vicious blades at the end. Corelle imagined they must be ceremonial weapons, quite useless if somebody attempted to gain illicit entry into the building, since the poles would be so unwieldy, they would be useful only in the retrieval of a child's ball from the branches of a tree.

They approached the doors, and the guards did not attempt to prevent their entry. Beyond the doors lay a large courtyard with a vast array of flowers planted throughout it. Corelle did not know what variety of colourful flowers grew in the winter seasons. Had they also been imported from the south? Signs guided visitors around the buildings around the courtyard, though Corelle could not imagine how visitors who could not read were expected to find their way around. She had met the Duke and thought he would not be much concerned with those citizens who could not read, since they would be unlikely to pay levies.

A sign told them the Ducal Secretary could be found through a door to their left, and they agreed to start there, since the Secretary must manage appointments and other mundane tasks, but they were incorrect. The Secretary controlled the Duke's personal finances, but they were directed to administration offices where, an aide assured them, they could seek an appointment.

The layers of bureaucracy in the Ducal Highhome staggered Corelle, and every person they encountered appeared to have undergone extensive training in obstruction. They struggled to progress past the first clerk, and it turned on Raolos's stature as a former Portreeve, together with a vague recollection that the Duke had once visited him in his rooms, to win them an appointment with the next clerk.

As they debated with the overbearing woman, a guard entered the office, summoned, or by chance; Corelle could not tell. She glanced at him, and he made straight for her and thrust his face into hers. She stood her ground, and he snarled, "I know you. You threatened us in the home of this man."

Corelle worried how this turn would affect the outcome of their request. "I do not recognise you."

"I recognise you. It astonishes me you would present yourself here. Do you seek to hang?"

"That I do." He seemed taken aback by the reply. "I should hang for all I come here to confess, and if the Duke will not hear me, then he should hang next to me."

Raolos raised a hand to his forehead, but Corelle committed to the strategy. Belligerence might still fail, but politeness would also be a waste of breath. The guard glanced at the woman, who shrugged. They appeared uncertain of the situation, and Corelle had them on the back foot.

She pressed her advantage. She straightened to her full height, some way below the guard, who towered over her. "It matters not. If the Duke will not see us, we will ensure the Durfolk know he turned a blind eye to the heinous crimes of his Bailiff, which I carried out on his behalf. They may hang me, but if they do, they will march for the Duke afterward."

With a nervy laugh, Raolos intervened. "My colleague exaggerates." Corelle cursed his lack of patience.

The guard turned to Raolos. "You seek audience with the Duke on the matters this woman has mentioned?"

Raolos straightened and took control of the situation. "That I do. A few moments of his time to outline allegations of such outrageous corruption, I guarantee he will wish to hear the tale told in full." Raolos stood erect before the man, his position and manner an intimidation to those used to servitude, as Corelle's dagger might be to those unused to violence.

"Wait here." The guard spun on his heels and strode from the office. They waited as colour returned to the face of the clerk, and she shuffled journals and ledgers about on her large desk.

The guard returned. "The Duke's Senior Assistant will hear your plea. If, as you claim, the Duke must hear you, it will be so." They took a step toward the door he had entered from, but he held up a hand. "The Senior Assistant will see Raolos. He will not see you." He fixed Corelle with a pointed stare.

Raolos protested. "That is ridiculous, for she is the most important piece."

"Then she should have taken thought for that matter before she threatened the Duke, his Bailiff, and his men."

Raolos tutted, and Corelle regretted her anger and impetuosity when the Duke had visited Deineike. She had been furious and frightened, but her behaviour had been unpardonable, and now it might return to plague this pivotal moment.

Raolos followed the guard while Corelle and Synna waited. Raolos soon returned, and as he walked through the door, Corelle could not decide if the briefness of his visit with the Senior Assistant suggested a good portent or an ill one. Two guards strode in behind him.

Raolos approached her and whispered in her ear. "The Senior Assistant read the letters from the Bailiff to Styrrach, and I told him you would testify to Styrrach's nature. He agrees the matter is most grave and will take us to the Duke."

He paused, and Corelle felt he had left something unsaid. "I hear a condition in your silence."

Raolos's face turned red, and he clenched his teeth. "It is ridiculous. You are to submit to a search for concealed weapons, and if you threaten him again…"

Corelle laughed. "My life is forfeit?"

"That it is."

She had arrived prepared to confess to terrible crimes that would see the Bailiff hanged for his involvement in the atrocities the Guild had carried out, and the thought she might be hanged for a threat to the Duke held no terror for her. The search would be an unnecessary drama, but she would not throw away this one chance. They might never have another.

She turned to the guards. "I accept the conditions, but I will not submit to a search by a man." She pointed to the clerk. "This woman will search me."

The woman's face reddened, and she protested, but a guard swept aside her bluster, and the woman rose from behind the protection of her desk. She ran her hands up and down Corelle's tunic, careful not to touch her breasts, then repeated the foolish exercise on Corelle's trousers. When she sat down, Corelle bent to her boot and produced the dagger the woman had missed. She handed it to one of the guards with a smirk.

They would not permit Synna to attend, since they considered him no more than a bodyguard. The guards led them through a series of corridors, each guarded by Ortwood doors, until they stood in an office as big as the parlour in Raolos's home. Four clerks sat behind enormous desks, and one of the aides passed through another Ortwood door. The two guards flanked Corelle, both armed with short swords. It seemed her words at the house about the inefficiency of the weapons had not been heeded.

The Ortwood door opened, and the aide beckoned them through. The Duke sat behind a massive desk of dark, stained Ortwood with no chairs visible for visitors to sit. Portraits lined the walls of an office so vast, Corelle imagined it would take a day to walk from one side of it to the other. She could not comprehend the excesses of power. The Duke gazed on her with undisguised contempt. Two women sat at smaller desks to one side of the room, scribing tools and journals before them.

Corelle pointed toward the women. "I suggest they record addresses and names only. The tale I will tell you must not be scribed, for if it came into the hands of Durfolk, it would shake their beliefs, and everything they hold true would be cast into doubt."

The Duke considered this for a moment, then he spoke to her. "Begin your tale. We will scribe nothing until we hear the bones of it." The use of "we" puzzled her. Would he also scribe as she spoke? She had never wondered whether the Duke could read or scribe but imagined someone so important would possess such skills.

"Before I begin, there is one other matter I wish to rectify. Raolos is a good and decent man who missteps on occasion. The Bailiff fabricated charges against him, and somebody else paid women to testify against him. There is conflict between him and me, but I say this. I am a garment maker, and he is a bolt of fine cloth with some minor imperfections. You refused his appeal out of your anger at me, I think. You made a mistake, and you should reinstate him without further delay."

The Duke flicked his gaze to Raolos. "We will consider these words once we have heard all you have to say."

Corelle drew in a breath. "The reason I urge you not to scribe all I will tell is this. I am a killer, a member of a clandestine group known as the Guild. At the behest of a man I will name, who has links to the Portreeves of four of the cities of Dur and the Bailiff himself, the Guild kills Durfolk. Those who are killed obstruct the financial exploitation this man perpetrates on the citizens of Dur daily." The Duke's mouth dropped open, his eyes wide. "Do I have your attention?"

The Duke seemed shocked by her words, but with some effort, he regained his composure. "You will indicate to the scribes such information as you believe we should record. Begin your tale."

Raolos stepped forward and placed the letters on the Duke's desk. "These letters show links between the Bailiff, several Portreeves, and a man named Styrrach." The Duke pulled the letters toward him and scanned the scribing on them. The first one contained the Bailiff's instruction to Styrrach to meet him at "RT."

"What is 'RT?'" The Duke did not pause to look up.

Raolos replied. "It refers to The Riverside Tavern." On the voyage south, Synna had told them Balgow took occasional meetings at the tavern, and Gill had mentioned it to him after the attack at The Duke's Seat, or the tale might have had a weak start. "I am sure investigation into that tavern will confirm the Bailiff and the Portreeve of Alcmouth met with Guild leaders there many times over the years."

The Duke did not reply as he flicked through the letters and read them with no expression on his face. After a while, he picked them up and squared them together before he handed them back to Raolos. "Some evidence is self-explanatory. Many of the letters appear cryptic, some less so. Why is this?"

Raolos answered his question. "We are not certain. We have discussed it, and the less cryptic letters refer to incidents and meetings some time ago. We believe they became more guarded in the way they communicated as their business grew."

"Some of the letters are addressed to Styrrach, and some to Balgow. Who do you claim these people to be? It is not against any law of Dur for a person in power to have business interests. I have many personal business interests, for instance, as I am sure you do."

Corelle felt best placed to answer the question, and she spoke before Raolos could reply. "They led the Guild. Balgow led the Guild here, in Alcmouth. Styrrach killed him and assumed control here, but in truth, Styrrach ran the entire operation. He controlled the Guilds in Ryl, Zhanghar, Alcmouth, and Torric. He received vast sums of coin from sums remitted to the Bailiff by businesses involved in a scheme to inflate the prices of goods imported from overseas and sold at exorbitant profits."

The Duke's gaze turned to her, reluctant to behold her, it seemed. "You can prove this?"

The Bailiff would have ordered the ledger destroyed by now, or so Corelle believed, and Klordia had gone to Dur City, and she lacked confidence in this part of her story. "A ledger exists, or did exist, and it showed the sums remitted to Styrrach. A friend of ours, an employee of the Bailiff's Tally Master, saw it in the Bailiffs tally office. The Bailiff will now have destroyed such evidence, I fear."

"He would do this why?"

Corelle ignored the unusual way the Duke had asked the question. "Because he knows I am determined to expose him, or worse."

He raised his dark, bushy eyebrows. "Worse?"

She shifted, uncomfortable now she had come to the part that damned her. "Duke—"

He interrupted her. "My Duke."

"What?"

"The proper way to address me is 'My Duke.'"

Of all the things she might lay before him, it seemed ridiculous for him to insist she call him by this pompous term. "You do not have a name?"

"That I do. The proper way to address me is 'My Duke.'"

She stared at the ceiling as she fought to control her temper. "Duke, this tale will make more sense if you permit me to tell it in order. To jump around like this will waste time and confuse matters."

He glared at her, and she held his gaze for a tense moment until he waved a hand at her. "Continue."

Corelle began with the story of her time in the Guild in Zhanghar and left nothing out. She told him of all the gests she had carried out and some others she knew of, careful to include the one referenced in one of the letters. The gory details of all the deaths she told him about could be verified and would provide evidence of the involvement of both her and Styrrach.

Corelle explained how she had been shrouded but had killed Arella to escape the Guild. Some of those in the room gasped when she confessed to the murder of the woman she loved, and tears fell from her own eyes as she told it. She did not tell the story of the mariner in Torric because it had no impact on the guilt of the Bailiff, nor did she name Wilash or Klordia, and she would not be drawn on it as she admitted she had killed the Portreeve's man in Alcmouth as part of the gest on Klordia. When she spoke about the attack in Raolos's office and of the Guild members sent on more than one occasion to kill him and his family, she refused to name Synna, but she mentioned she had been handed the tunic of a Bailiff's man as further proof of the Bailiff's complicity. She confessed to the murder of Adijon in the inn in Ort. As she told the Duke the details of the attack on her and Deineike in The Duke's Seat and the subsequent death of Deineike, she became light-headed, and Raolos caught her as she swayed backward.

By the time she had recounted the tale of the murder of Elger, Gill, and Styrrach, she could no longer contain her sobs. The full horror of her life, poured out in the tale, sickened her, and she could not guess how Durfolk would react if they heard it. Corelle had laid bare a tale of immense horror and painted herself as a remorseless monster who would kill for any slight. All true, she reflected as she finished.

Raolos begged the Duke to bring a chair for her as she bent forward, her hands on her thighs, and she struggled for breath between her incessant sobs. As an aide went for a chair, only her cries shattered the silence in the room, and the others stared at her in disbelief. When the chair appeared, she slumped into it, her head bowed as her tears dripped from her face onto her trousers.

After a lengthy silence, the Duke cleared his throat as if he wished to ensure he could still speak. After all else, he had heard things nobody in Dur could have imagined in their worst nightmares. "A tale such as this can never be made public. My thanks for your discretion about the scribing of these details. The things you have heard must remain in this room. They must be repeated to nobody."

His words confused her, since she had not heard the words—she had said them. When she looked up at him, however, he gazed around the room at all present.

Raolos spoke, his tone angry. "You must summon the Bailiff and have him answer these charges."

The Duke appeared uncomfortable. "Ah. My Bailiff is on a leave of absence. In truth, we have not seen him for some days, and none know his whereabouts. You had the right of it, I think. The death of this Styrrach spells the downfall of much that has turned for many years. I fear Glailam has taken his ill-gotten gains and fled."

Raolos set his jaw and seemed unprepared to admit defeat. "Then you must act against the others named. Jorinda will give you addresses of Guild locations, and you must replace the Portreeves. Any Guild leaders must be apprehended and hanged."

The Duke gazed at Raolos and knitted his brows. "You call her Jorinda, yet she calls herself Corelle. I do not understand this."

Corelle explained the names. "I have used both names. Corelle is my name, by my parents' choice."

He nodded. "Raolos, you urge me to act against the people named by Corelle. In truth, I cannot."

"What?" Corelle's head snapped up as she stared at him with venom in her eyes and her heart. "You are the Duke, are you not? The most powerful man in Dur? How can you not act on all you have heard?"

"Our law is clear. I am the Duke, but I have no judicial power. That power is vested in my Bailiff, in part. For the most part, it resides with the Portreeves. They are the upholders of the law. The Bailiff can, of course, direct them on points of law such as the things you have laid bare here today. I cannot."

She gasped. "You can do nothing? Why then have I poured out my ruin to you?"

"My dear, you had no other sympathetic ear in all Dur, by your own admission. All have been bought by this Styrrach."

Only his arrogance might exceed her anger, and she spat a frustrated response. "Then you cannot order me hanged for my confession?"

"That I cannot. My Bailiff can, or a Portreeve. I cannot."

Corelle exhaled a bitter breath. "Then I may as well leave. I have wasted my breath, and our time."

The Duke raised his eyebrows. "I do not suggest you take this course of action. My guards—the ones you insulted—may be inclined to ignore the finer points of the law, and you are unarmed. There is, however, another issue I wish to address. You asked me to reinstate Raolos. The Bailiff indicted him on charges of behaviour unworthy of one of his status, and he appealed to me as the last right of appeal left to him, since my Bailiff had convicted and impeached him. Do you know how many appeals a Duke has ever granted throughout the history of Dur?"

Corelle did not, and she shook her head.

"Seven. Since the formation of the Duchy, seven appeals have been granted. The Duke has no power to overturn a Bailiff's decision but can ask the Bailiff to allow his leniency as a mark of respect. No Bailiff refused to honour those seven appeals. You had the right of it. I declined to pursue Raolos's appeal, in part, because of you. Raolos had been impeached for questionable conduct, and since the company he kept threatened me and my men, I felt disinclined to pursue his appeal. I did not believe anybody of suitable character would travel with such a companion."

She thought she had grasped his implication. "You cannot reinstate Raolos?"

"That I cannot. My Bailiff could, if he heard fresh evidence and felt so inclined."

"If only he had not fled south to live a life of luxury." Corelle sighed, frustrated. "If you had acted when I urged you to hang him, he might not have escaped."

"I could not have hanged him. If I had the power to hang him, I would hang you this very morning. Our laws are clear. The Duke is head of state, not head of judicial matters."

Corelle turned to Raolos. "Let us leave. This man can do nothing for us, and I have laid bare the worst beasts of my nature for naught. I have work to do, and it seems none can hang me for it once it is completed."

The Duke had not finished. "Do you know what I do have the power to do?"

Corelle's fury drove her sarcastic reply. "Choose which trousers you will wear tomorrow?" More gasps echoed around the room.

He gave a small laugh. "Not always, in truth. Certain occasions demand certain formal dress, you see. What I do have the power to do is remove and appoint a Bailiff as my head of all things magisterial and financial as they pertain to the Duchy."

Corelle's hopes rose. "Does the Bailiff's power pass to you then, if you remove him?"

He laughed again. "That it does not. I must appoint a new Bailiff if the current one is no longer in office. Do you know—"

"Four." Corelle hoped to interrupt his long-windedness.

"One. More than two hundred years ago. A philanderer and a thief, it turned. Every other Bailiff has retired with grace or died in office." He pulled a parch toward himself and began to scribe, only the scratch of his scribing tool audible for some time. He laid the scribing tool down and rang a bell on his desk.

A man scurried in and bowed to the Duke. "My Duke."

The Duke turned to Corelle. "You see? 'My Duke.' This is the proper manner of address." He turned to the man. "My seal, if you will."

The man bowed again and ran from the room. He returned soon

enough with a seal and a bowl filled with melted wax, suspended above a small candle. The Duke pushed the seal into the wax, stamped it on the parch, then signed it with such a dramatic flourish, Corelle thought his signature might be a sketch of her.

"Let this be entered into the records and let the Sergeant take the appropriate actions." The man picked up the parch, bowed again and ran from the room once more.

The Duke turned to Raolos. "I have signed a warrant to remove Glailam from the office of Duke's Bailiff. The Sergeant will send for the Bailiff's sceptre, and it will be brought here to be passed on to another, who will become the next Bailiff."

The elaborate rituals of power had Corelle bewildered. "The Sergeant will assume the role then?"

The Duke laughed again. "That he will not. He is my cousin. His role is as symbolic as my own. He controls the records of the Duchy and presides over the formalities at the end of one Bailiff's tenure and the start of the next. It is a simple job, and he lacks the competence to do, it in truth. Family." He smiled.

Corelle put little trust in the good nature of Styrrach and his partners. "What if Glailam has stolen the sceptre?"

The Duke shook his head. "It is held in a safe three rooms from here. It is handed to the Bailiff, then taken back and stored in safety. It is a very old and very important piece of Dur's history. We do not even trust our Bailiffs that far." He laughed aloud, and several of the others joined in.

They waited for some time, and Corelle grew impatient. She could lie motionless for hours at a time to gather intelligence for a gest, but she had no patience for the pomp and verbosity of the Duke and all the apparatus of state.

Long moments later, the Ortwood door opened, and a man entered. "My Duke, your Sergeant." The man gave a deep bow.

A short, rotund man dressed in a fancy uniform of yellow with vast swathes of brocade embroidered onto it entered the room. He carried a small golden rod with a large, bulbous head. Set into the rod were many precious stones that glittered in the lantern light. The man approached the Duke, and spoke once he reached the desk. "Cousin."

"This is a formal occasion, Sergeant." The Duke seemed to strive to control his impatience with his relative.

"Ah, of course. My Duke." The Sergeant's cheeks turned a fiery red.

"Sergeant, I have removed Glailam from the office of Bailiff of Dur. Do you bear the sceptre?"

The Sergeant held up the item in question, a small glint of triumph in his eyes. "That I do."

"Then I must appoint a new Bailiff." The Duke explained the procedure for the benefit of Corelle and Raolos, which involved the nomination of a new Bailiff from Portreeves who are in office at the time. He nominated the Portreeve of Dur City, but Corelle raised an immediate objection based on the time it would take to summon him from such a far-flung corner of the land. She feared it would take so long the miscreants would have ample time to flee.

The Duke nodded at her. "I understand this. More is at stake than your claims, however. There is the future good governance of Dur to be considered." He paused. "There is, however, clear provision in our law for another nomination for the position of Bailiff." His pointed stare never left her eyes. "Any citizen of Dur present at the time a new Bailiff is nominated may also nominate anybody they see fit to assume the position. In such a rare case, a decision would be required. I am, therefore, compelled to ask whether any here wish to nominate another as Bailiff of Dur." His eyes remained fixed on hers as he spoke, and she guessed his intent. It was an excellent hand, and he had played it well.

Corelle stood. "Duke." He frowned. She sighed and decided this might not the time to score further points against his ego. "*My* Duke, I wish to nominate this man, Raolos, as Bailiff."

Raolos gasped and the Duke seemed shocked. A horrified tone came to his voice. "Why, this is unheard of. A citizen's nomination competes with my own. Remarkable. Who are you to nominate this man?"

"I am Corelle, a citizen of Dur." She hoped she had recalled all the points he had made.

He betrayed no amusement at the bizarre situation he had crafted. "Very well. Sergeant, two nominations have been made, and a decision must be cast. Our laws are clear. The nominee must be present, prepared and able to accept the nomination. By some oversight on my part, I have neglected to invite my nominee to the ceremony. I instruct you, in accordance with our laws, to ask this citizen's nominee if he will accept the position."

The Sergeant produced a parch from within his tunic and turned to Raolos. "Raolos, if you are prepared to accept the nomination of this citizen and become Bailiff of Dur, please read aloud this oath." He offered the parch to Raolos, who stared at it in disbelief.

Raolos turned to Corelle, his expression one of incomprehension. "What of the charges of my misconduct?" She shrugged.

"Raolos." The Sergeant sounded testy. "If you are prepared to accept the nomination, please read the oath. If you are not prepared to accept it, another will be nominated in your stead at some later time."

Raolos took the parch and read the scribing in silence. He hesitated, and Corelle feared he might refuse after all the bizarre games the Duke had played to arrive at the moment, but he cleared his throat and read aloud from the parch. To Corelle, the words were meaningless, filled with "shall uphold," and "serve in good faith," and other ceremonial language. The oath could benefit from some simplification, but Raolos had finished, and she had understood little of what he had read out.

The Sergeant handed Raolos the sceptre, and he took it. He

turned and held it out toward Corelle, but one of the guards grasped it instead and handed it straight back to the Sergeant.

The Duke scribed on a fresh parch and finished with another sketch, mayhap of his new Bailiff this time, before he pressed his seal to the document. He rang the bell, even though the aide stood next to him. The man bowed. "My Duke."

"Let this be entered into the records." The Duke handed the parch to the man and he scurried out. "Congratulations, Bailiff." At the Duke's words, all in the room clapped their hands.

THIRTY
A HARSH SENTENCE

Dur's new Bailiff mumbled some words of thanks to the Duke and grinned at Corelle. "We must go. We have much work to do."

"One matter I must bring before my new Bailiff." The Duke's sombre words echoed around the room, which fell silent as he spoke. "I heard a confession here today before many witnesses. This woman"—he pointed at Corelle—"confessed to many heinous acts of murder. You must deliver a verdict on her crimes now you are Bailiff. Do you wish to hear testimony of what she admitted to?"

Corelle frowned in confusion and fiddled with the hem of her tunic, deep in thought. Could this be some fresh play designed to use the pomp of state to absolve her of guilt, or would the Duke compel Raolos to hang her? He must harbour bitterness about the threats in the house and her earlier refusal to call him by his proper title.

Raolos made it clear he would not play the game. "That I do not. I will pardon her."

"Our laws are clear." Corelle glanced away and pressed her lips together. She had lost count of how many times the Duke had used the phrase, and, after all else, it baffled her how he could be so certain of all the laws of Dur. "A person not found guilty of a crime may not be pardoned, since there is nothing to pardon them for. Serious charges were laid, and you must deliver a verdict. I remind you, the accused confessed to these crimes by her own tongue."

Raolos seemed overcome with sadness at this turn. "Then I find her guilty of murder, and I pardon her."

The Duke tutted. "Our laws are clear. You may not find her guilty, then pardon her for no apparent reason. For the theft of an apple, the punishment might be an hour or two in the stocks. For murder, the punishment is death by hanging. Once the verdict is handed down, the sentence must be carried out at once unless the convicted person wishes to appeal to a higher authority. As the Bailiff has declared the verdict, there is only one higher authority in the land to whom the convicted might appeal. Her Duke."

All eyes turned to Corelle, and an expectant hush descended on the room. She knew what everybody in the room expected of her, but without Deineike, life had lost its appeal, and she intended to disappoint her audience. She drew herself up to her full height and stared ahead, silent.

Raolos whispered in her ear, his voice urgent and compelling. "Jorinda, you must appeal to the Duke. You have but one chance."

Corelle had made up her mind. "I have confessed to the murders of more people than I can keep track of, my own lover among them. I do not deserve leniency. I trust it will not take long to find a noose."

Several people began to talk at once, and one of the scribing women began to cry. Raolos leaned close and whispered in her ear again, his words fast and laden with desperation. "Jorinda, you have confessed to terrible things. I knew of some of your past, but your words shocked even me. I beg you to appeal." He hesitated, then continued. "Deineike would beg you to appeal. She would say you have confessed, but you do not deserve to die for your mistakes. You have work to do yet. I beg you again—appeal, for Deineike's sake."

Deineike's face filled Corelle's mind. The sparkle in her blue eyes, the laughter, the look of ecstasy as they made love, the concern as Jorinda wallowed at her darkest. She saw Deineike in the bed in Torric as she forgave her for the murder of Arella, the woman they had both loved. Deineike had beseeched her many times not to talk of her own death. Would she have urged Corelle to appeal? Raolos had the right of it; if Deineike had been in the room, she would not wish her hanged. Corelle had been a disappointment to many people throughout her short life. She would not be a disappointment to Deineike at this moment. "I appeal." She spoke the words in a small, timid voice, and an eerie silence fell over the room once more.

The Duke studied her for some moments. "Corelle, you have appealed against your sentence of death for the crimes of murder. You have today served the people of Dur with great honour, but your crimes are a stain on this great land and cannot be overlooked with ease. I will not ask my Bailiff to pardon you." Many present gasped at his words. "Instead, I will ask him for clemency. In recognition of the aid you rendered to us in the exposure of our trusted office bearers' complicity in the murders you have committed, I will ask my Bailiff to commute your sentence from death to banishment. I will ask him to exile you from Dur, on pain of death should you return." Raolos tried to object, but the Duke held up a hand. "Bailiff, will you allow my appeal for clemency?"

Raolos glared at the Duke. "I wish to pardon her."

"Our laws are clear." The Duke leaned forward and stared at Raolos. Their proud, obstinate eyes locked, and neither seemed prepared to give ground. "She came here prepared to hang, man. Is this a worse alternative? This woman is a killer. By my mercy, she can live, but I do not wish death to walk the streets of Dur, ready to strike down any who anger her."

Corelle imagined Deineike would have approved of the Duke's logic. Her menace had no place among decent folk, so for now she would live until she went wherever she travelled to afterward. She laid a hand on Raolos's arm. "It is fair. We must leave. The sand falls, and I have information you will need if you are to apprehend those who did not flee when they heard of Styrrach's death." She turned to the Duke. "Any who remain must be taken into custody and Raolos will need time to send men to carry out those tasks. Once the criminals learn of Raolos's appointment, they may slip away."

"That they may, but I am required to proclaim the appointment of a new Bailiff." The Duke paused for a heartbeat. "I find my schedule so filled with events of state, I shall not be able to issue any proclamation for two days." Corelle coughed. "I mean three days. I must issue the proclamation then, however."

Corelle smiled at him. "My thanks."

He did not return the smile. "One pass at most, young woman. Do not return. Dur holds nothing for you. I remain sorry about the death of your lover."

The peculiar events of the morning left Corelle light-headed. She had poured out her crimes, but she still lived, banished from her own land. Raolos had been appointed Bailiff, a turn she would not have anticipated in her wildest dreams. The development pleased her, although the Duke's openness to the idea surprised her. Raolos would be an admirable Bailiff and would serve Durfolk with fairness and honesty, she had no doubt. The cities and towns implicated in Styrrach's scheme would see decent Portreeves appointed, and the prices of the exotic goods from the south would reduce and be more available to all. One day, a woman might even become a Portreeve, since Raolos appeared open to it.

To her frustration, Corelle had not fulfilled her vows. The Bailiff had escaped it seemed. If she had tried to kill him after she took Styrrach, his debt for the life of Deineike might have been paid. Instead, he would live a life of wealth, while Deineike had gone to the flames. Corelle had somehow not been hanged, but she could take her own life at any point. Her own survival vexed her less than the escape of the Bailiff.

They had arrived uncertain whether they would be admitted to see the Duke on such short notice, yet they had achieved so much against all their expectations, and she saw the day as a success despite her fury that the Bailiff would not be hanged in the square. They found Synna, and as they rode back to the inn in their coach, they told him what had turned. His surprise rendered him speechless as they revealed each new twist, and he pounded Raolos on the back when they explained the news of his employer's appointment as Bailiff.

He beamed at Raolos. "It is well deserved." When he learned of Corelle's exile, his disappointment crushed him. "I am sorry. An unhappy turn."

She shrugged. "Preferable to the alternative, many would say, were they in the same position."

Raolos leaned forward and spoke in a soft voice. "Synna. Everything I heard of you before today, I heard as a private citizen. See to it your new Bailiff hears nothing of your past." Synna nodded.

The coach reached their inn, and they gathered in Raolos's rooms. Corelle scribed all the addresses of Guild buildings she could recall along with the names of those she knew to be implicated. She requested some more of Styrrach's coin since she had been banished from Dur, and Raolos urged her to take as much of it as she could carry.

"You have much to do," she said to Raolos. "I regret I cannot assist you with your tasks, although in truth I never expected to."

"I have Ibie and Synna, and soon enough we will have Portreeves who will once again work for the people they represent, and not themselves. Where will you go?"

"I know not." Corelle shrugged. "I believed this would be the day I learned where we travel to afterward, if anywhere. That knowledge is not to be mine for a time."

Raolos appeared to hesitate. "Take Pettra with you." He looked down at his feet.

His words stunned her, and she glanced at Synna, who seemed as shocked as her. "She is your wife."

"That she is." Raolos sighed. "While you attended to Styrrach, she spoke of nothing but you. She claims she loves you."

The words, though not a surprise, deflated Corelle, and hardened her resolve to have no more to do with Pettra, but she chose not to hurt Raolos further. He need not know his wife had already spoken to Corelle of her love. "She is confused, nothing more. Even if she believes it, I feel more certain than ever. I am not right for her. Two women have said those words to me before, and both are now dead on my account. I cannot inflict that fate on Pettra also."

Raolos waved a hand in the air in dismissal of her argument. "Coincidence, nothing more. I do not read anything into this. I married her, and I forced her into my bed in the process when she desired to lie with a woman. Her station, her background, the expectations of her parents, these things all played on her, and she became trapped. She suffered me, and I do not wish to return home from every busy workday to a wife who suffers me and dreams of you."

Corelle wiped at her eyes. "She told me she knew of your affair and welcomed it because you did not pester her for dalliances she took no enjoyment from."

He nodded, his face a mask of dejection. "I will make no excuses for myself. I trapped her. She is a beautiful woman, and it helped my ambition to have her on my arm. I did little enough to help her."

"You cared for her. Do not berate yourself. It is not your fault she is the way she is. None of us choose it or ask for it. To do so would be madness in a land where we are viewed as deviants."

A look of determination replaced his misery. "That must change. A great deal must change in Dur. I have much more to achieve than to bring these miscreants to justice. Take her with you. She needs you."

Corelle refused to entertain the idea, convinced she would be Pettra's ruin. She shook her head. "I am not good for her. You know my nature and might guess at the terrors that tear at my mind from all I have become. I would not lay that upon her."

"She needs you. She is a child."

Corelle scoffed. "She is twice my age."

"That she is, but she is still a child." Misery returned to his face. "Does she urge you to hurt her?"

"That she does. I cannot bring myself to strike her, though she begs me to."

A tear rolled down his cheek. "Then you are better for her than me, and she needs you."

"Raolos—"

He held up a hand. "Do not defend me. I gave in to her requests. Mayhap I punished her for something I suspected about her. She might hold herself to blame for all that has turned for her, trapped into a marriage she did not relish, forced to take Raopul on as her own son. Who knows?"

The conversation saddened Corelle. "I do not plan to return to Ort."

He brightened somewhat. "You would do me a favour, and more than the care of Pettra. You could carry letters for me. Ibie must be summoned to Alcmouth to aid me, and Raopul and the staff must prepare to journey here. Pettra too, if she will not go with you." He paused. "She will go." The new Bailiff fell silent again.

Corelle did not want to take Pettra. Until Raolos had asked her, the thought had not occurred to her, and she did not want to be trapped into it through Raolos's ruse that she would be a courier for him. "I cannot bring myself to take Pettra. The violence does not sit well with me."

His emitted a bitter, accusatory laugh. "I find that strange. You are the most violent person I have ever known."

"That I am. I am a puzzle even to myself."

Raolos shrugged. "You may guide her to find love that does not demand such perverse pleasures."

Corelle stood. Her discomfort increased as every moment passed. "Why are you so keen for her to leave with me? She is your wife, after all else."

Agony and sorrow swam in his gaze, and a tear ran down his cheek. "I have told you. I no longer wish to be an inconvenience who stands in the way of her true desires. I also want her to find joy. She has earned it. None can deny that."

Corelle tired of the argument. Raolos appeared determined to ignore her own wishes in the matter. "I am sorry Raolos. I cannot help you with Pettra. My fates are written in some other way."

Dejection filled Raolos's eyes, then he called on the formidable inner strength Corelle had observed before. "Will you take the letters for me, at the least?"

She sighed. It seemed uncharitable to refuse. Raolos could not take them—he must devote his time and energy to the capture of as many of those who had benefited from the Guild as he could. Synna could not go, or Raolos would have no protection. He had trapped her, despite her efforts to the contrary. "That I will. Send them to my room when they are scribed, and I will sail north with them tomorrow."

He nodded. "And Pettra?"

Corelle shook her head. If Pettra did love Corelle, her love would lead her down the same dreadful streets Arella and Deineike had trodden before her, and Corelle's conscience could not carry any more of the burden of guilt that would bring. "I am the wrong person to help her. I may unlock worse elements within her. As the expression goes, '*When one lies down with monsters, one must eventually become a monster.*'"

He gazed up at her, sorrow in his eyes, but pride too. "Deineike did not."

Corelle pictured Deineike's smile, the dark hair that framed her face, the beauty lit from within by her gentle nature and thoughtful disposition, the blue eyes that flashed as she said, "I love you."

She walked to the door but stopped, turned around in the doorway, and smiled. "That she did not."

THE END

NOTE FROM HAYLEY

The Vermilion Saga ends with this book. It has been rewarding but also challenging for me to bring my debut series to life. I stumbled at the start, but from the second edition of The Vermilion Ribbon, I discovered Jamie Flack's artwork, and the three covers he created revealed his unquestionable talent.

I cannot thank those of you who read my words enough. You took a chance on a new author and allowed me to bring Corelle into your consciousness. It is humbling to see people buy the books, or read them on Kindle Unlimited. Thank you, from the bottom of my heart.

2025 will see Corelle return. There will be a number of books following her life from the end of The Vermilion Saga. I hope you'll stick with her, and I look forward to seeing you again. To learn about the next books, please subscribe to my newsletter on my website (links at the end of the book).

ACKNOWLEDGMENTS

"Dune Road"
    Performed by Catherine Porter
    Written by Catherine Porter and Kevin Malpass
    © Dune Road Discs 2021
    Lyrics reprinted by permission

Cover by Jamie Flack - https://www.catandcrown.com

Cover models:
Corelle/Jorinda - Erin https://www.instagram.com/afaerytalecos/
Deineike - Katya https://www.instagram.com/katyafern/

Map and scene divider created by André Barbeto

Edited by Jo Crivelli

SPECIAL THANKS

Special thanks to:
Ailsa, as ever, for her patience and her love.
Catherine Porter, for her beautiful soul, and for the use of Dune Road.
Jo & Rob, Danny & Wendy. Support such as yours has no price. Thank you.
Jamie, Katya, and Erin. We set the bar high on the first two books, but we cleared it again.
Tam & Danae, for their valuable friendship. What happens in Blue Eyes, stays in Blue Eyes.
Jo, for her editing skills and perception.
André for the map and scene divider.
My constant champions, Bec and Bianca.
Everybody who has read my books. Thank you from the bottom of my heart for taking that chance.
Christopher Cross. One of these days, you'll make it into one of my books.
Rosie, the cutest, sweetest natured cat ever.

LINKS

Here are some links I hope you will find useful.

My website: https://hayleyprice.net

(More links on next page)

Listen to Dune Road on Spotify: https://open.spotify.com/track/ 2AEKOPKRtFNp1dg5UQGZUk?si=0294ce688de849ec

Please leave a review for this book at: https://geni.us/ TheVermilionTriangle

www.ingramcontent.com/pod-product-compliance
Lightning Source LLC
Chambersburg PA
CBHW030511120726
47904CB00005B/1422